Personal Habits

Personal Habits

SHANNON LEWIS

DOUBLEDAY & COMPANY, INC.
GARDEN CITY, NEW YORK
1982

Copyright © 1982 by Shannon Lewis
ISBN 0-385-17279-6
Library of Congress Catalog Card Number 81–43416
First Edition
Printed in the United States of America
All Rights Reserved

One

WHEN SHE MOVED, the satin sheets rustled with a glamorous, moneyed sound, but they were wrinkled and hot. Damn satin, she thought. It's like ice when you first get into it, and after you slip and slide around on it for one night, you have to change the whole bed because it looks terrible.

She raised one eyebrow and her eyes sparkled with wry humor. Or the housekeeper has to change the bed. Which is definitely better.

It was a pleasant little thought with which to start a day she had been dreading.

The other side of the big bed was empty, the sheets cold again, but that did not relieve her feeling of being hot and sticky. Impatiently, she tossed the covers aside and got up, padding naked across the deep burgundy shag carpeting to the bathroom. All she wanted to think about was sinking into a clean tub.

She pushed the little button beside the door and a silent wash of light flooded the room, reflecting from the smoked-mirror walls, the gold faucets, the gleaming black marble fixtures.

Mine, she said silently, reminding herself before this day began. This is the world I have created for me.

She began her morning rituals.

The body she examined in the mirror was firm and slim, almost tomboyish, with flat hips and small, high breasts. And only seven hundred calories a day will keep it that way, she reminded herself grimly, pinching a tiny fold of flesh at her waist that might be hiding a treacherous ounce of fat.

The face in the mirror was youthful, elegantly pale, the skin tight on the bone, with slanting brows and smoky eyes somewhere between green and gray. They were the kind of eyes that challenged a man to stare into them, trying to guess their exact color. Heavy, dark hair, almost black, hung in a tumbled mass to her shoulders, waiting to be sleeked back into the classic chignon she frequently wore.

Poised, polished, ladylike. Ivory Talbot Reynolds.

She leaned forward and studied the faint network of fine wrinkles and puffed flesh around her eyes more closely. Not so young and lovely, that. It's time for the eye job, I've put it off as long as I can. What's the matter, sissy, scared of a little pain? Scared to have the plastic surgeon pull the stitches out of your eyelids?

The thought made something shrivel in the pit of her stomach, but she looked into the mirror very deliberately and forced herself to grin. What the hell! It won't be the worst thing that ever happened to you.

When she grinned, the sculptured features dissolved into an impish face that was somehow more familiar to her, though not beautiful at all. It was a face she allowed no one to see but her bathroom mirror. For just a few moments, every morning of her life, she looked into the mirror and plain Imagene Tutt from Anson, Texas, looked back at her. In solemn ritual, the two exchanged a conspiratorial wink.

The ring of the telephone startled Ivory as she emerged from the bathroom. She tensed with the hostility she always felt toward sudden noise. I should have that bell replaced with a chime, she thought. Or a flashing light. My conscience might let me ignore a flashing light at least long enough for Monique to answer it in the kitchen.

In two strides, she reached the baroque french telephone and lifted the receiver quickly, pleased to hear its raucous voice interrupted in mid-ring. Before the other person could speak, she knew who it had to be.

"Hello, Sharon," she said.

"Miss R.? It's Sharon MacCandless," a flat midwestern accent informed her unnecessarily. Sharon was unable to begin a telephone conversation without firmly pinning down the identities of both parties involved. Ivory suspected she even began her calls home that way: "Mrs. Mac-Candless? It's your daughter, Sharon MacCandless."

"Yes, Sharon," Ivory sighed.

"You wanted me to call you as soon as I came in?"

"That's right."

"Well, I just came in."

Ivory waited. Communicating with Sharon took time. If you interrupted, she never heard you but went right on with her preprogrammed recital of the tedious minutes of her day. If you had the patience to wait, eventually she got to the meat. Ivory had made patience a virtue, but today it was especially difficult.

"When I got to my desk, the light was on," Sharon babbled, "so as soon as I opened the daybook—I know you like me to do that, first thing—I called the switchboard and Helen gave me your message. So I'm calling. What can I do for you, Miss R.?"

Ivory closed her eyes. Develop laryngitis, she answered silently. "You're going to have to juggle my schedule, Sharon. I may not be back from the board meeting at the hospital at my usual time; there's sort of an emergency situation there. It would be a good idea to postpone that meeting with the Save the Whales group until tomorrow, and you'd better set my lunch date with the writers for . . . no, maybe we'd better skip that too, this once. I just don't know how long I may be tied up."

"But you never miss your monthly lunch with the writers!" Sharon protested.

"There's always a first time; I'll make it up to them."

"And you've got a show tonight. Richard will be here to do your hair and if you're late for that, well, you know how upset he gets. He could just walk out, then what would we do?"

Ivory drummed impatient fingers on the tabletop. How nice for Richard, to be allowed the luxury of temperament. Something is very wrong with my life if a hairdressing appointment has the same priority as life and death at the hospital. But I can't blame Sharon for thinking that, can I? In our business, the way my hair looks may *be* a matter of life and death.

"It'll be all right, Sharon. Don't worry. I can go on with a chignon if necessary. Just clear me a chunk of time from eleven o'clock onward, I don't know exactly how long. At least a couple of hours. And adjust everything accordingly."

She could imagine Sharon staring in horror at the daybook, with all those neat, segmented slices of time that controlled the lives of those in the television industry. Sacrilege to pull out a big undefined amount of it.

"What'll I tell people?" Sharon asked, sounding helpless.

"Tell them where I am and that I can't be disturbed. I'll get to the studio as soon as the meeting breaks up."

"What if Doctor Scott calls?"

The name sent a small stab of pain through Ivory. "He won't be calling," she said.

"Oh. Is he going to be at the meeting, too?"

Why did the girl ask so many questions? "Just do what I asked you to, Sharon. I'll be in as soon as I can."

"What about Mr. Everhardt?"

Clinton Everhardt, producer of "Headliners." The ultimate authority, the voice of God. "If he wants to see me, that's just too bad, Sharon—though don't put it that way to him. He's the one who got me on the board at the hospital in the first place; if it weren't for him, I wouldn't be in this mess."

"Just a little favor, Ivory"; that's what Ev had said. "It won't take much of your time. Sit in on a few board meetings, let them use your name on the letterhead for fund raising." Since Allenboro Memorial was Michael Mitchellson's pet charity, and Mitchellson was president of the Lincoln Broadcasting System, what better way to make a few additional points with the powers that be?

That's how the game is played; work all the angles. Except angles have sharp edges, sometimes, and someone can get hurt.

With difficulty, she extricated herself from Sharon's ongoing babble and hung up the phone. It rang again almost immediately. She glared at it. Unintimidated, the instrument went on demanding until she answered it.

"Miss R.? It's Sharon MacCandless again. Look, I hate to bother you, but I just remembered you've already had a call here this morning, from somebody named Sister Immaculata. Would that be a nun? She wanted to know if I expected you in. Is she a friend of yours or is she talent?"

A chuckle broke Ivory's tension. Talent. What an apt description of Sister Immaculata—of Penny. "No, Sharon, she's not anyone who's guesting on the show, just a . . . an acquaintance."

"Will you call her? I said you'd get back to her . . ."

"Thank you for the message, Sharon. Good-bye now."

She pressed the receiver firmly back into its cradle, hearing Sharon's voice until the very last moment, questioning, protesting. "But Miss R., I don't like to leave it like that. I mean, the poor woman sounded sort of upset, like it might be important, and I assured her you'd . . ."

Hanging up on Sharon was the only way to deal with her. If only it were that easy to deal with Penny. And with Nathan Scott. There was no point in returning Penny's call; there was nothing to say to her until they faced each other in the hospital. Faced each other like surgeons at an operating table, with the options of life and death the issue and two . . . no, three careers cut open and vulnerable in front of them, waiting for the knife that would kill or cure.

Ivory shuddered. That was an unpleasant analogy. So many . . . killings . . . might be prevented if she could somehow make it go her way this morning. If she and Penny didn't tear Nathan Scott to pieces between them.

She glanced at the rumpled bed, still fragrant with the familiar, loved scent of his body. But fragrant wasn't the right word. The emotions between them last night had been too bitter, they must have left their own unpleasant odors. Even the heated sex, more like rape than love, could not overcome that.

We may never make love again, she thought, staring at the bed. Something twisted and tore inside her.

Like something alive being ripped out of her body.

Sickened, she turned away from the telephone table just as Monique rapped on the bedroom door. "You want some breakfast?"

"I'm not hungry, Monique. Just coffee, please."

"I could do eggs. Maybe eggs Benedict? Fresh fruit, cereal, a croissant?" Worlds of Gallic seduction shimmered in Monique's Parisian voice.

Ivory had a mouth-watering flash of piping hot eggs Benedict but steeled herself against it, resenting her own indestructible appetite that could make its demands even at a time like this. "Just coffee, Monique," she said firmly. "And a small glass of grapefruit juice."

Monique's silent disapproval carried through the closed

door with a force stronger than words. Cooking was her passion, both vocation and avocation, and she had spent half her adult life compiling a mammoth cookbook of recipes of her own invention. Her job as Ivory's housekeeper gave her unlimited access to an expensively equipped kitchen and charge accounts at New York's best markets, and she looked fondly on Ivory as the patron saint of her cookbook. It was her great sorrow that her employer was on a perpetual diet and refused to be a guinea pig for new recipes. Monique consoled herself, however, with the certainty that Ivory was starving herself into a sickbed and would eventually require brimming bowls of thick soups and loaves of crusty bread to rescue her from the brink of the grave.

Ivory stepped into her closet. It was actually a room, large enough to sleep a couple, designed by a decorator and meticulously fitted out to store the vast wardrobe required by a major television personality. On hangers padded with satin and scented with Ivory's signature perfume hung suits and dresses of silk and wool and linen, Charmeuse and cashmere and crepe de chine. Dinner gowns glowed in jewel tones. There was not a color or fabric that did not perfectly complement Ivory's complexion and skin texture. Beside the light switch, a list, printed in Ivory's precise block lettering, described each outfit and its complete set of accessories, down to the shade of nylons and the numbered drawer containing the appropriate jewelry.

Ivory reached for a summer-weight silk suit, hanging with its contrasting blouse, then drew back her hand. Black and white. The habit intruding, unbidden, after all these years. An odd choice for this particular day.

Instead she chose a coral silk sheath with a matching bolero. She carried the outfit to the mirror and held it in front of her, seeing the glow of the color reflected on her pale skin.

Too pale.

Without makeup, her face looked stripped and vulnerable. She hung the dress over a chair and went to her makeup table, reaching hungrily for the cosmetics that would transform her into Ivory Talbot Reynolds.

When she went into the spacious living room overlooking Central Park, the drapes were still drawn. She did not open them. A diffused light filtered through their loose weave, and a jagged gray outline, that might have been mountains or skyscrapers or any fantasy landscape, hung in the middle distance. At least it wasn't flat. No one could mistake the view out that wall of windows for the prairies of Texas.

Ivory did not have a penthouse, though she could have afforded one and many stars of her status would have demanded that type of accommodation. But Ivory continued to live in the same apartment she had bought during the fledgling days of "Headliners," when no one was sure if the show would be a success or not. Then, the apartment had been too expensive for her, a gamble on a future that might be nothing more than a castle in the air. It was an extravagant indulgence she had allowed herself, knowing if the show failed she would always have the memory of once having possessed a beautiful home of her own.

"Headliners" proved to be the hit of the season, surprising everyone but Clinton Everhardt, who insisted he had known it all along. Ivory's salary soared and she could have lived anywhere she liked, but by then the apartment was truly home and the very thought of exchanging it for something else frightened her in an obscure way. Instead she furnished it with all the elegant things she had always wanted, the Georgian breakfront and Waterford chandeliers, deep sofas covered in velvet, heavy glass tables and Impressionist art.

Monique emerged from the brick-walled kitchen wearing a determined expression and carrying a silver coffee service augmented by a large goblet of something that wasn't grapefruit juice. Ivory looked at it suspiciously.

"What's that?"

"Something I made for you special."

"It has froth on top," Ivory accused.

Monique managed a Gallic shrug without tilting the tray. "Perhaps. From the egg, may be."

"Egg!" Ivory's scandalized tone enumerated the calorie and cholesterol count of one demon egg.

"Just a little one," Monique wheedled. "Like a bird's egg, so small it was," she added, to make it plain no one could expect any harm from such a charming miniature.

Ivory was not placated. "What's in there besides that hummingbird's egg you're trying to foist off on me?"

"A little fresh pineapple, not much. Orange juice. Perhaps a touch of cream."

"Cream!"

"For your *skin*. I tell you and tell you, you need fat or you will get wrinkles in your skin. And you need more padding elsewhere, too," she commented, continuing an old argument between them. She put the silver tray down on a small table in front of the windows and cast a meaningful glance at her employer's figure. "If you had more padding, everything would get better for you. Men do not enjoy bony women in bed, bruising them."

Ivory sat down and poured her coffee. She sipped it immediately; it was strong and hot and seemed to be absorbed directly into her bloodstream, sharpening her senses. "I haven't had any complaints about my bones in bed," she said defensively.

"Doctor Scott left before dawn," Monique said with satisfaction, considering her point proved.

"Not because I'm too thin!"

"Think what you will," Monique told her with another expressive shrug. "But it is a known fact—American women do not understand men."

Ivory was amused. "I suppose you do? You're the one who's divorced, not me."

"*I* divorced *him*," Monique pointed out, "*because* I understand men."

Ivory smiled at her. "Go on back to your kitchen and start working on that veal piquante you were telling me about. That's what's really important around here, and you mustn't let anything else get in the way."

Monique's deep-set eyes glowed. "Ah, you see why I must take such good care of you? Where else would I find someone so generous? Now drink this nice drink and I will leave you in peace." Placing the glass directly in front of Ivory, she headed back toward the kitchen, her duty done. Her departing back made a firmly self-righteous statement.

Ivory sipped the scalding coffee and tried to ignore the glass with its lacy circlet of foam, but its fragrance undercut the smell of the coffee. Her mouth began to water. There was probably honey in it too, damn it; Monique was a firm believer in raw honey. Ivory put down the cup and lifted the glass—just one small sip, to make Monique happy.

To think about food as pleasurable is to encourage gluttony. To deny yourself is a gift to God.

She drained the goblet and licked her lips. The drink was sinfully delicious.

Hell, she thought belatedly. Now Monique will try to pour something down my throat every morning until I look like a blimp on-camera. If I didn't have this business with Penny and Nathan on my mind, I wouldn't have let myself lose control like that.

Penny and Nathan. Why did I automatically list her first?

Because Penny always came first, as if by divine right, from the very beginning. It never occurred to anyone to question that. Golden, perfect Penny. Just looking at her you knew that she was the one who would win all the prizes, have all the friends, marry the town millionaire, and live happily ever after.

Penny. Sister Immaculata.

Nothing turned out the way we expected it, did it, Penny?

When Ivory stepped from the shadowed interior of her apartment building into the glaring heat of midtown New York in July, she tried to brace herself against the shock, but it hit her like a battering ram. Radiating from no particular source but every possible surface, the heat melted makeup and puddled armpits.

Eddie, the doorman with a kid's name and an old man's face, appeared at her elbow, abashed because she had beaten him to opening the door.

"What's the thermometer say, Eddie? It's like the tropics out here."

"Sure is, Miss Reynolds. S'posed to go into the upper nineties today. Wonder if we're going to have one of those killer heat waves like they had in Texas a few years back; 'member that? Temperature in the hundreds for months and all those people died."

Ivory's throat went dry. The convent must have been like an oven then, in spite of its thick walls and the big old trees surrounding it. How the nuns must have suffered, those who still wore the full habit. All those layers of cloth . . .

"I remember, Eddie." Was Texas going to be a universal topic today? Monique had made some reference to it too, just as Ivory was leaving the apartment—something about having bought a side of meat "as big as Texas" to perform her culinary experiments upon. It was a joke of the Fates, occasionally repeating the same subject over and over without reason. One day she had mentally recorded five separate references to Errol Flynn in one afternoon, though there was nothing about him in the media to stimulate nostalgia. Yet thoughts of the dead movie star had definitely been in the air, like the millions of electronic images circling the globe on countless pathways. And people picked up on them.

As people today might pick up on the heat, the South, Texas . . . she knew before it had begun that she would encounter one reference after another today, a constant resurrecting of the old land and the old memories.

Don't be superstitious! she scolded herself. This isn't Texas, this is New York. Texas was Penny's place, *this* is mine.

Yet it was hard to realize that everything had come down to a test of strength between them, and harder still to imagine she could hope to win. Not against Penny.

"Limousine coming for you today, Miss Reynolds?"

"No, Eddie, I'll take a taxi. I have other stops before I go to LBS."

Ivory had grown to dislike the limousine and avoided using it whenever she could. She hated sitting in that shining gray box with its little glass portholes, while people on the sidewalks craned their necks to get a look at the Celebrity, the Occupant. The sense of intrusion into her private world upset her more than she had ever been able to explain to Ev, who insisted she use the limo for her daily trips to and from the studio. It was a small game she played, a little rebellion, avoiding his dictates. She much preferred the anonymity of a tinny, smelly, jolting taxicab, with a driver who could not be impressed by anyone. That restored her feeling of membership in the human race. Riding in the limousine was like walking down the street in a nun's habit.

The veil is a privilege. It affords automatic respect. To assume the veil is to assume the dignity and authority of a symbol.

Eddie reluctantly ushered Ivory into a taxicab and gave the driver her destination—"Allenboro Memorial Hospital, y'know it?" Eddie had a professional suspicion, fostered by years of being a doorman, that taxi drivers were borderline psychotics uniformly possessed of a homicidal mania. He hated putting any of "his people" into a taxi and sending them unprotected into the streets of New York.

Why would that nice Miss Reynolds, a lady like her, want to take a taxi when she had a limousine available to her any time she wanted it? No explaining some people!

The cabdriver had a portable radio beside him on the front seat. It added its own static to the rattle and bang of the taxi; sounds of life. His eyes met Ivory's in the rearview mirror. "Last night's ball scores," he told her. "You wanna lissen? I can turn it up. We really creamed them Rangers, didn't we?"

Without waiting for an answer, he launched into a scathing appraisal of the Texas team, its strengths as he saw them and its much greater weaknesses—according to him—and talked happily all the way to the hospital. Ivory sat back in the seat with folded hands and downcast eyes, hearing the occasional "Texas" slung over his shoulder like a stone.

The taxi passed through a blur of quick, hot scenes: apartments and hotels, a Nedicks on the corner, camera stores, pawn shops, monolithic office buildings, a black man wearing a silver-lamé toga and operating a shell game, a dry and desiccated park, a cluster of tenements, a sweeping view of oily river, and then the curving drive to the front entrance of the Bishop Allenboro Memorial Hospital, a brick building of modest formal demeanor befitting a privately funded hospital with a strong inclination toward research.

"Here y'are, lady. You visitin' somebody?"

Ivory stared up at the impassive face of the hospital. Life and death behind slatted blinds.

"I have business here," she replied.

In the past eighteen months, she had come to Allenboro Memorial a number of times to attend meetings, always feeling a little out of place among the older, more socially linked members of the board of directors. Recognizing her as a proxy for the powerful head of the Lincoln Broadcasting System, they had been kind enough to her, willing to overlook her rather gaudy celebrity, patient with her as she learned the entrenched viewpoint. If any of them had been aware of her developing affair with Doctor Nathan Scott, they had not mentioned it. If any of them had learned of the special relationship between Ivory and Sister Immaculata, head of the nursing staff, they had not brought it up during board meetings. Ivory had been treated with the unfailing politeness and faint patronization to be expected from the oldest, bluest blood in New York Catholic society. In return she had smiled, agreed, taken notes, and afterward "dropped in" to Mitchellson's mahogany-paneled office atop the LBS Building, to keep him appraised of the hospital's comfortable financial situation and growing reputation in the medical community.

Aside from the time required, it had been a simple enough duty, one of the many unrelated tasks that seemed to become necessary as one ascended the pyramid of success. So many things were asked of her; so many demands were made on her resources, and she had always said yes, always made the extra effort, gone the extra mile.

Like Penny.

Penny.

Getting out of the taxi, Ivory handed the driver a bill without even looking at it and murmured, "Keep the change." If she had been paying attention, his surprised "Thank *you!*" would have warned her that she had vastly overpaid him, but all her attention was focused on the building itself as it squatted in the sunlight, waiting for her.

Somewhere inside it was Penny; Sister Immaculata, who always won.

Beautiful golden Penny, beloved Penny, who had become Ivory's deadly enemy.

Two

THE LITTLE GIRL had not awakened until the third time her father pounded on the door, his voice rough with anger. "Imagene! If you don't get up right now, I'm gonna drag you outta that bed!" She opened her eyes regretfully and stared up at the ceiling, where a large water stain made a passable imitation of a map of Africa on the discolored wallpaper. She got out of bed very slowly and took off her faded cotton pajamas. A frayed seam hooked on one of her hangnails, tugging at tender flesh. She caught a glimpse of her naked self in profile in the tall mirror behind her battered old-fashioned dresser, and though she had never paid any attention to her reflection before, this time she stopped to look. She saw flat pink buttons on a narrow chest, a round little tummy thrust out in front, round little buttocks thrust out behind. The whole figure resembled a pudgy question mark, but the child didn't have any answers.

An hour later, she and her father emerged from a shabby frame bungalow, the neighborhood eyesore, and got into their car. The Tutt house was of the same construction as its neighbors, modest little houses built in the late thirties, their lawns and gardens long since established, their sycamore saplings grown into handsome trees that shaded the street. But the other homes were well cared for, with mowed lawns and fresh paint when needed. The neighborhood was not affluent, but it was respectable. And proud.

Only Barney Tutt's house had peeling paint and tall weeds.

The back Ford coupé was never parked in the Tutt garage; there wasn't room. The space was taken up by work benches littered with unfinished projects and abandoned inventions, none of them having to do with home repair. The car sat out, summer and winter, and by nine in the morning of an early September day, it had already filled with heat.

As soon as Imagene got in, she rolled her window down and tried to rest her arm across the top of the door, but the hot metal blistered her skin and she withdrew it quickly. She glanced hopefully at her father to see if he had noticed, but of course he hadn't.

He put the car in gear and they rolled down the driveway and out onto Belmont Street, turning left. They drove through a residential neighborhood much like their own, with neat little houses and porch swings and lawns baked to yellow-beige, the customary shade of Texas grass in the summer. Imagene looked wistfully at the houses, imagining complete and happy families inside.

After several minutes, she asked, "Is it very far to St. Mary's?" She wasn't really curious. She just wanted to hear the sound of a voice.

"Too damn far," her father replied gruffly, not looking at her. "After this, you can ride the bus. I haven't got time to fool with you. Next week we'll get you moved into the dormitory and you'll be living there full-time."

She sighed, a deep, adult sound unexpected from a ten-year-old, and he glanced at her then in annoyance. He saw a plain little girl with sallow skin and teeth permanently discolored from the hard mineral water she had drunk in one of the towns of her early childhood, some sad little corner of New Jersey or Illinois or Missouri where Barney had fled in search of elusive success, only to find himself jobless and broke when the liquor he loved destroyed each small security.

Seeing that she had his attention, Imagene tried to press the advantage. "Why do I have to live at St. Mary's?" she wanted to know. "I don't want to live with all those strangers. I won't know anybody there. Why can't I stay home and take care of you?" Her voice rose, pleading. "I can keep house for you. Mama taught me. Then I could keep going to public school, where I know the kids and . . ."

Barney slammed his foot on the brake, sending his only child lurching toward the dashboard. "I'm telling you for the last time. You're not staying home! Underfoot all the time, making trouble. And if you learned how to keep house from your Mama, that's no recommendation!" He checked himself, forcing his voice to be a degree more kind. "It was your Mama who wanted you to go to St. Mary's in the first place; you got to respect that. We got no choice. Besides, what makes you think you could take her place? Nobody could do that. My Nora . . ." His eyes filled with self-pitying tears. His paraded grief for his dead wife was more enjoyable than the living woman had ever been; it companioned his days, it explained his failures and supplied a new excuse for his drinking. It was giving him a chance to get his child out of the house and into someone else's hands —his homely little daughter with her mother's face and accusing gray-green eyes, always watching him. Judging him. Damn the child.

"Don't you want me to be with you?" the little girl asked wistfully, already knowing the answer but unable to hold back the question. She knew the fight was lost. Sending her to boarding school at St. Mary's had been her mother's deathbed pledge, the only expression of a spirit otherwise too weak to fight for life. Nora Tutt had taken to her bed and let the cancer devour her without a struggle, preferring that crucifixion death to an existence of endless quarrels and ceaseless disappointments. Barney was a self-destructive man who had failed at business and drunk his way out of a dozen jobs since marrying Nora in her native Ohio, and their married life had been spent one jump ahead of the sheriff's eviction notice, or bankruptcy court. Nora's strong Catholic upbringing demanded that she remain his wife and go down with his ship.

But Nora was capable of one small mutiny. Before she fell ill, she had taken out a life insurance policy on herself with the last remnant of a small inheritance from her father. That policy was a life raft for Imagene; a lawyer had arranged that it be used to send the child to a Catholic boarding school in the event of the mother's death. Welcome death had caught up to Nora Tutt in Texas, and now her foresight would free her child from Barney's inevitable destruction.

"Don't you want me?" Imagene repeated.

Barney didn't answer his daughter, nor did she expect him to. That question had gone unanswered every time she asked it. He stared fixedly at the road ahead. Why did the girl have to argue about everything? Why didn't she just accept and shut up? At least when she was out of the way he could have some buddies over, kill a few bottles, have a few laughs. Or drink alone in the bedroom he and Nora had shared, if that's what he felt like doing. Drink to lost and lovely Nora in her lace wedding dress, safely imprisoned in time and a silver frame.

The car jerked and picked up speed. They swung out onto River Road, driving through a newer and more prosperous area featuring white-painted brick Colonials and stucco Moderns with rounded corners and glass-brick windows. Beyond them broke the first wave of the newest residential architecture to reach Anson, Texas—split-level California Ranches sprawling across treeless half-acre lots.

The end of World War II had meant new money for Anson with the conversion of the old defense plant into a plastics factory, and other businesses were moving into the area as well, drawn by the Sun Belt promise of limitless growth. The houses they passed were larger, and the attached two-car garages held Cadillacs and Lincolns.

The black Ford Coupé passed a handsome brick home with the new cedar shingles that were the latest status symbol. Fully grown trees had been planted on the lawn, as it was called out here, although in the Tutts' neighborhood the same space would have been referred to as the front yard. Beneath one of the trees, a doghouse had been built, a little model of its human counterpart, complete with cedar shingles and shuttered windows. Imagene stared at it in wonder. What kind of people could build such a house for a dog? She knew instinctively that they did not have yellowed linoleum on their kitchen floors, nor battered oak furniture with shiny varnish. Imagene read all the magazines, avidly poring over pictures of stylish rooms with smiling inhabitants in *House Beautiful* and *Southern Living*. She liked to pretend that she was looking at scenes from her own home and her own family. Entering them in her imagination, she found a happier life than she knew with Barney Tutt in the house on Belmont Street.

She gazed with aching hunger at the expensive houses they drove past. Permanent homes. My own beautiful home.

Beyond the last curving street, with its raw cement curbs and raped earth devoid yet of house or shrub, waiting like an open sore to attract the new money, the prairie lay. It reached to the horizon in a smooth beige sheet, its only punctuation the staccato lines of an occasional barbed wire fence. Country. Texas. Empty, tumbleweed territory, it was

the stubborn enemy from which man would wrest a liveli-
hood and ultimately a victory, smearing its clean, free face
with his towns and his industries. The prairie was already
shrunken, invaded by an alien called Progress, but it still
had its allure, its beckoning horizon that could lead to anywhere.

Imagene thought of throwing open the car door and
jumping out, running as hard as she could across the baked
earth toward that lovely, distant Anywhere. She would run
like a jackrabbit and he would never catch her; she would
vanish down a hole like Alice in Wonderland and live with
the prairie dogs, who chuckled and romped together and
kissed each other; she would double back when it got dark
and knock on the door of the house with the cedar shingles,
to ask if they wanted a little girl to raise.

The car turned onto a dirt road marked by an unpainted
wooden bus shelter. The road was rutted and dry, lined
with mesquite trees. A cloud of dust boiled up behind the
Ford. Ahead Imagene could see a dark-green mass, thick,
not bleached out by the pervasive heat. As the car drew
nearer, it took shape and revealed itself as an elm grove surrounding a black wrought-iron gate. Across the top of the
gate were the words ST. MARY'S ACADEMY.

"Here we are!" Barney exclaimed with relief.

They drove through the welcome shade of the elm trees
and onto an asphalt parking lot. Beyond the parking lot was
the main building of the academy, a multiwinged structure
of red sandstone, turreted like a castle, with a broad portico
surmounted by a statue of the Madonna holding out her
Child. Pigeon droppings streaked her marble robes. The
face of the Virgin Mother was blank and pure, a heavy-lid-
ded, expressionless oval that could never have convulsed in
childbirth or shrieked in death agony. She held her child
out like a sacrifice.

At the base of the east wing opposite the parking lot, a
flight of steps led downward to a basement door, yawning

into darkness. Imagene watched as a line of little girls in white gym shorts and singlets emerged from the side entrance and marched in silent obedience into that gaping maw, going without protest into nothingness. They disappeared as completely as if they had never existed.

In the stuffy attic of the Tutts' rented bungalow, Imagene had read and reread the old newspapers and magazines left there by previous tenants. She lost herself in them, trying to shut out the sounds of her mother crying or her father swearing in the rooms below. The yellowing news accounts and glossy magazine ads had shaped her perceptions of the world. There she found the wire service pictures that had once sent shock waves around the planet.

Grainy images in shades of gray and black, relieved only with dead white tones like a fish's belly, the obscenely naked flesh of the doomed. "Belsen," the captions read. "Auschwitz." Stacks of cordwood with arms and legs. Stolidly obedient lines of people naked or clad only in their underwear, being herded into yawning doorways. Many of them had been children like herself, or those little girls who had just vanished into the sandstone building.

She had studied those pictures with morbid fascination, seeing in them some clue to life itself, some dreadful, obligatory destiny. "Don't look at those nasty things, they'll give you nightmares," her sick mother had told her. "Besides, that's just Jews. It doesn't happen to Catholics. Not anymore."

Imagene had taken the pictures to Barney, curiosity overriding her fear of his customary rejection. But this time he at least glanced at what she held. "Those are killing chambers," he said bluntly. "Nobody wanted all those kikes, so the Nazis marched them into big rooms disguised to look like something else and pumped a lot of poison gas in there through pipes and killed 'em all."

"Even the children?" she asked in horror.

"Sure, why not? Kids make a lot of trouble, ask a lot of

questions, always get in the way." He grinned suddenly, enjoying her fear. "It's a good way to keep from being pestered all the time."

Now Imagene watched that line marching without protest into the bowels of the red sandstone castle (disguised to look like something else!) and fear clutched her heart like a hand.

"Please, Daddy, don't make me go in there!"

Barney was already halfway out of the car. "You don't know what's good for you," he told her. "You ought to be grateful for the chance to go to a fancy private school like this and hang around with the kids of all the high mucketymucks. Maybe you'll learn some manners." He had come around to her side and reached in to pull her out. She leaned away from him but it was no good. He grabbed her shoulder and yanked hard and then she was standing on the asphalt beside him, the safe shell of the Ford behind her, the massive and malign entity of the academy waiting.

"Please!" she begged once more, her heart in her eyes.

"Your mother made me promise on her deathbed. You had to have this fucking education, and you're gonna have it, by God! Nora's blood money is gonna give you this, y'know that? Salted away a little insurance policy all this time, money I could have really used, just to send you here. Should have been my money, given me a fresh start somewhere . . ." His voice trailed away in self-pity and he pulled Imagene after him up the stone steps, passing beneath the portico and the blind madonna with her infant sacrifice. A nun opened the double oak doors before he could knock and smiled sweetly at the frightened child.

"Come with me, dear," she said gently. Then she looked at Barney Tutt. "Has she never seen a nun before?" she asked.

They followed her down echoing corridors to the office of the Mother Superior. There Imagene sat in a lump of panic while her father stumbled through the enrollment procedures. "Catholic? Oh yes, Sister, all of us. Especially my dear Nora. She never missed Mass. I was the backslider, you know, pressures of business and all that, but she made me promise to atone for it; yes, she did. And to see that our little girl had the kind of education she'd had, in a fine school like this. She graduated from a school like St. Mary's, my Nora did; oh, she was a smart one. She went to a lawyer all on her own without even telling me," he chuckled fatuously, as if it were a fine joke on him, "and got this insurance policy money all tied up so it would pay Imagene's tuition through the twelfth grade. What do you think of that? My poor Nora . . ." His voice quivered and broke. Mother Superior hurried around her desk to pat his shoulder comfortingly and offer him a glass of water from her own carafe.

Meanwhile Imagene sat forgotten on a straight-backed chair in the high-ceilinged room that resembled a Victorian parlor. "My wife had to die to send our little girl to this school; I couldn't afford it myself!" Barney wailed, while the nun struggled to soothe him, but Imagene wasn't listening. She was staring with wide eyes at a cluster of pipes that emerged from the white-painted radiator in the corner and ran up the wall and through the ceiling. To go where? To do what?

Gas them with pipes. That's how you get rid of the unwanted, the children who ask too many questions and cause trouble.

There was a rustle of cloth beside her and Imagene looked up, startled. The Mother Superior was smiling down at her and holding out her hand. Her face was as rosy as if freshly scrubbed—not shrunken and pasty as Mama's had been—and her robes had an exotic smell about them, a fragrance of starch and spice. The white wimple framing her face was immaculate, starched and pressed to an ivory sheen.

"Come with me, Imagene," she said gently, "and I'll take you to meet your new teacher and classmates while your father and I finish our discussion." Barney sat quietly hiccuping, his face averted. "You're going to be happy with us at St. Mary's," the nun went on, reassuring the poor motherless child who stared at her with such frightened eyes. "Believe me, Imagene; soon you will have a lot of new friends."

Three

THE MOTHER SUPERIOR delivered Imagene to the classroom that would be hers and introduced her to the teacher, Sister Barbara, a younger, smaller nun, with glinting glasses and a gentle smile. Imagene was in no condition to differentiate between nuns, however; to her they were equally forbidding forms swathed in black. Exotic, remote, incomprehensible. They seemed to be watching her like dark birds of prey, waiting for her to reveal some vulnerability.

As she stood in the doorway, the faces of her new classmates turned toward her and she searched them for signs of friendliness. But there were none. She saw closed faces, hostile, quick to tease or hate, the faces of a pack already formed and prepared to savage any intruder.

Sister Barbara, who thought of them only as an ordinary class of little girls, sometimes naughty but basically nice, did not see that at all. She thought they looked at the new child with curiosity. "This is Imagene Tutt, young ladies," she said, pushing the girl forward. "She is joining this class and I want you to make her welcome."

The children's faces turned on their necks like sunflowers on stalks, following Imagene's progress across the room to an empty desk. The desks were of old-fashioned golden oak, affixed to elaborate wrought-iron legs. Generations of initials were carved in the varnished desktop. A glass bottle turned iridescent by decades of spilled ink was sunk in a well in the upper-right-hand corner. The desk was wide enough to be shared by two students, and the far side of it was already occupied. Imagine, used to the smaller, more utilitarian single desks of public school, looked at the strange furniture with misgivings. It could be mistaken for a form of trap.

"Sit down, dear," Sister Barbara urged. "I understand you won't actually be starting class until tomorrow, but you might like to sit with us for a while this morning and get used to our procedure. Now I want all of you young ladies to introduce yourselves to Imagene in turn; this is a good opportunity to practice our manners, isn't it?"

One by one, the girls turned and looked at Imagene as they recited their names. Not one name stuck in her memory. She smiled a frozen smile at each and nodded, repeating a string of meaningless syllables. The girl in the other side of the desk sat and stared at her.

The introductions over, the class returned to its study of the complications of the written word. Imagene's deskmate, at the nun's urging, furnished her with a sheet of lined paper and a pencil, and the grudging explanation, "We're practicing Palmer method."

Imagene had never heard of Palmer method—it might be artificial respiration for all she knew, in which case she might soon be in need of it. She was faint from anxiety and tension.

Palmer method proved to be a style of handwriting requiring the fingers to be still and the arm to do all the work. Copying an alphabet painted at the top of the black-board, the students wrote individual letters in flowing long-hand, with the rhythm of synchronized machines. Imagene, feeling beads of sweat break out on her forehead, struggled to imitate them.

The dark, lanky girl sitting next to her giggled. "You write like a crab," she said.

In the car going home, Imagene sat pressed against the door, staring out the window. Barney spoke to her a time or two but she did not answer. Having carried his paternal duty as far as he cared to, he said nothing more, and they drove into town as two separate, unhappy realities locked together inside one automobile.

St. Mary's required its students to wear uniforms, neat jumpers of that red-purple color fashion then labeled "ma-roon," and white blouses. Barney was outraged at the cost, and more upset still when Mrs. Hammond from across the street, who sewed, told him it would take two weeks before she could get around to making uniforms for Imagene.

"Well, if you can't wait, you can always order 'em from one of the department stores," Mrs. Hammond sniffed. "Sev-eral places in town carry them, I think. Cost you twice what I'll do 'em for."

"We'll wait," said Barney.

So for two weeks Imagene underscored her difference from the other girls by wearing the shabby, cheap clothes her mother had purchased from the least expensive of the mail order catalogs. Her uniformed classmates, the daugh-ters of doctors and attorneys and successful businessmen, had closets at home filled with clothes from the more fash-ionable department stores their families patronized.

If several girls were talking when she approached, they fell silent, but after she had passed by she could hear them giggling. Under Sister Barbara's watchful eye they were polite, but in the dormitory and on the playground they were cruel.

"Where did you get those clothes—Goodwill?"

"What kind of accent is that you have? You're not from Texas, you talk funny. Does everybody talk that way where you come from? What are they, hillbillies? Or *Yankees?*"

"That's it, you're a Yankee. A Northerner. A foreigner! What are you doing here?"

At first Imagene tried to join the other girls at mealtime, but soon she found herself sitting alone at one end of the table, morosely eating the excellent food the nuns prepared. It was the only pleasure in her day, and she began to look forward to it with almost feverish appetite. As long as she kept her eyes on her plate and seemed preoccupied with her meal, she was in a safe place, set apart from the others, and something nice was happening. The more she ate, the longer she made lunch last, the longer she could put off going out on the playground and trying to find something to do by herself.

She was not invited to join the games of the other girls.

The nun in charge of playground supervision did not try to force the newcomer into the closed circle of her classmates. It was her experience and belief that these things resolved themselves eventually, and adult interference could only make matters worse.

"The child must learn how to make friends on her own," she explained to Sister Barbara, who agreed with her.

And at the end of two weeks, the day before Imagene's new uniforms were ready, the matter did indeed resolve itself.

Penny came back to school.

Penny, known on the school records as Elaine Endicott, was the undisputed queen of her class, and had been since the first grade. Penny had missed two weeks of school in order to accompany her parents on a business trip to the East Coast, where Kellam Endicott was arranging financing for the enlargement of his plastics factory, the newest booming postwar industry in Anson. The nuns never objected when Penny missed school to travel with her parents —a common occurrence—because the child always took her books and her assignments with her and returned as well-prepared as any of her classmates.

For a student like that, a girl whose report card was a monotony of A's, special dispensations were made.

On that Monday, the first bell had already rung when Penny swung gaily through the door and into the classroom, but Sister Barbara said nothing about her tardiness. "Elaine, my dear!" she exclaimed with genuine pleasure.

"Hi, Penny!" "Hey, look at you!" "Penny!" the girls cried, vying for attention. Everyone was eager to be noticed, to have Penny's acknowledgment as a seal of approval.

"Who's that?" Imagene whispered to her seatmate, the dark, lanky Sybil Baxter.

"*My* best friend," Sybil boasted.

Almost every girl in class, as it turned out, claimed Penny as a best friend, a claim Penny never denied. Friendship was her specialty. Penny Endicott was the sort of child who would be desperately sought within the next decade for television commercials, to advertise toothpaste or soap or shampoo. She was a natural golden blonde, with curly hair and wide blue eyes. Her skin was fair and free of blemishes; her teeth were straight and without cavities. She was a made-to-order child, as lovely and perfect as a doll.

To Imagene she was a fairy-tale vision, like the glossy, beyond-reach rooms in the magazines she pored over. Penny might have stepped out of one of those *House Beautiful* sets, loved and treasured, life as it should be lived.

But Penny was too real to be captured in a still photograph. She was so full of energy that she glowed, she bounced, she charmed everyone. Her sparkling eyes and ready smile were irresistible and she knew it.

"The miracle is, the child seems quite free of conceit,"

Sister Angelus had once commented to Sister Benedict. "Elaine has it all, yet there isn't a mean or selfish bone in her body. That child is truly blessed by the Lord."

"It happens that way sometimes," Sister Benedict acknowledged. "I have no doubt our Elaine is meant to do something splendid with her life. The Lord doesn't give all those gifts without a reason."

The day Penny returned, things began to change for Imagene. On the playground at recess, with all her friends clustered around her, Penny noticed the lonely child loitering by herself near the swings. "Who's that?" she asked.

"Oh, that's just Imagene Tutt, the new girl. She's from up North someplace, a Yankee. You wouldn't like her."

"I don't know that," Penny said, and started toward the swings.

Imagene was startled to see the golden girl approaching her. It was bad enough to be bullied by the others; it would be dreadful to have this paragon pick on her.

Penny looked at the anxious face, the all-wrong clothes, the awkward posture of the new girl in class. Imagene Tutt looked like a friendless mongrel expecting to be kicked. She was, beyond question, the least attractive girl in the class.

Penny put on her friendliest smile. "They say you're from the North," she began warmly. "I think that's neat. My mother's from Pennsylvania, and I just love to hear her talk, she has such clever ways of saying things. Tell me, don't you think Texas people have awful accents? When we go anywhere, I always notice." Before the astonished Imagene could think of a single answer to this flow of words, Penny had linked her arm and begun walking with her across the playground, still chattering companionably as if they had known each other for years.

Penny had a strong curiosity and a deft way of asking the most personal questions so as to solicit the most revealing answers. Without giving the appearance of prying, she soon found out about Nora Tutt's death, Barney Tutt's infatuation with the bottle, and Imagene's extreme and painful loneliness.

"Hey, that's really awful for you," she said with brimming sympathy. "I don't know how you can stand all that; you must be awfully brave."

Imagene, who had never been accused of being brave, felt the first pangs of schoolgirl adoration.

A few minutes later, sides were chosen for a softball game, with Penny naturally captaining one of the teams, and her first choice as a player was Imagene Tutt.

As simply as that, the door was opened and Imagene was invited inside.

It took her a while to get used to it.

With Penny's stamp of approval, the other girls began to accept her willingly enough. They quit teasing her about her accent and her teeth; they checked homework assignments with her or borrowed notebook paper. The hazing was over.

The world of the convent school was different from anything Imagene had known, in any of the towns she had lived during her brief, miserable childhood. Girls at St. Mary's were generally from the "better families" in Anson, at least the better Catholic families, and their conversations were larded with unfamiliar references to a standard of living Imagene had only dreamed about. They took ballet lessons, piano lessons, voice—Penny, of course, had almost perfect pitch—and their parents sent them to exclusive summer camps, far from the heat and dust.

And always, always, they competed with one another in a silent, sadly desperate competition of one-upsmanship that was but a reflection of the adult world their parents inhabited. Who had the most expensive shoes; whose father drove the fanciest car; who had her own horse, her own piano, her own real pearl necklace. They came from a Texas society that was learning to define itself by Things Possessed. Postwar affluence was settling like golden dust over much of the state, and people were obsessively aware of every nuance of status.

It might have surprised some of the parents to realize just how strongly their children felt the weight of that preoccupation.

Nora Tutt's legacy had guaranteed her child an entry into that world of privilege, but none of the trappings.

It was Elaine Endicott—Penny—who set the style for girls in the elementary grades of St. Mary's. When Penny abandoned the standard two-ring notebook for a three-ringer, within a week every girl in her class had done the same. Only Imagene did not make the switch. Penny, noticing, bought a new notebook for her friend and gave it to her one afternoon. "But I thought tomorrow was your birthday! Are you sure it isn't? Oh darn; now where did I get that idea? Look, go ahead and take this anyway, will you, and then when your birthday comes I just won't give you anything, okay?"

As soon as Penny announced she had read *The Three Musketeers* and wanted to act out the story during recess, there was a rush on Dumas in the school library that flustered Sister Ignatius, the septuagenarian librarian. Soon swashbuckling adventurers swarmed across the playground and practiced swordsmanship on the stairs.

Penny, of course, was D'Artagnan, encouraging her comrades to "Hit harder! Cut him off at the knees!"

Imagene, as Athos, accidentally drove a stick sword into the upper arm of Mary Ellen Casey and was forbidden afternoon collation for the rest of the month. Sister Barbara admonished her, "Violence always comes to a bad end." But no one lectured Penny. "She's so creative," Sister Magdalene told Sister Mercy. "It would be a shame to stifle that."

The nuns tried to avoid showing favoritism, but in Penny's case that was difficult. She reflected their highest hopes for all their girls, and when her enthusiasms overstepped the bounds of accepted behavior, she took discipline with such willing grace it negated the value of punishment.

Other girls were not so lucky. The ideas were Penny's, but it was always someone else who got in trouble carrying them out. And more often than not it was Penny, loyal Penny, speaking up for her friends, pleading their cases with outwardly frowning, inwardly amused nuns, who got punishments lightened.

There was nothing Penny would not do for her friends. She loaned money, rolled up hair, listened patiently to their complaints about parents or schoolwork, handed out copies of test answers guaranteed to be right to those who had to take an exam for the second time (she was never caught, of course), and set an example the other girls struggled constantly to equal.

In some cases, it did some good. Imagene, who had been an indifferent scholar, began concentrating on her schoolwork and pulled her grades up from C's and D's to B-pluses. She also slept on metal hair rollers, hoping to acquire a facsimile of Penny's soft curls, and awoke with blinding headaches and a mass of dark frizz. When the nun in charge of the dormitory made her stop, Penny comforted her by saying, "I think straight hair's a lot better, really, 'Gene. Mine curls up something awful when it gets wet, I look just like a poodle. I'll bet your hair will be just gorgeous when you grow up, you'll wear those sophisticated styles like Audrey Hepburn."

If she had questioned it, which she did not, Imagene might have wondered why Penny really did seem to favor her over the prettier, more popular girls in the class. To Imagene, Penny's friendship was a gift from the gods, never to be examined or doubted. When other girls said, "Penny's my best friend," Imagene comforted herself with the knowledge that Penny was just being nice to everybody. "I like you best; I really do," Penny had told her more than once.

34

"Isn't it nice of Elaine to be so friendly with that homely little Tutt girl?" Sister Mercy said to Sister Magdalene.

"Elaine's the sort who's always picking up strays," Sister Magdalene replied. "Last year, when I had her in my classroom, she adopted that poor Hammersmith child; remember her? The one with the absolutely ferocious stammer? Really took the girl under her wing, they were practically inseparable. Paula Hammersmith went home with Elaine for Christmas vacation last year, in fact. But then her family moved to Houston. It must have been hard on Paula, leaving a friend like Elaine Endicott who'd done so much for her."

From the time Imagene moved into the dormitory used by elementary-grade pupils at St. Mary's, Barney only visited her once before the end of the school year. That was the day he came to take her home for a miserable Thanksgiving weekend which she spent in the attic with her magazines and her schoolbooks, while Barney and some "friends" played poker and drank in the living room below, amid a welter of bottles and overflowing ashtrays. The house stank, and so did Barney. When Imagene returned to the convent school, it no longer frightened her; it was a welcome sight, a safe refuge.

Penny's father, Kellam Endicott, was more available to his daughter. The Endicotts lived on a vast acreage, miles north of Anson, and like many parents of St. Mary's pupils, were too preoccupied with their own lives to develop genuine family ties, but Kellam Endicott had a habit of dropping by the convent on weekends and whisking his daughter off to political barbecues and the sort of events that appeared in the Sunday society section of the Anson *Bugle*. Whenever she knew her father was coming, Penny became a bundle of nerves.

Every dress had to be tried on, her hair had to be brushed and pinned and arranged in every possible way, and at the last moment, when the sister rang from downstairs to say, "Your father is waiting for you in the reception parlor, Elaine," Penny would cast a stricken look in the mirror and start all over again with a different dress and a different way of wearing her hair. If it had been anyone but Penny, the other girls would have laughed at the spectacle of an overanxious fourth-grader primping as if for a grownup date.

The first time Endicott came to St. Mary's, Sybil told Imagene about him with rolling eyes. "He is really *neat!* I mean, I wish my daddy was like Mr. Endicott. Every time he comes here to get Penny, he brings a box of candy, a big box, just for this dorm, and he doesn't treat us like kids at all. You'll see. When I get older, I'm going to have a boyfriend just like Mr. Endicott."

So when Penny's father was announced as waiting below for his tardy daughter, Imagene was not surprised that all the girls in the dorm offered to go down and "keep him company." What did surprise—and flatter—her was Penny's reaction. "Uh-uh," said the blond girl firmly. "I want Imagene to go. 'Gene, you entertain my father until I finish getting dressed, okay? Tell him I'll just be a minute and . . . before you go, tell me honestly, how does this blue jersey look? Will he like it?"

Kellam Endicott was waiting in the Victorian parlor known as the reception room. As Imagene came down the stairs, he stood up and smiled. He was a tall, broad-shouldered man, booted and holding a Stetson in his hand, and even a ten-year-old girl could see that he was handsome and feel the power of his charm. He had Penny's golden hair and blue eyes, plus the added contrast of a deep tan carefully maintained year-round at considerable effort.

When he saw the plain little girl coming toward him, there was a flicker of quickly masked disappointment in his eyes, then he gave her a broad smile and a courtly bow. "So this is the new little lady my princess has been telling me about! Imagene, isn't it? Come over here and sit by me and tell me all about yourself."

Imagene had the distinct impression that he was being nice to her out of duty rather than inclination, a feeling most children are familiar with in the presence of adults. So why did the other girls think he was so wonderful?

She sat down beside him on the old-fashioned red brocade sofa, folding her hands in her lap ("Make a cup and saucer with them, dear") as the nuns had taught her. She paused before answering. "I don't know all about myself," she said, after considering his request. "I'm not quite eleven yet."

Caught by surprise, Kellam Endicott rewarded her with a genuine smile. "Will you know more when you reach the great age of eleven?"

Imagene chewed her lip and the question. "I don't think so. I suppose you have to be old enough to die before you can know all about yourself, and by then it's too late to do anything about it."

Kellam Endicott roared with laughter; not the calculated, aren't-we-good-ole-boys-together laughter of the would-be politician at barbecues and smokers, but real belly-shaking guffaws. "How old did you say you are?" he asked her afterward, still chuckling. "A hundred and ten?"

Just then Penny came running down the broad oak staircase, breathless and smiling. "Here I am, Daddy! I really hurried this time, see? You said to wear something blue so I put on this dress, is it okay? I mean, is it what you want?" She hurried across the room like an eager puppy coming for praise.

"Yes, that'll do all right," Endicott told her, giving his daughter a perfunctory hug. "This is an airport dedication we're going to, and we'll be meeting your mother there. She said she's wearing a blue suit and I thought it would look good to have you both in the same color, more of a family group. Got a couple magazine photographers coming to do a little layout in color." He shot back his cuff and looked at his watch. "We better get going. Nice to meet you, Imagene." He turned and walked briskly from the room, with Penny trotting beside him. He did not seem to be aware of the way his child gazed adoringly up at him.

Imagene stood alone in the empty parlor, hearing their fading footsteps echoing down the hallway.

A father and daughter, doing things together. Well, of course, a girl like Penny would have a father who wanted to be with her, to share things with her and take her places.

If I were as pretty as Penny, if I could do all the things Penny can do, I'd have a father who loved me, too, Imagene thought. Why does somebody like Penny get everything, when I don't have anything?

And then, because she was Imagene and had seen enough self-pity to sicken her of the emotion forever, she put the thought aside and turned her attention to something else.

For the first time since coming to St. Mary's, she was alone and unsupervised in the reception parlor, looking directly at the massive central staircase with its wide, inviting banister. "Someday when nobody's around I'm going to slide down that banister," Penny had said. "It's absolutely forbidden, and I'll bet it's the best sliding banister in the world."

Tingling with anticipation, Penny's words urging her up every step, Imagene climbed to the top and looked down. She kept expecting a nun to appear, but none did. From the head of the long staircase, the banister looked unexpectedly steep. It gleamed with loving waxing, the work of generations of nuns.

It would be very fast.

Breathing heavily, Imagene—who had never slid down a banister—slung one leg across and tried to steady herself before letting go. But she was inexperienced and misjudged her timing. Before she was ready, she was flying downward with a sickening rush. There was no newel post at the bottom to stop her, merely an elegant left-turning curve, and she hurtled off the banister to land on her tailbone with a sickening thud at the foot of the stairs, all breath knocked out of her.

Nuns came running then, of course, from every direction, and she was hugged and scolded and ultimately punished by being kept indoors all weekend, while Penny and the others played outside in the last golden days of the late Indian summer.

Imagene was watching from the dormitory window when Penny hit the last home run of the season. After she crossed home plate, she looked up at the nearby building and saw Imagene, nose pressed against the window glass. Penny grinned and waved at her friend, then impulsively abandoned the game to come running indoors and thundering up the stairs to share and lighten Imagene's exile for the rest of the afternoon.

Four

AUTUMN faded into the gray days of winter, not yet cold, for winter came late to Anson, Texas, but dreary enough to keep children indoors much of the time. Imagene grew accustomed to living in a dormitory with other girls. On occasion she missed the privacy of her attic retreat and her own uninterrupted thoughts, but most of the time it was nice to feel herself part of a family. When she commented on it though, other girls who had siblings at home jeered at her. "Listen, 'Gene, if you had to live with a snoopy kid sister or two, you wouldn't think it was so great!"

"I always wanted a sister," Penny told her quietly. "I think it's nice, too."

History and geography and English, catechism and math and phys. ed. Diagram sentences. Where does an adjectival phrase go? Write letters home that were never answered. Choir practice. Confession on Fridays, a nervous listing of the small venial sins possible to schoolgirls. ("Imagine what it would be like to have to confess a mortal sin?" "Oh, I couldn't! I could never . . .") Holy days of obligation. Volleyball.

Christmas was coming and there was a crèche to be prepared, and the retelling, ever new, of the old miracles.

Penny asked Imagene to spend Christmas with her at the Endicotts' estate, a sprawling "gentleman's ranch."

Imagene was astonished. "Are you kidding?"

It was late afternoon; the girls were returning to the dormitory from choir practice in the chapel. Fading light lay in flat planes across the playground, illuminating dust motes but giving no warmth. There were black shadows beneath the trees at the edge of the softball field. The students walked in small groups, one occasionally breaking away from one set to become satellite to another.

Penny had just issued her invitation when Betty Sue Metzger joined them. "What are you talking about—Christmas?" she asked, mental antennae quivering.

Penny nodded, noncommittal.

"Are you going to invite someone to your place this year like you did last year?" Betty Sue asked eagerly. Everybody knew the Endicotts kept a stable full of registered quarter horses for guests to ride, and Betty Sue preferred horses to anything, even Rock Hudson.

Betty Sue was a pretty girl with heavy, mahogany-colored hair and a flirtatious giggle.

Penny looked rueful. "I wanted to ask you, Betty Sue," she said, not letting her eyes meet Imagene's. "But your folks always take you to the Bahamas, so I knew it wouldn't be any use."

"Oh, I think I could get out of it. I'm sick and tired of lying around on those same old beaches getting sand in my shorts. I can call home tonight . . ."

"Oh, dear," Penny lamented, "this year is definitely out. I've already invited somebody else and she's accepted. You know how it is. But next year for sure, okay?"

Betty Sue nodded, obviously disappointed but unable to keep from returning Penny's guileless smile. "Sure, I know how it is. Next year's great."

Betty Sue drifted off again to join a different group, and Imagene said to Penny, "I hadn't accepted; I don't even know if my father will let me do it. Why'd you tell her that?"

Penny's voice was urgent. "You just have to come, 'Gene; I don't want Betty Sue or any of those other girls. Promise me you'll do it. Promise me!"

Those other girls. Imagene knew who she meant. The girls like Penny, with their pretty faces and their nice clothes; the "in" girls who had gone to St. Mary's since the first grade, who had already visited numerous times in each other's houses, knew the same people, repeated the same jokes. Pretty, popular, secure girls like Penny, who had it all.

Yet Penny was turning her back on them and deliberately offering special friendship to Imagene. It was the highest honor the lonely little girl had received in her life.

When Imagene nervously telephoned Barney from Mother Superior's office, he had no objections. He was relieved to anticipate a Christmas spent without his daughter's eyes following him everywhere, seeing where he hid his bottles, watching as he stumbled on the steps. "You go on and have a good time, hear?" was his only parental comment.

Kellam Endicott came for the two girls himself and drove them to the Endicott estate. His big silver Cadillac awed Imagene. It looked as if it had never been used, the paint so glossy it might still be wet. The upholstery smelled new—an odor she had not encountered in an automobile before. Barney Tutt's succession of cheap cars were used when he bought them. Imagene sat beside Penny in almost speechless silence as the Cadillac sped along the highway out of

Anson, then began zigzagging along rural roads, past the acreage of "gentleman's ranches" with white-rail fences and unfamiliar breeds of show cattle.

"Those are Brangus—that's a Brahma-Angus cross," Penny said, playing tour guide. "Those big white cows are Charolais. French, you know. Daddy says we may get some of those sometime, isn't that right, Daddy? The governor raises them, you know, and the governor's a friend of ours. Well, of my father's, really."

For the first time, Endicott entered the conversation. "That's right, princess," he added. "Him and me are like that." He took one hand off the wheel and raised it with two fingers overlapped, to show his proximity to power.

Ahead of them loomed a large estate gate, with a professionally painted sign showing a logo of bluebonnets beneath the words SKYFLOWER RANCH. The car turned in, and Imagene heard the unfamiliar rumble of a cattle guard as they drove across it. "What place is this?" she asked Penny.

"Home, of course," was the reply.

A long drive lined with ornamental fruit trees, leafless in mid-December, circled through manicured pastures to the house. When Imagene got her first look at the Endicott residence, her heart went out to it in one great surge of love and longing.

It was a sprawling white-frame structure, casually patterned on Mount Vernon, with Colonial columns adorning the front and a pair of self-consciously symmetrical wings angled to embrace the lawn. Behind sparkling windowpanes, every shade was adjusted to the same level. Foundation plantings had been shaped and pruned with mathematical precision. No stray leaf or forgotten tool marred the perfection of the landscape.

Penny's home looked just like the cover of a magazine. She had been born and raised there; she had never lived anywhere else. She could look forward to living in that same house until she was grown, then being married from it to move into a home of her own, not too dissimilar in cost and style—her father would see to that.

Imagene Tutt had lived in several houses like the shabby bungalow on Belmont Street. She had lived in apartments over garages and in basements; there were times when home had been a trailer court or a seedy motel on the outskirts of a town.

Her father had seen to that.

She stared at the Endicott house as a sinner might stare at the gates of heaven, never expecting to enter, not even truly believing, but with tears in the eyes and a lump in the throat.

Some deep pride, surfacing for the first time, told her to act as unimpressed as if such places were her accustomed environment. Head up, she followed Penny and her father into the house, resisting the temptation to stare at the crystal chandelier in the entrance hall or the oriental carpet underfoot. Because she was not paying attention to those things, her keen ears picked up a whisper not meant for them.

Under his breath, Kellam Endicott was asking his daughter, "Why didn't you invite Betty Sue, or that Lewis girl? You know I like them. Wouldn't you have had more fun with girls like that?"

Penny shook her head. Her answer was unintelligible.

Imagene fought to keep tears from welling in her eyes. Mr. Endicott hadn't wanted her at all—he wanted one of the other girls; Amy Lewis with her dimples and her saucy charm.

That's all right, Imagene told herself. Penny wants me.

She had never seen a household like the Endicotts'. Servants appeared and disappeared like magic, silent and well-trained, polishing and straightening a room the moment it was empty and then whisking themselves away if someone approached. Imagene wondered how they liked having to be invisible. Her father wanted her to be invisible.

Mrs. Endicott would not appear until dinner, an elaborate meal served by a Mexican cook in a starched uniform, and then Mrs. Endicott just smiled and ate and said very little. It was as if she were under orders to be invisible, too.

Penny's room was a chamber designed for a princess, with a white four-poster bed and starched organdy curtains tied back with blue ribbons. Penny tidied the room herself with fanatic zeal, as if she expected to be graded on it. She had made neat labels and taped them beneath the handles of all the drawers, listing their contents, and she kept a notebook describing every outfit in her closet and its accessories. "It's important to be organized," she explained to Imagene. "We go to a lot of places and have our pictures in the paper and all, and Daddy wants to be sure we look just perfect all the time. He says the more organized you are, the fewer mistakes you make."

It was a strange holiday. Imagene watched, puzzled, as Penny exhausted herself showing off for her father. But no matter what she did, it was never good enough to please Kellam Endicott.

He kept a chart hanging on the front of the upstairs bathroom door, marked off in ruled columns punctuated with occasional gold stars, but more often studded with black x's. Every day some new notation was added to it, and Imagene asked Penny about.

"That's my elimination chart," Penny explained, blushing slightly. "If I have a good . . . bowel movement by ten in the morning he puts a gold star on it, but if I don't I have to eat prunes and bran and sit on the toilet till I have something to show him."

Imagene was appalled. "That's awful! You mean he grades you on your . . . your . . . and puts that chart up where everybody can see it?"

Penny nodded. "That's to make me try harder. Sometimes he tells my friends about it; sometimes he even shows it to his guests. Don't look that way, 'Gene; don't you understand? He does it because he loves me! He wants me to be healthy, that's all."

Imagene did not understand. Kellam Endicott might indeed love his daughter, but it had nothing to do with the kind of love Imagene had always imagined other fathers—not Barney—might show their children. Endicott never touched his child, never even kissed her good night. Their only physical contact was the frequent, savage spankings that followed her failures to live up to his standards. Shoes unpolished or a minuscule breach of conduct could bring on the spankings, with Penny turned over her father's knee and a hard hand slamming again and again across her bare buttocks. Then there was always a hasty pushing away, a rejection of both the child and the touching.

He did not push other little girls away. The house seemed to be filled with them throughout the holiday—ten- to fifteen-year-olds, the daughters of friends and business associates invited to come and "see Penny," to share the stables and the game room, the heated swimming pool and the Mario Lanza records.

More than once Imagene overheard Kellam say to his wife, who was an older, thinner version of Penny, with streaked ash-blond hair, "We've got to get more young people over here for Penny, you hear me? Get on the phone and call somebody, will you?"

Mrs. Endicott would give him an unreadable look, somewhere between fear and defiance but containing deeper, darker emotions. When he stood his ground and held her gaze, she always made the calls.

Penny idolized him and blamed whatever problems her parents had on her mother. "She's never made him happy, you know," the girl confided to Imagene as they lay together in the white four-poster. "My parents don't even sleep in the same room anymore."

On Christmas Eve, Penny broke the porcelain angel that topped the Christmas tree. The tree had been brought from town in Mrs. Endicott's station wagon and set up in the living room, its tip almost touching the high-beamed ceiling. It was the first flocked tree Imagene had ever seen, a lush spruce sprayed thickly with a white chemical substance to give the appearance of snow. The lights made it sparkle with a fairy-tale beauty. At that moment, Imagene vowed that she would never have a plain green tree, once she was grown up and in charge of her own life.

A photographer from the newspaper arrived to take pictures of the family and the house for the Sunday supplement. Christmas, Texas-style. Kellam Endicott stood in the center with an arm around each of his women. "My two best girls," he called them, beaming into the camera. Penny, trying to snuggle still closer to him, jostled the tree somehow and it swayed. The antique figurine had not been fastened securely enough; it came loose and smashed on the tile floor.

"That's all right, honey, don't worry about that for a minute," Endicott said for the photographer's benefit, but after the man left he took his daughter upstairs and beat her with his belt. Imagene stood outside the closed door of the bedroom, frightened by the sounds of violence but more frightened by the fact that Penny did not cry.

Afterward, Penny showed her the angry welts on her buttocks, crimson stripes across the pale skin, oozing blood. Penny seemed proud of them.

When Mr. Endicott wasn't around, Imagene could pretend to herself that she and Penny were sisters; that she too lived in this beautiful house, amid these lovely things. Mrs. Endicott was nice to her then, in a quiet way, and even the servants seemed more friendly. The cook made cakes and fudge and sent them to the girls' room with big pitchers of cold milk. Penny and Imagene played the last games of little girlhood together: paper dolls and movie star and nurse. Penny liked nurse best.

"There are nursing nuns, you know," she told Imagene. "We read about them last year. Sister Magdalene told us it's one of the most noble vocations, taking care of the sick. Like being an angel of mercy. I take care of my mother when she's sick sometimes—she gets the most awful head-aches—and I like doing it. 'Gene, have you ever thought about being a nun? I mean, really?"

Imagene considered. The nuns occasionally spoke to their pupils of the privileges and obligations of the religious life, but they never minimized the sacrifices required nor attempted to glamorize their vocation. Nevertheless, there was not a girl at St. Mary's who had not at some time daydreamed, however briefly, of following an idolized teacher into holy orders.

Except for Imagene Tutt, who had never thought about it at all. She was going to have a beautiful house and a white-flocked Christmas tree.

"Gee, Pen, are you serious?"

"Of course I am. It would be wonderful, I think. Have you ever seen anybody happier than nuns?"

The two girls were sitting on the floor at the foot of Penny's bed, with an assortment of paper dolls designed to represent ballet dancers arranged between them. They looked with unseeing eyes at the dolls, picturing other life-styles. They thought about being nuns.

Imagene imagined voices raised sweetly in chapel, floating on waves of incense. She remembered watching her teachers walking in silent companionship along the garden pathways, hands serenely folded at their waists, obviously sharing something very special.

Nuns. Timeless, ageless, full of grace, assured of heaven, living intimately with a loving Father . . .

The paper dolls were put back into their labeled drawer and the two girls spent the rest of the afternoon being nuns instead, wearing veils made of carefully pinned pillowcases. At first they were nurses but then, to be fair, they tried being teachers, and Imagene solemnly intoned basic Latin and English grammar while Penny rearranged furniture to simulate a classroom peopled with her expensive collection of Madame Alexander dolls.

"We could do it, 'Gene," Penny said. "We could take our vows together when we grow up and be nuns; then we'd always be friends and have each other. What do you think? I really want to do it, you know?" She squeezed Imagene's hand. "And I want you to do it with me."

Wanted. Wrapped in it, lapped in it as in a satin comforter, Imagene lay in bed that night and pictured herself and Penny as nuns. Wanted; together; chosen by God.

Five

TEXAS THRIVED in the fifties. Industries were spawned and exploded into unprecedented growth. Everyone seemed to be making money. Almost everyone. Land developers were carving up the prairie in earnest, spreading a network of concrete grids like right-angled spider webs across dry acres not yet surrendered by the scorpion and the horny-toad. Stands of feathery pale-green mesquite were cut and burned, to be replaced by tract houses landscaped with oleanders and creeping juniper. Frustrated gardeners from Virginia or Ohio struggled to grow azaleas and roses in unyielding caliche clay, only to see them droop and die in the hostile environment.

In the five-and-dime store on the wrong side of town, where he was assistant manager, Barney Tutt did a brisk business in the new plastic decorator items, flowers and wall plaques and household unnecessaries produced by Endicott Products, Inc. But there was never quite enough money to cover his personal bills after he took his liquor money off the top.

The fifties were years of change. While the students at St. Mary's Academy were entering puberty, a war bearing the quixotic label of "police action" was subsiding into inconclusion in distant Korea. In Germany a destroyed nation was rebuilding itself upon foundations financed by the puritan consciences of its conquerors. In Hollywood a girl once called Norma Jean Baker was rebuilding herself, complete with euphonic name and platinum hair, into the sex symbol of the age.

Under a tropical sun in Indochina, an administrative center known as Dienbienphu fell to the Vietminh, and the French tricolor was hauled down to be replaced by a Communist flag. That same day, seventh-graders at St. Mary's Academy were dancing with each other in the gymnasium to a Kitty Kallen recording of "Little Things Mean a Lot."

Penny Endicott, the first girl in her class to develop breasts, had received a distinctive brown-and-white-striped Neiman-Marcus box from her mother, containing an assortment of dainty silk-and-lace brassieres. She let every girl in the dorm try them on, though she was the only one who had enough to fill them.

Imagene Tutt began to gorge on doughnuts and candy, hoping her figure would swell into curves like Penny's. As the weeks passed, Penny grew even prettier, and Imagene only grew pudgy.

On the third floor, where the sixteen seventh-graders shared double dormitory bedrooms, crucifixes competed for wall space with framed photographs of Elvis Presley. Proscribed by the nuns, bootlegged copies of "Heartbreak Hotel" throbbed with raw sexuality beneath tented quilts meant to muffle the sound, while giggling girls crouched over the portable record player, sighing in rapture.

Lines began to form to use the telephone, and there was a daily rush for the mail. Soon feverish correspondences were being carried on with boys met during Christmas vacation or Easter break, boys from St. Luke's, St. Joe's, Sacred Heart. Boys who would attend Loyola and Notre Dame.

Penny Endicott reigned unchallenged on the third floor. The setter of style, the smuggler of Elvis records, she was the center of every group. Penny had been promised her own car as soon as she learned how to drive and already her classmates looked forward to their turns behind the wheel, knowing Penny would share. She would not have to wait for her sixteenth birthday and the formality of a license. Kellam Endicott had friends; exceptions could be made.

Everyone told Penny their secrets; she was the school confidante. She had a habit of smiling encouragement and then just waiting quietly, never questioning, merely being a sympathetic presence that said, I'm here if you want to talk. Trust me.

And trust her they did. Every girl in the class took her problems to Penny at one time or another—not enough allowance from home, an untimely outbreak of pimples, a mad crush on the most divine boy in the entire whole world. Penny understood and kept the secrets. She loaned money and dispensed Clearasil and dictated charming love letters.

"How do you do it?" Imagene asked her once. "How can you be so patient with people? We never get to spend an undisturbed hour studying without somebody coming in here wanting help with an assignment or some other dumb problem, but you never get mad, you always act like you're glad to see them and just dying to help. It burns me up, but you don't seem to mind at all."

Penny smiled. "My father's a politician, remember? Or he's trying to be. That's one of a politician's tricks, making people think you really care about them, acting like you believe they're as important as *they* think they are. If you do that, other people think you're wonderful."

Imagene felt chilled. "You mean it's all an act? Those girls think you're their friend, Penny!"

"And I am. I give them what they want, don't I? In return they give me what I want."

"What's that?"

"Popularity," Penny said simply.

"But what about real friendships?"

"You're my real friend, 'Gene," Penny said with convincing warmth. "I really mean it. I'm comfortable with you, I don't feel like I have to compete with you all the time."

Imagene smiled a small, rueful smile. "No, I'm certainly no competition for you," she said in a voice so low Penny didn't hear it. They were in the rest room between classes, taking turns puffing on a cigarette—a cigarette!—Penny had miraculously produced from the pages of an algebra book under the very nose of Sister James. Imagene, glimpsing the contraband and Penny's quick, wicked wink, had understood the message: Meet me in the rest room and we'll do something naughty.

The cigarette was more unpleasant than naughty. The pleasure was only in the breaking of rules. Smoking it made Imagene cough and for the rest of the day her mouth would taste, as she said in her own mind, like dirty socks. But sharing the little wickedness with Penny was part of what their relationship was all about. The two faces Imagene saw reflected in the mirror above the row of white porcelain sinks was another part. One belonged to a blue-eyed blonde with a heart-shaped face and dimpled chin, a lovely child who was destined to be a beautiful woman, thanks to an arrangement of genes and chromosomes over which she had no control. The other face was that of a chubby brunette with drab skin and mottled teeth, framed in a halo of bushy hair; the sort of fairy godmother who made Penny even prettier by her proximity.

On a deep level, Imagene had come to understand and accept her role, and the natural jealousies she felt had been so long submerged in love and admiration for Penny that she was not aware of them. It did not even seem unfair that the friendship was in some way conditional upon her homeliness. After all, that was what she had to offer. In return she was Penny's special friend. Whatever happened she was included, and wherever Penny went she was invited.

By keeping Imagene at her side, Penny managed, sometimes, to move the Betty Sues and the Amys out of her immediate area, where they would not compete with her for her father's attention. With only Penny or Imagene to choose between, Kellam Endicott paid a little more attention to his daughter.

As a result, over the years since she first entered St. Mary's, Imagene had spent an increasing amount of time at the Endicott home, taking her Easter break and Christmas vacations with Penny. She was Penny's confederate, Penny's ally against forces she did not, could not, understand. And when the Endicotts gave a formal dance for their daughter at the Silver Lake Country Club, Imagene Tutt was the first St. Mary's girl to be invited.

"I've never been to a dance, Penny. I don't have a long dress or anything; I don't even know a boy I could ask to take me," Imagene protested. She could not bear to think of the embarrassment of telephoning some boy and being turned down.

But Penny merely grinned. "Oh, silly, don't worry about all that. This is just a practice dance, sort of, so when we get a little older and go to proms we'll know how to act. There'll be plenty of boys there from the country club, and they'll dance with all of us. You'll see. You'll have a good time. If you just call your father and explain it to him, he'll let you have the money for a dress."

He didn't. He subjected Imagene to a long, drunken tirade, punctuated by tears, in which he blamed her for everything from selfish extravagance to her mother's death. It was Mrs. Hammond from across the street who ultimately supplied the girl with a formal gown, out of pity. Not new, not even in style, it was the outgrown dress of one of her own daughters, a shiny peach satin that threatened to rip at every seam. "I'm too fat for this," Imagene said sadly, gazing at her reflection in the mirror. She looked like an over-stuffed pink sausage.

"Nonsense, dear, you have a lovely little figure," insisted Mrs. Hammond, who was softhearted and nearsighted. "You'll be the belle of the ball."

Imagene was not the belle of the ball. She sat uncomfortably in a dim corner of the room, so her fat wouldn't be so obvious, and tried to look as if she were used to being at a country club dance. She nursed her glass of ginger ale and smiled at everyone who passed by, and to make it look as if she had a genuine excuse for being there, she took off one of her shoes and rubbed her foot continually, wincing with the pain of one who has danced too much and suffers from blisters.

It was a good act. No one noticed; no one was paying any attention at all to the plain little girl sitting off in a corner. Only Penny came to hunt her out from time to time, bringing some pimpled boy in tow.

"Imagene, this is Clarence Freebarger. He's been dying to meet you," Penny would say, just before dancing away with another football player or track star. Imagene and Clarence would stand or sit together briefly, struggling to find words to say to each other, then the boy's eyes would light with relief and he would exclaim, "I'll get you something to drink!" as he rushed off in search of yet another ginger ale. The soda delivered, Clarence and his successors pretended they had urgent business elsewhere and Imagene was once more left alone, rubbing her foot and giving a grim imitation of a girl having the time of her life.

The evening seemed to last for years.

Later, Penny asked, "Didn't you enjoy that? Aren't you glad you came?"

"Wonderful," said Imagene. "I had a wonderful time, Pen."

Penny, still glowing from her own triumph—even Kellam Endicott had commented on the number and social status of his daughter's conquests—had been too busy to pay close attention to Imagene during the evening, aside from towing boys into her vicinity as a well-trained hostess should. But now she heard something pained in her friend's voice, something bordering on sarcasm.

"'Gene, are you sure?" she questioned carefully. "That you had a good time?" A frown creased her smooth forehead. To have let her friend be neglected through her own carelessness was a monumental social gaffe. She was suddenly worried and anxious. Had her father noticed?

Imagene saw the quick concern on Penny's face and rose to the occasion with a gallant, elaborate lie that grew out of her own concern for Penny's happiness, and in spite of the knowledge that she was committing a venial sin. She had already come to suspect that some sins weighed less heavily on the soul than others, and some could be discounted altogether, if they were in a good cause. Comforting Penny, who had so often comforted her, was a very good cause.

"I had the best time I've ever had, Penny," she said with convincing honesty, forcing herself to meet and hold Penny's eyes. "I got asked to dance more than I wanted to—I got this blister on my heel, darn it—and three boys took down my phone number. Didn't you see that cute one with the crew cut—Ralph-something, I think he's LaVonne's cousin? He would hardly leave me alone."

After they had gone to bed, she lay wide-eyed in the dark, listening to Penny's rhythmic breathing across the room. Never again, Imagene thought. I won't go through anything like that again. I'll learn.

I'll learn. Like Penny learned from her father. Now there's a rumor he's going to run for the state senate next year, so obviously he knows how to make people like him. And Penny knows. I'll learn to be popular too.

It seemed so cold-blooded, so calculating, that something inside the girl shrank from the task, but the memory of that endless humiliating evening spurred her on. I don't have to like myself very much if only other people will love me the way they do Penny, she thought. That will be enough. Just to be loved. And Penny has the secret.

The only secret Penny did not have was that which would make her own father love her, and this puzzled Imagene. How could a man be so cold to such a perfect child? If I were like Penny, Imagene thought, my father would have loved me. But there was no understanding the ways of fathers. Girl children in their terrible vulnerability needed that love as they needed air to breathe, but there were no guarantees of obtaining it. Not even for Elaine Endicott, who knew all the secrets.

Imagene began studying Penny as seriously as she studied algebra or Latin. She copied the tilt of her head and practiced her exact smile in the mirror for hours, steeling herself against the reality of her own plain, wistful little face, trying to see only Penny's assured beauty in the reflection.

All the St. Mary's girls tended to model themselves on Penny, but none went as far as Imagene Tutt. Penny, aware of it, was benevolently amused. She began helping Imagene with those finer grace points no one had shown the girl before. She coached her in telephone flirtations—unnecessarily, since no boy ever spent hours on the telephone with Imagene—and she searched through fashion magazines, looking for styles in hair and makeup that the two girls could experiment with on weekends at the Endicott estate.

So much attention, like water to a parched daisy, began to bring something to life in Imagene Tutt. Something new. Her eyes sparkled—perhaps it was just Penny's mascara—and her sallow complexion took on new color. With a mighty effort of will, she stayed off doughnuts and fudge and turned down bread at meals, until a hint of a figure began to show itself through her babyfat.

And the very next semester, a new girl came to St. Mary's; tall, bony, big-nosed, a girl who made even Imagene look attractive by comparison. And suddenly Penny had a new chum, and Imagene was on the outside again, looking in.

They were still roommates, but Penny spent more and more time with the storklike Amanda Wheeler. When Imagene complained, Penny was touchingly remorseful.

"Gosh, 'Gene, I didn't think you minded. I thought you of all people would understand. Amanda doesn't have anybody, do you realize that? I mean, look at the poor thing!"

Imagene felt betrayed, but she did not blame Penny. It was her own fault, as always; some lack in herself, some blemish—or perhaps a fading of blemishes in this case.

She could not bear to think of Penny and Amanda walking to the lockers together, giggling over some private joke, or sitting together with their heads bent over a single textbook. It was still worse to imagine Amanda going home with Penny for holidays, home to that beautiful house that had come to be her own home in her secret dreams.

She wrote a poem about blue eyes and cheeks like peaches and hid it between the pages of her roommate's notebook. When the handwritten sheet was discovered in class, Penny read it, then glanced up with a quizzical smile, her eyebrows slightly lifted. She looked like a questioning angel. "You wrote this?" she mouthed silently.

Imagene nodded, blushing furiously.

That night in their room, Penny gave Imagene one of the impulsive hugs that was almost a trademark of hers, then let one hand stray down Imagene's neck and into her blouse.

A door slammed in the hall. The telephone rang; someone turned on a shower.

Imagene felt soft fingers brush across her nipple, bringing

it erect. Her mouth was dry. She stared at the closed door of their room, seeing the panels where the mahogany stain was streaked and the wax shone unevenly. She felt rooted to the spot.

Was this a new condition to Penny's friendship? Was this a test she could not afford to fail?

It was too much for her. She was an ignorant adolescent girl, unprepared. Unfamiliar emotions swamped her and her body made its own choice without conscious direction, shuddering away from the exploring hand.

Penny pulled back instantly. "I'm sorry, 'Gene," she said with a breathless little laugh. "I didn't mean anything by that. Sometimes I do crazy things; I don't even know why. But you understand, don't you? You've always understood."

Imagene stared at her, wordless.

"Imagene? Say something, will you? I told you I'm sorry. I don't know what came over me. But we're still friends, aren't we? Best friends?"

There was a note of pleading in her voice. Penny, pleading for Imagene's friendship? Without understanding why Penny should now be the supplicant, Imagene pressed her advantage. "You have Amanda," she said.

Penny waved her hand. "Amanda's all right, but she's certainly not my best friend. To tell you the truth, I'm beginning to think she's the most stubborn, opinionated girl I've ever met. You can't tell her *anything*. And she's not totally trustworthy, either. She told Mother Superior that I let her copy one of my papers. I'm really sorry you think I've been neglecting you for her, but things will be different from now on, I promise. Just say we're friends again, 'Gene. Please. I need you."

That last statement was torn still bleeding from some sore place inside of Penny, and Imagene, who had so many similar sore places, recognized it. Her whole heart went out to Penny in a rush. "Oh, Pen, of course we're friends. Best friends, always. You don't ever have to worry about that."

The tension left Penny's face and she smiled, that irresistible candybox smile. For just a moment she had been afraid her impulsive act had cost her the uncritical, worshipful love she had come to depend upon. The love that made up in a small measure for her father's rejection of her own adoration. But looking at Imagene's face, she knew that everything was all right, there was still at least one person who thought she was . . . perfect.

From that night on, however, she dropped the affectionate hug from her repertoire of mannerisms.

Six

IN TEXAS, in that region known as Tornado Alley, people heard what sounded like the approach of a giant train and hid beneath their beds or cowered in their storm cellars while their houses exploded. A man tried to drive his new car into his garage only to watch in disbelief as the garage perversely backed away from him, sucked into the funnel of the tornado. A woman emerged from her shower stall, dripping wet, to find that all that was left of her house was a bare wooden floor studded with broken pipes. The storm had taken everything, leaving her shocked and naked on a bare stage, without so much as a towel.

The sun burned through seven blazing months of summer; a copper disk in a melting sky. Hurricanes in the Gulf of Mexico brought massive flooding that made it impossible for farmers in East Texas to get into town to cash their drought-relief checks. Then the brief, bitter winter came slashing down from the Panhandle, encasing everything in a sheathing of ice as deadly as it was beautiful.

Eisenhower was President, the Soviets were preparing to launch the first Sputnik, and Penny Endicott offered her virginity to a Mexican laborer who worked for her father.

Male-female relationships were the principle topic of conversation at St. Mary's when the nuns were out of earshot. Conversations were larded with Donny-this and Bobby Joe-that. In the spring, Imagene and her classmates would be graduating, and more than one hand sparkled with diamonds. But Penny, incredibly, was not among the engaged. Neither was Imagene Tutt, to no one's surprise including her own.

There was considerable speculation about Penny's romantic life, and her refusal to discuss it with them provoked her friends into giggling flights of fantasy. "Is he someone from out of town, an older man?" "A movie star, I'll bet; can't you just picture him with Penny?" "How about some oilman's son, working as a roughneck on a drilling rig to learn the business from the ground up?" LaVonne guessed, rolling her eyes.

Penny wouldn't say.

Imagene was aware of a simmering excitement beneath the surface. Penny had a special glow about her, a sparkle in her eyes like that of a child willfully doing mischief. "Who are you seeing, Pen?" Imagene begged to know. "Come on, you can tell me. I won't breathe a word to anybody, cross my heart."

The two girls were alone in their shared room on the third floor of St. Mary's. The bookshelf between their beds was crammed with copies of *St. Augustine* and the lives of various saints; books on history and algebra and *My Friend Flicka*. Jammed behind that impressive façade were rolled-up movie magazines and a well-thumbed copy of *Lady Chatterley's Lover*. Penny had propped a mirror in the window so she could experiment with makeup in natural light. "It's just someone I met, 'Gene," she said casually.

Imagene, who had learned the technique from watching Penny, said nothing, just smiled encouragingly and waited. Eventually, Penny began stuffing words into the vacuum between them.

"I don't talk about him because Daddy would have an absolute fit if he found out," she explained. "He would never, I mean never, let me hear the end of it. I have to keep it secret from him; you must understand that, 'Gene. You know my father."

"I know him well enough to know you shouldn't keep secrets from him. You're right; he would be awfully angry."

"You better believe it. Oh, he has his own secrets, of course, things he thinks nobody else knows about."

"What are you talking about?"

"My father's pretty little secrets." Penny narrowed her eyes slightly, and there was contempt and jealousy in her voice. "I've been watching him, you know, for a long time. You can't live in a house with somebody for your entire life without finding out a lot of things about them that they think no one knows." Just talking about it brought back the tingle of excitement she had felt since she first began spying on Kellam Endicott, getting a vicarious thrill from observing actions she only partly understood. In the beginning, some instinct had warned her that her father's behavior was going beyond unspoken boundaries; as her body and emotions developed, they were influenced by what she saw and what she gradually guessed. Spying on her father came to be a game, one of the most exciting of all games, but she never condemned him for what she saw. Because he was her father, her idol, she accepted Kellam Endicott's behavior without question.

All of the sex things, all the things that made Penny's body tingle and her heart race, became exciting only if they were forbidden and dangerous, as her father's sexual activities were forbidden. The clean-cut, socially acceptable young men who courted her in their polo shirts and white bucks made her feel nothing. They were just the safe ones, the ones her parents would allow her to see.

Miguel was different. No one would have sanctioned any relationship between the princess of the Endicott estate and Miguel with his scarred face and sweaty hands, his thick accent and moist, strangely innocent dark eyes.

Miguel had murmured, *"Madre de Dios!"* when she slipped out to him in the twilight that first time and took off her clothes in a thicket of mesquite trees. He had looked at her then as a man might look at a saint.

But he had not treated her like a saint.

Penny smiled. "I'm better at keeping things secret than my father is, even," she boasted. "Nobody knows about Miguel; I've seen to that, right under Daddy's nose. Nobody until you, 'Gene."

Imagene thought she said "Michael." "Are you serious about this boy?" she asked. "I mean, if you really like him, why would your father take it so hard? Are the two of you going steady?"

Penny barked a laugh without amusement. "Going steady? With Miguel? Oh, that's wonderful! Imagine Miguel coming to the front door with a corsage and taking me to the country club dance!"

Imagene was stunned. "Miguel?" she echoed. After spending years in Texas, she knew very well the sharply drawn lines one did not cross. Our kind of people; not our kind. Us; them. Even Barney recognized such distinctions. Though he had slipped from assistant manager of a five-and-dime to clerk in a failing shoe store to kitchen help in an even less successful café, he had always been quick to say he worked "not in the Mex district, thank God!"

Imagene stared at Penny. "You're dating a Mexican?"

Penny laughed. "Don't look like that! Miguel doesn't have horns and a forked tail. He's really rather a doll except for a bad scar on his cheek, but I don't mind it. He got it in a

knife fight in Laredo when he was only thirteen." She related that with pride, as another girl might boast of her
boyfriend's football injuries.

Imagene's social life consisted of rare dates with the
brothers of classmates, unsuccessful ventures during which
she was rigid with nervousness or inclined to break out in
off-putting giggles. She found it hard to take seriously any
boy who might be interested in her; they always seemed
like second choice, the sort of boys who could not get a date
with Penny.

Penny had it all, the football heroes and the millionaire's
son, and now she was involved—secretly!—with a dark and
dashing Mexican, of all things, with a scar on his face!

When she got over her first shock, Imagene was thrilled
by the romance. Penny was Juliet, her Romeo a boy denied
her by blood and social conventions. Imagene's imagination
immediately concocted a beautiful love story for the two of
them. "Are you just desperately in love with him?" she
asked Penny.

The blond girl twisted a lock of hair through her fingers
and released it in a perfect curl as she considered her answer. "I honestly don't know, 'Gene. I don't know what
being in love is supposed to feel like. It's exciting to be with
Miguel, more exciting than anything I've ever done in my
life, and maybe that's what being in love means. That kind
of excitement. It's the way my father gets excited about
. . ." She broke off and turned her face away from Imagene.
"About his . . ." She bit her lip and fell silent.

"His what?" There was a new tension in Penny; Imagene
could feel it. Something to do with her father; something
she had not meant to say. Kellam Endicott seemed to be a
constant source of hurt and disappointment in his daughter's life, and Imagene had come to hate him for that. If he
had done something new to cause Penny pain, she wanted
to know. Damn the man.

"Your father gets excited about his *what*, Penny?" she

urged. This conversation, in some strange way, was all about Kellam Endicott. Miguel seemed incidental, at least to Penny.

"Nothing, I shouldn't have said anything. Forget that." She still wouldn't meet Imagene's eyes.

"No, Penny," Imagene insisted. "You've got to tell me. I'm your best friend, aren't I? We always help each other? What has your father done now?"

Penny sighed and let it go. "Oh, it's nothing new. He's been this way all my life. Him and his girl friends. His very particular kind of girl friends. The only thing that seems to excite him, outside of politics. The only thing he's interested in. Not me, not Mother, just his . . . his pretty secrets." Her voice turned more bitter from word to word, like fruit shriveling and rotting in speeded-up time. "Oh, it's all right for him to want something he shouldn't have, and take it, too. That's perfectly all right. He's Kellam Endicott. He can do anything he wants, can't he? But I shouldn't. That's different. I have to be his princess, nice and shiny-clean and perfect for the photographers. The press. The voters.

"Well, I am his daughter, 'Gene," she exclaimed, turning suddenly to face Imagene with blazing eyes. "And maybe I want something I shouldn't have, just like he does. And maybe I intend to have it, just like he does!" Her vehemence was edged with defiance.

Imagene tried to bring the conversation back to a level she understood. Penny was talking about something else, something . . . frightening. Something that should be left secret. Imagene, who had stood to one side and observed over the years, knew and did not want to know what Penny was talking about. Undiscussed, kept away from the light, it might never become a reality. "What about love, Penny?" she asked. "Do you love Miguel, or do you just . . . I mean, do you want him because you can't have him?"

"I've always wanted the things I can't have. Why want something easy?"

"So you love him? And he loves you? Is that what you mean by wanting?"

"It's the same thing, 'Gene. Being wanted means being loved. Miguel wants me. Do you know what I'm saying?"

Imagene, who had never felt loved—or wanted—by any male, bowed her head in acknowledgment. "I guess so. What happens next, Penny? Are you going to marry him? I mean, are you going to elope to Oklahoma or something?" She stopped abruptly and stared at her friend with stricken eyes. "But I thought we were going to be nuns together!"

A spasm of guilt crossed Penny's face. "I thought you'd forgotten about that. That was kid stuff, 'Gene. Don't you know that? We all talked about being nuns at one time or another; it was just pretend. And it was my idea anyway, as I recall; I never thought you were serious."

"After we made those plans, I sort of . . . well, I took it for granted, I suppose. It was something to look forward to. If we're . . . if I'm not going to enter the convent with you, I don't know what I'm going to do with my life. I don't have anyplace much to go, after we graduate."

Penny's expression softened. "You can do anything, 'Gene. You're brighter than you think you are. You can have any kind of life you want if you just put your mind to it." It was meant as a sincere assessment; not flattery. "And besides, I don't think I'd make a very good nun. Poverty, chastity, and obedience. How could I live up to that? How could I go back to being a virgin?"

"Go back?" Imagene was very still for a moment. "You mean you actually . . . do . . . it?" Penny would know what she meant by "it." Everyone knew what "it" was. All the girls claimed complete and sophisticated knowledge of "it"— in the abstract, of course—to one another, while simultaneously striving to convince the nuns by word and deed that they had no knowledge of or interest in "it" whatsoever. The truth, as always, lay somewhere in between. To Imagene, with her limited social contacts and the boarding school acting as a buffer between her and the realities of life, "it" was still largely mystery, part unimaginable mechanics and hydraulics, part D. H. Lawrence, part giggles. Embarrassing and tantalizing.

And Penny was doing it. She gazed in awe at her friend.

"Of course we do it," Penny said impatiently, surprised at the other girl's naiveté. "What else would Miguel and I have in common—homework assignments? He's a laborer on my father's land, 'Gene. He's not somebody I could have a regular date with. Or marry, for that matter. But he's crazy about me." She threw back her golden head defiantly, looking wild and beautiful and reckless.

So that was the new standard, the new ideal. In some unnoticed moment, Penny had slipped away from Imagene into a new world; a world she could not hope to enter. There were no hot-eyed, dark boys hiding in the night, waiting for Imagene Tutt.

As for the dream of the two of them becoming nuns together, that was like all of Imagene's dreams. Ephemeral, fading. Glossy four-color ads in a magazine collecting dust in an attic somewhere. The real future loomed ahead, coming at her like an express train, suddenly too fast, with no way of knowing what it held. Judging from the past, the best she could hope for was a colorless existence, trying to survive, always on the fringes of life.

Something strong and stubborn rose up in the girl.

No. There has to more to it than that. I don't know what, but I will have *something*. I will!

The week before graduation, Imagene found her roommate sitting on the closed toilet seat in the bathroom, crying. Her face was red and blotchy and her eyes were swollen. It was the first time Imagene had ever seen Penny cry and it frightened her. She dropped to her knees and threw her arms around her friend. Something far at the back of her mind noted that it was the first time in months she had embraced Penny.

"Oh, 'Gene, I'm pregnant!" the blond girl moaned, burying her ravaged face in Imagene's shoulder.

"You're kidding." She knew as soon as she said it that it was a dumb response, but Penny was in no condition to judge her.

"I wish I were," the other replied in a muffled voice. "God! I wish I were! But I went to a doctor—not our family doctor, a stranger clear across town, and it's definite, all right. I'm caught." She shuddered in Imagene's arms.

To her own vast surprise, Imagene's mind was clear and cool, racing over the possibilities, already accepting the impossible and trying to make sense out of it. "Have you told Miguel?"

Penny drew back and looked at her. "Are you crazy? What good would that do?"

"He should marry you."

Penny shoved free of the cradling arms. "That would be just wonderful, wouldn't it! Can you see me married to some wetback and giving him a baby every year? My father would just love that, wouldn't he? He wouldn't give us a dime; he would forget he ever had a daughter."

"But Miguel would want to marry you. You said yourself he's crazy about you."

"I don't even know that he would be willing to. Sure, he's crazy about me. And I guess he'd think I was a wonderful catch—until Daddy cut us off cold. Then what? Do you know what my life would be like then? Uh-uh, 'Gene. Marrying Miguel is definitely out. I'm not going to spend the rest of my life in some shack in the Mex district." She began crying harder, making no effort to wipe away the tears streaming down her face or the mucus running from her nose in a glistening thread. "It was all just a game!" she wailed. "A game. It wasn't supposed to . . . I never thought . . ." The tears enveloped her and she dissolved into them, crying helplessly in rage and frustration.

Imagene could think of nothing to say. The glossy color pictures in the magazines were crumpled up and distorted. Real life wasn't like that at all.

It must not be that way. Not for Penny. Penny's world must be protected; the fairy tale must remain intact.

"I'll help you, Pen," she vowed.

"How?"

"I don't know yet. But I'll find a way," she added with grim determination. A brand-new feeling of strength, almost of superiority, flooded through her. There must be a way, simply because she would not accept less.

She telephoned Mrs. Hammond. No longer Mrs. Hammond-who-lived-across-the-street, because Barney's descent into the bottle had taken him from the bungalow on Belmont Street to a meanly furnished room at the edge of the downtown area. But Mrs. Hammond had remained a friend, the closest thing Imagene had to a mother figure. Now Imagene spoke to her over the phone in cautious phrases, explaining Penny's situation with carefully chosen words and without naming names, letting Mrs. Hammond jump to the conclusion that it was "poor little Imagene" who was in the most desperate sort of trouble a young girl could have.

Practical Mrs. Hammond had an answer—the only answer possible for a girl pregnant by a Mexican, according to Mrs. Hammond's own social mores. "You need the name of a doctor, dear," she said gently. "A safe, reliable doctor. And those aren't easy to find. But I think I know of one. I'll tell you who to call."

As simply as that, a solution appeared. Imagene felt a wash of relief. Inexperienced as she was, she still knew what kind of a doctor Mrs. Hammond was referring to and what service he would perform. Abortion was not a subject for open discussion at St. Mary's, but it was a dark reality known to be available for those unthinkable strangers who might need such help.

Except now it was for Penny, not a faceless stranger.

Behind the closed door of their room, she told Penny about Mrs. Hammond and the possible arrangements.

For one brief flash, there was hope, even relief, in Penny's eyes, but then she recoiled in horror. "I couldn't, 'Gene! That's a mortal sin! What are you trying to do to me?"

"I'm trying to help you, Penny. It's the only answer."

"Not for me, it isn't. I don't want my soul to burn in hellfire forever!"

"Do you really believe that's what would happen?"

Penny looked doubly shocked. "Of course, don't you?"

"I'm not so sure," Imagene told her thoughtfully. "If God is a god of love, would He do that to us?"

"It's the only punishment for murder."

"We have to murder cows and chickens in order to eat meat," Imagene replied. "I don't think we'll go to hell for that."

"Sin is sin," Penny told her with conviction. Faced with the prospect of God's awful retribution for the breaking of the ultimate law, she had gone, as she always did, to extremes.

Imagene's mind raced back over all the numerous small sins, the venial sins, Penny had committed in the course of their friendship, and had urged her to commit. There had been no pangs of conscience then.

"Fornicating is a sin, too," she reminded Penny, "but that didn't stop you from doing it with Miguel."

Suddenly Imagene thought she could see a graduation of sin more complex than the simple division of mortal or venial; sins that sent one to hell or merely condemned the sinner to an indefinite sentence in purgatory unless confessed and absolved. There was a full spectrum from murder—and was abortion murder, if necessary to save oneself from an impossible life?—all the way down to the simple thoughtless white lie used to spare someone else's feelings.

In her fear and distress, Penny could not be expected to follow such thinking. She only needed help, and she needed it now. To pay back for the many times she had helped Imagene when there was no one else to do it; the money loaned, the sympathy offered, the friendship Imagene had clung to as her only reason for having a positive self-image.

Penny was crying in great hiccuping sobs. "No abortion," she gasped through her tears. "I just couldn't go through with it, 'Gene. You've got to understand."

"Of course I understand. It's all right, Pen, honestly. We'll think of something else. Try not to make yourself sick, okay? Stop crying like that and we'll think of something else."

But I don't know what, she added in her mind. Damn it, Imagene thought with a fierce anger. Damn it all to hell.

Penny did look ill. There were dark circles under her eyes and a greenish tint to her skin. Nausea, perhaps. How early did morning sickness start?

"Well, if you won't have an abortion," Imagene said, her mind desperately searching for alternatives, "that means you're going to have the baby. And that means you'll either have to tell your father or somehow keep him from knowing about it altogether."

"That's it! That's the only way! I'll go away somewhere and have the baby. I'll let him think I've just run away from home—he'd forgive me for that, in time. When I come back and seem repentant. I'll go away now, before I start to show, and you'll help me." Her sobbing slowed to sniffles.

The thought of Penny running away hollowed the center of Imagene's stomach. "You can't go off all alone, scared and . . . in trouble. I'll go with you," she volunteered eagerly.

Penny shook her head. "No. That's definitely out." She was thinking fast now. "As soon as they know I'm gone, Daddy'll have people out looking for me, and two of us would be a lot easier to trace than just one. I can't take the chance. But if I can get far away, and stay away long enough, to have the baby and give it up for adoption, then I can come home. I'll have plenty of time to make up some sort of story. It will have to be something people would believe, even if they didn't approve, like going to Hollywood to try to get in the movies, a crazy thing like that. But I'll need money, and you'll have to back up whatever story we decide on . . ." Her eyes narrowed, calculating. "I've used up this month's allowance, and I couldn't take any money out of my savings account without my parents knowing, they're cosigned on it or something. But there is some money I could get hold of, probably enough . . ."

Breathlessly, she outlined her plan to Imagene, working it out and enlarging it as she spoke. It had the exotic allure of all Penny's plans. There was money in the cashbox in her father's study; Kellam Endicott always kept a sizable amount of cash around the house. "It wouldn't be stealing, Imagene, that's not theft. Not from my own parents."

How odd, Imagene thought, that Penny is so concerned with sin and morality now. Why didn't she think of all this before? But she said nothing, just offered her support.

Penny decided to return home for the weekend, picking a time when she felt certain both her parents would be out of the house. She would pack her warm-climate clothes, as if she were really going to California, and take the money from the cashbox. She would leave a note. Imagene, when questioned, would admit that Penny had been dreaming for a long time of trying her luck in the movies. Drawn into the plan, blindly committed to give whatever support was asked, Imagene began inventing the details of the story that would make it believable. Penny did not seem able to fasten her mind on trivia; she could not foresee such questions as "Did she take the train? Or a bus? Surely she didn't hitchhike!" Nor could she prepare answers. But Imagene could and did, surprising herself with her own calm surety, her ability to invent plausibly. Maybe it would work, after all.

Penny would go to St. Louis instead of California, to the

Catholic home for unwed mothers there which had been a charity of the St. Mary's Sodality. She would dye her hair en route and use another name. She would leave her car in the parking lot at St. Mary's, for it was too distinctive; her father would have the state police looking for it and she would never make the Oklahoma border.

Plans, details. They worked it out. If it was preposterous, they did not realize it; if it was doomed to failure, they fortunately did not know.

"As soon as I get the money, I'll come back here, 'Gene, and we'll go into town together as if nothing's wrong. Like we're going for a soda or something. I'll have my suitcase stashed . . ."

"Behind the hedge across the road from the bus stop."

"Yes, behind the hedge. I'll get it and catch the bus, and when I get to St. Louis I'll call you right away, so you'll know."

"You won't forget?" Imagene asked urgently. "I'm going to be terribly worried about you, Pen; you know that. I just wish you'd let me go with you."

Penny was resolute. "No," she said, looking with more tenderness than ever before at the face of the one person whose love she had always counted upon. "I don't want to get you into this any deeper than necessary. You stay here and get your diploma, 'Gene. I'll be back in a few months and then . . ." She smiled wanly. It was very hard to imagine what would happen then.

The next morning was Saturday. Most of the girls had someplace to go for the weekend; Imagene was left almost alone in the dorm, trying to pretend she was studying. Penny had left right after breakfast. If all went well, she should be back by noon. But noon came and went and the Thunderbird did not wheel into the convent parking lot, spitting gravel. Imagene went to the window every few minutes to check, feeling a growing chill of apprehension as the afternoon wore on.

Penny had been delayed at home; her parents had been there after all, she'd had no chance to get the money; she would call. She would call soon.

The phone in the hall rang occasionally, but never for Imagene. The afternoon faded into soft-blue twilight, into evening and night without end, while Imagene paced and worried. Should she call? No, better to wait to hear from Penny.

Oh, Penny . . .

On Sunday morning, before Mass, she could stand it no longer. She called the Endicott house and listened to the phone ring and ring. At last an unfamiliar voice identified "Mistah Endicott's rezdence."

"Is Penny . . . is Elaine there?"

"No ma'am, I doan think so. They all gone."

"All? Together? Do you know when they'll be back?"

The voice was guarded and dark with suspicion. "Nome, I cain't say. You got bizness with Miss Penny?"

"I'm a friend. Imagene Tutt."

"Oh. Yes. Well, she gone away with her folks, I doan know when they be back. They gone on a trip. You call nex' week or so, hear?"

Imagene held the phone away from her face and stared at it. A trip? Call next week? Without even knowing what frightened her, she was afraid. She walked slowly back to their shared room. A stack of Penny's sheet music lay forgotten on the desk. Her clothes still hung in the closet above a neat row of polished and treed shoes, precisely graduated from high heels to loafers. A faint scent of Potpourri lingered on the air.

Seven

SHOCK WAVES reverberated through St. Mary's when the school was informed Elaine Endicott would not be attending graduation. The news came in the form of a telephone call to Mother Superior, a message she promptly relayed to the faculty and they as promptly passed on to their students. All found it hard to believe.

According to Mother Superior, "The Endicotts are in New York City right now, on their way to Europe. It seems Mr. Endicott has an extremely important business matter to handle in Europe, one that will take several months and has come up quite unexpectedly. He thought it would be an excellent opportunity for Elaine to see the Continent, sort of a graduation present, so the whole family is going. Unfortunately, they were not able to delay their departure long enough for Elaine to take part in the graduation ceremonies. We will have her diploma forwarded to her, of course, and we shall all miss her presence very much, but I think we should be thankful that she is having this grand opportunity to spend several months abroad with her parents. That sort of trip is an education in itself, you know."

It was a diplomatic speech, but it did not hide the fact that Mother Superior was as puzzled as everyone else. The school was a-buzz. The girls assumed Imagene would be better informed than they, and she was barraged with questions she could not answer. The excitement of Penny's sudden departure, with its attendant glamour of mystery, quite overshadowed the graduation itself.

Imagene felt as if she were sleepwalking through the ceremonies. Something terrible had happened to Penny, she felt certain of it, but there was nothing she could do about it, no one she could even tell without betraying her friend. Mrs. Hammond, who attended in lieu of Barney Tutt ("I just knew that man wouldn't show up at his own daughter's graduation," she told her friends. "Drunk again, I'm sure") watched the girl with aching sympathy. She thought she knew why Imagene had red-rimmed eyes and seemed so apathetic. When she had a chance, she pulled her aside for some gentle interrogation.

"Have you been to the doctor, my dear?"

Imagene shook her head.

"Surely you understand there isn't too much time. If it's money, I can't help you there, but perhaps . . ."

"It isn't for me," Imagene said wearily.

Mrs. Hammond patted her hand. "All right, if that's the way you want it. Goodness knows, it's a miracle you have any pride left, with a father like yours, but still. There you are, and good for you. This friend of yours, then, has got to do something right away; you must understand that, Imagene!"

"I do understand," Imagene said miserably.

The sun shone fiercely hot, and the white dresses of the graduates wilted limply against their clammy skin. The bishop made an interminable speech. The ceremony was held in the garden, with students and guests perched on metal folding chairs, and immediately followed Mass, so no one had a chance to eat beforehand. Imagene felt faint.

Mrs. Hammond, hovering, suggested, "My dear, I certainly don't think you should go to your father's place in your . . . ah . . . condition. When this is over, wouldn't you like to come home with me for a few days? While you decide what to do next?"

There was no need to go on pretending. Penny's problem was out of her hands. "Thank you, but that really isn't necessary," she told the solicitous face peering at her from beneath the brim of an ancient straw hat, its black faded to purple in the beating sun. "I've already made arrangements for the summer. I'll be staying here at St. Mary's to help with the tutorial program." Mother Superior, who also did not want to see Imagene go home to Barney Tutt, had offered the opportunity the night before, and Imagene had grabbed it as a lifeline.

Once again, Mrs. Hammond thought she knew what was going on. The nuns were going to shelter the poor thing safely behind the high walls of the convent. Well, everything was all right, then. No need to worry. She could go back to Belmont Street content, her duty done.

So Imagene had a home for the summer, a familiar home peopled by familiar faces, and work to do to keep her busy. She had the advice and counsel of the nuns, who urged her to apply for a scholarship to a nearby Catholic college, and she had occasional notes and phone calls from classmates, recounting the details of their own lives, their new freedom, their various bright futures. All she lacked was Penny.

And then, suddenly, Barney was gone, too.

The day they buried Barnard Tutt, it poured rain. The sky was gravid with clouds piled in layers from horizon to horizon. The wet earth at graveside smelled of fertility and mortality. Few people stood beneath the green funeral awning; the sparse collection of flowers sent by acquaintances and distant relatives was an embarrassment to Imagene.

The service was brief, as if the priest knew that no one really cared. Imagene tried to picture her father lying inside the closed coffin, but all she could think about was the embalming. All the body openings stuffed with cotton. Barney, plugged up to keep him from leaking. Finally, eternally pickled. She was glad the lid was closed. She did not want to see the face that had disintegrated into that of a stranger, marred with broken veins and the peculiar velvety complexion of advanced alcoholism.

When he was dying, when even he at last had to admit he was dying, he had sent for her. The ward where he lay smelled of other men, dying. The enamel on the hospital bed was chipped and the iron showed through. "Cirrhosis of the liver," the doctor had said. "It's only a matter of time. We're doing all we can."

They didn't appear to be doing anything much. Who goes to extra effort for the poor? Barney lay shrunken beneath the sheet; his eyes were bleary and frightened. Imagene tried to smile at him, but he didn't respond. "You out of school yet?" was his only greeting. His voice was a scratchy whisper.

She nodded. Who was this man? This stranger? Where was the pain she was supposed to feel?

"You have any of that money left?" he asked, not calling her by name.

"No. But I'll be all right," she added, although she realized he had not asked the question out of concern for her welfare. It was a question he asked every time he saw her. It meant: Can you give me money for a bottle? The resentment burned deep in him; the insurance money that should have been his, wasted on this gawky girl, giving her a convent education when the free public school should have been good enough for her.

He closed his eyes and his breathing became stertorous. His hands lay atop the sheet and she looked at them because it was easier than looking at his face. They were thin and darkly veined, and the nails were broken, but at least they were clean. The hospital had cared for him to that extent.

And then something in the shape of those hands looked familiar to her and she looked down at her own hands, the same square palms, the same long, blunt-tipped fingers.

My flesh is formed of his flesh. My blood is his blood.

Part of me is dying.

Suddenly stricken, she reached out and lifted his hand, feeling its coldness and trying to warm it between her own palms. Barney opened his eyes and looked at her through gummy lashes. "Nora," he said.

"I'm Imagene, Daddy."

"My Nora," he said again. His hand moved convulsively in hers and seemed to be trying to return her tender pressure. He squinted his eyes as if struggling to see across a vast distance. "Imagene?"

"Yes, Daddy. I'm right here."

"Don't want you. Want . . ."

She tried to break through the fog gathering around him and touch him, just once; exchange the caring bonds that would hold a memory of her father, somehow, when he was gone. How little time was left to love and be loved! "I'm here, Daddy," she said, calling out to him. "I'm with you."

He pulled his hand free of hers and made an impatient gesture with it, then began plucking senselessly at the bedclothes. His eyes roamed the room, but never fixed on her face. "I could have made it if I'd had a little help," he said in a petulant voice. "But you took my money. You took what I needed. You let me down when I needed help."

"I didn't let you down, Daddy! I wanted to help, but you sent me away, remember?"

He focused on her one last time. "Imagene," he said. And then, so clearly that she could not mistake his words, "You were never good for anything but trouble." Then he closed his eyes and went away, and the room smelled of disinfectant, and old men dying.

Standing at his grave, watching others turn and leave with the enviable freedom of the noninvolved, she could think of other things she should have said to him. But there was no point in saying them to a polished box and a sodden scattering of flowers.

Mrs. Hammond, who never missed a funeral, had not missed this one. "I've buried three husbands, so it's gotten to be a habit," she explained, running her eyes in disbelief down Imagene's figure. The child certainly wasn't showing, though she should be by now. Or had she miscarried? She bit her lip and resolved to mind her own business. The rain began blowing sideways, driven by a fierce wind off the prairie, and she gave Imagene a last pat before making her way back to her battered old coupé.

Imagene stared into the grave and wondered how long she was expected to stand there—expected by whom?— before it would be all right for her to leave. Should she kneel and cry, crouching grief-stricken by her father's grave in the rain? It was a theatrically appealing image—the kind of gesture Penny might have made—but it would be too hypocritical. Imagene knew, with bitterness and regret, that she was not truly grief-stricken, merely saddened by lost opportunities. And relieved, too, on some level of consciousness. There need be no more striving to try to please Barney Tutt. She stood passively, looking down, waiting for some inner mechanism to signal release.

There was the depressing business of going through the rubble of Barney's personal effects and explaining to his creditors that there was nothing of value. She left the damp and characterless furnished room that had been Barney's, switched off the hall light, and returned the key to the weasel-faced landlady with a feeling of disinterested efficiency. Barney, and what he had been, were no longer a part of her life. She could not mourn him, but knew she would spend the rest of her years missing the father she'd never had. And there was nothing to be done about that.

Mother Superior welcomed her into that same office by which she had first entered St. Mary's, still with its Victorian stuffiness and the radiator pipes running . . . somewhere. Imagene didn't pay any attention to them. She sat across the desk from the nun, eating brown-rimmed cookies and drinking tea.

"What will you do now, my child?"

"I wish I knew, Reverend Mother."

"Have you decided about going to college? There's still time to apply for that scholarship we spoke of before."

Imagene looked into her tea cup. The liquid was glowing dark-amber, framed by a shell of fine porcelain. "I'm not sure I'm ready to go to college. I mean, what would I study? I don't know what courses I'm going to need to take because I don't know what I'm going to do with my life."

Mother Superior looked across the desk at the strong-boned, intelligent face. Not just another pretty girl, with a family behind her and a wedding ring in her future. There was something else for Imagene. Perhaps God had a plan.

"At your age, my dear, surely you have had dreams . . . ?"

Imagene was reluctant to trot out her make-believe before the established complacency of a real nun, but it was all she had to offer. "Penny and I used to talk about joining a religious order together," she said shyly. "Somehow I just took for granted that it would happen, eventually. I guess I never gave a lot of thought to doing anything else."

At the mention of Penny's name, Mother Superior lit with a soft glow. "Ah yes, Elaine might have had a true vocation. What a loving spirit that girl had; so generous! And a sense of humor—a sense of humor is a saving grace in a convent, you know." She smiled at her own small joke. "But what are your feelings now, Imagene? Your own true desires? Do you feel called to the religious life for yourself, not just because of friendship or admiration for someone else?"

Imagene tried to see both directions of her life at once: forward and backward. The past seemed to be one long succession of swallowed hurts, with only Penny to brighten it. The future loomed unguessable. Marriage? Who would ask her? A job in an office, or behind a counter? A life spent with her nose pressed to the candy store window, watching others live richly?

In the world beyond the convent walls, women were beginning to demand more opportunities and options. But Imagene Tutt had been raised in a backwater, and the changing current had not touched her yet. She saw few alternatives.

She gave the answer Mother Superior seemed to want. "There's nothing I want more than to love God and serve Him. I can't imagine any other life."

Mother Superior was obviously pleased, and Imagene felt the small pleasure of success. Her own success. But the nun restrained her enthusiasm. A young woman should neither be pushed nor led, and such decisions were sometimes made in the heat of an emotion that would later fade. She talked to Imagene seriously and at length about the demands of a religious life. Listening, the girl felt a growing excitement at having this possibility presented to her alone. Her own choice; her own achievement. A thing she could do that Penny had not. *Penny, why didn't you ever call me?*

When she remained firm in her intention, the steps were outlined for her. "You should talk to your parish priest first, Father Christopher, I believe, and he will advise you as to which order might be suited to you. Or, based on his knowledge of your nature, he might advise against such a step altogether. Of course, it would be pleasant if you were to join us, the Sisters of the Good Shepherd. But each of us must find her own way."

The way proved harder than Imagene had anticipated. There were times when she would have given up, had it not been for an inner voice urging her to go through with it and succeed, as Penny would have done. To show Penny that she could. To show Barney, watching from wherever he was. If he was bothering to watch.

There was the question of which order to consider. Among the religious orders, there was as much diversity as existed in the characters of women outside the walls. There were teaching orders, such as the Sisters of the Good Shepherd or the Sisters of Loretto at the Foot of the Cross; more worldly orders like the Immaculate Heart of Mary; missionary orders for the adventurous, such as the Foreign Mission Sisters of St. Dominic; nursing orders similar to the Sisters of Gethsemane. For a girl uncertain yet of her own nature, familiarity seemed safest, and Imagene applied to the head of the Order of the Sisters of the Good Shepherd.

Mother Superior's last words of advice to her were, "I'm sure you will make us proud of you, Imagene. Just learn to curb your more, ah, uninhibited impulses, and develop a true spirit of obedience."

Mother Superior had not forgotten the day Imagene glued all the erasers to the blackboard. Or slipped red ink in the washing machines. Or slid down the banister into the entrance hall. Or dropped a water bomb from the roof just as the archbishop was arriving for his annual visit.

Imagene stood with downcast eyes, exactly as Penny would have done, and murmured, "Yes, Reverend Mother. Thank you." Exactly as Penny would have done.

Her application to the order having been processed, she was given a formal interview in a hotel lobby, like a job applicant, without familiar surroundings to shelter her or convent walls to apply their own psychological pressure. She wore a gray cotton skirt and a jacket posing as flannel, and was terrified someone would notice the child hiding in her adult's body. But she gave the answers Penny would have given and the interview went well.

Because of her homeless, jobless situation and her convent school background, she was able to skip some of the preentrance requirements, such as the period of living "on the outside" while following an abbreviated version of the convent's rule of life. With a medical certificate in hand to prove she was of sound body—nobody questioned the soundness of her mind—she applied to the novice mistress in the order's motherhouse in a small town in Missouri, and her period as a postulant began.

The motherhouse was redbrick, nestled behind an ivied wall, and Imagene was disappointed because it lacked sandstone turrets and the air of a medieval fortress.

She arrived with two small suitcases and a cardboard box tied with string, containing all the relics of her childhood that she cared to keep.

Earthly possessions weigh down the spirit as it travels the road to God.

She ruthlessly divested herself of the small collection of personal property, keeping only her parents' wedding photograph and a silk scarf that retained a fading fragrance of Potpourri.

Her life, which had seemed so empty a few months before, was full again. Full to overflowing with the all-powerful presence of Sister Dominic, the novice mistress, as well as a routine in which every minute of the day was immutably shaped by tradition. "The Sisters of the Good Shepherd require a year of postulancy, Imagene," Sister Dominic explained, "before you can become a novice. During that time, we will get to know you, and you will get to know what Our Lord expects of those who give their lives to Him. You may leave at any time during this period and there will be no questions asked and no reflection on your character."

Those were the words she said, but that was not what Imagene heard. She heard: If you leave, you will have failed. Failed as your father would have expected; failed as Mama failed to survive.

She threw herself into the life with all her energy. Postulancy was a hard time, both emotionally and physically. The food was even plainer than that served at St. Mary's, where the appetites of affluent children had been considered to some degree in planning the menus. Hard physical labor was expected as a test of devotion. On a raw October day, with a high wind blowing, the novice mistress sent Imagene into the courtyard to rake leaves, an impossible task which lasted for hours and accomplished nothing.

When Imagene protested, Sister Dominic said gently, "You have accomplished a lot. You have persevered, strengthened your character, resisted the temptation to lose your temper, and made a sacrifice of your labor to God. I would call that quite a day's work."

Imagene lay on her narrow, hard bed that night, in the tiny cell whose only ornament was the crucifix on the wall, and felt a glow of personal satisfaction.

I'm making it. They will keep me; I'll have a home.

She wrote a letter, her first since arriving at the motherhouse, and mailed it to the Endicotts' address at Anson. It was a long letter, painstakingly rewritten a number of times. Each time she began afresh, she intended to write cheerfully, glowingly, of her own small success and her happiness, but somewhere in mid-letter her words became bitter and accusatory, blaming Penny for deserting her, demanding to know the reasons.

It was not a letter she would like to receive; it was not the letter she wanted to send Penny. It seemed to her to be full of whining and self-pity, and so she stayed awake far into the night, working over it until at last she had the sort of bland, chatty note that would skillfully disguise all trace of heartache. Surely Penny had come home by now.

Surely Penny would answer. Explain.

There was no answer.

88

When she had been a postulant for three months, one of the other postulants left the order unexpectedly. It was a matter of much discussion and speculation until the novice mistress explained, "Marjorie was not cut out for the Sisters of the Good Shepherd. She has determined to go to the Benedictines."

The postulants looked at one another. They had accepted a life of sacrifice, but the total isolation of the Benedictine seemed to them like the final slamming of a door. It had the glamour of ultimate commitment, but there was something daunting about it, a sense of being asked for more than one could give.

Sister Dominic told them, "A solemnly enforced and total enclosure, such as the Benedictines enjoy, removes all temptations and makes virtue easier. It is, in its way, the straightest path. But it is not for everyone; it is what the desert was to the hermit."

I could never do that, Imagene thought. I couldn't spend my entire life behind one set of walls, never seeing the world again.

She had not seen very much of the world, but she was aware of it. Outside. Sometimes the postulants went into the city for brief expeditions that would be denied them during their period of novitiate, and occasionally, as she crossed the courtyard after evening prayer, she would look up to see a flaming sunset crisscrossed by the grid of telephone wires and poles on the other side of the wall.

God and Alexander Graham Bell, she thought once. Sharing the sky.

If she chose to be a teacher within the order, and to be assigned to a school similar to St. Mary's Academy, years of further training still awaited her, although all members of the order did not teach. But she put off making that decision. There were so many commitments to be made first. At the end of her year of postulancy, she would enter the novitiate and feel for the first time a real sense of belonging to the community of nuns. She yearned for the experience and dreaded it. That, too, would be a door slamming.

There were times when the months of postulancy dragged. So much study, so much prayer. So much kneeling with uncushioned knees, while the mind wandered . . . until recalled to its devotions by guilt or a hissed warning from the novice mistress.

Among many other lessons to be learned were the ancient traditions regarding the habit itself, the name and reason for each separate garment, the way in which it was to be put on and taken off, the history that bound it to the nun like a kind of skin, wrapping her in a special aura with a power of its own. All the little details. The belt. The crucifix. The headdress that came in eight separate layers. As a practical necessity, the nuns had developed a system for pinning each layer to the next so the entire construction could be lifted off in one piece at night and kept on a broom handle in the corner of the cell.

Imagene laughed the first time that was demonstrated.

There were times of complete beauty, too; periods of intense serenity beyond anything she had imagined, when the romance of her vocation and the promised communion with God bestowed radiant happiness. Some of the nuns, particularly the older ones, wore that lingering happiness on their faces all their lives. Seeing them made Imagene hungry for what they had.

At last the trial period was over and the group of postulants, somewhat diminished in number, submitted their formal requests to join the order. After being considered and accepted by the Mother General and her council, they were welcomed into the novitiate with a simple ceremony and clothed in a short version of the order's habit and veil.

They were then allowed to choose their new names in religion, names embodying virtues they hoped to emulate or saints they admired. Imagene chose Catherine, after St. Catherine of Siena. "Sister Catherine," she whispered to herself in her bed at night, over and over, waiting for something inside her to answer to that name.

The period of the novitiate was a time of added restrictions and increased sacrifice. Novices were never allowed to leave the enclosure; mail was limited, and read by the novice mistress. Hard physical work remained. And study. And prayer.

Imagene—the new Sister Catherine, who still always thought of herself as Imagene, in spite of her best intentions —struggled to be docile and obedient. But it was hard.

Sister Dominic told her charges, "No one is going to be a successful nun unless she's touched with fire."

Imagene looked at the faces of her fellow novices. Were any of them touched with fire? They all seemed quite ordinary, scrubbed and white-coiffed young women in identical habits, with identical expressions of dutiful attention. She saw no fervor burning in them.

She imagined how Penny would have looked in that group, leaning slightly forward as she always did during a lecture, her lips parted as if she could not get enough, her eyes bright. Penny knew how to look as if she were touched with fire. She had confided to Imagene once, "If you make them think you're really eager, teachers assume you know the answers and they skip you and ask somebody who doesn't look prepared. I try to do everything a hundred and ten percent all the time. It makes a terrific impression."

Imagene leaned forward on her elbows and let her lips part slightly, as if Sister Dominic's words left her breathless.

The novice's day was divided into half-hour segments, each filled with some opportunity to improve soul, mind, or physical well-being. Prayer and study alternated with the labor of caring for the convent and its inhabitants, and each aspect of the religious life was expected to be lived with love, an offering to God.

Imagene studied Church history, lives and writings of the saints, philosophy, and underwent continued reinforcement of the lessons in deportment she had learned as a postulant. How to walk, stand, sit, speak, be silent. How to be a nun.

And why.

"You enter the convent not because you choose to, but because you are chosen," Sister Dominic said again and again. "You must feel that anything less would not be enough."

Imagene tried hard to feel that way. Sometimes she was aware of, wrapped up in, enraptured by, the great sense of peace and fulfillment the convent offered.

And other times were soured by doubt and frustration, when she was certain that the nun's life was impossible for her, that her spirit would never submit and adjust. She broke small rules willfully, secretly, and then confessed days after, burning with shame at her rebellion.

"An extroverted personality is best-suited to the contemplative life," Sister Dominic told her novices. "That is perhaps the reverse of what you would expect. But a nun needs emotional energy; she must have the qualities of self-confidence and enthusiasm, and a zest for life. This is not a pallid profession; we are in the business of joy, of taking joy from doing God's work."

Imagene listened to the descriptions and tried to make them apply to herself. But they sounded more like Penny. Penny, smiling and cheerful, her pure, clear soprano soaring in the choir, her generous breathless rush to help, give, offer, achieve.

Imagene redoubled her efforts to be the perfect novice; to become the perfect nun.

Take no pride in your personal achievements; they are only manifestations, through you, of the power of God.

Imagene lay beneath the crucifix on her wall at night, willing herself to ignore the hardness of her bed and the coarseness of her sheet, and tried to understand the difference between feeling humble and feeling inferior. She fell into a deep sleep born of physical and mental exertion,

long hours, and wholesome food, and lay lapped in silence
until five in the morning, when a knock on the door and the
call of the sister ringing the handbell awoke her. "Blessed
be God," announced the disembodied voice, and Imagene
answered back, fighting up through layers of fuzziness,
"Blessed be His Holy Name."

In addition to her other duties, she took her turn in the
garden, and in the dairy barn, for the motherhouse was a
self-contained community, capable of functioning and pro-
viding for itself, independently of the world beyond the
walls. Imagene enjoyed caring for the cows. There were
three beautiful golden Jerseys, with triangular heads like
fine Arabian horses, and liquid eyes that glowed with gentle
intelligence. They tolerated her awkward efforts at learning
to milk with bovine good humor. Their breath smelled of
clover. The dairy barn was airy and spacious, and sometimes Imagene fantasized running away from the convent
and becoming a farmer, in a house with big rooms and
green pastures beyond the windows.

The nuns' cells justified their name. Each little cubicle
was a characterless whitewashed box, seven by nine feet,
furnished with a bed, a chair, a pine chest, and a crucifix. In
a mirror reversal of the competition among girls at St.
Mary's for the most strikingly decorated room, the nuns
strove wordlessly to have the most barren cells. It was surprising to discover how difficult it was to achieve a state of
visual ascetism. A wrinkle on the blanket could produce an
unnecessary pattern. A handful of daisies in a water glass
was an embarrassing opulence. Imagene was unlucky; beyond her small window, a plum tree grew like a delicate
Japanese print etched against the sky. No amount of interior
starkness was sufficient to counteract that exquisite grace.

One novice, more fortunate than her sisters by their
newly acquired standards, had a smaller cell than the
others. It was wedged into an angle formed by a disused
stairwell and had no window at all. It was like a stigmata, a

sign that here was a special soul, privileged to bear additional hardship and offer greater sacrifices.

On each floor of the chapter house where the novices lived, there was one bathroom. Imagene and eleven others shared theirs in turn, soaking in a massive footed tub from a bygone era. The toilet had a mahogany seat, dried and roughened from years of being scrubbed with disinfectant, and an overhead water tank with a pull-chain. The wash basin was marble, but there was no mirror.

A nun needs no mirror. She gives up such vanities and contents herself with reflecting the love of God onto others.

The floor was covered with black-and-white linoleum blocks, well waxed, but during her third week as a novice Imagene made a discovery. She dropped her toothbrush and it skidded under the tub. When she crouched on the floor to reach for it, she could see that the area beneath the footed tub harbored an unsuspected wilderness of dust and puffballs.

It was a teeming jungle surrounded by a sterile black-and-white desert. When Imagene reached under the tub, feeling gingerly around in the debris, she heard something move, and when she snatched her hand back a small life form scuttled away in fright. A roach, perhaps, or even a tiny mouse. Some living creature was going its own way, abiding by its own laws, unnoticed in that otherwise sanitized atmosphere.

Imagene told no one about her discovery, and when it was her turn to clean the bathroom she stopped the mop short at the edge of the tub. Each time she entered the room, she checked to see that the small haven was undisturbed. It gave her a peculiar satisfaction to think of it flourishing there, outside the law. As long as it was safe, it seemed easier for her to submit to the other disciplines imposed by the community: the regimented hours, the silence at meals, the constant self-restraint. There was a secret haven, known to her alone, to which she could magically flee if the going got too tough. Some playful part of her mind imagined herself shrinking to thimble size and dwelling in the velvety darkness, protected by the four ball-and-claw feet of the tub, communing with a mouse.

Novices were never praised, nor did they expect it, but as time passed Imagene began to acquire a degree of self-confidence. She could endure the work; she learned to concentrate on her prayers; she even began to enjoy her studies and the feeling of stretching her mind to admit new knowledge.

Nuns, whether novice or fully professed, were discouraged from forming close friendships, so that their full love and attention could be reserved for God. But they took turns walking with one another, and studying and meditating together, strengthening the bonds of communal sisterhood. There was little discussion of background and none of status in the society beyond the walls, for those things no longer mattered. Free of the world, closer to God, the nuns turned their minds to more important subjects. They worried about the poor and the sick; they prayed for the entire troubled entity of mankind. They joined together into one faceless voice, beseeching their heavenly Father for his goodness and mercy for those less fortunate than they.

One faceless voice, anonymous. Later, for some, individuality might reassert itself and demand expression. But for now, there was a sense of family and of belonging, of being a part of one whole, that Imagene cherished. She still did not feel called, but she felt wanted.

When she had been a novice of the Sisters of the Good Shepherd for eleven months, Elaine Endicott arrived at the motherhouse.

Eight

IMAGENE would always remember the day Penny arrived at the Motherhouse of the Sisters of the Good Shepherd. It was a day of endings and beginnings, like the day she herself had arrived, sitting tensely in the taxicab and puffing with frantic greed at one last cigarette. She had stared out the window at the closed gates of the convent as she used to stare at the homes of others, imagining the love and security they contained. Then the convent gates opened and she began to make a new life for herself.

A life that was to change again, when Penny came.

Imagene was working in the refectory that day, clearing the tables after breakfast. Sunlight poured like melted butter through the small-paned windows lining the east wall of the long, cheerful room. Beneath the beamed ceiling, the walls were painted a fresh white that reflected the summer light. The big tables were of oak, blackened with the patina of generations of use, lovingly washed and wiped by generations of nuns. Backless benches ran the length of each table. Nuns seated on them could either see the view from the windows or admire the large mural of Christ as the Good Shepherd which covered most of the real wall. It had been painted by a Sister Luke in the nineteenth century, in the rich colors and sentimental style of the period. It showed a tender, almost effeminate Christ, cuddling the Lost Lamb.

Imagene moved along the benches, picking up the white stoneware plates and bowls and stacking them on a tin tray. The morning meal had consisted of wheat toast, cold cereal, and fresh fruit, with hot tea for those sisters who drank it. White pottery pitchers were set at each end of the table and kept filled with cold water from the convent's own well. Imagene was trying to learn to drink nothing but the sweet, pure water—and finding it hard going. Sometimes in the late afternoon, she had an almost religious vision of a Coca-Cola in a curving green-glass bottle; frosty; beaded with moisture.

Sister Veronica peered around the edge of the swinging door leading to the kitchen. "When you're through clearing away, Sister Catherine, please set a fresh place at the first table, will you? We have a new novice joining us today, and they just called down from Mother General's office to tell us she's had no breakfast, nor any meal at all since yesterday noon, poor soul. I thought I'd give her an egg and some good hot oatmeal."

Imagene was surprised. Convent rules were strict; no meals except at set times, and no exceptions. All nuns must eat the same fare. Yet here was an exception being made— and for a mere novice!

Sister Honoria accompanied the novice to the refectory, arriving just as Imagene finished setting the place. "Ah, Sister Catherine, I'm glad to see you're here," Sister Honoria said. "Perhaps you would be kind enough to keep Sister Immaculata company while she eats, and then show her around the chapter house? I have to get back to the office;

it's one of those days." She smiled and Imagene smiled back. Sister Honoria stepped aside then, to make way for the introduction, and Imagene found herself staring with disbelief into Penny's eyes.

"Sister . . . Immaculata?" she asked incredulously.

Penny nodded and held out her hand. She gave no sign of recognizing Imagene. Yet it was Penny herself who was almost unrecognizable. The short novice's veil hid most of her hair, though one blond tendril had escaped and clung to her temple. Her rounded figure was not concealed beneath the habit; it was gone, replaced by an emaciation even the folds of cloth could not disguise. She was deathly pale, with dark shadows under her eyes, making them appear larger and bluer than ever. Her cheeks were hollow, the dimples melted away. She had the withdrawn expression of a person whose mind is totally elsewhere.

Sister Honoria completed the introduction and left them together, unaware of Imagene's shock. Trying not to stare at her dreadfully changed friend, Imagene brought the food from the kitchen and served Penny, then sat down beside her, unable to contain herself any longer. Her questions tumbled out faster than anyone could answer them, but Penny was making no effort to answer them anyway. Nor was she eating; she picked at her food indifferently and pushed the plate away after taking a few bites.

Imagene was saying, "Why didn't you at least call me? I don't understand that. I waited and waited but I never heard from you, and I thought we had everything all planned . . ."

Penny looked at her for the first time. She said, in a flat voice, "There was no reason to call you. There was nothing you could do. There was nothing anybody could have done. But that was a long time ago and I don't think about it anymore; I'd rather you didn't, either. Your name in Christ is . . . Sister Catherine now, I believe? It's nice to see you again, Sister Catherine."

She turned away from Imagene and began folding her napkin neatly, squaring its edges with the edges of the table.

Imagene watched her, suddenly speechless. Who was this stranger living behind Penny's face?

Napkin folding completed, the young woman now known as Sister Immaculata—Immaculata? for *Penny?*—said, as to a new acquaintance, "I would appreciate it very much, Sister, if you would just direct me to the chapel now."

Imagene struggled to find words, and when they came they were not the right ones. "Yes, sure. I mean, of course, if that's what you want to do. The chapel. But first we ought to find the novice mistress and have her assign you your room, so you'll know where to put your things."

"I have no things," Penny's new colorless voice answered. "And it doesn't matter where I stay. Just take me to the chapel; to Our Lord's house."

It must be some sort of peculiar dream. "All right, I'll take you," Imagene mumbled, standing up quickly, so awkwardly that the bench was shoved backward by her calves and made a scraping noise on the stone floor like fingernails on a blackboard. Imagene shuddered, but Penny didn't even smile.

There was no further conversation between them as they left the refectory and crossed the little park to the chapter house and its adjoining chapel. Penny's manner forbade conversation. She paced steadily, staring straight ahead. She was like a person alone. Imagene felt baffled and shut out.

When they came to the open doorway of the chapel, a glow greeted them from within as the morning sun turned the stained-glass windows to ruby and topaz and sapphire. When Imagene found the prospect of a life spent in the convent unbearably limiting, she liked to come to the chapel and kneel in silence, letting the beauty of those colors and the fragrance of the incense soothe her spirit. She might arrive thinking resentfully, "I'm here because I have nowhere else to go," but an hour of peace and beauty in the chapel made it seem less like a life sentence and more like a privilege. "I'm lucky to be here; lucky God wants me," she could ultimately tell herself, and be comforted.

Now Penny stepped past her as if the chapel were her own private world, and she entered without inviting Imagene to join her. She crossed herself with holy water and dropped to her knees in the nearest pew, instantly immersing herself in prayer.

Imagene lingered by the doorway for a few minutes, though it was obvious she had been forgotten. She returned to her regular duties with a queasy feeling in her stomach and a mind that would not concentrate, but only repeat the questions Penny had refused to answer.

The noon meal was the largest of the day, the nuns' dinner, and they would not all come together again in the refectory until they met for a light supper before bed. Imagene watched eagerly for Penny, but the other girl didn't come. No wonder she's so thin if she's not eating, Imagene thought, worried.

After the meal she approached Sister Dominic, unable to contain her curiosity any longer.

"The new novice?" Sister Dominic said. "Oh yes, that would be Sister Immaculata. I understand there's rather a delicate situation there. She served her period of postulancy abroad, in the south of France, I believe; a rather abbreviated one, actually. But she has convinced Mother General that she has a true calling, and because of her extreme devotion and some . . . ah . . . aspects of her history that I was not told, Mother General allowed her to enter directly as a novice. She was very impressed with her."

Of course. People were always impressed by Penny. The Mother General of the order was known for her personal asceticism, although the order itself was not as insistent upon abject poverty as some. The Sisters of the Good Shepherd were allowed a few small luxuries; there were even some carefully selected novels in the library—Jane Austen and Gene Stratton Porter. But the new Penny—this Sister Immaculata, with her wasted body and her martyrlike detachment—might represent some inner vision Mother General had of the perfect nun. The old Penny—cheerful, outgoing, bubbling with gaiety and high spirits—would not have pleased Mother General half so well.

Sister Immaculata didn't look as if she would ever try to persuade a postulant to smuggle in a Mars bar for her.

Imagene saw Penny in chapel that evening but there was no opportunity to speak with her. It was only after supper, when the novices retired to their cells to perform their personal devotions and prepare for bed, that the two met face-to-face in a place where they could talk. The common room adjoined the bathroom, and as Imagene entered it on her way to bathe she met Penny returning, face still damp and toothbrush in hand. Penny was wearing a cotton gown and a flannel robe too large for her, and her blond hair was pulled severely back from her face, held by a rubber band that split and tore the fragile gold.

"Penny . . . I mean, Sister . . ." Imagene began uncertainly, "can't we . . . won't you talk to me?"

The other young woman paused with a polite smile on her lips but not in her eyes. "Yes? What is it?"

"Surely we have things to say to each other . . ."

Penny's smile did not fade, but it cast no warmth. "Oh, I don't think so, really. What would we talk about, the past? That's far behind us now; I don't want to be reminded of it and I shouldn't think you would, either. You used to tell me how unhappy you were as a girl in Anson—do you want to dredge all that up again?"

"I'm not talking about childhood, Penny, I'm talking about what happened two years ago. I was so worried about you when you disappeared like that, Pen. You can't imagine! I thought something terrible had happened to you.

Why didn't you ever write, or send me a postcard at least, something?"

Penny stood with slightly lifted eyebrows, watching from a remote distance as Imagene's emotions came boiling to the surface. "Something terrible did happen," she said, "and I didn't want to talk about it. I still don't. Can't you respect that and just let it be?"

"But you walked away from commencement and all our plans and everything!" Imagene wailed. She was no longer a self-possessed young novice, cultivating serenity like a garden of roses; she was once again an abandoned child, reacting with baffled rage. Mother, father, friend—all beyond her control. They seemed to possess weapons of indifference which she did not. But she was not a child any longer; she knew there were ways to hurt back, and for the first time she deliberately used one against Penny.

"What about your baby?" she said suddenly, throwing the words at her friend like a weapon. "What did you do with the baby?"

That got through Penny's shell. Her pale face turned paler; bleached and white like the linen in the laundry. She grabbed Imagene's shoulder and dug her fingers in with surprising strength for one so frail. "Be quiet," she hissed between her teeth. "Don't you dare say that. Somebody might hear you!"

Imagene knew an advantage when she saw one. That was another lesson she had learned from Penny: make the most of every opportunity. "If you won't talk to me now, I'll keep on asking for an explanation until you do," she threatened, surprised at her own audacity. "Sooner or later somebody will hear us, but I don't care. I just want to know why you left me the way you did."

Penny's hold on her arm loosened. She was not remote anymore; she was close and quiet and tired beyond her years. "All right," she said in an exhausted voice, "I guess you have a right to know, if anyone does. But not here and now. We have to be really alone someplace, where no one can overhear us."

That presented a small problem. Sister Dominic was strict about not allowing her charges to pair off, particularly in private. She explained that the prohibition was to keep them from forming exclusive friendships of sufficient intensity to drain off a little of the emotion that should be channeled to God.

Imagene thought briefly, then suggested, "I'm going to be working in the vegetable garden this coming week. If you tell Sister Dominic that you need some sun and air, she'll believe you. You look like you really do. Ask her if you can do a little gardening. We can talk there. No one can overhear and the novices are almost expected to chatter among the cabbages; it's one of the few privileges we get."

The old, sly expression peeped briefly at her from Penny's eyes. Once they had planned much innocent mischief together in the same way, only then it had usually been Penny's idea and Penny's plan. Except Penny never got caught. Imagene was the one who got caught, always.

The next afternoon a hard-driving rain kept everyone inside. Gathered in their common room to read or write letters, the novices began to talk among themselves, using human voices to shut out the sounds of the storm. The discussion drifted around to their various reasons for having joined the convent. Only Sister Immaculata sat apart, in a chair by the window with a book on her lap, her face closed to any offer of companionship.

"I came because I always knew that was what God wanted for me," the sturdy nun called Sister Angela said complacently. "I never had any doubts about that. What was hard for me was leaving my dog." The others laughed. "No, I mean it! I'd had him since he was just a puppy and when I became a postulant he was getting old, white around the muzzle. I tried to tell him I was going away, but he didn't understand. Mother wrote me that he used to go up to my room and sleep on my empty bed. He was put to sleep the day after my Simple Profession—all his organs seemed to fail at once. It's strange, but it still hurts me to think about that."

Imagene, who had never had a dog, could feel Sister Angela's pain. She could imagine the animal she would have loved so much, lying faithfully atop the bed she might have had in the lovely house she had so often dreamed for herself.

"The thing that hurts me sometimes is knowing I'm never going to have a family of my own," said small Sister Rose.

"We're all part of one family now," someone reminded her.

"Oh, I know that; that isn't what I mean. I'm talking about having a husband and babies. I think about that a lot, still. I wonder if it means I'm not ready to be a nun."

"I guess we all think about it sometimes," another novice interjected. "We wouldn't be normal if we didn't."

A voice spoke suddenly from the leather chair by the window, startling them all. Sister Immaculata said, with absolute certainty, "The love of just one man isn't enough. To love one you would have to reject so many. I prefer the limitless love of God."

They stared at one another. "What a way to put it!" Sister Andrew said finally. "That really makes you stop and think, doesn't it?"

Sister Immaculata took no further part in the conversation, but they were all aware of her, aware of that silent presence whose thoughts seemed to occupy a higher plane than theirs. They began to watch her and wait for her rare comments. As the days passed, there was a subtle movement among the novices, like an undercurrent drawn by a powerful force. Somehow, without making any obvious effort to do so, it was Penny who was setting the standard again. The other novices seemed to sense a rarefied spirit in her and it attracted them strongly. She never complained or appeared tired; she seemed almost unaware of her surroundings, as if she already walked with God.

Sister Dominic sent the newest novice to work in the garden with Sister Catherine. "The poor girl has been ill, I think," Sister Dominic told Sister Honoria, "and it will do her good to spend some time out of doors. Besides, Sister Catherine is such a go-getter she'll do most of the work herself, so Sister Immaculata can't overdo."

On the next sunny day, the two novices went together to the gardener's little square brick "hut" and were given hoes and bug sprayers, and baskets for gathering any ripe vegetables. They walked in silence to the garden plot. It smelled of tilled earth and sun-warmed tomatoes. They set their baskets down at the end of the first row and began systematically chopping at the crop of new weeds that had appeared between the lettuces and the summer squash. Imagene demonstrated the technique and Penny grasped it immediately. They were alone in the garden, except for the occasional bumblebee or earthworm.

"Now we can talk," Imagene said, working close to Penny, keeping her face turned toward the earth and the weeds. "I won't tell a soul, Pen; you know that. Just tell me your troubles the way I always used to tell you mine. It'll make you feel better. I promise."

Penny stooped and cut and stepped forward, stooped and hacked at a dandelion and stepped forward again.

"I went home to try to get the money," she said with no prelude. Her voice was so low Imagene had to strain to hear her. "I told the housekeeper I needed to collect some things for my graduation. She didn't pay much attention; she just told me my parents had gone to town, then went back to work. I went to the place where my father kept his cashbox and took out all the money in it. I had to break it open with his letter opener, and I broke that too. But there was only a hundred dollars inside, not nearly enough.

"I didn't know what to do. When he came home he'd see the cashbox was broken, so I thought I'd better take it with me and let him think someone had stolen the whole thing. There were always people in and out of the house, and we didn't keep the doors locked. You know, Texas hospitality. Anyway, I took the box upstairs and put it in a suitcase with some underwear and things, but I still didn't know what to do. I couldn't live very long on that little amount of money. You remember how I was then, so spoiled I thought it took a lot of *things* to make me happy." Her words were flat with contempt; contempt for the lovely things Penny had always had, and Imagene had always wanted.

She continued, "Then I remembered that Friday was payday, so maybe Miguel still had some money. I don't remember what story I intended to tell him. I suppose I wasn't thinking too clearly at that point. My only clear memory is how terrified I was that my father would find out I was pregnant by a Mexican. His lily-white princess. I wasn't thinking and I wasn't paying much attention to what was going on around me. I got back in my car and headed for the bunkhouse where Miguel lived; I didn't even notice Daddy and Mother in the Cadillac, coming up our drive.

"When I got to the bunkhouse, Miguel was just coming out. I ran over to him and started telling him some story, something stupid. I had my hand on his chest, trying to flirt with him, you know, being persuasive, and then I heard a screech of tires and a car door slammed."

The sun was beating down on their backs. A single drop of perspiration ran down Imagene's nose and clung to the very tip.

Penny said, without ever looking up, "My father came toward us, and when he saw him Miguel stepped backward, away from me. It must have been a very guilty gesture. Daddy yelled, 'What the hell's going on here?' and Miguel got scared and ran back into the bunkhouse. Then my father knew something was really wrong. He grabbed my shoulder and spun me around and began asking me a lot of questions. He'd forbidden me ever to go near the bunk-house, and I could tell he was furious. He was shouting at me and he slapped me, no harder than he'd slapped me a hundred times before, but for some idiotic reason I cried out. And Miguel came back out of the bunkhouse then, with a knife in his hand. He swore in Spanish and lunged be-tween us, pushing me away from Daddy, and then there was blood everywhere. Blood spurting, and my father yell-ing, and my mother screaming somewhere off in the dis-tance."

Penny's voice was as emotionless as if she were describing the action of her arm chopping weeds, the hoe rising and falling, rising and falling. Imagene worked beside her, weeding, spraying, her eyes blind to everything but that distant Texas landscape, with its baked earth and the long, low silhouette of the frame bunkhouse.

"My father got away from Miguel—he knocked him down, I think—and dragged me to the car, and I suppose we drove back to the house. Mother was sobbing, and I could smell blood, thick and sweet, sickening. Did you ever think how much it smells like copper?" she asked idly.

"What happened when you got to the house?" Imagene asked in a strangled voice.

"We all went into the living room, and my mother was dabbing at Daddy with her handkerchief, just that silly scrap of linen trying to stop buckets of blood from pouring out of him. The servants came running, but he chased them all out of the room and insisted he could take care of it him-self. It turned out the wound wasn't that bad; it bled terri-bly because it had cut a vein, I suppose, but it was basically superficial. No real damage; he just wound up with a stiff muscle in his upper arm and an ugly scar across his chest.

"Anyway, he sent Mother to get gauze and tape. He insisted she not call a doctor, he said it would be too em-barrassing for the family to have to explain about a knife fight with a Mexican, one of his own hired hands. When she was out of the room, he kept demanding to know what I'd been doing down at the bunkhouse, and what involvement I had with Miguel. He automatically assumed the worst.

"That was what upset me the most, you see. It was true, but he couldn't have known that. He just assumed it; he assumed that I had done the most degrading possible thing, according to his point of view. He called me a tramp and a whore and he said he'd beat all that nonsense out of me once and for all.

"That was when I lost my temper completely; I suppose I went a little crazy. What right did he have to say those things to me? I knew what he was. I knew why he always wanted my friends and classmates around, so he could pick out the pretty ones and hug them and pet them and put his hands all over them. I knew about the poor girls from the other side of town, the ones he picked up in his car after work and bought cheap dresses for, and perfume, and took for drives. Drives. Oh, yes, I knew about all that. Miguel told me. Miguel had seen my father with a very young girl in his car, cuddled tight against his side while he drove. It hadn't even surprised me, hearing that; it just made me furious that he thought he had the right to call *me* names.

"I lost my head then. I wanted to hurt him enough to even the score for all the times and all the ways he'd hurt me. I screamed it all out at him, about Miguel and the things we'd done together, about the baby, everything. And it was wonderful. It was wonderful to see the awful, sick look he got on his face, and the way his mouth sagged. It was worth it all just for that moment, to know I'd cut my own knife right through his guts."

Imagene could not reconcile the gaunt nun with her calm, uninvolved face with the horrors she was recounting in that emotionless voice.

They reached the end of one row and turned down another. Penny said, as if to the heads of cabbages. "Daddy hit

me on the jaw with his doubled fist. He knocked me halfway across the room and I slammed against the leg of the
piano somehow. It knocked me out, which was a blessing,
because I really think he would have killed me otherwise.
When I came to he was gone and Mother was bending over
me, crying, and I had the most terrible pain in my back. She
helped me get upstairs to my room, and she told me that
Daddy had gone out to get some other men and go after
Miguel. I don't know if they ever found him or not; no one
told me. Perhaps they dispensed a little Texas justice and
left him lying in a ditch somewhere, covered with six inches
of dirt and a tangle of barbed wire.

"But somebody died that night that I'm sure about; my
baby. I lost it in my bedroom, with the door locked and my
head in Mother's lap. She took the best care of me she
could, but she was afraid to call the doctor for me, because
of Daddy. I didn't realize until then how terrified she truly
was of him. I suppose her spirit had been broken for a long
time.

"That night is just a blur of pain and voices. In the morning, when I felt a little better, I found out Daddy had come
home and fired all the servants, given them enough money
to go off on long vacations far from Anson, where they'd
never tell what had happened. He made reservations for the
three of us to go to Europe immediately, so no one would
ever know, so Kellam Endicott could go on being a big shot,
with the potential scandal swept tidily under the rug; me,
the dead baby, everything out of sight. And Mother helped
him. The family name, that was what meant the most to
her. She cried a lot and popped pills until she sounded
drunk and couldn't walk straight, but she did what he told
her to do.

"By the time we got to London, I had a high fever. They
checked into the Dorchester and let a doctor look at me
then, but of course it was too late."

There was a finality in her voice as if she were describing the end of the world. But no pain; no feeling at all.

"What do you mean by too late? Because you'd already had the miscarriage?"

"Not just that. By the time I got medical attention, I had a severe infection. Mother meant well, but she was no nurse. It was a long time before I was well again, and they told me I would never have any more children. By then my mother was in the hospital herself, overdosed on blue pills or yellow pills or something. While she was convalescing, my father took me to Switzerland. For a change of scene, he said."

There was some emotion in her voice then, but Imagene did not recognize what it was. A dark sound, bitter, sarcastic, indicative of intense and complex reactions to something beyond Imagene Tutt's range of experience. But before Penny could go further with her story, the Angelus bell rang and something shuttered closed in her face as she set aside the now unimportant history of her worldly life and replaced it with the contemplation of the one Father Who never failed His children.

Standing beside her, head bowed, shaken, Imagene was not thinking of the Annunciation of Christ's Incarnation, nor of any of the aspects of divinity.

Another pair of nuns approached them, chatting companionably as they came to take over the second shift of garden work, and Sister Catherine and Sister Immaculata parted company, each headed for separate duties indoors. There was more to Penny's story, but it would have to wait for another opportunity to be told, and Imagene was not certain she wanted to hear it. She had a sense of something uglier still, waiting. Something beyond the ability of her love for Penny to whitewash.

Nine

LIFE IN THE CONVENT moved at a different pace from that of the world beyond the walls; God's time, perhaps. Work to be done, prayers to be said, Mass and Confession and long hours of meditation that filled the soul with peace, as pure water fills an empty pitcher.

Imagene Tutt did not possess an easily pacified soul. She longed for the beauty and serenity of the life, but at the same time she continued to feel the presence of the outside world, and not necessarily as a hostile environment. Life was going on out there. When she sat immobile, hands folded in her lap, eyes cast down in the classic posture of meditation, imps of curiosity were tugging at her. What had happened to Penny? What was happening to other young women, the girls of their class, dating, marrying, raising families, holding jobs?

Instead of long conversations with God, her imagination insisted on creating alternate lives, and showing them to her in vividly colored mental vignettes. She struggled against

the temptation, aware that serene, self-possessed Sister Immaculata seemed to suffer from no such distractions. Whatever had happened to Penny in the past, she appeared to
have wiped it from her mind completely; after that aborted
disclosure in the garden, she never offered to discuss it with
Imagene again.

Several weeks had passed before chance threw the two of
them together again, in a situation where there was little
likelihood of their conversation being overheard. Sister Immaculata had begun to gain strength, her cheeks were
filling out, and she had begun insisting on doing her full
share of physical labor, as did the other young nuns. One afternoon she and Sister Catherine were assigned together to
the laundry, in the basement beneath the refectory.

Imagene hated the laundry. *How can one hate God's
work?* Easily. She hated the smell of steam and dirty water;
she hated the backbreaking strain of lifting heavy wet
habits out of the tubs; she hated the way the flesh of her
hands itched and cracked afterward. I could never be a
martyr, she thought to herself. Ever. And she was secretly
glad that the days of martyrdom seemed to be far in the
past.

Unlike some of the other nuns, who did such work without complaint, Imagene complained often, not with a whine
but with a sarcastic pleasure taken in the very act of airing
her grievances. "I don't see why we have to work like
coolies when there's a perfectly good laundry down on
Acacia that could do all this, and probably a lot better. Do
you really think this is the most productive way for us to
spend our time? I mean, don't you suppose we'd be doing
just as much good visiting the sick?" No sooner had she said
that than she laughed at herself. "Come to think of it, I
don't like being around sick people, either. How can Christ
possibly find a good use for me?"

The day she and Penny found themselves together, bent

over the laundry tubs, she said something similar and was shocked by the look Penny gave her. The blue eyes were like chips of dark ice. "You should thank God on your knees for this," Penny said in a savage whisper. "You have clean work to do. *Clean.* You have a marvelous opportunity for the expiation of sin through sacrifice, and you should appreciate it."

"Of whose sins?" Imagene couldn't help asking.

"Of your own, for starters."

Imagene straightened up with a sigh and rubbed her aching back. "Frankly, Sister, I haven't had much opportunity to commit that many sins." Damn it, she added silently to herself, surprised at the sudden welling of resentment.

"Count yourself fortunate," Penny said in a low voice.

Imagene bent back over the tub. "Sister . . . ?"

"Yes?"

"You were telling me . . . in the garden . . . do you remember?"

"I remember." Her mouth was a noncommittal line.

"I couldn't help thinking about it, wondering how you got from being on a vacation with your father in Switzerland to being a novice here. I just can't put it together in my own head, and I feel that something more happened first, something that's really hurt you."

Penny looked at her then. Her eyes were empty; almost hostile. "Are you just curious, or do you really care?"

Imagene was stung. "Oh, Penny, you know I care! I've been so worried about you, for so long! I tried to find out what happened, tried to get in touch with you in some way, but I just couldn't. For all I knew you were dead, and no one was telling me. It was awful!"

"Yes," said Penny. "It was awful."

She hefted a mass of steaming black cloth and wrung it savagely, then plopped it into a rinsing tub. She wiped her hands on the blue apron pinned over her habit and turned to face Imagene, her eyes looking beyond them to the door. "Does anyone else ever come in here?" she asked in a guarded voice.

"I doubt it. It's not exactly a favorite gathering spot. The only nuns I've ever seen in here are the ones working on the laundry, and for this hour, that's us."

"All right," said Penny, "I'll tell you. This one time, because I suppose I owe you that much. But then I will never speak of it again, not to you or anyone else, and I want you to give me your promise you won't tell anyone what I've told you. Never. Do you promise?"

Imagene was surprised at the vehemence behind those words. "Yes, of course, I promise! You know I wouldn't break my word to you."

"All right, then." Penny took a deep breath and looked beyond Imagene, into the past. "My father tried to make it up to me, in Switzerland," she began. "He wanted to be sure I was on his side again, so I would never tell anybody and disgrace him, ruin his political chances. He took me to the best restaurants and resorts, he bought me trunks full of clothes and all that overpriced jewelry they sell to rich American tourists. He kept urging me to buy, eat, enjoy, but I just didn't have an appetite for any of it. I felt hollow.

"And then one night there was a lot of brandy, enough to blur all the sharp edges and make everything seem much less important somehow. It was almost like a religious ecstasy; I was floating above the world and nothing hurt anymore, I could do anything and it didn't matter. I was so free. There was no such time as tomorrow and no such thing as consequences. Just drifting, and colors swirling, and laughter about nothing at all.

"When I tried to stand up, my legs were rubber. He practically had to carry me back to our hotel. He took me to my room, but I couldn't even take off my own dress; my fingers couldn't manage the buttonholes. He undressed me himself. I can still see his face leaning over mine, flushed from the brandy, and the way his eyes looked. His fingers were cold, I remember that very clearly. And his hands were shaking.

"Then he got into bed with me."

Imagene stood rigid with shock. The quiet basement room was an isolated pocket of protection from reality. In glittering resorts with fairy-tale landscapes, people like Kellam Endicott did unspeakable things. There were obviously two worlds; the surface world worn like a nun's habit, concealing what lay beneath, and the bizarre, hidden world that had turned Penny into a burned-out shell of a woman, reciting a terrible litany in a room smelling of bleach and laundry soap.

"God, Penny!" Imagene whispered.

"Yes," the other answered with cool detachment. "God. I ran away from Kellam Endicott and came to God.

"Do you know what my father said to me? He said it was all right because I was ruined anyway. Those were the exact words he used. I wasn't drunk enough to ever forget them. Ruined anyway. He was so excited he was panting like an animal, groaning, heaving on top of me. He said he would teach me what lovemaking was really like. He said, 'I have a big present for my little girl.'"

"Did you scream for help?" Imagene asked, revolted by the picture in her mind.

Penny shook her head. "He was my father, don't you understand?"

The awful thing was, on some level Imagene did understand. Had she been in Penny's situation, loving her father as much as Penny had loved Kellam Endicott, she might not have screamed either. That was a hard thing to realize about herself, but somewhere along the way—perhaps in all those hours spent staring into the mirror and trying to see Penny's face instead of her own—she had learned to be brutally honest with herself. I wouldn't have screamed either, she thought. I would have been terrified and disgusted, but I wouldn't have screamed.

"What happened then?" she made herself ask, hoping there would be some comfort for Penny somewhere in this awful recital.

"Later, when he had to go out on business, I got some clothes and took the jewelry he'd bought me and went out and sold it. They gave me a fraction of what everything cost originally, but I didn't care. I just needed enough money to get away. I went to the nuns, to a convent outside Lucerne, because that was the nearest place I knew of. I told them just enough of my story to get them to take me in. Eventually, they arranged for me to go to a convent of this order in the south of France. There I had a new name and a new identity; he could never find me. I wanted nothing but God, then; just to be a nun and live with God. But I came to see that that was a kind of cowardice, hiding out in France, so I asked them to send me back here."

"Has your father tried to find you?"

"Apparently not. I don't think he made much of an effort at all. I suspect he hopes I'm gone for good, out of sight permanently. We're dead to each other now. All of that no longer exists for me. I'm free of men and their world." She gave a contented little sigh, like a housewife tidying up the dirty laundry and putting it out of sight in a hamper. She half-turned away from Imagene, making it obvious she had gone back to work, that the conversation was finished and the subject closed.

Imagene could not ask any of the questions burning the back of her throat. After a few minutes of pretending to work, she escaped from the laundry room, up the shallow whitewashed steps to the sunny garden just beyond, and stood in the yellow light, letting it wash cleanly over her. A breeze rippled the hem of her habit. She found she was holding her rosary in her hand, not telling the beads, just holding it in a clenched fist.

Penny came up the steps behind her, drying her hands on her apron. "You're still here?" she said with surprise.

"I've been thinking about what you said in there."

"Well, don't. I assure you I never think about it anymore, and this is the last time I ever intend to say anything about it to anybody. I told it to my confessor in Europe, a poor little man who could hardly understand a word of English. I doubt if he had a clue what I was telling him. But he gave me absolution. I have that; nothing can take it away from me."

"Surely Mother General must know . . ."

"She knows I was raped in Europe, nothing more. And she will never ask. That's the beauty of the convent; the past really is dead here. And if you were ever my friend, you'll let it stay dead. You'll understand how important it is to me that we never discuss this again."

If you *were* my friend? Past tense? "I'll never mention it to you or anyone, Pen," Imagene said.

"Sister Immaculata," Penny corrected her sternly.

"Sister Immaculata. Yes."

After that day in the laundry, Penny undertook to establish a distance between them. She lived behind walls of her own choosing and treated Imagene no differently from the other nuns, remaining evenly polite and coolly friendly with all of them. Imagene made a sincere effort to reestablish their relationship on the old footing of caring and sharing lives, but Penny rebuffed her by acting as if they had never shared anything. Two strangers, newly met and with nothing in common. It was almost as if there were some stain on her that made her unacceptable for Penny's friendship. Imagene was the confessor, now burdened with the guilt, and there was no one to whom she could pass it on. Penny walked pure and free, cleansed, and shunned Imagene for her knowledge.

Forced to take an objective, outsider's viewpoint, Imagene saw how impressed her fellow novices were becoming with Sister Immaculata. She watched, as one watches a familiar play, while Penny's influence spread throughout the

novitiate and even among the professed nuns. Without appearing to make any bid for attention, Penny moved, as she always had, in a spotlight, followed by admiring eyes.

Sister Angela once commented, "Sister Immaculata seems to be listening to some other voice, have you noticed that? She's never totally with us, though no one could deny she is a great help and comfort to the entire convent. Knowing her is like knowing someone who may be canonized someday."

Nobody laughed. It did not seem impossible that the quiet, austere nun, her beautiful face purified by some unknown suffering, might become one of those specially blessed by God's grace. She seemed limitless in her ability to pray and study, to sacrifice herself, to help others, to do the hardest tasks gladly. With a gentle gravity, she encouraged the admiration of others simply by not discouraging it. As time went by, only Imagene found herself immune to Sister Immaculata's drawing power, and began to go her own way, seeking some other ideal to follow.

Her two years in the novitiate were spent in constant trial as Imagene's desire to be a good nun struggled against a rebellious spirit that resented folding its hands and bowing its head. She could not seem to conform without question to the shaping forces of tradition. She insisted on asking, "Why?" too many times, even for the patient novice mistress. "You should have been born a boy, so you could be a Jesuit," Sister Therese Luke snapped at her one day.

Daydreams overtook her at the least appropriate moments. She still found herself thinking of houses, homes, although she now lived in a more architecturally elegant building than she had ever expected to occupy. Still, during Mass or meditation, or late at night when her tired body sometimes refused to sleep, she caught herself imagining big solid one-family houses or elegantly furnished apartments, rooms filled with beautiful things, soft furniture, intimate and beloved personal belongings that spelled Home.

At other moments, she found herself envisioning the

world beyond the walls, with all its ugliness and shock, but
still tantalizing, a wild place with unlimited possibilities, as
exotic and alluring as the world Alice discovered down the
rabbit hole. Penny's experience had shocked and shaken
her, but it had not destroyed her own appetite for life nor
her curiosity about it. She could tell herself, again and
again: If you were out there, Imagene, you'd probably wind
up in some miserable low-paying job, a bored and lonely old
maid to the end of your days; you're lucky to be here instead. Still, part of her remained unconvinced, and hungry.

In spite of these tugs and pulls, and the vague dissat-
isfaction that never went away, she tried hard to be an obedient nun, glad in the service of God. But with Sister Immaculata's outstanding example always before her, it grew
harder and harder to feel confident of her own abilities. As
the time approached when those novices who were deemed
ready were to make their Simple Profession, the young
women were all involved in a period of self-examination
and last-minute doubts, but none felt so insecure as Imagene.

Simple Profession meant graduating from the novitiate
and being fully accepted into the community as a professed
nun. The new nuns would be Clothed, then, in the traditional habit of their order; their hair would be shorn and
they would officially begin their lives as Sisters of the Good
Shepherd. Only one commitment would still remain to be
made: the final, binding, Solemn Profession, the ultimate
and irrevocable offering of oneself to God.

Between Simple and Solemn Profession as much as five or
ten years might pass, during which the nun would renew
her vows every year. Throughout that time she would be free
to reconsider her decision, up to the day of Solemn Profession itself, but the form of the temporary commitment and
its intention were exactly the same as that of the permanent
vow for which it served as apprenticeship.

Before Simple Profession, the novices were considered
and reviewed by the Mother General and her council, and

that weeding-out process resulted in the loss of two of their number. To her own surprise, Imagene was not one of them.

Mother General said to her, "We are aware that this has not been an easy time for you, Sister Catherine. Both poverty and obedience seem hard vows for you. You keep wanting to add material pleasures to your life here, and we have spoken before about the difficulties you experience with submission. You are slow to accept the authority of others and quick to take initiatives that are not yours to take. But we will help you, Sister. We will all work together to strengthen and beautify your soul."

Once again Imagene promised herself to work harder, to mortify the flesh and subdue the spirit, that rebellious spirit that sometimes painted lurid pictures in her brain and dreamed wild dreams of palaces and princes, of beautiful material things that she would never have.

It all seemed so easy for Penny. She glided through convent life on a straight track, untouched by temptation, everything tasted and put behind her. Sure of her destination, she sped toward God, and a bevy of followers strove to live up to her example.

Only Imagene knew what it had cost Penny to arrive at that station in life, and sometimes she looked at her former friend speculatively, wondering how much of what she saw was genuine.

In the common room, the novices talked among themselves more earnestly than ever before, hammering out their beliefs, fighting off their doubts.

"Celibacy!" little Sister Mary Patience sighed. "I don't know what it means not to be celibate, yet here I am, taking a vow to give up carnal love forever. Now I'll never know what it's like. The whole world is preoccupied with sex and I never got any more than a good-night kiss on the front porch with closed lips."

The others laughed.

"I'll tell you what celibacy means," offered Sister Angela. "A vow of chastity is a way of clearing the decks for action." Sister Angela's father was a career naval officer. "By remaining celibate, we can be sure that nothing comes between us and God. We give all humanity a claim on our love, instead of just one person—that's what Sister Immaculata says."

Sister Immaculata was not with them. She had no doubts to air, apparently. She was in her cell, praising God and praying for mankind, and they were all aware of it.

Imagene brought up the subject that had been bothering her for weeks. "We're going to go through a wedding service; that's what Simple Profession amounts to. We become Brides of Christ, with veils, flowers and all. I know it's beautiful and a great honor, but don't you think it's—well—sort of like admitting that we're appendages to a man, instead of people in our own right?"

The others looked at her in surprise. "What do you mean?"

"Just that everything we do is dictated by men. The whole female community of nuns is governed by the all-male hierarchy of the Church. Doesn't that bother any of you?"

"I never thought of it that way," said Sister Mercy, "but I have no objections. My father was the ultimate authority in our household, almost like the Pope, and it made me feel very safe and secure knowing he was in charge. Besides, we'll have our superiors and Mother General; we're not directly answerable to men."

"No, but our superiors are," Imagene argued. "The bishops and the cardinals have the last say. Our whole future is in the hands of men, and how can we trust them not to neglect us . . . or be tyrannical? It's nice to think there's someone loving and wise and good who cherishes us and will take care of us, but how can we be sure? Shouldn't we have more responsibility for ourselves?"

"There is One we can trust, Whose love never fails us,"

said a voice behind her. Penny stood in the doorway. "You
need only put yourself in Christ's hands and He will give
you everything you should have."

The other novices looked at Penny admiringly.

They were too close to Simple Profession; Imagene
dropped the argument. It was like picking at a scab; if she
tore it open, it might bleed and ruin everything. But the
questions lay unanswered in her mind. Penny herself had
said she was free of men and their world. Two visions of
convent life, one of freedom, one of subservience to the male
authority figure. Which was right? And which was right for
Imagene?

She could only hope that understanding would come to
her with the habit, and peace descend on her in the form of
the bishop's blessing.

Some of the novices invited their relatives to attend the
ceremony, as they might have gone joyously to any wedding. Imagene had no one to invite. Penny also extended no
invitations, and notified no one of the event about to take
place.

The novices went on retreat for the final few days. Once
that retreat would have lasted three months, the time required to sew a habit by hand. Like a trousseau. Then the
waiting time was over at last and the day of Simple Profession arrived.

On a radiant spring morning, the novices appeared together before the bishop. Dressed in bridal white and lace
veils, carrying bouquets of white roses and baby's breath,
they marched in radiant procession down the aisle and knelt
in prayer at the bishop's feet. As they repeated the vows of
Simple Profession, they felt the hush of a great mystery descend upon them. Imagene was embarrassed to find that she
could not concentrate; she heard Sister Mary Patience's
voice catch in a little sob of happiness.

Their vows completed, the newly professed nuns trooped
silently to an anteroom where their bridal finery was re-

moved and replaced by a simple black habit. Then they knelt in turn at the feet of their abbess as she cut their hair with shears held close to the skull.

As their hair fell away, the air seemed shockingly cold to their denuded scalps. When no one was looking, Imagene ran her hand over her head and felt the prickle of harsh stubble. But the down remaining on Penny's skull was soft and golden, and a beam of light from the clerestory window turned it into a halo. Looking at it, the other shorn nuns imagined that they too were beautiful.

Ten

NEWLY PROFESSED NUNS were assigned to various convents throughout the order by the Mother General. Some nuns expressed preferences for a particular community; most were content to leave their fates in the hands of their superiors. Sister Angela grinned through her freckles as she said, "I think that's the most exciting aspect of it all. We're being sent out on uncharted seas, so to speak. Brand-new lives in totally unfamiliar surroundings. What an adventure!"

"I hope they're not too unfamiliar," commented Sister Mary Patience. "Adventure is fine for you; you're used to it. I sort of like to feel at home, you know?"

"You will," Sister Immaculata assured her kindly. "You'll be in the home Our Father provides for you wherever you go. What greater security could any of us ask for? Besides, one convent isn't all that different from another, Sister—you'll see."

Sister Mary Patience bit her lip doubtfully. "Are you sure?"

"I give you my word. I've been in convents in both France and Switzerland, and I can assure you that you could walk into one of them and almost feel you were still here."

Trust kindled in the other nun's eyes. "Then I won't worry," she said with relief. Sister Immaculata gave her a fond smile.

To their surprise, both Sister Catherine and Sister Immaculata were assigned to the Convent of the Holy Child, in Texas, the only nuns to be sent back to their home state. When they heard the news, Imagene expected Penny to make an objection—surely she wouldn't want to be that close to her father after what had happened. But Penny seemed unconcerned. "I won't be going outside the convent," she assured Imagene. "He'll never know I'm in Texas, and that's the way I want it. I told you, he doesn't exist for me anymore, nor I for him."

"But this is a teaching order! What about finishing your education and getting your degree? You can't do that without leaving the convent; we'll have to go the university for at least part of the time."

"I'm just not ready for that yet," Penny told her. "I've already talked it over with Reverend Mother and she understands. Not every sister of our order becomes a teacher; you know that. I simply don't feel called to that particular service."

Imagene, who did not feel "called" to anything, nodded. "You'd make a good teacher anyway," she said lamely.

"I suppose so." Penny's voice was indifferent.

The Convent of the Holy Child was not as large as St. Mary's, but the buildings themselves were older. They were situated on a slight rise called Murphy's Mountain by residents of the nearby town of Lickskillet, which was itself no more than the proverbial "wide place in the road," famed only for the quaintness of its name. But a broad new highway flowed like a swift river toward the metropolis of Dallas and its neighbor, Fort Worth, and on her first day at Holy Child Imagene found herself glancing out one of the windows on the second floor and being comforted by the highway visible in the distance, leading outward to Life.

The two new nuns were joined by a third, Sister Angela of the freckles and the adventurous spirit. "Imagine this!" she exclaimed, quite delighted with her assignment. "Texas! *Cowboys!*"

The others laughed. "I doubt if you'll be seeing many cowboys here," Imagene told her.

"Oh, I don't need to see them. I can just think of them out there, galloping over the sagebrush."

Penny and Imagene looked at each other and smiled.

Imagene was surprised at the nature of that exchanged glance, the comfortable familiarity of two old friends, insiders amused together. For the first time in many months, she allowed herself to think that she and Penny might pick up their friendship again, altered by circumstance but still warm and special. And as the days passed and they settled in, they did seem to be more comfortable with each other than they had been at the motherhouse. Nuns are discouraged from pairing off, but when they were brought together by the daily routine, Penny was sometimes the first to smile, and usually offered conversation.

But it was not the same Penny; there was no use pretending otherwise. The nun with Penny's face was still and always Sister Immaculata, and at Holy Child the other nuns responded to her as surely as they had at the motherhouse. These were older women, members of an aging and shrinking community, and they welcomed the new nuns as an infusion of life, with love and without resentment. From the beginning, however, it was apparent that Penny was something special. She could enter into their theosophical discussions and was soon leading them, while Sister Catherine and

Sister Angela sat quietly at the edge of the conversation, hands folded, lips silent, very aware of themselves as newcomers and too young to have valuable opinions. Accepting and accommodating itself to the new members, life in the convent altered and shifted, swirled around them with subtle gradations of emotion and adjustment, and then settled comfortably into a new pattern, a strengthened whole that did not recognize their individuality but was the better because of it.

It became clear that Sister Immaculata was a traditionalist, totally committed to her vows of poverty, chastity, and obedience, perfectly at home in a community of nuns who seemed to have never questioned either their calling or their rules. The restrictions of convent life did not weigh heavily upon her; indeed, they were not heavy enough, for she was always seeking ways to sacrifice more. She ate more sparingly, slept less, spent more hours in prayer than anyone. Her spiritual strength seemed inexhaustible. Her entire being focused on the convent and way of life it represented.

Sister Catherine, Imagene, found herself at the opposite pole. In spite of her best intentions and her sincere desire to emulate Penny's performance, her own interests persisted in turning outward. As a professed nun, she now had access to newspapers and magazines, as well as the radio in the common room, and she discovered a passionate interest in news. Any news—world or local, any word or voice that brought drama into the serenity of the convent. The other nuns suffered her degrading addiction as they suffered Sister Stephen's dreadful puns, with practiced forbearance.

Imagene began urging the Mother Superior to enlarge the convent library to include recent writing reflecting the spirit of the times, such books as *The Shoes of the Fisherman*, *Silent Spring* and *The Group*. *The Shoes of the Fisherman* made it; *The Group* did not. Mother Superior made a general comment at dinner one day about the deplorable increase of what she called tasteless novels being offered the general public; Sister Immaculata, catching Imagene's eye, said in a clear and positive voice, "No amount of trashy material will endanger a truly healthy soul. Novels like that really serve no purpose in a convent library, however," she added, warning Imagene with her eyes to agree by remaining silent. Penny, once again helping a friend, showing her what to do, how to be.

Long-ago Penny, in a dormitory bedroom, giggling, explaining, "Boys are just as scared of us as we are of them, 'Gene; prob'ly more. All you have to do is tell them what they want to hear. If you listen, they'll give you plenty of clues."

Tell them what they want to hear, Sister Catherine. Play the game. Follow the rules.

She couldn't.

Imagene was surprised at how loud and self-conscious her voice sounded in the refectory. "I'm starting courses at the college next week, in the kind of world those novels are telling about, where people read and are influenced by books like that. And I'm going to be a teacher, teaching children who will go out into that world, not stay sheltered in a convent. Don't you think it's a mistake for me to try to keep blinders on?"

"Your purpose as a teacher will be to guide your students to a better life, not wallow in filth with them," Mother Superior said sharply.

"There are a lot of good contemporary novels about human relationships . . . about *sex*" (she was aware of the indrawn breath of shock among the older nuns) ". . . that aren't wallowing in filth. All I'm saying is that we should have access to some of them, to help us keep in touch with the world." She saw Penny staring purposefully at her, sending her signals, but she ignored them. "Things are changing out there, Reverend Mother, and like it or not, we're going to be influenced by them!"

Mother Superior pursed her lips and shook her head.

"You are very young, my dear," she said, a condemnation in-
stead of an explanation. "We will not discuss this further.
Sister Stephen, will you please read to us? Perhaps St.
Thomas Aquinas would be appropriate this evening."

Penny kept her eyes on her food and did not look toward
Imagene again.

Lyndon Johnson was President and Texas jokes were the
latest fad, particularly among those nuns who were not originally from Texas. Even the older nuns allowed themselves
to smile at Johnson's beagles; at his showing off his scar; at
his outrageous, larger-than-life Texanism. After the tragedy
of the Kennedy assassination, which had driven a number of
women into convents seeking something stable in a world
gone mad, it was a relief to laugh about a President instead
of crying for him.

In Vietnam there was little to laugh about, and young
men died in jungles and rice paddies while the American
mass media took up the antiwar cause with as much enthusiasm as had once been given to urging the destruction of
Hitler and Hirohito. Now war itself had been declared the
enemy.

On college campuses and among those who could receive
"Greetings!" any day from their government, the unrest
grew. It was no longer unpopular to be radical. The only
unpopularity accrued to those who tried to take the middle
ground and urge restraint.

Sister Catherine had begun her courses at the nearest college. Sister Angela was sent farther afield, all the way to
Dallas, to take special instruction in educating the handi-
capped, a vocation she had long desired. Mother Superior
let it be known that she felt some distress because neither
young woman could get the necessary educational requirements in full without spending at least some time in a secular school, but Imagene was glad.

College. The word had a magical sound. Nora Tutt's be-
quest would never have stretched for college tuition, and

Imagene could never have devoted herself exclusively to her studies enough to get a full scholarship. But now she was going to go to college. She felt the nostalgia of sharpened yellow pencils and crisp fall days; she found herself more eager for school than she had ever been before.

College turned out to be quite different from her mental pictures of it. Gone were the rolled bobby sox, the June Allyson co-eds, the jalopies and malt shops and clean-cut young men with nothing more serious on their minds than panty raids. This was a different generation from that of the movies Imagene had watched avidly as a child, dreaming herself into a world she thought closed to her. These students were intense, scruffy, hard-edged, many of them fanatics in search of a cause.

To Imagene's surprise, they granted her a kind of automatic respect as someone who had already found her cause, no matter how far removed from their own. She was treated with the deference they accorded anyone outside the mainstream, but she was not befriended, because she was perceived as having nothing in common with her classmates, and at first she thought this was true. She sat in classrooms and auditoriums among them but not with them; she yawned through interminable lectures in stuffy lecture halls beside them but apart from them, automatically segregated because of the habit she wore. Joking died away when she approached. Girls of her own age spoke to her as they would to someone a generation older, never including her in the secret language and current fads of the young. If a passing breeze carried a fragrance similar to that of burning oregano, pleasant/unpleasant, the other students exchanged guilty glances and tried to distract her attention. College girls were wearing jeans to class, and many of the boys were letting their hair grow to a length that reminded Imagene of the mural of the Good Shepherd at the motherhouse.

During the opening of the Second Vatican Council in Rome in 1962, Pope John XXIII had remarked, "We are going to shake off the dust that has collected on the Throne of St. Peter since the time of Constantine and let in some fresh air." Pope John had died before that dream could be realized, but the Curia, the cardinals who govern under the Pope's direction, continued to urge religious orders to look to their sources and return to the pioneering spirit of their founders.

In 1965, Vatican II called for a revitalization of all religious orders, including the approximately 360 orders of nuns in America at that time. As America was searching its collective soul about its involvement in a war on the other side of the world, men and women in convents and monasteries were devoting much prayer and soul-searching to their own futures. Community workshops and discussions about spiritual renewal were arranged. Some orders went so far toward modernization as to modify their dress and rewrite their rules and customs.

The Sisters of Loretto at the Foot of the Cross were the first to give up the traditional habit altogether, in favor of simple suits. The Sisters of the Good Shepherd chose the middle ground, just shortening their habits to a modest below-knee-length. Some of the younger women wanted a complete return to secular dress ("The habit was originally intended in the Middle Ages to make us look inconspicuous!" they argued), and even some of the older, more philosophic nuns were willing to accept a drastic change, but the women in their middle years, the Mothers Superior and General, could not.

Sister Immaculata agreed with them. She even resented the shortening of the habit, telling her circle of influence, "We're lowering our standards by raising our hems." It became something of a catchword in the community and ultimately influenced the decision to go no further with modernization.

The first day Imagene attended classes in her new shortened habit, she was aware of the students' staring. In the rest room, she made sure she would not be interrupted by jamming the door shut and then climbing up on a lavatory counter to get a look at her newly visible legs in the mirror. They were prim in their black stockings and tied oxfords, but her ankles were slender and her calves had an obvious curve.

She smiled hesitantly at her reflection in the mirror, as at a new friend. Later, when she caught a bearded young man eyeing her legs with interest, she felt a pleasure she did not report to the priest in Confession.

Unrest was in the air. Now that change had begun, it fed on itself, gaining momentum and demanding more change. An American group, the Conference of Major Superiors of Women's Institutes, sent a unanimous petition to Rome asking for representation on the all-male commissions that regulated the lives of Catholic nuns.

That request was ignored.

The dissension invading campuses and classrooms began to affect Imagene as well. It was impossible to avoid the feeling of revolt because it permeated the very air she breathed during her school day. She listened to the slogans and catchwords and they excited her. She enjoyed the drama; she found that she was hungry for a cause—any cause. The rebellion of youth had bypassed her in her own struggle for survival, but now it caught up with her with a vengeance. It began by expressing itself in a growing resentment of masculine domination of religion.

She started introducing her fledgling philosophies into the evening discussions in the common room at Holy Child. Some long-suppressed anger against men welled up in her and would not be denied. Men like Barney Tutt, who had rejected his daughter. Men like Kellam Endicott, who twisted their children into unrecognizable beings. Men who started wars. Men who controlled the lives of women. She said, "The power structure of the Church was conceived by men and for men. The Father, the Son, the Holy Ghost. Men are priests and we are servants."

The others looked at her in surprise. Some of them thought about what she said. Some complained to the Mother Superior.

In the college rest room one day, Imagene took off her headdress with its layered veils and starched white wimple, and looked at her close-cropped hair. Some of the older nuns still shaved their heads bald. "Why should women have to make themselves ugly deliberately?" she asked the reflection in the glass.

Later she asked the same question in the common room. Overhearing her, Sister Immaculata answered, "Sister Catherine, you're rebelling when there's no need to rebel. The walls, the habit—these are things that set us apart as special; they don't make us second-class citizens."

"I'm not so sure. I think they're just ways to keep us from being involved with life. Maybe that's fine for you, but . . ."

"You should be grateful for the protection of your calling," Sister Immaculata told her.

"I don't need protection. I need to have some sense of control over my own life."

"You have surrendered that control to God," she was told. "You must allow Him to guide you."

I have surrendered that control to men, Imagene thought privately. A masculine God and his masculine priests. The Bible was written by men. She thought of the press, of radio and television inveighing against the war in Vietnam.

Media manipulation. That's where the power is; that's where it's always been. In the hands of the men who control our histories and influence our thoughts. Men tell us what's good for us and what to believe.

With the gentleness used to reprove an impetuous child, Mother Superior and the older nuns began to remind her of her vows of obedience and the dignity of her vocation. But their arguments were the traditional ones, of obvious male construction. They answered none of Imagene's questions. All they did was politely demand her silence.

She longed for someone to talk to; she wanted to lie in the dark with Penny, whispering across the space between their beds, exchanging confidences. But the Penny she knew had become Sister Immaculata, who would not understand.

She tried. "Sister, don't you ever feel any . . . doubts about your vocation? Honestly?"

"Doubts? No."

"But surely we all feel them sometimes," Imagene protested.

Penny's expression was as tranquil as that of the marble madonna standing above the portico at St. Mary's. She had gradually gained back some of the weight she had lost, and her face was as lovely and unlined as it had been in childhood. It was incredible to Imagene that none of the traumas Penny had experienced should show in her face. Only occasionally, in rare, unguarded moments, Imagene thought she caught a glimpse of some deep pain hiding there, but Penny would never talk about it.

"I've never had any doubts," said Sister Immaculata. "I know exactly where I belong. And with whom."

"I envy you," Imagene told her, saying it aloud for the first and only time in their lives.

"Our Lord has been good to me," the other nun said complacently. "He has shown me the true path."

Imagene wanted to grab her and shake her. She wanted to say, "This is me you're talking to, Penny; you don't have to put on an act with me!" But she didn't. What if it wasn't an act? What if such piety really existed, and she was the only one so spiritually limited as to disbelieve?

"The longer I stay in the convent," Imagene said aloud, "the harder some things are for me to accept."

"That's because you go outside. It's totally corrupt out there, in *their* world. You're being tempted into questioning your values. But listen to me, Sister. Here in the convent is where women really have autonomy and power. The monastic enclosure liberates us, can't you see that? Oh, granted, our superiors pay fealty to the male hierarchy, but you and I don't have to deal with them. We're a self-contained community of women here. We've deliberately chosen celibacy to free ourselves from the enslavement of childbearing; we have each other for companionship; we have our work, our prayers, the Sacraments, and the never-failing love of God, the only real Father. We don't need anything else."

"I do," Imagene said in a voice so low Penny could hardly hear it.

"What? What do you need that you're not getting from the religious life?"

Imagene lifted her head and Penny saw an expression of baffled frustration in her eyes. "That's just it. I don't know!"

Penny's face softened, just a little, and something fond and familiar looked at Imagene from the big blue eyes. "Oh, Sister, you are having a hard time adjusting, aren't you? You should have asked all these questions while we were still in the novitiate," Penny reminded her. "That was the time and place for them. Your life has progressed past that now."

"But it hasn't. That's just the problem! I'm just now finding out what the questions are!"

"Don't ruin things for yourself," Penny warned her, her voice suddenly very serious. "I'm warning you: you could do yourself more damage than you realize. This is the best of all possible worlds, Imagene." (Imagene!) "Believe me, I know."

"Well, I don't know, damn it!" Imagene exploded. "I don't know anything! And I want to!"

She went out alone into the small garden next to the chapel, a peaceful place of crape myrtle and fading grass spangled with dandelions, a jungle of little yellow lions. She sat on a bench of cedar wood, gray with age and service, as

gray as the stone walls rising behind it, and fingered her rosary. Bees hummed, moving among the fleshy-pink blossoms
of the crape myrtle. Pollinating, perhaps? Did bees do that
to crape myrtle?

Pollinating. Carrying life.

I shouldn't have sworn like that at Penny.

She tilted her head back and gazed up into the bottom-
less blue sky.

God's not going to strike me down for it, though. In a
way, I almost wish He would, then at least I could be certain He's paying attention. Are You listening, God? Damn
it. God damn it. God damn it to hell.

Unperturbed, undisturbed, the sky burned on, a hellish,
unrelieved blue.

The antiwar protesters became more organized, marching, making speeches, battering the Establishment with
the weight of their youth and energy. Imagene gravitated
toward them, hungry to be part of the pulsing life they
radiated. It was not because she fully understood their
cause; she did not, at first. She was not even certain the war
was the total mistake they claimed. She had grown up with
World War II, and glory on Iwo Jima, relived in articles
and stories read and reread on sweltering, lonely afternoons.
But she learned. She was told that war turned young men
into cannon fodder to satisfy the greed of old men. She
learned that the munitions czars callously manipulated the
rise and fall of nations. She listened intently when one of
the most blazing of the new firebrands, a gaunt, bearded
man in his late twenties named Robert Osmond, stood on a
platform and shouted that her parents' generation had sold
her own down the river. For profit.

"War is bad for children and other living things!"

Osmond—known as Rob to his devoted followers—was a
possessor of the new charisma. The antithesis of the classic
hero, he made courage synonymous with suicide and offered

love as a panacea for all the wrongs of the world. Broad-spectrum, unlimited love. Stop the guns, ban the bombs, throw your arms around one another and love. Love.

Sister Catherine listened, wide-eyed.

The marching, the cheering, the posters in primary colors, all represented the crest of a new wave of evangelism, a crusade that could silence inner questions and release tension in a mighty roar of anger, and she could be part of it, if she chose. She could belong.

The day came when Sister Catherine stepped onto a platform and made her own speech denouncing the bloodsucking bureaucracy. The fat cats, the munitions makers. The men. She was cheered and patted on the back by feverish boys with Galilean hair and told that she was "Right on, Sister!" She was given a can of warm beer and she drank it, feeling deliciously wicked.

Rob Osmond himself hugged her, then stood beside her, holding her hand, while the crowd swayed and sang. "That was a heavy thing you did," he told her. "You're really speaking out for love. I never expected anything like that to come from a tight-assed establishment like the Catholic church."

His proximity was exciting, beyond the excitement of the speeches and the fervor of the massed mob. He was wearing Levi's cut-offs, and when he walked away from her to speak to a group of girls in similar uniform, Imagene found herself watching the backs of his legs. The tendons behind the knees seemed like columns, protecting an unsuspected vulnerability. To her astonishment, she wanted to touch those legs.

It was terrible to think that such a man might be sent off to war, as cannon fodder.

Aware of her eyes following him, he looked around at her and smiled. The air seemed heavier then and it was hard to breathe.

Imagene Tutt was twenty-five and she had just come to life.

There were other rallies and other demonstrations, always with Rob Osmond center stage, and soon with Sister Catherine as much a fixture as he. They talked, when there was time. Of the movement, of philosophy, of the power of love. Their conversations were always in the abstract, but the way Osmond looked at the young nun was not abstract. Imagene was aware of it and frightened by it, but she awoke each day hoping she would see him again.

She did not discuss these feelings in the confessional.

Osmond had other girls around him, always, and Imagene knew, without letting herself dwell on it, what services they performed. There was something pagan involved. A priest with his servitors, his priestesses, ministering to him. In every way. Sharing in the all-encompassing love.

She tried not to think about it, but her dreams became lurid with suppressed sex and when she was near Rob Osmond her palms sweated. She began skipping classes to go to the rallies.

Mother Superior was upset. "Sister Catherine, you are behaving irresponsibly. If you continue, we will be forced to withdraw you from college and that would be a loss. You have so much to contribute as a teacher; a good intelligence and abundant energy are gifts from Our Lord, meant to be used constructively. But you're wasting them, my dear! Our order has strict rules against becoming involved in politics, and what you're doing only points out the justification for those rules."

"I feel an obligation to speak out against injustice," Imagene tried to explain.

"I understand that, and it does you credit. But believe me, you will be far more help praying for mankind than haranguing people from platforms."

Imagene meant to obey. That was her vow and she intended to keep it, no matter how hard. The difficulty was part of the willing sacrifice offered to God. And she was fully aware of the simmering danger of her attraction to Rob Osmond; there was another vow threatened. Celibacy had no place in Rob Osmond's credo. She forced herself to stay away from the rallies and redoubled her efforts at her studies.

But in 1967 more American men died in Vietnam than in all the previous years of that war, plus an additional 53,000 supposedly noncombatant Vietnamese. The Pentagon proposed a policy of increased aggressiveness, and the youth of America, led by Rob Osmond, among others, howled in rage.

The Dow Chemical Company, which incidentally made napalm, sent recruiters to Imagene's campus and a fight broke out that put many of her classmates in jail. That night Imagene did not return to the convent. She stayed on-campus to stand with the others around a roaring bonfire and chant the slogans of dissent and disillusion, and when the cameras moved in for close-ups they focused on her rapt face.

Suddenly Sister Catherine was news.

Microphones were thrust in front of her and she was asked her opinions of the protest movement, civil rights, migrant labor, even the early stirrings of the women's liberation movement. She answered them all and the press loved it. She was articulate and photogenic, her strong features revealing unsuspected beauties to the camera. The contrast between her habit and her views provided high drama and the journalists scented it quickly. AP and UPI wrote feature stories about her, and local and national television clamored for more coverage of the young nun who couldn't be kept quiet.

But they could keep her quiet, of course. Mother Superior sent for her and told her in no uncertain terms that her days of notoriety were over. She was being withdrawn from college, her teaching career canceled by her own actions, and henceforth she would remain behind the walls, serving God in more private ways until she learned the proper humility and freed herself of her wicked lust for attention.

"By whose directive?" Imagene demanded to know.

"I have heard from both His Eminence and His Excellency," Mother Superior replied, placing the responsibility on the cardinal and the archbishop. The Establishment. Imagene stood with her teeth clenched and her head up, refusing to look humble.

"I've done nothing wrong," she said. "I merely said what I thought, as any citizen of this country has a right to do."

"But you are a citizen of the community of God," Mother Superior reminded her. "The temporal world is no longer your home."

"I don't recall giving up my American citizenship," Imagene answered stiffly.

Mother Superior was a plump woman with kind brown eyes and a firm jaw. The eyes took precedence over the jaw now, expressing loving pity for the rebel spirit that must be returned to the fold. "My dear, please listen to me. We have only your best interests at heart. I realize that, perhaps, you haven't had enough experience of the world to put things in their proper perspective, and it's not surprising that these feelings are surfacing in you after all this time. Our human natures are very strong. You haven't chosen the easy path, being a nun. I can understand that because it's not easy for any of us to turn our backs on the world."

It's easy for Penny, Imagene thought, steeling herself against the other woman's kindness. She had begun to realize she was too susceptible to kindness. When Rob Osmond offered her half of his sandwich . . . No. Don't think about that. And don't think about Penny, either. I can't be her kind of nun.

Mother Superior continued, "Sister Catherine, if you cannot keep your vows of obedience, surely you realize . . ."

She lifted her hands and turned them, palms up. The unspoken alternative was plain: conform or abandon the veil. "Please, my dear, go on retreat for a while. Several days or weeks; take as long as you need. Pray to God to guide you and make His will manifest in you. Ask Him to grant you the grace of submission. I urge you in the strongest terms to renew your vows, not only to the order but to yourself and Christ."

She went back to the college one last time, to pick up her books and say her good-byes. She did not try to explain what had happened. A wall of embarrassment seemed to exist between herself and her classmates now, but she could see the admiration in their eyes. To some of them, she was a martyr.

Penny would have enjoyed that, being a martyr. It made Imagene uncomfortable.

Rob Osmond and some of his followers were in the coffee house across the street from the campus. They parted deferentially to allow Imagene to move into their center, surrounded by her new celebrity.

"I'm leaving school," she told them, her eyes on Osmond's. "The convent's withdrawn me from the course."

"Bastards," Osmond said between his teeth. His eyes blazed. "They don't have the right to do that to you!"

She bent her head slightly. "I gave them the right," she said. It was an admission of weakness.

"Well, you don't have to accept it now! Tell 'em to take their habits and their rules and stuff 'em!" Osmond dug into his jeans and pulled out a piece of paper on which he quickly scrawled something in pencil. "Look, you don't even have to go back there tonight. You can stay with us. We're pulling out of here tomorrow anyway, got another scene to make, more places to spread the word. And we're going to be staying here," he tapped the paper with a dirty fingernail, "at this sort of commune run by some friends of mine.

You can come to us there, anytime. You're part of us, you know."

He hadn't said: "Come to me." He said: "Come to us." She met his eyes questioningly but his expression was unreadable. In one moment of supreme courage she could accept the paper and the commune and whatever it implied and change her world totally.

Slowly—very slowly—she folded the paper and put it in her purse. "Maybe later," she said, hating herself for her cowardice and dependency. "I . . . don't think I'm ready right now."

"Anytime," Osmond said cheerfully, accepting her decision without argument. She longed for him to urge her, but he did not. He smiled. "You need me, you know where to find me." He turned to the others and resumed the conversation that had been interrupted by her arrival. When she left, they took it as casually as if they would see her tomorrow.

The convent seemed more eager to have and hold her.

She was sent to a lovely retreat house, surrounded by pine woods and plowed fields of red clay. Television cameras and protest marches seemed a million miles away, on some other planet. But in the unbroken quiet that was meant to be a retreat from the world and into God, she found that the world would not be silenced. She lay sleepless at night, staring into darkness and listening to the voices in her head.

If I stay in the convent and take my final vows, it will be like sleepwalking through life. I'll be living in an out-of-step world controlled by archaic traditions and nostalgia.

And I'll be cared for, as I used to imagine other girls were cared for. And loved. Loved in some ways, but not in others.

Rob Osmond's burning fervor; his voice ringing above the crowd.

What's it like to join a commune? Is it like this? Are there any differences, other than men and women living together? Would I be happy? Would I be protected?

In the convent, I'm . . . happy enough. Really happy, sometimes. And protected; protected by the walls and the veil, protected from rejection.

But who can really be protected in this nuclear age? Radiation will go right through brick walls and layered habits. The old securities people used to trust in are gone, and what's left? God?

In the convent, there is time to examine everything, myself included. Time to be peaceful. Time to learn, and pray. All the time in the world, with the Hereafter thrown in for good measure.

So easy.

So hard.

Sitting inside the walls with all of life going on outside. Rowdy, raucous, full of uncertainties, but still life, growing unchecked like some kind of cancer, perhaps, but growing. Not sitting still. Stretching. Open to possibilities.

Reverend Mother would say I was risking my immortal soul. Is that possible?

Is the risk part of the excitement? Is that a temptation of the devil, that excitement, or just life calling to me?

I don't know.

She returned to the convent and nothing had changed; Rob Osmond had left the city, but people there were dancing the Watusi and watching a movie called *The Graduate*. Kids not involved in antiwar protests spent their time playing with Frisbees and experimenting with sex and pot. Even businessmen in offices were wearing their hair longer, looking like middle-aged Beatles. The area's first abortion clinic opened defiantly and very briefly.

The TV cameras found Sister Catherine in the milling, yelling throng outside, caught between picketers and defenders, and a reporter interviewed her with her back to the wall and her eyes very bright.

"Women have a right to their own bodies!" Imagene heard herself insisting as she stared into the camera lens. "There should be free abortion clinics all over the country, where women could go with confidence and without shame. So much misery would be spared!" *Penny. Oh, Penny.*

The camera loved the planes of her face and the quality of her skin, so that the woman shown that night on television screens across the nation appeared beautiful. Nun Favors Abortion.

Mother Superior sent for her again. This time the determined jaw prevailed over the sympathetic eyes. "I have spoken with Mother General this very morning," she began briskly, as she would start sweeping a dirty room. "This time you have gone much too far, Sister Catherine. Advocating murder! Publicly! It is almost impossible to believe, yet I am told millions of people have seen you. A Sister of the Good Shepherd, defending abortion!"

Imagene stood with her hands held stiffly at her sides. Her voice was very controlled as she replied, "I have to stand up for what I believe. Didn't the saints do that?" There was less conviction than stubborn pride in her voice, but Mother Superior did not realize it.

"Are you equating your defense of willful murder with the courage of the martyrs?" The older nun was shocked.

"No, of course not. But I believe that no one has the right to a woman's body but that woman herself. She should be protected against the consequences of an unwanted pregnancy just as she should be protected against rape. The Church has authority over our souls, but we should be sovereign in our own bodies."

Mother Superior felt as if she were on the verge of fainting. It was like seeing her own child physically attacking the pillars supporting Church and Family with a club, destroying the secure walls of orthodoxy that kept the barbarians at bay. Who could guess what evil might come slithering through the broken walls?

"Sister Catherine," she said through tight lips, "you speak of a woman's rights to her own body. What about the rights of the unborn child, the vessel of God, to its body? What evil force has convinced you it's permissible to rip that innocent little being from its safe home and destroy it?"

Imagene struggled with the answers to that argument, the things she had heard. "It's not a person yet, it's just a fetus . . ." she began, but Mother Superior cut her off with a voice like a lash.

"That 'fetus' you would kill contains life; therefore it contains the spark from the Creator. It has a soul."

"I don't know that!" Imagene said desperately. "It can't be proven!" Prove it to me; give me something I can be sure of! she begged in her mind.

Mother Superior stared at her with embarrassing pity for a long time. Then she said, "I am very much afraid that a mistake has been made here. Two mistakes: ours and yours. I will speak with Mother General again this afternoon and I imagine she will want to meet with her council to discuss your situation. It is very possible, Sister, that you are just not cut out to be a nun at all. We might be doing you a grave injustice by expecting too much of you."

Imagene retreated to her cell. She had to pass the chapel on the way, and she started to go in, but then she wondered why. What would I pray for? Unquestioning faith? Reverend Mother is right; I don't think it's in me.

She sat on her narrow bed with her hands folded on her knees and tried to create a quietness within herself, hoping that God would in some way speak into that quietness.

Beyond the walls of her room, the life of the convent flowed on uninterrupted, a broad river, certain of its destination. No television set intruded, bringing in discord. Still, most of the other nuns were already aware of what had happened the day before at the abortion clinic. If Imagene left her room, she would see them glance at her and then look away, unsure of how to act toward her until a decision was made for them by higher authorities.

She stayed in her room and waited. Once she went to the window, feeling as if her lungs were bursting for lack of air, and smelled the fragrance of baking chicken coming from the kitchen. Her stomach knotted; another rebel, unwilling to submit. The childhood chubbiness was long since pared away, but the appetite remained, a battle to be fought endlessly.

She could not bring herself to go to the refectory. It was one thing to stand in front of a TV camera, addressing strangers she would never see. It was quite another to face her sisters in God across a table.

If only she could talk to Penny. She walked back and forth across the room, subconsciously measuring it. How small it was! Had she never noticed that before? How quickly it grew dark as the light faded! She could go out in the hall and wait for Penny—one nun would never enter another's cell without her permission—and then they could talk. She actually went as far as opening her own door and looking down the hall, hearing the soft silence of the rooms waiting for their returning occupants.

She clenched her fists and went back into her own cell, shutting the door behind her with a firm gesture. Stand on your own, Imagene. Even Penny can't help you with this. Quit trying to be a copycat. Find your own way and follow it.

Oh, Penny! she mourned in the growing twilight.

She sat in silence and the smell of lemon polish, and at last heard the whisper of their habits coming down the hall, and the murmur of voices. No footsteps paused at her door. She could picture them passing by, their folded hands hidden by their sleeves, their faces free of tension. People on the outside rarely had that look. They appeared bored or anxious or angry as they rushed through their uncertain lives, seeking some kind of security, either physical or emotional.

Why am I throwing all of this away? she thought.

Stupid pride.

But I have to be right about something!

Now that it was no longer a certainty in her life, she suddenly saw the full beauty of the religious community, as the face of a dying loved one will reveal unsuspected beauty too soon to be lost. She remembered the way they had all laughed together at the freak snowstorm last winter, hiking up their habits and hurling snowballs joyously at each other, as excited as any Texas schoolchild who rarely saw snow.

She thought of the long, stimulating discussions she had so much enjoyed in the common room; she felt again the radiant joy of receiving Mass in the company of her sisterhood; she recalled the poignance of going to the small cemetery beyond the grape arbor and laying flowers on the graves of those who were still, in some way, very much a part of life in the convent. She had felt immortal then.

Now she felt vulnerable and very mortal.

What if I am asked to leave? What will happen to me? Who will take care of me? Will I be able to take care of myself? How? I've never done it!

She imagined herself running down the echoing halls and bursting into Mother Superior's office, begging for mercy. "I didn't mean it. I take it all back! I don't know what made me say those things. Just forgive me and I'll never do it again!"

But just as she had lacked the courage to throw everything over and join Rob Osmond in his tumbleweed lifestyle, renouncing the security of the convent forever, she now lacked the fortitude to make that final, ringing denunciation of the world itself. The power of active choice seemed beyond her. It would have to be made for her. She was attacked by a dreadful passivity that left her as helpless as a child, waiting for others to direct her life.

The question of abortion haunted her, now that the heat of the moment had cooled and her passion with it. Facing the cameras, she had been so sure; hearing the applause of the crowd, she had felt so inspired. But alone in her cell, she could hear the echo of Mother Superior's words and she could even hear Penny's own voice, protesting abortion as sin, denying herself that escape.

Oh, Penny, I did it for you! she wanted to cry aloud to the girl who wasn't there. But she was no longer sure, even of that.

She hugged her arms around her midriff and bent over, rocking in a kind of agony. It was far too late for abortion to save Penny. And would Penny want saving? Wasn't she infinitely happier now than she might have been, had her life gone in another direction? Who could know?

Devoured by doubt, Imagene sat in her cell and waited for judgment.

Eleven

THE COMMUNE was actually a few miles outside of Dallas, down a winding dirt road between the straggling suburban outskirts of the metropolis and the stubborn resistance of doomed farming country. When she got off the bus, she stood in the road, feeling very small and frightened, a woman who had come to the end of the world and was about to jump off. The area looked poor, unpromising, and her one small suitcase seemed suddenly very heavy.

A sign, roughly painted on a board, offered an arrow and the words PEACE VILLAGE. Imagene followed the direction pointed out by the arrow, finding walking difficult in the rutted clay road. The sun beat down on her and she could smell her own sweat. Her clothes seemed too flimsy to protect her from the environment, yet her cheap flannel skirt, bought in anticipation of the autumn still to come, stuck to her damp slip and was unbearably hot beneath the waistband.

I'll have to get something lighter and cooler to wear, she

told herself. Probably everybody here wears jeans. I'll look like a freak, an old maid schoolteacher.

Well, that's what you are, Imagene.

For now. Until something happens to change that . . . to change you.

A cluster of ramshackle buildings appeared on her right. Badly in need of paint, with torn screens on the windows and junked cars in the yard, they looked like a squatter's settlement. Imagene felt a moment's revulsion. It was the sort of place Barney Tutt might have moved into in one of his worst periods. Yet another sign, similar to that on the highway, proclaimed, PEACE VILLAGE—LOVE IS HERE!

She hesitated at the edge of the compound. Shouldn't someone come to greet her, as at the convent? She could see a couple of slatternly girls washing something in a galvanized tub at the side of one of the shacks, and a bearded youth, in faded jeans with the crotch torn open, sat on the front porch, his legs sprawled so she could see something pink that must be his genitals. He made no effort to hide himself as she approached, and she struggled desperately to look anywhere but at his lap. He grinned.

"You lookin' for somebody, lady?"

"Rob Osmond. I'm . . . a friend of his. He said I could come here if I needed a place."

Without moving, the boy shouted, "'Nother one'a Rob's chicks here. Anybody spectin' her?"

A young woman, in an ankle-length dress of faded cotton, a crying baby clutched to her chest, came to the door of the shack. Her hair was stringy and her eyes were dead. She looked at Imagene without interest. "No," she said.

Imagene felt panicky. Where else can I go? What can I do? *Who will take care of me?* She took out the piece of paper he had given her and waved it at them. "But he said I was to come here if I needed to!"

The boy took the paper from her hand and examined the writing. "That's Rob's, all right," he told the girl in the doorway. "I guess it's okay. We can use another pair of hands, can't we?"

"We don't need another mouth to feed," the girl replied. "Unless she's got money. You got money?"

"A little," Imagene said defensively. "But I'm used to hard work."

The boy barked a harsh laugh. "Oh, we don't go in for much *hard* work. Sometimes we have to go into town and raise money for the movement, that's all. Would you be good at that?"

She wanted to turn and run away. But there seemed nowhere else to go. "I suppose so," she answered. "I've never tried."

"You got family you could write and ask for money?" said the girl in the doorway.

"No."

"Hmmph." All interest lost, the girl swung around and vanished into the shack. Imagene and the boy looked at each other.

"This *is* Peace Village, isn't it?" Imagene asked. "I mean, is this the place Rob told me about, where antiwar protesters come and . . . and everybody looks after everybody else?"

The boy grinned. "Love, right? Sure, we got lots of love here, and we all take care a each other. We're not all uptight about marriage and the draft and all that shit, if that's what you wanna know. Anybody's welcome here who thinks the war is a buncha crap and wants to make a protest. This is like another world, you know? I mean, we've all dropped out, we don't want any part a that shit anymore. Don't pay no attention to Darlene, she's just in one'a her moods. Rob said you could come here, that's good enough for us." He stood up lazily, the grin widening. "A course, you'll need a place to sleep. You can sleep with me tonight; my old lady's off someplace with Rob."

He stood insolently, waiting for her to come up the broken steps to him. "You're a tad old for me, actually," he commented. "I like a young chick. But I'll show you a good time. That's what we're all about here, y'know? Good times, doin' your own thing . . ."

Imagene's feet were walking backward and she hadn't even realized it. "I've made a mistake," she said in a strangled voice.

He started down the steps after her then. "No, you're in the right place."

She was shaking her head from side to side. "I'm not, I'm sorry. Oh God, this is not the right place!" She was almost running, terrified that he would catch her and hold her, but he just stood watching her and laughing. "Suit yourself," he called after her. "I'll tell ol' Rob you couldn't wait. What's your name, anyway?"

She was out in the road again, the baked, rutted road, with no place at all to go and only emptiness stretching before her. From somewhere deep inside herself, she found a moment's defiance, because that was all she possessed.

"Penny!" she shouted at him.

She started back up the road toward the highway. Maybe she could catch a bus there, into Dallas.

The big blue-and-silver Greyhound raced down the highway, swallowed her up, and took her to the city. Any city would have done; any big, crowded city with people. Dallas just happened to be nearest, and she had so little money. She crouched in a seat behind the driver, feeling dirty and rumpled, trying to reach ahead with her mind and picture herself living in Dallas.

Somehow.

The skyline rose like a mirage above the flat prairie, shimmering with heat haze, sharp vertical towers thrusting out of a horizontal plane. Seen from a distance, it looked like a fairy-tale place, gleaming with wealth.

The bus terminal was depressingly gritty, and by the time

she got there Imagene had a throbbing headache. She made herself concentrate on the one small pleasure she could create in her immediate future: a hot bath. She would find a room, hang up her clothes, brush her teeth, and scrub herself clean.

Then she would have to take charge of her life, all by herself. There were no options left. And in some strange way, that made her glad. It's time, Imagene, she told herself.

In a phone booth at the bus station, she searched through yellow pages softened to the texture of old rags by much fingering, trying to find a hotel within the downtown area that lived up to its advertised "reasonable rates." When her small stock of change was almost depleted, she was given a reservation she could afford at a place called the Palm Court, on Ervay Street. The girl at the ticket counter assured her that Ervay Street was not too far to walk.

She was glad to walk; it was the best way to get some feel for the city. Beyond the bus station was an area occupied by small manufacturers and wholesalers in dark-brick buildings still stained by the smoke of another era. Beyond that again was a fringe of pawn shops and narrow doorways leading to fly-by-night businesses too transient for expensive overhead signs. A few blocks more and she was in the retail district.

The late afternoon was cloudless and hot, denying the calendar. Store windows brimmed with autumn, with sheaves of brittle corn and plaster turkeys and cornucopias overflowing with silk scarves or costume jewelry or artificial fruit. One shoe store featured a giant pumpkin in the center of its display, surrounded by delicate slippers with see-through plastic high heels. Cinderella's coach at 12:01, Imagene thought.

She walked slowly, studying the windows as if they were textbooks. What were women wearing this season? What colors were the lipstick, the makeup? Were eyebrows in or out? How high were hems? How high were prices?

Good God, the prices!

How strange it was to have to worry about these things. As she walked through the bustling streets, she became aware of the details that set her apart from the swirl of tired, perspiring shoppers. Her clothes were dowdy by comparison with most of theirs, her growing-out hair looked like an unpruned bush, her lack of makeup identified her as an alien in the kingdom of Neiman-Marcus and Sanger-Harris.

She paused in front of a small shop and gazed at the assortment of blouses and skirts in the window. Just those simple items, but so many different styles and colors! How could one choose?

She drifted on to the shoe shop next door, again struck by the enormous selection. Her eye began adjusting to the nuances of style and she found herself starting to select one pair over another. That one had a heel she liked; those were of very soft leather, looked comfortable; and oh! look at this pair! Gleaming gunmetal patent leather, and what a graceful shape!

She was smiling a little to herself as she walked on up the street.

It seemed a very long way; probably that girl in the bus station had never walked it, herself. You could tell an out-of-towner anything. The little suitcase seemed to have gotten bigger and heavier, banging uncomfortably against her legs. Then the first cool breeze of the oncoming evening skittered down the concrete canyon, cooling her face and reminding her that summer was really over. The long, hot summer of self-doubt, of retreat houses and hours spent on her knees in chapel, of defeat and loss.

Her small pleasure evaporated when she saw the Palm Court. The chipped tiles of its Moorish façade gave it the appearance of someone in a faded *Arabian Nights* costume, peering from between two sober businessmen neatly attired in buff-brick. A garish pink arch framed the doorway opening onto a tiled vestibule. The floor was littered with the bodies of hundreds of dead crickets carelessly left there since the preceding night, when they had been drawn by the neon sign overhead. The small, brittle bodies crunched beneath her feet and Imagene shuddered. She would have turned away, sought some other hotel, but she was suddenly desperately tired. Too tired to search anymore.

Brush my teeth. Take a hot bath.

Barney Tutt would have stayed in a place like this, she thought.

The clerk at the desk met her eyes with the bored, cynical gaze of clerks in cheap hotels everywhere. He looked at her white face and her figure in the straining blouse. He liked to see a woman in clothes that were too small for her. Taking a calculated risk, he leaned across the desk as he handed her the key, and caught her fingers with his own. He smiled at Imagene as if he knew some dirty secret about her.

"You lookin' for a little company . . . later?" he asked.

She snatched the key and fled toward the single elevator.

The corridor of the third floor was narrow and badly lit. A soggy-looking red carpet ended halfway down the hall. Imagene's room was numbered 322, and the final numeral had lost one of its nails so that it hung upside down on the layered paint. When Imagene put her key in the lock, the door refused to open.

She began shaking helplessly. She turned from side to side, as if seeking aid, but then she realized the only available help was probably the leering desk clerk. She jiggled the key in the lock with silent desperation, pleading with it to work. Just this once. Please, God. Let me get this door open. Let me in. Oh, please, let me in!

The door swung open and a rush of stale air came out to greet her.

The room was small and drab and dirty. After the neat

freshness of her cell at the convent with its sparkling clean window and its faint perfume of furniture polish, the hotel bedroom seemed filthy; obscene. It had splotched wallpaper in chalky turquoise and battered blond Danish modern furniture, patterned by cigarette burns. A single framed print over the bed showed two children with hyperthyroid eyes, staring out at the room with identical expressions of victimhood.

The bathroom was little better, but at least it had been spared any attempt at decoration, leaving it plain and utilitarian. There was a mirror over the sink with a leaf-shaped dark area at the bottom where the silvering had peeled off, and there was a dark ring in the tub Imagene didn't want to think about.

She turned on the light above the mirror and studied her reflection. That's me, she thought. That exhausted woman is me. I thought she was just a girl, but it looks like someone's come in the night and stolen years away from her. Away from me.

Her eyes stung but remained dry. The face in the mirror was pathetic.

If I saw someone like that in the street, what would I do, turn away from her? No, I'd try to help, in common human decency. Even if I weren't a nun.

Am not a nun.

She put out one hand very slowly, and the image in the damaged glass reached toward her in response, groping like a blind thing. Their fingertips touched on the cold surface of the mirror.

"Hello," Imagene said to the unfamiliar face. Softly, so she wouldn't frighten it. It looked as if it could be easily frightened.

Its lips shaped the word and sent it back to her.

"Don't look so hopeless . . . Imagene," she whispered, trying out the sound of the name. It didn't fit the face in the mirror. The woman in the glass looked at her without recognition. Not Imagene, then. Imagene was somebody far away and long ago. Dead, perhaps.

Gassed by the Nazis.

The self-pity she expected to see reflected in the mirror wasn't there. That woman wasn't bemoaning her fate, her stiffened body tossed like cordwood on all those other corpses, waiting for immolation. The woman in the mirror merely looked drained and lonely, a waif on a street corner who didn't know where to find shelter.

She needs friends, poor thing. Where are they, the friends who should have comforted her, the family who should have protected her from the holocaust?

She looked deeply into the mirror at the nameless person who was no longer Imagene Tutt but who had no other identity.

The face watched her. It was not dead after all, that face. Life still glowed somewhere in the gray-green eyes. She saw to her surprise that she was not unattractive. She had never been a pretty girl, but the passage of time had brought finely sculpted bones to the surface of what had been a pudgy, platter-shaped child's face. Her eyes were enormous and compelling. She stared into them and they stared back, waiting for her to say something.

I have to make the first move, she thought. That one in the mirror never will. I'll have to take the responsibility for both of us.

"You look like you could use a friend," she said to the mirror woman. To her horror, the face crumpled with sudden anguish, hurt at last beyond all bearing.

Imagene was frightened. "God?" she whispered once, feeling faintly ridiculous. No one answered.

The woman in the mirror was still waiting, helpless until she could make some decision for both of them. They could stand there for hours, staring at each other. They could stand there until she starved and fell unconscious on the grimy linoleum, and no one else would care.

She swallowed hard against the fear rising like a flood in her throat, and spoke aloud to her only ally. "It's going to be all right," she said in a voice scarcely above a whisper. She cleared her throat and spoke again, louder, taking courage from the sound of a human voice in that place of emptiness.

"It's going to be all right," she repeated to the face in the mirror. "We're going to make it, damn it! I don't know how yet, but we will, just stick with me." She wasn't going to cry, not anymore. She willed the face in the mirror not to cry. "Let's get a bath and some sleep and we'll make a fresh start in the morning," she advised it.

Incredibly, she saw a dim hope being born in those watching eyes. The woman in the glass believed her. Knowing that, she could almost believe herself.

"We'll be just fine, you'll see," she promised, making the words a vow. Looking deliberately into that other face, she forced a big, confident wink.

No one else would ever know the effort it cost her. But the face in the mirror knew.

Job hunting was a lesson in humility. Every prospective employer knew just what kind of person was wanted for a given job, and that person never fit the description of Imagene Tutt. When personnel managers learned she had been a nun, they became self-conscious ("I'm afraid you wouldn't be happy here, we're a pretty relaxed gang, you know, some of the men . . . not that I approve of that, of course, it's just the way things are"), or hostile ("We just don't have the budget to make appropriate arrangements for you. Why not go to your own people?"), or intimidated, or rudely curious—anything but receptive.

It was as she had feared. No one wanted Imagene Tutt.

Maybe the name was part of the trouble.

Her money was almost gone. She could get in touch with the bishop, make arrangements, but she didn't want to do that. The ties were cut; let them remain so. She searched the want ads desperately, looking for anything.

Anything?

HELP WANTED—DOMESTICS.
Live-in housekeeper, must be reliable
and willing to work. Room with bath,
air conditioning, private entrance.
Call 555-8047.

I need a place to live. I'm reliable and I'm willing to work, Imagene thought. And there's nothing dishonorable about being a . . . a domestic. It would be a lot more dishonorable to keep on taking the Church's charity.

Nervously, she went to interview for the job in University Park, an affluent neighborhood north of even more affluent Highland Park. The house was a handsome brick ranch on a sweeping lawn, with professional landscaping and an air of being comfortably removed from the mundane struggles of life. The prospective employer, an elderly doctor's widow with a bad case of arthritis but otherwise good health, was obviously surprised to see a young, intelligent, white woman applying for the position, but when Imagene explained her background Mrs. Colby was delighted.

"My dear, I think you're absolutely perfect! I can't help thinking you're a godsend! The last girl I had, oh, I just can't tell you . . ." Rolling her eyes heavenward, she did proceed to tell Imagene, at length, with details and gestures. Imagene, who had nothing better to do anyway, and enjoyed the comfortable, serene feeling of the house, sat with folded hands and listened. Eventually, at Mrs. Colby's request, she went into the big birch-paneled kitchen and fixed two tall Waterford crystal tumblers of iced tea, which she carried back to the living room and another hour of conversation.

She heard about the late Doctor Colby—"An absolute saint of a man, my dear. He never thought of himself; that's why he worked himself into an early grave, don't you know"—the children, the grandchildren, and the arthritis. A gentle flow of cool conditioned air moved through the house like a benediction. By late afternoon, Imagene Tutt had a job.

The convent had finished the training her mother had begun, and Imagene had little difficulty keeping house to Mrs. Colby's requirements. Cooking was somewhat harder. There was a shelf full of cookbooks in the kitchen to make the art sound easy, but obviously they lacked such basic information as how to keep white sauce from curdling or the way to make "real Texas" chili without making it "hot"—a constant request of the doctor's widow. With dogged persistence, Imagene tried to turn herself into a good cook. She read, stirred, sampled, and felt her stomach pressing against the waistband of her skirt. But when she tried to cut back on her own eating, Mrs. Colby complained.

"Eating alone is such an 'old lady' thing to do, don't you know, almost as bad as drinking alone. It makes for bad habits. I want you to sit with me, my dear, and let's have a nice chat while we eat, that's best for the digestion. And here, take more than that, you're not eating enough to keep feathers on a sparrow. I like to see young folks with a good appetite. That's what the doctor always said, don't you know. As long as people have a good appetite, there's plenty of life in them."

Mrs. Colby's real need was for someone to talk to, and in return for a room of her own, more luxurious than any she had ever possessed, and an adequate salary, Imagene was glad to oblige her. She enjoyed taking care of the house. Sometimes, while polishing furniture or hanging quilts in the sun for an airing, she found herself whistling, off-key and happy. Why did people look down on domestic service? At those moments, it seemed a most satisfactory occupation to her, a profession like any other and better than many. She had done much harder physical work in the convent, and had less sense of freedom.

Mrs. Colby's neighbors were surprised at the arrangement. They were used to "colored help," although now that, as they whispered to one another over back fences, "black folks had gotten so uppity," the kind of domestic servants they had always hired seemed to be in short supply. Several made blatant efforts to try and lure Imagene away from Mrs. Colby, and Imagene was amused.

She felt valuable. It was a wonderful feeling.

But at night, when she sat at the little skirted dressing table in her pale-pink bedroom (Mrs. Colby thought all bedrooms should be pink, with flowered fabrics), Imagene looked at a discontented face in the mirror. It wasn't the job; she was happy enough in that and thankful to have it. The source of the discontent was herself. That waiting face still did not have a name or an identity of its own.

The bedroom included a little Queen Anne writing desk ("So you can keep in touch with your friends, don't you know") and Imagene took a sheet of paper from the small supply in one of the drawers and began jotting down different names, seeing how they looked on paper, saying them to herself to hear how they sounded. If she liked one, she went over and said it to the face in the mirror.

One of the names was Ivory.

At first it sounded pretentious, but it stuck in her mind. Ivory was a name with a definite identity, an image; that of something lovely and valuable.

Like Immaculata.

She smiled to herself, feeling at last she had hold of a tiny piece of her future, shaped to her own desire. Ivory it would be, then. Ivory . . . Talbot, not Tutt. Talbot sounded aristocratic, the name of someone who had never been poor or embarrassed.

She went back to the desk and began her first letter. She wrote it five times, achieving a paragraph or two and then crumpling the paper in anger to start over. She could hear the words clearly in her mind, but when she saw them written they seemed stilted and conveyed the wrong meanings. At last she settled for the simplest words possible, stripped of any emotion that might be misconstrued.

"Dear Sister Immaculata," she wrote:

"I regret our parting on such an angry note. Please accept my apologies.

I have a job here in Dallas and am doing all right. My address is on the envelope if you ever want to write me. The name may be different, however. I am going to start saving some money so I can have my name legally changed, because I never liked Imagene Tutt and now I don't have to answer to anybody, I can call myself whatever I like. When the change is made, I will write you again and tell you about it.

Best wishes to you and all the sisters,

Ever your friend,

Imagene"

She was actually surprised when Penny answered, in a letter almost as carefully worded as hers. But at least the contact was reestablished, and suddenly she felt less alone. It was all right; she could change her name and cut herself off from the past, but Penny was still there, like a thin umbilical cord, reaching backward, anchored in the familiar, and she was glad.

Mrs. Colby was amused by the proposed name change. "I was christened Cora, you see," she explained in one of their interminable afternoon conversations, accompanied by the clink of iced tea glasses and the endless mindless barking of a collie dog in the backyard next door. "But my last name was Borris, and Cora Borris sounded awful. My middle name was Hannah—that was worse. As soon as I could, I started encouraging people to call me by my nickname, June Bug, and of course that stuck and I've been June Bug ever since, even to the doctor. Which was a pity in a way, don't you know, because once I got married I saw that Cora

Colby would've sounded real nice. But it was too late then. I'll always be June Bug." The little old lady smiled radiantly, her face dissolving into a net of wrinkles containing an impish sixteen-year-old's spirit.

Imagene smiled back.

Listening to Mrs. Colby was an education in itself, not only for the history the old lady related, which was considerable, and not all of it the tedious recountings of dead-and-gone family, but also because it was teaching Imagene a trick that had served Penny in such good stead. She was learning to focus on others, to listen with the rapt attention Penny had always given.

Some of Mrs. Colby's stories were fascinating. Once, after receiving a long distance telephone call from one of her daughters in Abilene, she got off on the subject of telephones. "When I was just a little girl, telephones were still new here; not many folks had them. That was the year of the big Elks convention downtown, I think 1909 or '10, somewhere in there. My momma was going to take me to town to meet Poppa and have dinner at one of the hotels. Our phone had just been put in, and the maid had finished dressing me when it rang. After Momma talked for a little while, she told the maid to change my clothes, we wouldn't be going to town. I was little, but I remember how disappointed I was. Years later, Poppa told me what happened. Land sakes, I was shocked!"

Imagene leaned forward, as Penny would have done, and urged the old lady on with her expression and her interest.

"It seems there was a rich family lived way out on Munger Place, I think, and they had this gardener they'd had for a long time. One day he up and raped their little five-year-old girl. Didn't kill her, I don't think; I can't quite recall anymore, but I know he hurt her terribly. The police arrested him and put him in the old jail, and a mob of white men went down there and got him out. They dragged that darky all the way to the intersection of Elm and Akard, where there was a big double wooden arch the Elks had put up. And they strung him up on that arch.

"This happened the day we were supposed to go downtown, and naturally Poppa didn't want us to come into anything like that. He said later that mob was just crazy. They actually cut pieces off that man for souvenirs, can you believe it! His ears, and hunks out of his legs, and . . . oh well, I just can't say. But to me, the worst of it was what happened after they took the body down. Those souvenir hunters went right on trying to have a piece of what happened to remember it by. They gouged so many hunks of wood out of the brand-new phone poles on the corners that those phone poles had to be replaced. Can you imagine it, people crazy enough to destroy telephone poles just to have some souvenir of a lynching?"

Mrs. Colby sighed and sipped her tea. The ice clinked against her porcelain teeth at the rim of the glass. "I do believe," she added, "that was the last lynching in Dallas, thank the Lord. But you know, I've never forgotten about those telephone poles. Now, what kind of folks would do a thing like that?"

Crowds, Imagene thought. Mobs, chanting and yelling, carried away by the spirit of the moment.

In her next letter to Penny, she recounted the story without comment as an interesting historical anecdote, something that could fill a page without being too personal. She was reluctant to be personal with Penny. The connection was not broken, but it was very changed.

Penny wrote back immediately: "They should have lynched him. I told you the world was evil and corrupt, and that's just one more example of it. People hurt each other cruelly and nobody seems to care anymore. What good does it do to care? It just gets you hurt. I see now that I hurt you, 'Gene, cutting you off the way I did, but that only proves my point. I didn't want to cause any pain. I hope you can understand that. I was just trying to protect myself, and I'd advise you to protect yourself the same way. It's one thing to love people in the abstract and pray for them. I can handle that. And I can use it to make up for some things. But I don't ever want to love somebody so much they can let me down again."

I didn't let you down, Penny, Imagene thought. But in her answering letter, she didn't say it.

They were writing regularly now, exchanging the trivia of their lives, and Imagene faithfully signed each letter with her new name.

Ivory.

Your friend, Ivory.

At last Penny began to use it.

"Dear Ivory," she wrote. "I marked my calendar to remind me of the date your name change would become legal. It was nice of your Mrs. Colby to introduce you to her attorney so that such an intimate matter could be handled by someone you know. I was amused that you and your employer celebrated by spiking your gin with iced tea, or vice versa. You write very witty letters, did you know that?"

But immediately after that compliment, she moved to the topic of all Penny's letters—Penny herself. She had never bragged and she did not now, but every week seemed to bring the diffident recounting of some new honor or accomplishment that loomed large in the small landscape of the Convent of the Holy Child. Mother Superior had assigned her to be the permanent reader during the evening meal. The bishop himself had given her a scapular from Lourdes. There was concern that she might be exhausting herself through prayer and fasting beyond that expected of a nun.

"Of course, I'm perfectly healthy," she wrote, "but they keep on worrying about me, anyway. It's touching but quite unnecessary. It's important that I set a very high standard for myself, Ivory—you understand that."

Yes. I understand that.

She wrote back: "Do take it a little easier, Sister, and don't overdo your fasting. You've always had a tendency to go too far." She did not mean to sound critical, only caring.

Penny did not answer that letter for weeks. When at last she did, her reply was frosty. "Don't presume to give advice about things you can't possibly understand," she wrote. "You don't know what you're talking about. I am very fortunate to be strong enough to make the sacrifices God asks of me, and if I am called upon for still greater sacrifices, I will gladly accept. My whole lifetime cannot possibly be enough to atone."

Atone for what? Ivory wondered, holding the letter. Penny was much more a victim than a sinner, and what she went through certainly should have balanced the scales. Why does she go on trying to justify herself to me—as if my opinion mattered—and being absolutely masochistic with herself?

Ivory continued to worry about her friend, but she kept her worries to herself and offered no more advice. Instead she tried to fill her letters with interesting tidbits from her conversations with June Bug Colby, and such harmless topics as the details of her daily life and a Texan's endless preoccupation with the weather.

Mrs. Colby had never asked her to wear a uniform, but when she had enough money to start buying a few clothes, she automatically bought matronly, safe dresses in navy or black or charcoal-gray, long-sleeved shirtwaists with buttons down the front, anonymous shifts and tents, uniforms without style. In the stores she told herself they would be the easiest to accessorize. They were undemanding. In the fitting rooms she watched herself in the mirror, not knowing what she expected to see, vaguely displeased but unsure how to change. She carried her characterless purchases out of the store, past racks of bright silks and youthful jerseys, and she looked at these things with love, as she looked at the pictures in the fashion magazines. She just could not envision them on herself.

One day she sat next to a man on a bus—a middle-aged, worn little man with deep creases on his forehead and an apologetic look about him, and the two of them made bland small talk. As they chatted, glancing occasionally at the smeared windows through which neighborhoods appeared and disappeared like acts of faith, she realized the man was assuming she was of his own generation.

He was approximately the age Barney Tutt would have been.

Shocked, she got off at the next shopping center and went into an unfamiliar department store. Holding her courage tightly in both fists, she said to a salesgirl, "I want to see some dresses, or skirts, something. But they have to be . . . bright. Dashing."

The girl looked bored. "Maybe a lighter shade of blue?" she suggested, making it easy on herself, noting that her customer wore a nondescript navy cotton with mid-length sleeves and a mid-length hem. Dowdy, her eyes said. I'll sell you another dowdy one.

"No! I mean, well, I want something like that over there." The woman in navy pointed at a cherry-red sundress with a halter top.

"For yourself?" the salesgirl asked in surprise.

"Yes, for myself." And then she added, rather strangely, "For Ivory Talbot."

She spent a long time in the fitting room, trying on the red dress, and when she came out at last she was smiling.

She thought Mrs. Colby might disapprove, but the old lady's eyes lit with pleasure at the sight of the dress. "I used to have one like that," she said. "Well, maybe not so bare in the back, we didn't wear them that way then, but I do remember red was the doctor's favorite color, and he loved me to wear that red dress. Now, don't you clean house in that. Save it for having fun in, don't you know."

Save it for having fun.

And then Mrs. Colby suffered a stroke, a terrible ax slicing down through her body that left half of her twisted and paralyzed, her speaking ability lost, all those long afternoon conversations strangled in her throat, and only her sixteen-year-old's eyes glared from her face, still speaking, betrayed and enraged.

Her children came to take care of her, to make the inevitable arrangements for a nursing home and the long, slow descent into oblivion for June Bug Colby. Two daughters, from Abilene and Wichita Falls—daughters who had never found time to visit before—arrived to survey the old lady's property with calculating eyes and ask probing questions about the likely length of Mrs. Colby's survival. They did not seem cheered when the doctor told them, "Why, she could be with us for years. Aside from her impairment, she's in robust health and her mind is as keen as ever; she can still get a lot of enjoyment out of life. If perhaps one of you would be willing to take her . . . ?"

Ivory later overheard one of the daughters say to the other, "It's just a dratted shame you can't put down old people the way you do old horses, when they're no use to anybody anymore."

Mrs. Colby's son arrived shortly after both women vigorously declined to care for their mother. A bachelor, he could not take her either, he explained with genuine regret. "I just bought me a little television station in West Texas, something I've wanted to do for years, and it takes up all my time. It's almost a one-man shop at this point. Mama thinks I'm some sort of tycoon, but I'm really just a slave to that station." He smiled apologetically at his mother and Ivory. "But I'll see that you get the best care, Mama. You can count on that. The best that money can buy."

Twelve

BUFORD COLBY was a slightly built, sandy-haired man, with a sunken chest and an incipient potbelly. His face was ageless: it never had looked childlike; it could never appear mature. He was the sort of colorless male for whom a homely woman might gladly settle.

Something in Ivory Talbot warmed to him as to a kindred soul. Important man or not—by his mother's boast, at least— he was quiet and diffident, and Ivory went out of her way to try to make him comfortable during the difficult days of decision making and getting Mrs. Colby located in an expensive, trustworthy nursing home. Afterward, he expressed his thanks, pressing her hand shyly.

"We owe you a great debt, Miss Talbot," he said in a voice like rustling papers. "It is Miss Talbot, isn't it? I thought Mother said in one of her letters that your name was . . ."

"It's Talbot. Ivory Talbot. And you don't owe me anything, Mr. Colby. I was very fond of your mother, and I just did the job she hired me to do."

He smiled. "I don't know about that. Mother could be difficult. She'd talk your arm off if you let her."

"I never minded."

He narrowed his eyes slightly. "You really mean that, don't you? Well, like I said, we owe you, and I want to see that you at least get a new position as good as the one you're losing. I have some friends who need a . . ."

"I appreciate that," Ivory told him, "but I don't think I want to take another job as a housekeeper. This one was perfect, a good job when I needed it and had no job experience, but I think I'd like to move on now, try something else."

"If you have no other job experience, what do you think you might do?"

What would Penny have said to a question like that? Ivory hesitated, then drew a deep breath and mimicked Penny's confident smile. "Anything," she said. "I have a good mind and I can learn fast."

Buford Colby pursed his lips together with his fingers. He took a pair of reading glasses out of his vest pocket (He must be the only man in Texas wearing a three-piece suit these days, Ivory thought), polished the lenses, and tucked them back in the pocket again, absentmindedly. Then he said, "Well, we could use a trainee at the station. Did Mother tell you I've gotten into this little TV station out West? Nothing glamorous, you understand, and I'm just learning the business myself, but like I said, we owe you. Would you be willing to consider it?"

Would she! Ten days later, Ivory Talbot had a furnished room in an old Victorian house on the outskirts of still another little Texas town, and a job as all-purpose trainee and gofer at KXAS, Channel 5.

It was another uprooting, another sudden new beginning, but this time it was easier. Maybe it's because we've had some practice at it, Ivory thought, looking at the face in the mirror. It was a more relaxed, less frightened face. It had moments of near-beauty, but she didn't see them because she had never expected beauty. It was Ivory's face, not Imagene's, however—and she liked it.

She had to furnish a résumé, with her convent history spelled out in painful detail, but Channel 5 was indeed a small place, with a haphazard filing system and no real personnel manager. The résumé disappeared, unread, into some drawer someplace, and Buford Colby never mentioned it to her.

He did mention lunch, and then an occasional dinner, asking shyly as if he expected a rejection. He had never married, and the first time Ivory ate lunch with him at the Silver Streak, she could understand why. The man was almost unable to talk to a woman at all. His only topic of conversation was business, the station, the lack of advertisers, the genderless trivia of their shared interest. If any other subject threatened to surface, he fell silent and played with his food.

Nevertheless, she liked him, and at first she was very grateful to have at least one male social contact. She felt that any date was better than none, and Buford Colby could not be described as scraping the bottom of the barrel. He was polite and he made a good living, especially by the standards of a dusty town that existed only to supply a feudal system of sprawling ranches with feed and farm machinery. To spend big money, the ranchers and their families jetted in their private planes to Dallas or Houston.

She wrote Penny: "The town doesn't seem like much after Dallas, but it's nice to be able to walk almost anywhere I want to go, provided the temperature isn't over ninety-five or we're not having a dust storm. I'm learning more all the time, and I've been promised the opportunity to learn almost every aspect of television. That's what a struggling little outfit like this is good for, I suppose. I seem

to work a minimum of twelve hours a day, but there's nothing new about that. And I am having fun. Television is exciting."

She didn't say more; she didn't want Penny to think she
was boasting to make herself feel better. The work was fun,
however, and she was learning about everything, about
cameras and lights and news stories, soliciting advertising
and reading budgets and even taking a turn at the switchboard, explaining to some furious rancher's wife why her favorite soap opera had been preempted for network coverage of a moon landing.

She was also learning about men, slowly and painfully.
Buford Colby, nice and undemanding as he was, left her
feeling exhausted at the end of their evenings together. Lou
Ellis at the switchboard complained about having to fight
her boyfriend off, but that was never Ivory's problem.
Buford made no advances. The nearest he came to it was
looking hopeful when he bade Ivory good night on the front
porch of the house, and then finally, on a night bedazzled
by fireflies reflecting a desert sky full of stars, he put his
arms around her. Very tentatively, as if he thought she
would shove him away. When she did nothing, just stood
waiting in his embrace, he patted her clumsily on the back.
"Why, you're just a little thing," he said, awkwardly hug-
ging her in an embrace more like a father's than a lover's.
"Somebody should be taking care of you."

Ivory felt a sudden flare of anger. Too late! It was too late
for a man to say that, in that paternal, gentle, flabby way.
Flabby! The time had long since passed when she actively
sought such a response from a man. Every atom of her
being now cried out for something else, for a strong and
passionate lover to match the throbbing life of the summer
night.

Not Buford Colby.

With a sense of regret, she gently freed herself from his
embrace. "I can take care of myself, Buford," she said. Per-

haps it wasn't true yet; she wasn't sure. But she would make it true.

He accepted her rejection without resistance, and that made her perversely angry. Surely she was worth a little more effort than that!

That night she told the woman in her dresser mirror, "I don't have to settle for Buford Colby. I don't have to settle for anything. I can have the things I really want. I *can*."

Her brave speech made, she sat down on the end of the bed and stared blankly around her. "But how?" she asked the quiet room.

Bit by bit, she was learning the arts of womanhood. She let her hair grow and got a permanent. She began painstakingly assembling a wardrobe for Ivory Talbot. She bought fashion magazines and the new, glossy periodicals just beginning to tell women how to live lives in places other than the kitchen and the bedroom.

When uncertainty plagued her, she tried to imagine how Penny would act. She began reaching out to other people as Penny once had, collecting friends by displaying an interest in them, listening and encouraging as she had with Mrs. Colby. She taught herself to focus on strangers, to give at least the superficial appearance of caring, and soon she found that people she would have once dismissed as boring were often very interesting, once you got beneath the surface. She bought a simulated-leather address book with the name Ivory Talbot stamped on it in gilt letters, and soon it was full of names.

Friends.

Drawn out of herself, she began to feel more and more a part of the world she had been forced to rejoin. Forced? she wondered. Or did I really choose it myself? Will I ever know?

Though her relationship with Buford Colby had settled into a placid business friendship, with no disturbing ripples, she began to discover she was hungry for the sharp edges and strong planes of a male mind. Years spent in the company of women had left her with an aching for that different intellect and point of view. She looked at herself in the mirror and tried to see her as a man might see her. Not bad—not as bad as she had once thought. But could be better. Would be better.

She devoted herself to a regimen of diet, exercise, and self-improvement that soon reduced her to unbearable hunger pangs and desperately sore muscles. She faced herself in the mirror and winced. "You're a disaster area, kid," she told that other face. "You have just got to shape up."

When she couldn't stand it anymore, she bought a huge box of Turtles, a local candy consisting of dark milk chocolate poured over clumps of pecans. She ate the entire thing in one sitting, glorying in gluttony, then went back on her diet. She promised the face in the mirror, "When you can't stand it anymore, we'll do that again."

One morning Buford Colby said to her, with the surprised tone of one who has just made a discovery, "I'll bet you'd look good on television, Ivory! Those bones . . . look, Bob Wallace wants to take a couple days off next week and do some fishing in the Gulf. How would you like to have a try at the noon news? It's mostly just housewives that watch it, anyway. If you have trouble, nobody'll complain."

Why do you assume I'd have trouble? Ivory thought but did not say. Because I'm just a woman?

She came in early and read the sheets again and again, familiarizing herself with every word, so that when she sat down at the desk and faced the camera lights, she was relaxed and confident. "Good afternoon, this is Ivory Talbot with the noon news." She did not say, "substituting for Bob Wallace."

The housewives loved her. They called the switchboard to say how pleased they were to see a woman doing the news for a change. A lot of those who called were Ivory's friends, but the girl at the switchboard didn't know that. She dutifully passed on the news that Ivory was a hit.

A few months later, Ivory was able to write to Penny: "I'm going to have my own TV show! It's a sort of experiment, because no one has done anything like it in this area, and we're all excited about it. It's called 'Consumer 5,' and we'll be focusing on consumer issues."

Penny wrote back: "I am very happy for you. It sounds as if you've found your place in the world, after all. I wish we had a television set at Holy Child so I could see your show, but I don't suppose Mother Superior would think consumer issues were very important to our way of life."

Our way of life. Above all that. I won't let her get to me! Ivory vowed. Maybe she didn't mean it that way; I'm probably just hypersensitive.

She was accepting dates for dinner with the brothers and friends of friends. She had barbecue at Red Momma's and chicken-fried steak at the Silver Streak and learned to enjoy the rodeo on Saturday afternoons. She studied the creature called Man and decided she liked him, in general, if not yet in the specific. They weren't all like Barney Tutt, or even Buford Colby.

She played around the edges of sex, embarrassed to be still a virgin in her mid-twenties. After three glasses of beer and an intense embrace in a parked car with a steamy windshield (Mrs. Dougall ran an old-fashioned boarding house, no gentlemen allowed upstairs), her body was sending her disturbing signals and she allowed herself to fantasize about the formerly forbidden.

Not yet, but maybe someday.

Maybe soon.

It was almost time.

She moved from the furnished room to a tiny rented house of her own, closer to the TV station. If she had taken another woman to share the house, she could have afforded to buy more furniture, but she was reluctant to let any other woman so intimately into her life. She lived happily alone, with a bed and a chest and a secondhand couch, and she learned to strip and refinish used furniture from one of the experts she interviewed on "Consumer 5." The little house began to take on a color and style of its own, and Ivory lavished her pent-up love on it through many do-it-your-selfer weekends.

On Sunday mornings she attended early Mass unfailingly, until one day when she slept right through her alarm, exhausted from painting the kitchen until four in the morning. When she woke up, she waited for the stab of guilt, but it didn't come. Instead she packed a picnic lunch for herself and carried it down to the bank of the muddy little creek known as Hickory Falls—there were no hickory trees within a hundred miles—and ate her lunch contentedly while whatever God there was minded His own business in a glorious blue sky. After that, she did not give up going to Mass, but she became less rigid about it.

What would Penny have said to that? She didn't ask.

Penny wrote: "God has been so good to me! I only regret that my opportunities are so few to repay Him. I have begun praying that He will show me some new way to do His work."

It was pious and prissy and Ivory never doubted Penny meant every word of it. I could never write a letter like that, she thought. Yet there were other times, other letters, when the old Penny peeped through, in small, wistful glimpses that touched Ivory's heart. The letters seemed almost more important than the person who wrote them; that nun in Holy Child wasn't Penny. Penny was an occasional sentence, a note of concern, a cheerful greeting on a piece of plain white stationery.

"Dear Ivory. Sister Justinian took a bad fall on the stairs yesterday and skinned her knees just the way we used to do when we were girls together. For some silly reason, I told her spit would stop the bleeding, the way I used to tell you, and she very seriously applied it. The bleeding stopped immediately. So much for perfect faith."

It was impossible not to remember the small Imagene Tutt crouched over her own skinned knees, on the verge of tears, and Penny ministering to her. Spit and love had stopped the bleeding then, too. And Penny's eyes had sparkled with mischief, knowing even at that young age that the secret wasn't in the spit.

The largest local advertiser with KXAS was an affable man named Tony Castellano, a self-made millionaire busy turning acres of sand and sagebrush into "Castels in the West," a misspelled, overpriced, exceedingly successful development. Since their first meeting, his wife Sylvia and Ivory had been friends. Sylvia was a sun-streaked, tanned-to-leather blonde, with a relaxed air and no pretensions whatsoever. Ivory genuinely liked her. When Sylvia invited Ivory to "a little bash at our place, honey. Supper and drinks and then we'll all push each other into the pool," Ivory accepted.

"You'll be right glad you did," Sylvia told her with an unmistakable wink. "I've invited somebody real special for you."

Ivory hesitated. "Not a blind date, Sylvia? I hate that. I've tried it a couple of times, and it's like being a prize pig with a sign saying 'Available' hung around my neck."

Sylvia whooped with laughter, bubbling up from deep in her belly like Permian Basin oil. "Honey, I promise you're not the prize pig at this party! That honor goes to our other guest, only you can't rightly call him a pig. More like a very choice stud bull, and he's a definite blue ribbon-winner. Now, don't look like that, I promise you you're gonna have a hell of a time. You'll thank me for this one."

It was the usual Texas dinner party, with bourbon and branch for the men (those who fancied themselves as pace-setters requested Chivas Regal instead) and bloody marys as thick as congealed blood for their women. Steaks were incinerated on a mammoth poolside grill, and the air was heavy with billowing smoke and the scent of carbonized beef. Sylvia's idea of a little party involved a horde of old cattle money and new oil money and the newest development money, attired in Italian silk suits and ostrich-leather boots. They swirled through the rooms of the Castellanos' white adobe hacienda, pinching each other's wives and bellowing progressively dirtier stories.

Ivory hated it, and resented Sylvia for having invited her. She stood alone in a corner by a plastic potted palm, holding a glass in her hand and waiting for the melting ice to dilute the mess sufficiently to make it drinkable. She had not yet been introduced to the prize Sylvia had promised her and she had just decided to pour her drink into the palm tree and leave, undoubtedly unnoticed in the milling throng.

"If you're not Ivory Talbot, I'm going home," a man's voice said in her ear. "This is the dullest party I've been to in a month of Sundays."

Startled, she turned and looked up, and up, into the smiling face of a man who might have posed as the quintessential Texan. He was tall and broad-shouldered and gorgeous, a creature of turquoise (turquoise!) eyes and toothpaste-ad teeth, and he was smiling down at her in a way that must have melted a hundred female hearts.

"You *are* Ivory Talbot, little lady?" he asked, making a slight, courtly bow.

A thousand female hearts, Ivory silently amended.

"Guilty," she told him.

"Then why don't you and I go sit down someplace and figure out what we're doin' in such a mess of borin' people?" He smiled broadly at her and caught her deftly by the elbow, steering her toward a couch out of the general traffic flow. As soon as they were seated, he introduced himself.

"My name is Randolph Reynolds—Randy, to everybody who matters. And just lookin' at you convinces me you matter, little lady. Yes indeed, I can see that you are somethin' really special."

He was overpowering, a man of practiced charm and tremendous physical presence, and he knew it. He was too much and she was not yet enough; she could no more resist him than she could resist the great dust and sand storms that blew like the hand of God across the high plains. She sat captivated, perfectly aware that he was using a line on her that he must have used countless times before, but she was eager to hear and believe it. This spectacular man was trying to impress *her!*

If only they could see me now, she thought. Imagene the wallflower.

If Penny could see me now.

He brought her a plate of food, a fresh drink, and his full attention. He appeared not to notice the admiring glances of the other women; he appeared to see no one but Ivory. With boyish modesty, he described himself as "a country fella runnin' his daddy's business."

"What kind of business?" Ivory asked.

"Oh, a few oil leases up in Wyoming, just a parcel of Shoshone Indian land on the Wind River. It don't amount to much, but it keeps me busier'n I like to be." He grinned engagingly. "But let's don't talk about me. I know all about that. Let's talk about you. Somebody told me you have your own television show, a pretty little thing like you! Is that true?"

His teeth fascinated her. They were white and square, perfectly even, and they gave the same impression of strength that the rest of his body radiated. Such teeth could bite into life as into an apple and let its juices run sweetly down the throat.

When he suggested they leave the party early, her

numbed mind could think of no objection at all. "I'll go make our excuses," he told her. "You just wait close enough to the door so we can make a clean getaway, all right?"

Ivory made her way through the crowd and into the red-tiled foyer. She was out of sight there and had no way of knowing the conversation that took place when Randolph Reynolds found Tony Castellano.

"Me and that little gal from the TV station are goin' home, Tony," Reynolds said with a broad smile. "Tell me, ole buddy, were you stringin' me about her, or was she really a nun?"

Castellano punched his friend on the arm. "She was a nun all right, you old hound dawg! That's what interests you about her, isn't it? Something really different for your trophy case? Well, you can trust me to steer you right, 'cause I got it from a trophy of my own, that cutie-pie Lou Ellis up at Channel 5. That girl is as curious as all outdoors, and she reads everybody's personnel file."

"I be go to hell," said Randolph Reynolds softly. "A nun. A professional virgin. And she just got out of the convent a while back, you say?"

"Last year."

Reynolds slapped his thigh to produce a flat crack like a rifle shot. "Then I would say that young lady is just about to do some livin'! Yessir, I would definitely say she is all *ready!*"

Meanwhile, Sylvia Castellano had been looking for Ivory. She appeared surprised to see her guest standing by the front door in the attitude of someone on her way out.

"Ivory, honey, you're not going home already? You haven't even met the fellow I promised you!"

"I think I have, Sylvia."

"Oh no, you couldn't, he just came in through the patio. Here, Doctor Scott, come over here a minute, will you? There's someone I've been dying for you to meet."

At Sylvia's signal, a dark young man entered the foyer,

wearing the slightly embarrassed look people sometimes do when they are party to arranged introductions. He was in his mid-thirties, with a lean and craggy face, something like that of a young Abe Lincoln. Definitely not handsome, was Ivory's first thought—nothing like Randy Reynolds. But his eyes were kind and there was strength in his jaw and sensuality to the curve of his mouth, and she liked his looks enough to give him a genuine smile instead of a social one.

"This is Nathan Scott, Ivory," Sylvia explained. "He's quite a brilliant doctor, I understand. He's been at Baylor, but he's going back East this fall, isn't it? I thought there would be time for you two to get to know each other before that, because you're really . . ."

"There you are!" Randy's voice boomed, interrupting. "Oh, hi, Sylvia. I was just lookin' for you to tell you I'm stealin' this little lady for the rest of the evening. Hope you don't mind. Ivory, did you bring a sweater or somethin'?"

Ivory shook her head. "No, I just came like this." He was guiding her out the door. She threw a hurried smile at the Lincolnesque young doctor and saw Sylvia making obvious signals to her, which she ignored. Let Sylvia matchmake with somebody else! "I'm sorry we didn't have longer to chat, Doctor Scott," she said politely before the closing door separated them.

"So am I," he replied, with genuine regret.

Randy had a new Thunderbird; Penny would have loved it. He took them for a roaring drive through the Texas night, gunning the powerful engine until the echoes shivered the starry silence. The wind blew Ivory's hair, but she didn't care. Randy was laughing, and she was laughing, and they were going at a dangerous speed and she loved it, rocketing down the highway, alive. Alive!

She wanted the ride to last forever, partly because she was enjoying it so much and partly because she dreaded the inevitable wrestling match when Randy took her home. Or would there be a wrestling match? This time, with this spectacular man, why not just give in and find out what it was all about? Why be the only one who was missing out?

To her astonishment, there was no wrestling match. When at last he took her home, Randy made no coy comments about coming in for coffee or one for the road; he didn't grab her and try to paw her; he didn't even force a kiss. He stood very close to her, close enough to hear the pounding of her heart, she thought, and clasped one of her hands in both of his. Very slowly, he raised the captive hand to his mouth and kissed it. Then he touched her lips with his forefinger and promised, "Next time I'll put one there." Turning on his heel, he strode jauntily back to the Thunderbird and roared away.

She stared after the car, feeling dizzy.

The next day she upset her director by pouring a can of pork and beans onto the table instead of onto a plate, and missing her cues more badly than she had on her very first, nervous day as hostess of "Consumer 5."

"What's the matter with you, Ivory?" the director asked. "Spring fever?"

Her eyes were sparkling. "Something like that."

"Well, take an aspirin or something, will you? Thank God you've built up a loyal audience that trusts you, or they might think you were on the sauce."

Sylvia Castellano called her. "I never meant for you to wind up with Randy Reynolds, honey!" she complained. "That man is definitely wrong for you."

Ivory's voice was chill. "Really, Sylvia? Why? Don't you think I'm in his league?"

"I should hope not! Listen, honey, he's had at least two wives that I know about . . . no, I think that's three . . . and he has a reputation with women that . . ."

"I don't want to hear all this, Sylvia. I'll form my own opinions, if you don't mind."

"Don't get huffy! And don't be stubborn, either, Ivory; I'm telling you this for your own good."

The thread of Ivory's temper snapped. "I'm tired of other people giving me advice for my own good! This is *my* life, and I'll live it my way, thank you. I'll see whom I want to see, *thank you!*" She hung up abruptly, then found herself staring at the phone. That was a tacky thing to do, she told herself. Sylvia was only trying to be a friend, and you're the one who wanted friends.

But I want Randy Reynolds, too, she admitted. And what if he doesn't call? What if he doesn't want me, and last night he was just being nice to plain little Imagene Tutt?

She concentrated on the telephone, willing it to ring. But it didn't.

The next day a florist delivered three dozen roses—yellow, not red—to Channel 5, for Miss Ivory Talbot. Randy Reynolds's card was attached, and a brief note. "These are different because you are different. I'll pick you up tonight at seven."

It began to rain in the early afternoon and Ivory went home from the studio in a drenching downpour, but by the time Randy came for her a silver-gilt sunset was glimmering through shredded gray clouds. It heralded a radiant evening. Randy drove sixty miles to a restaurant capable of serving a decent filet mignon and imported champagne—not vintage, however—and paid the dazzled little combo a small fortune to play only romantic music for the entire evening.

Ivory sat at their table, fingering the thin stem of her wineglass, thinking: Here we have Ivory Talbot, TV personality, out on a date with a handsome millionaire. This must be somebody else's glamorous life I've stumbled into by mistake.

But if it is, please, oh please! don't let me wake up!

Randolph Reynolds courted her with a barrage of presents and gradually increasing physical intimacies that always stopped just short of what she expected. He was skilled at arousing a woman to a fever pitch and leaving her there, dangling, until she had no power left to resist. He did

not know that only Ivory's painfully acquired self-discipline
kept her from showing him just how ready she was.

She intrigued him. She was obviously intelligent and he
didn't care for smart women, but beneath her apparent maturity he could sense the innocent child. That innocence
drew him like a bird dog on point.

She really believed him when he told her how unhappy
his other romances had been—he noticed that she liked that
word, romance—and when he said his wives had mistreated
him, she believed that, too. She allowed him to play southern gentleman, a role he had never tried before, and he enjoyed it . . . for a while. He kissed her directly on the lips
on their third date (Date! he thought, amused. Like kids!),
and it was not until their next evening together that he actually went inside her house with her. Then they only sat
together on the couch and did a little modest petting,
enough to make Ivory's cheeks flush but not enough to send
Randy to one of his other "lady friends" for relief afterward.

He sent her an endless supply of candy and flowers, tele-
grams at two in the morning, boxes from Linz Bros. and
A. Everts with what he called "gewgaws" inside. The first
time Ivory opened one of these jewelers' boxes and found
herself staring at a sapphire pendant, she nearly dropped
the box.

"I can't take this, Randy!"

"Sure you can. I like to see a woman all gussied up when
I take her out."

The program, the pressures, the sudden small fame that
meant women recognized her and asked her advice in the
A&P—and Randy Reynolds. It was too much; she wasn't
prepared for it. She went into a state of emotional overload.

That was when he asked her to marry him.

She was so unready that she gave him no answer at all.
Frightened of her own reactions, she telephoned the Convent of the Holy Child and asked to speak to Sister Immaculata on a matter of some urgency. "I have to see you,

talk to you," she explained. "Something's come up and I just have to talk to someone who . . . who really knows me."

"Come and see me," Penny said in a voice a shade more warm than that cool nun's voice Ivory remembered. "I need to talk to you, too."

Thirteen

THEY FACED EACH OTHER in the small anteroom that served as a reception room for the Convent of the Holy Child. It was a strange sensation, being within convent walls again. The air had a certain quality of stillness she recognized, and a mustiness she did not remember. Perhaps it had always been there, that thin smell of stagnation, faintly sour, like faded flowers or undisturbed dust in an attic. Ivory felt uncomfortable.

Penny smiled like a gracious hostess across the cups of tea they were sipping. "I'm glad you've come back for a visit after all this time," she said.

"It does seem like a long time, doesn't it?" Ivory looked around. "It feels as if I left the convent ages ago, and it really hasn't been that long. But so much has happened."

"You wanted to talk to me about something?"

"You're all the roots I have, I guess. At a time like this, a girl likes to talk to her family, and for me, that's you."

Penny smiled. "I'm flattered. But you could have had a much larger family, Imagene . . . Ivory."

Ivory shook her head. "No. I tried, but the convent was never right for me."

"It isn't right for me, either," Penny said astonishingly. Ivory lost her grip on the cup handle and spilled tea into the saucer.

"What did you say?" she asked, hardly believing what she had heard. "Are *you* leaving the convent?"

"Yes, in a way. I'm leaving Holy Child, but not the religious life itself. I've applied for transfer to another order, the Sisters of Gethsemane. I'm leaving the Sisters of the Good Shepherd because everything is too easy for me here."

"I don't understand." That's not fair! a small voice inside Ivory's head protested. How could it be too easy for her when it was too hard for me?

"I could stay here the rest of my life and be perfectly content, as long as I didn't actually have to teach," Penny explained. "But that wouldn't accomplish anything. And after a lot of praying and soul-searching, I discovered I really don't have a vocation for teaching. I'm not comfortable with children for some reason. In time I came to realize that I have a strong urge toward the complete enclosure, the purely contemplative life. More than an urge; a compelling desire."

Yes, Ivory thought, you always were given to extremes.

"The increasing secularization in the convent bothered me," Penny went on. "You were one of the first rebels, but certainly not the last. There has been a lot of talk about expanding our horizons and having more interaction with the community, and recently some of the nuns have even suggested wearing makeup so they would look like everybody else outside the walls.

"Frankly, I am appalled by that. The pettiness, the instability of such attitudes! *Professed nuns*, wanting to trade a life of privacy in God's company for a lot of cheap materialistic values." Penny shuddered delicately. She did not meet Ivory's eyes; she did not have to. Her words condemned Ivory with the others.

"Listening to them," she said, "I realized that what I wanted was the exact opposite. I wanted to submerge myself in the traditional ways, to become a Cistercian, a Benedictine, to set myself completely apart from all the temptations of corruption." The perfect oval of her face seemed so untouched by life that it was impossible to think of it in terms of ever having experienced temptation or corruption.

"I spent many hours in prayer, and at last the selfishness of that desire was revealed to me," she told Ivory. "A contemplative life would be a gift to me, not to God. I saw then that the greatest sacrifice I could make would be to go back into the world, not to avoid pain but to seek it out. Since I have no vocation for teaching, I have decided to go into nursing, and in order to do that I have applied for transfer to the Sisters of Gethsemane."

As she habitually did, Penny related this newest event of her life with a slight breathlessness that invested it with drama and tension. This was *Penny's* life; it had to be more of everything than anyone else's. Only when she had related the terrible tale of her miscarriage and her father's abuse had her voice been without emotion, and that, too, had lent its own drama.

By the time she finished speaking, through some alchemy her decision and the change in her life had become the central features of the conversation, and Ivory felt she had been summoned here to give Penny her blessing. Her own proposal faded into a commonplace event, an everyday happening to be related if the opportunity arose, but nothing like the unusual and momentous step of a nun actually changing orders.

"It's a big step, Sister," she said. "I know you've thought it all out, but are you sure you're not rushing this a little?

It's the rest of your life, you know; you don't want to make a mistake."

"I'm not making a mistake," Penny said, with a stubborn tilt to her chin that Ivory remembered from the past. "I know exactly what I'm doing, and I'm certain it's the right thing."

"How did Mother Superior take it when you told her?"

"Well, she was surprised, of course, but once she was convinced that I meant to go through with it she was very helpful and supportive. Most of the arrangements are already made; I'll be going into nurse's training in New York, and I'll join the order there. The Sisters of Gethsemane manage a very fine private hospital on the East Side, you know." Seeing the expression on Ivory's face, the nun curved her lips into a smile of irresistible sweetness. "It's dear of you to be concerned about me, Ivory," she said, "but you don't have to worry. I'm very lucky and very, very happy; I want you to know that and be happy for me."

"I am happy, of course . . . if it's what you really want."

"It is. I hoped you would understand; some of the others here don't. They seem to feel I'm rejecting them in some way, and that isn't it at all." There was pain in the big blue eyes and Ivory wanted to wipe it away.

"You have to do what's right for you," she said loyally.

Penny gave her hand an impulsive squeeze, and for a brief moment the broken past was healed and they were best friends again. "I'm so glad I still have you to count on," Penny said. "Now, what was this you wanted to talk to me about?"

Ivory had meant to tell her about the proposal, to discuss the kind of man she thought he was and her own feelings about him, to perhaps ask the other woman's advice. But she couldn't do that now. It would be too anticlimactic.

"Oh, I just wanted to tell you that I'm getting married," she said, trying to make it sound casual.

"Really!" It was an unflattering amount of surprise, and it spurred Ivory on.

"Yes, really. He's a genuine Texas millionaire, of all things, a great big handsome guy, simply terrific."

"And he wants to marry you?" Penny asked in a voice filled with barely concealed disbelief.

"Absolutely," Ivory told her, and smiled. "He's the catch of the year, and he's crazy about me." How wonderful it was to see she had surprised Penny for once! She extended her left hand. "The next time you see this, it will be wearing a diamond as big as a golf ball. I was hoping you could get permission to come to the wedding."

Penny's expression was rueful. "Oh, my dear, I wish I could, but I'll be going to New York in a very few days. I'm so sorry—I wouldn't have missed your wedding for anything, you know that. But you will send me clippings, won't you?"

"Lots of them," Ivory promised. Enough to knock your eyes out, she vowed to herself.

When she was home again, alone in her own little house, she thought about the extent of her rash commitment. Marrying Randy would mean a break with the Church, for he was a divorced man with living ex-wives. In the eyes of her faith, she would be living in sin.

Her faith. Her nebulous, flickering faith.

Hadn't she already begun the process of giving it up a long time ago, when she took off the plain gold band that marked her as a Bride of Christ? She looked at her empty finger and felt the loss of the symbol as acutely as a widowhood. There must be something to replace it.

Randy didn't give her a diamond, but an immense ruby set in platinum. "I'll guarantee you there's nothing like that west of Dallas," he promised her. The jewel glowed on her hand; it was so heavy she was constantly aware of it.

Lou Ellis and the other girls at Channel 5 looked at her as if she were a princess from a fairy tale.

There would be no Church wedding, of course; no white satin, no veil. She tried not to let her mind dwell on that small dream lost. Randy wouldn't have wanted it anyway. He told her, "I did all that down the aisle stuff, and it didn't make the marriage stick any better. We'll go to a justice of the peace and have a big reception afterward, and you can wear a long, fancy dress for that if you want to."

She didn't allow herself to want to; it wouldn't have been the same.

He brought her an envelope filled with color snapshots of his house in Houston, in the exclusive River Oaks section. If she had not already promised to marry him, that house alone might have persuaded her. It was a sprawling sweep of fieldstone-and-redwood, set in a Japanese garden of raked gravel and boxed azaleas and small gnarled oaks. It looked as expensive and as secure as a fortress.

But it was hundreds of miles away.

"Randy, what about my job?"

He laughed. "You're not gonna need any job! I can provide for my woman just fine, Iv'ry. All you gotta do is set yourself up in that nice house and entertain Houston society. There's not a one of 'em won't come millin' around to see what kind of a wife Randolph Reynolds got himself this time."

"But I love my job," she protested.

He brushed her objection aside with a wave of his big hand. "I got a full-time job for you at home," he told her. "Besides, were you plannin' on workin' once the babies start comin'? 'Course not; I didn't think so. So you might as well get settled in and get started learnin' how to be Mrs. Reynolds, and not worry about workin' for wages anymore."

It was the first time he had mentioned children and she had no arguments prepared against that.

A baby, she thought, with a quick, tender pain. A soft little person smelling like talcum powder, to hold and love . . .

He saw the surrender in her eyes. There was a key to

every one of them, a man just had to find it and mark it
down. Look at the way she was glowing now, like candles
had been lit behind her skin. Suddenly she was almost too
easy, and he felt the first familiar flicker of contempt for
her. There should be more sport in the game than that.

On the evening before their wedding, he brought her a
document to sign. He appeared embarrassed and apologetic,
more boyish than she had ever seen him. "I hate this, Iv'ry,
I honestly do, and if you balk right here and now I'll understand. But the fact is, I been wrong about women all my
life, and I've got this high-priced lawyer who has nothin' to
do but see I don't make any more expensive mistakes. I pay
him so much money for that I just have to take his advice,
you understand? He's drawn up this little financial agree-
ment, just a paper sayin' you won't make any claim on my
money—aside from what I give you outright, of course—until we been married ten years or have children, whichever
comes first. I hope you don't think this is my idea. It isn't;
it's just one of those business things that goes with havin'
money. Just about everybody I know does it, but I feel bad,
askin' it of you at all. I know you wouldn't try to take me
for a ride."

It seemed reasonable, even sensible. He would take care
of her in luxury beyond anything she had ever known, and
there would be children, of course; soon. Signing the agree-
ment readily seemed a simple way of proving he was right
about her integrity.

She signed the paper. It was another form of vow; a vow
not to be grasping or mercenary like the other women who
had pursued the Reynolds' money. It would be easy to live
up to it—it was a long way from poverty, chastity, and obedience.

They were married on a Thursday afternoon, a day of
cold sunshine and blustery February winds. Sylvia and
Tony came, and Buford and Lou Ellis and all her friends
from the station. "We've hired a replacement for you,

Ivory," her producer told her, "but I don't think she's going to be the crackerjack you were. If you ever want your old job back . . ." He laughed. She laughed.

A few of Randy's friends came; not many. Men who were involved with him in land or cattle or oil leases: men who smiled with cold eyes and kissed her perfunctorily on the cheek, men with hot eyes and dirty mouths who tried to feel her buttocks through the heavy skirt of her blue wool suit. Men who then cornered a willing Randy and engaged him in a long business discussion while she drank too much champagne and heard herself laughing too loudly.

This is the happiest day of my life, she reminded herself. Several times.

They flew to Las Vegas for the honeymoon. Randy had rented an enormous suite, dominated by a vast circular bed. In the bathroom was a sunken tub, heart-shaped. Big enough for two, as he pointed out. Ivory tried to smile, but her mouth was dry and her face felt numb.

Randy had begun unbuttoning his shirt even before the bellboy finished adusting the air conditioning to a bone-chilling low. He gave the man an ostentatious tip and almost pushed him out of the room.

"Now," he said to Ivory as he locked the door. His face was flushed and there was something different about him, a physical change. The easygoing, relaxed charmer had disappeared, replaced by a hard-muscled, tight-faced man who moved as if . . . as if he were stalking her. On the balls of his feet. Placing himself between her and the door. Pinning her with his eyes.

She gave a nervous little laugh. "I'm afraid I'm a bit frightened, Randy: you'll have to be patient with me," she said, embarrassed by the triteness of the remark.

But he didn't seem to mind. He actually appeared pleased. "Are you frightened?" he asked, drawing his lips back from his square white teeth into an expression that was not quite a smile. "How 'bout that?" he asked the room at large.

He reached out and put his hand on her breast with no preliminaries at all, just grabbing her like a melon in a store. She flinched and his smile grew wider, if a smile was what it was. He clutched her breast painfully, holding her so she could not move away from him, and thrust his other hand between her legs, grabbing her savagely. She almost cried out with pain and his eyes glittered.

"Not used to being handled like that, are you?" he asked. His heavy breathing overrode the *whirr* of the air-conditioner. "You're gonna have to get used to a lot of things from now on, Iv'ry. I'm gonna get you broke in right. Here, feel this for instance." He took her hand and guided it to the front of his trousers, pressing it hard against his swollen groin. "You're gonna learn to like that," he promised. "Oh, yeah. You're gonna learn to beg me for that."

She felt sickened. *Marriage is a sacrament.* Is that what they had been taught? Was this obscenity a sacrament? She struggled to pull away, but he wouldn't let her. He enjoyed her struggles. He laughed.

"That's more like it, baby! I was afraid there for a while you didn't have any spirit; woulda taken the fun right outta things. C'mon, fight me!"

The last thing she wanted to do was something that would so obviously please him. She stood still, rigid, trying hard not to be there at all. He crowded against her, pushing her step by step toward the bed until she lost her balance and they sprawled across it. His hands were all over her then, pulling her clothes away, and his mouth was hot and demanding on her skin. There was one moment, gone as swiftly as a startled bird, when she might have responded to him, for all the stored emotion and waiting sexuality of her sexless years was just beneath the surface. He could have ignited it, if he had been sensitive and caring, but he wasn't.

He was a hunter who had marked down his kill and meant to have it, without any appreciation for the fleeting beauty so soon to be destroyed.

For Randolph Reynolds the beauty, and the satisfaction, were contained within the cry of pain he forced from her with his first penetrating thrust. No other man had nailed this one; she was his alone.

Afterward, he was gentle with her. He brought a towel from the bathroom, wrung out in hot water and soothing to her sore body. He smoothed the spread over the bloody sheet, though not before Ivory had seen the look of triumph in his eyes. He called her honey and darlin' and ordered a dinner from room service when she told him she didn't feel like going downstairs.

She watched him move around the room as she would have watched a stranger. She felt no more for him than that. There was no mistaking the ice in her gray-green eyes when they locked with his, but he didn't mind. It didn't matter.

After they had been served dinner—he ate ravenously, she picked at her food then pushed the plate away—he announced that he was going down to the casino for a while. "You wanta come?"

She shook her head.

"You rest up, then. Take a hot bath, there's some of that bubble stuff in there. I'll be back in a while, you can count on that."

For the rest of her life, she would hate hotel rooms.

When they got to Houston, Ivory found her things had already been moved into the River Oaks house. It was as sumptuous as the pictures promised, an architect's showcase. A huge fieldstone fireplace dominated the oversized living room, where little islands of furniture were arranged on a sea of Spanish tile. Everything about the house was oversized, in a scale intended to dwarf and impress.

Trophies were displayed throughout the house and there

were gun cabinets in almost every room. The heads of murdered animals gazed glassy-eyed into eternity from every
wall. The housekeeper, a timid Hispanic woman named
Carmella, spent much of her time polishing the seemingly
endless array of fishing and shooting trophies that adorned
every available tabletop.

Photographs of beautiful women were hung in the halls
and bedrooms; photographs bearing intimate inscriptions to
Randy. He did not have them taken down when Ivory arrived, nor did he even bother to comment on them.

When she saw his house, Ivory understood Randolph
Reynolds at last. A nun was the ultimate sexual trophy,
something you could brag to your friends about, exotic and
rare as the skin of a near-extinct clouded leopard in Randy's
"den."

An apt phrase, Randy's den, she thought.

But a trophy once acquired loses its value, and the hunter
must go on to fresher game. Ivory was not heartbroken
when she realized he was seeing other women; he was giving them nothing she cared about. He treated her as well as
he treated the house and the trophies, and almost as impersonally, and she was glad of that; glad he hadn't made her
love him. Love would come from somewhere else. He still
came to her bed often enough to sire children, and she
focused on that. The promised reward, a beautiful home, a
family . . .

The months passed and she did not conceive.

She wrote Penny, "I am very happy here. We have a
lovely home and Randy seems to know everyone in Houston; all I have left to wish for are children, and I hope to be
able to write you soon with news about that.

"I'm so glad to hear your studies are going well and you
will soon have your R.N. From what you have told me of
Allenboro Memorial, it sounds like the perfect hospital for
you, and they are very lucky to get you. I hope you will be
as happy as I am here in Houston."

When she reread the letter, she crossed out that last sentence and wrote the whole thing over.

At first she had been afraid to use the charge accounts and the checkbook he had given her with no balance showing on the stubs. Unlimited funds. What could that mean? But Randy said, "Get whatever you want to," and seemed to mean it. For a man of his wealth it was an easy payoff, a small enough reward for appearing on his arm at parties, listening to the buzz of gossip, enduring the amused, speculative glances. Randy had made sure that everyone knew; it would have been no fun otherwise.

"A *nun,* can you believe it? Randy Reynolds married a nun! Isn't it delicious? I tell you, that Randy . . . you never know what to expect from him."

"That's the gospel truth. He keeps this town hummin', don't he?"

They smiled at her with their teeth but not their eyes. They treated her like what she was: a curiosity, this season's amusement, something that would inevitably be replaced by newer and more outrageous gossip.

One afternoon she was trying on a skirt in Sakowitz's and got a good long look at herself in the mirror. The woman reflected there had starved eyes.

Ivory went slightly mad. She bought everything, every gorgeous luxury that caught her eye, lingerie and shoes and peignoirs and hats and cosmetics and crystal perfume bottles and baskets of marzipan and Liberty scarves and beaded cashmere sweaters and . . .

It was a period of glorious gluttony. She could not get enough. She worried what Randy might say when he saw the bills, but she could not control herself. She bought more than she could ever use and reached for more still. She bought silk blouses and imported music boxes and gold cigarette cases, she brought home gift-wrapped presents for everyone at Channel 5 and mailed them with her new engraved cards, she ordered china and crystal and handmade Italian shoes.

When the bills started coming in, all Randy said was, "If you're gonna cost me so much, you might as well work harder for it. How about goin' huntin' next Sattidy? I got me some shootin' buddies I been tellin' about you."

Her first hunt was to be a rabbit hunt, usually too tame for the four big sunburned men in boots who tramped with her across the stubble of a corn field. Randy's big German pointer trotted around them as they quartered the field, its tongue lolling, its yellow eyes glinting.

A young jackrabbit was crouched in the stubble, revealed by its rounded contours amid the vertical lines of the dead stalks. When the dog got too close, the rabbit leaped into the air and bounded away across the furrowed earth.

Randy laughed. He followed the animal with his shotgun, and at the last minute, when the rabbit must have thought it had reached safety in the tall Johnson grass at the edge of the field, he pulled the trigger. The little creature was blasted into bloody scraps of fur and splintered bone.

"Pore dam' thang," Randy said with no pity at all.

Ivory turned to one side and vomited helplessly, deep wrenching spasms arising from deep inside. One of Randy's shootin' buddies came to help her, but instead of holding her head he let his hands roam over her helpless body, and in the red and roaring distance Ivory could hear the other men laughing. And Randy's voice, booming over the rest. Laughing. Encouraging.

"Go on, Si, warm her up a li'l! Nothin' like a li'l sport to get a woman in the right mood!"

She twisted away and ran from them as the rabbit had done, stumbling over the furrows, blinded by tears. She almost expected to hear the shotgun again.

The men eventually sauntered back to the jeep, where she sat shivering. They acted as if nothing had happened.

Their conversation was vulgar to the point of exhibitionism
and she knew it. They were joking and winking at one another and Randy was urging them on, enjoying her discomfiture, making it plain he didn't care how far his friends
went with her. He had her; now she was available to his
friends if they wanted her. Good ole boys together.

In self-defense Ivory wrapped a habit of icy disdain
around herself so that at last the drunken men realized she
would not cooperate, and sullenly they let her alone. But it
seemed it would be only a matter of time before it would
happen again, and this time Randy might not let her off so
easily.

She went on buying. She felt compelled to consume it all,
to grab the trappings of a fantasy life before . . .

Before what?

The Lord giveth and the Lord taketh away.

In November Randy and some of his buddies went to
Alaska to hunt moose. Ivory steadfastly refused to go. On
the last day of the hunt, one of the men mistook Randy for
his target and bagged him, a clean kill, through the head.

There was an inquest. The man who had shot Randy was
obviously very upset and everyone felt sorry for him; a mob
of similar sunburned men gathered around him to hit him
on the arm and mutter sympathetic obscenities. The
members of the Houston executive establishment gathered
in the courtroom were aware of the rules by which such
games are played, and did not draw attention to the fact
that Randy's killer would now move up to a higher position
in the holding corporation that controlled Randolph Enter-
prises, among other things.

Ivory sat swathed in black, with a veiled black straw hat
sheltering her face. She kept a little distance between herself and the curious spectators, and she was not listening to
the words of the coroner; she did not want to hear them.
Her mind instead kept going back to something she had

read or heard or perhaps even written at some time during her schooling, or in the convent.

In the dry, sterile air of the deserts of Arabia, the face of Woman is perceived as an alien intrusion. A being gifted with mysterious powers to enchant, to conceive, to bear, she must be wrapped in veils and hidden within tents or behind walls, not to shield her from men, but to shield the threatened male from her, from the unbearable possibility of her superiority.

Death by Misadventure was the coroner's ruling.

Randy's personal doctor stopped by to pay his condolences. "If Randolph had known this was going to happen to him at such a young age—still in his prime, you might say—I wonder if he'd have had me do that vasectomy four years ago?" the man speculated aloud. "It'd be nice if you had a son of his coming along, sort of a comfort at a time like this, Miz Reynolds."

Vasectomy. Four years ago. Her face was white with shock, but the doctor expected that under the circumstances. He patted her hand. "Or maybe it's just as well you're not in the family way. A shock like this . . ." He sighed. "The Lord works in mysterious ways. I tried to argue with Randy about the operation at the time, tell him he might regret it some day, but after that last marriage of his broke up he got pretty stubborn about the whole thing, and there was no arguing with him once his mind was set. You know Randy."

I do now, she thought.

The lawyers were quick to tell her she had no claim to the Reynolds' estate. The clothes, the jewelry—he had said he was getting her a car for Christmas but Christmas never came—that was all she had. She had signed the rest away to prove her integrity, and it would go to a fast-descending gaggle of Randolphs and Reynoldses whom she had never met before.

She received the news in a daze. She forced herself to keep her face calm and controlled, so the pain wouldn't show. She had nothing to offer them but ladylike dignity, so she hid behind that, wanting to scream and swear at the dirty trick that had been played on her. But she had made submission a habit; it was one she could not find the strength to break in her shattered emotional state.

She wrote Buford a businesslike letter, with any bid for sympathy carefully expunged. While she waited for an answer, she got a letter from New York, with the return address of the Sisters of Gethsemane. "I was saddened to hear of your loss," Penny wrote. "Please know that my prayers are with you, and a novena is being said for your late husband. Those of us in the religious life, with a Bridegroom who has triumphed over Death and can never be lost to us, are so blessed to have been spared the pain you are suffering."

Buford's reply came by telephone. "We have another hostess on your old consumer show," he told her. "Not as good as you were, Ivory, but I can't just kick her off, she's a divorced lady with two children to support. You come on out here and I'll find something for you though, I promise. At a time like this, you should be with your friends, back here in West Texas, where you belong."

It wasn't where she belonged and she knew it. It was a dusty little town in a part of the world she had grown to hate, and it seemed to her now to be a backwater, without excitement or promise. But maybe she couldn't expect such things; maybe the golden prizes were, after all, reserved for people like Penny, and when she reached for one she would catch only a brass ring, a Randolph Reynolds. No matter how much she longed to be someplace like New York, maybe she would never get any farther than another rented house in a small town, a job that paid the bills as long as she didn't want too much, and the hidden frustrations of a single woman growing older in a company of other such women, playing canasta, going to the movies together, looking forward to the next permanent and a new girdle.

Perhaps that was better than life in the fast lane, among the cannibals.

She told herself that. She didn't believe it.

True to his word, Buford Colby gave her a new job equal to the one she had left. Ivory Reynolds was the new anchorperson (how that title amused her!) of the noon news on a regular basis. She threw herself into the job with a passion. She took courses in the community college on television and on journalism, she spent hours studying the techniques of newsmen she admired on the big network programs, she channeled her mind and all her energy into at last making good at something, at just one thing, even if it was in a small town nobody ever heard of or would care about.

When someone proposed a date for her—"He's quite a nice man, Ivory, quiet, and he makes a good living selling insurance, I think"—she habitually refused. No more. No more hurt. Eventually, the proposals ceased.

She wrote her own news; she learned to dig out many of her own stories; she got over being secretly pained when she heard others say of her, "Oh, Ivory's strictly a career woman, no time or interest for anything else."

The times were changing. The label "career woman" was beginning to mean something other than spinster; there were those who saw it as a viable choice, a role to be preferred to that of homemaker, childbearer. Some women of inexhaustible energy even seemed able to combine the two, though not in small towns in Texas.

Ivory found doing her own research one of the most exciting parts of the job. She discovered a talent for digging up facts and following clues; a positive gift for knowing who to ask and where to look. Sometimes her discoveries startled her. Occasionally, they shocked her.

She sat up all one night, poring over a collection of clippings and articles from European tabloids as well as local

Texas papers, and then she neatly assembled them and put them into a specially labeled file which she kept in the bottom drawer of her desk. From time to time she took the file out and looked at it, but after that first long night she never reread it.

For Ivory, the months of hard work and dedication blurred into years, and she was no longer the anchor of the noon news, but the first woman to anchor the prestigious 6 P.M. news, as well as doing interviews with local politicians and the occasional lower-case celebrities who passed through the area on their way to someplace more exciting.

Penny wrote: "New York is a jungle. You can't imagine the things we see here in the hospital. God is demanding all my energy and all my courage, but what a joy it is to give it in His service! There are times I wish you were here with me, so we could talk as we used to. There is so much I wish I could share with you.

"However, I suppose your own job keeps you busy."

Ivory made certain that it did. She enjoyed the interviews most of all, and she worked unceasingly at perfecting her technique with guests. Listening with the rapt attention she had learned from watching Penny so long ago, she learned to fit herself to her guests like a well-worn shoe, adopting just the degree of reserve or earthiness that each individual would be most comfortable with. Her voice was warm and friendly but not prying, while at the same time it had an undertone of authority that insisted on an answer. I know all about you, that voice intimated. I understand. There is nothing you can tell me that will shock me and I will not judge you. Just tell me. Trust me. Tell me.

And they did.

She made herself everyone's friend and was exceptionally easy to work with. The time came when Ivory was doing occasional half-hour interviews with politicians from Austin and headline-makers from Dallas and Houston and San Antonio. The show was called "Headliners," and everybody watched to see who was on the hot seat and how much she could get them to reveal of themselves. The insanity of the sixties had faded into the hedonistic seventies, and celebrities had become the raw meat the public demanded to be fed. By the latter part of the decade, a talented interviewer like Ivory Talbot Reynolds was being besieged with contract offers from the big TV stations in major cities.

She was flattered; the offers were balm to a wounded ego. But she only mentioned them to Penny in passing because she did not want them to be minimized as her accomplishments always seemed to be by the nun's unconscious comments.

She did not accept the offers from Abilene and El Paso and Shreveport; she did not want to go back to any Texas city. She wanted to move ahead to something else, some *place* else. And she still could not quite believe that the chance would ever come, not for her. Because she wanted it so much.

Then one afternoon Buford Colby called her into the concrete-block cubicle that served as his office, smaller and more cluttered than that of the station manager or any of the other major personnel. A large color photograph of the new Mrs. Buford Colby, the former Lou Ellis, was prominently displayed on his desk.

"Ivory," he began in his whispery voice, running his finger around the inside of his shirt collar as he always did when nervous. "I don't quite want to tell you this, but . . ."

"What's the matter, Boo? Am I fired?" She asked the question as if in jest, not really expecting that to be the problem, but always prepared for that other shoe to drop.

"Oh sweet Jesus, no! Nothing like that! But I have the feeling we might be losing you anyway, I'm afraid. I've just been on the phone with this producer from New York, important fella, lot of hit shows to his credit. Name's Clinton Everhardt. He wants to take you to the Big Apple and make you a star."

Fourteen

NEW YORK. MANHATTAN. Before she had even talked with Clinton Everhardt, she knew she would take the job if he offered it to her. Suddenly she wanted it with an almost uncontrollable desire.

She wrote Penny a dozen letters, crumpled them all up, and threw them away. Finally she just said, "I may be coming to New York soon to see about a new job. If I do, I hope we can get together for a visit. So many years have gone by since we saw each other last and I'm sure we have a lot to talk about."

She did not mention the possibility of hosting a talk show. If the package was not sold to the network, at least she would not have to relate another failure to Penny. Penny had no failures. Sister Immaculata went from triumph to triumph; she had just been appointed as head nurse at Allenboro Memorial Hospital, an unprecedented promotion for someone so new to nursing. But Sister Immaculata was uniquely gifted; people recognized that. People always recognized that. Allenboro Memorial was her new kingdom now, where she undoubtedly reigned with charm and skill, impressing everyone with her abilities.

No failures for Penny.

Ivory agonized over her wardrobe, preparing for her first meeting with Clinton Everhardt. She hoped to draw confidence from her clothes, to impress the producer with tailored good taste. She wore a navy Chanel suit with a silk blouse and regretted that hats had been so long out of fashion; somehow a hat would have given her an extra touch of authority. He must not guess she was quivering Jell-o inside.

Clinton Everhardt was a chunky man in his mid-forties, going bald and not fighting it. He had a square shape to both skull and shoulders, and the features of his face were straight lines, not easy curves. His mouth was a slash between heavy jowls, his dark eyebrows were level, his eyes were set horizontally between heavy lids. It was a tough face and Ivory liked it. There was no deceptive charm to trick and trap.

"I want to do a serious talk show with a woman as host," he explained to her in what she would come to recognize as the New York way of talking: fast, sarcastic, take-it-or-leave-it. "Nobody's made a real success of it on a long-term basis because they haven't found the right gal. I think you can do it; I've watched you work. You're one slick interviewer; you're damn near as good as a confessional, Reynolds, and your personality doesn't encourage a hostile reaction in your audience."

There was no point in ducking it. "You know my background?"

He chuckled. "Yes, that's why I mentioned the confessional. Maybe that's why people open up to you; you've got some of that nun's aura left. We've got a lot of good gals in the business who have the brains and the background to do a show like this, but not one of them has that practiced serenity you project, and that's what I'm banking on. You'll be unique."

"I'm not as serene as I look," she told him, feeling a sudden compulsion to be honest.

"So? As long as you can give the impression of authority and sympathy at the same time and don't cost us a fortune in shrink's fees on the side, your personal life's your own. Or as much your own as it can be for anybody in the public eye."

"You seem to be pretty certain the network will buy the idea," Ivory commented.

"Nothing's ever certain in this business, Reynolds, but yes, I think we have a good chance. The pendulum is swinging, women are starting to have more of a voice in things, and I'm betting the time is right for a woman to do this program. I even want to keep that name you've been using— 'Headliners.' I like that, and that's what we want to have, the headliners of the day and you questioning them, getting them to open up. Not just small town politicians but international celebrities, senators, ax murderers, whoever makes the headlines. Newspapers and TV news give them superficial coverage from the outside; I want you to encourage them to tell their own story. That seems to be your special talent and we're going to capitalize on it."

My special talent. If only you knew, she thought. I learned it from somebody else. It's one of the bits and pieces I took from elsewhere to make up this person you see as Ivory Reynolds. Is everybody like that? Are we all deliberate compendiums? Even Penny shaped herself into an image she thought would please her father, and then again into an image that would please God.

She had to ask the question. "You don't think my having been a nun is a liability?"

He lifted his heavy eyelids and gave her a long, direct look. "No, but obviously you think it is. Why? It's certainly nothing to be ashamed of."

"I'm not ashamed," she shot back quickly. "It's just, well, I didn't make it as a nun. I've never tried to hide my background in the convent, but I've never advertised it, either. Yet it does seem to come out, and there have been some, ah, unpleasant repercussions. People react in strange ways sometimes."

"We won't try to hide it, either," Everhardt told her, "but I promise you we won't play it up if it makes you feel uncomfortable. Yet I'd better warn you, some people might recognize you somewhere along the way. I did."

She was startled. "What are you talking about?"

"Television is my business, remember? I watch. I notice faces. I listen. I knew who you were after the first ten minutes of watching your show; that face, that bone structure clicked, and I said, 'Oh yeah, that's the activist nun, the one on the evening news in the sixties.'"

Ivory was horrified. "You actually remembered me from that?"

The heavy face lightened into an amused smile. "There's a distinctly haunting quality about your face. Didn't you know that? Very unusual. What you have is better than beauty; it's star quality."

All those times I looked in the mirror, seeking beauty, she thought. And never finding it.

Star quality.

Maybe, just maybe, at last, this time, things were going to work out. Maybe she was finally on the right road.

And maybe it was still someone else's life she had blundered into, and she would lose it all. How funny it was that Clinton Everhardt perceived her as serene, and the camera invested her with "star quality"!

She asked one last favor of Buford Colby. "Could I take some of my files from the show—research, notes, that sort of thing? You'll never use them again here, and we might be able to do something with them in New York, if this thing goes."

"Sure," he agreed, "take whatever you want. You did your own research, anyway. I guess whatever you dug up is your property."

She arrived in New York City on a warm summer afternoon of blowing rain. It was love at first sight. The metropolis throbbed with all the color lacking in the endless beige of West Texas. Umbrellas bloomed, a riot of multihued blossoms amid the daffodil yellow ranks of scurrying taxicabs. The wet cement glittered with reflected light. The city smelled like rubber and orange rinds and wet paper; it tasted like grit; it sounded like a giant carnivorous engine in the process of stripping its gears; it roared with energy and life. Ivory wanted to throw her arms around the entire island of Manhattan and cry, "I'm here! I'm home!"

It seemed as if there were no end to the interviews and conferences and planning sessions required before the package, as Everhardt called it, was put together and ready for presentation. Ivory was groomed for her starring role like a racehorse. Specialists went over every aspect of her appearance, her voice, and her wardrobe, considering each in the light of the total image to be presented, the persona that would be sold as the hostess of "Headliners."

It was confusing and exhausting, but she loved it. For the first time, she understood the magic of being in the limelight, the star around whom all else revolved. She could sit in a room where others were discussing her as impersonally as a package of meat in a butcher shop, and she was not insulted. She did not cringe when her flaws were pointed out; at least somebody cared, somebody wanted to make her better. She had value.

Star quality.

Late one afternoon she found herself eating a quick lunch, alone for once, in one of the myriad ethnic eateries she had discovered. Under strict orders not to gain an ounce, she had searched for places that served good salads or lean fish, only to find that Manhattan was a brimming treasure chest of forbidden delicacies. To someone satiated with chicken-fried steak, a small café offering souvlaki or lasagna was irresistible.

Giuseppi's was a family restaurant run by three generations of cheerful, volatile Italians, who seemed to defy the odds by remaining trim although surrounded by mountains of pasta. The waitresses were not so metabolically gifted. As Ivory ate, her eye was drawn to one of them, leaning against the counter and staring across the room with an expression of inherent genetic boredom. She appeared to be chewing a cud. Clad in white nylon, her solid outthrust haunch resembled a bridge abutment. The line of her bikini pants, clearly visible beneath the taut uniform, divided continents of fat.

Ivory was suddenly angry with herself. "That does it," she said aloud, pushing away her half-finished meal of fettucini dripping with butter and cheese. "From now on, it's the health food bar for you, old girl."

She heard a rich, melodious chuckle, and looked up to meet the eyes of the man at the next table, who had apparently followed her own line of vision and was amused by her response. His face was strangely familiar. But then, she had met so many people in the past few weeks . . . better not offend anyone who might be someone. She smiled back, measuring out the warmth carefully so it would be enough for an acquaintance but not enough to invite intimacy.

He could tell she did not recognize him. His own smile deepened and he stood up, coming toward her. He was a tall, lean man of about her own age, with strong cheekbones and deep, naturally melancholy eyes, as if he had seen all the tragedies of the world. But his broad mouth was both sensuous and humorous, and it was impossible not to return his smile in kind.

"You don't remember me, do you?" he asked, holding out his hand. "I met you several years ago, in Texas, at an awful party given by some developer and his wife who were trying to get me to invest in a hundred acres of sagebrush. My name is Nathan Scott."

She remembered him then, surprisingly. That one long look across the Castellanos' foyer, that face like a young Abe Lincoln, not handsome but unforgettable. She realized she had never entirely forgotten him; she had thought of him more than once, over the years, wondering what might have happened if she had met him first that night and never gotten involved with Randolph Reynolds at all. And now here he was, in a little restaurant on the West Side.

"Of course I remember you, Doctor Scott," she said smoothly. "How nice to see you again, and here, of all places! If I promise to avoid saying it's a small world, will you join me?"

He chuckled again and brought his coffee and dessert to her table, and soon they were talking like old friends.

Ivory had already learned that sexual mores were very different in New York from those of a small town in the Southwest. Men and women seemed to fall into and out of intimacy easily, and there was something frightening about that. More than ever, she had been glad of her work and the long hours required; glad she could fall into bed exhausted each night and not have to think about going out; did not have to act sweetly feminine with some stranger.

She had kept herself safe from pain. She had not let herself realize she was lonely until Nathan Scott smiled at her. She told everyone she was too busy right now to get involved.

Yet from the moment Nathan Scott sat down at her table, she was very involved.

"What brings you to New York?" he asked, and when she told him, he replied, "I'm glad you're here. Somehow you seem to belong in New York. I just saw you once, but I thought at the time that you seemed sort of out of place in Texas."

"I felt out of place. I don't like Texas."

"Everybody's supposed to love Texas."

"Maybe I did once, but then I had so many unpleasant experiences there, it soured me. Now I hate to even hear it mentioned. But I love New York. It's everything I used to dream it would be."

Her excitement was contagious and a light kindled in his own eyes. "It is like a movie set, isn't it? And so full of energy, I can get high just walking down the street. I expected to hate coming here, but now that you mention it, I think I love it, too. Of course, I don't get to see all that much of it; I spend too many hours at the hospital."

"What hospital?"

"Allenboro Memorial, do you know it?"

It is a small world after all, she thought ruefully. Maybe there's no such thing as a cliché; only a truth. "I have a friend there, a girl I grew up with. One of the nursing nuns, Sister Immaculata."

"Oh yes," he said, and something flickered in his eyes. "Sister Immaculata. I know her." He abruptly changed the subject then, and Ivory, so familiar with the techniques of interviewing and of reading her subject's emotional responses, made no effort to change it back. For some reason, Doctor Scott did not want to talk about Sister Immaculata, and she was reluctant to insist. But she made a mental note; she would remember.

They talked easily, except for that; as comfortably as old friends reunited, and yet with the pleasant added tension of a man and a woman who found each other attractive. I have missed this, Ivory thought. I have always missed this. How wonderful it would be if this was where my life was leading all along, if I have come truly home, and here is a gentle and loving man whom I can trust.

Daydreams, Imagene, some stern inner disciplinarian reprimanded. Fantasies. Don't kid yourself again; remember your Texas millionaire.

The meal over and watches regretfully checked and double-checked, they parted after agreeing to meet again and continue the conversation. There would be dinner, and the theater, and then the mutual discovery of Central Park in the early morning, and Riverside Drive in the twilight. There was a skepticism in Ivory that had not been there before, so that now she was partly an outsider, watching and judging, defensive and aware. She would not be fooled again if she could help it, nor would she fall in love with love itself, nor a romantic image instead of the man behind it.

Not if she could help it.

The day the final contract was signed with the network, Clinton Everhardt called Ivory. "You know that apartment you were telling me about, Ivory? Buy it, baby! The contract's signed, the network loves it, and 'Headliners' is going to be on the fall lineup of the Lincoln Broadcasting System!"

When she hung up the phone, her hands were shaking. She made herself sit quietly and fold them in her lap. *Outward serenity is a sign of inner peace.*

I'm actually going to own my own home, she thought. My own. Home. Not a big house with an acre of lawn, but at least a nice apartment in a building with a good address. And a doorman; a *doorman!* And it will be all mine, my name on the certificate.

Imagene . . .

Ivory Talbot Reynolds.

A polished brass plate on the door, and monograms on the towels. Stationery with her address on it. Tear out walls, build in bookshelves. It's your own home.

That was when she telephoned Penny.

"That job I've been waiting for all this time has come through, Sister," she said. "And on top of that, I'm buying an apartment here in New York in a really nice co-op, so it looks like I'm here to stay."

"How wonderful! Perhaps we can get together soon and

celebrate. I'd really like that, Ivory," Penny told her. "I want to hear all about your job; goodness knows, I've been boring you for long enough with all the little details of mine."

Yes, thought Ivory, the boring details of your life. Not much. Caring for the sick, saving lives, winning the love and admiration of everyone.

"Could we have lunch together tomorrow, Sister?" Ivory asked aloud. "After this week, I'm not going to have any time for a while. Ev—that's my producer, Clinton Everhardt —has every minute scheduled for me for quite some time."

"I couldn't possibly come into town," Penny said with no hint of regret. "My own schedule won't allow that, I'm afraid, and even if I did, it couldn't be just the two of us. Sisters of Gethsemane always travel in pairs, you know." Her soft laugh rippled over the wires. "But why don't you come out here, to the hospital? We could have something to eat in the cafeteria and a little quiet visit in the nurses' lounge, that's easy to arrange."

The first time she saw Allenboro Memorial from the taxi-cab window, she thought: Yes, that's the kind of place where Penny would be. A neat brick building looking like old money.

Penny came to greet her in the lobby. Sister Immaculata, robed entirely in white now, smelling like snow and starch. The years were being good to Penny. If anything, she was lovelier than ever as maturity accented the perfect oval of her face, showing the good bone structure beneath the creamy skin. There were a few fine lines around her eyes, but they seemed to be caused by nothing more than the weight of her heavy eyelashes.

Ivory had worn her newest ensemble from Bergdorf's for the meeting. She wanted Penny to see her as she saw her-self, well-groomed, in the height of fashion, every hair in place. Successful and assured. But once again, looking at

Penny, she felt her assurance wilt a little. She had to struggle so hard to achieve what came to Penny naturally.

Penny gave her that warm, brimming smile she always remembered with love, but the nun paid no attention to her outfit at all. It did not seem to make any impression. "Ivory!" she exclaimed, holding out both hands in a familiar gesture. "See, I've finally gotten used to calling you that. How good it is to see you after such a long time—and to hear that you have a job at last, too. It must be dreadfully hard finding work these days, isn't it?"

Without waiting for an answer—or a job description—she tucked her hand beneath Ivory's arm and guided her toward the hospital cafeteria. "I'm afraid I don't have too much time," she apologized, "so it would be better if we get our meal first and visit while we eat. I never know when someone will need me and I'll have to go. You understand."

Once seated, with plates of alleged food in front of them, Penny apologized again. "Hospital food. It's quite adequate for me, of course, but you might not enjoy it very much. I seem to remember you always loved cheeseburgers, didn't you?"

"I don't eat cheeseburgers anymore," Ivory replied. "Last night I had *Champignons Farcis aux Crabes* at Dominique's."

"Oh really? How nice." Penny cut a tiny piece of bland fish and ate it, chewing with disinterest. She made no further comment on Ivory's culinary adventures.

Ivory could have forced the conversation. She had learned her profession well, she knew how to lead a dialogue and how to elicit responses. She could have made Penny ask her the questions that would have allowed her to spread her shining success on the table between them, to be seen and admired. But she did not. She had intended to do just that, but when the time came she found herself once more playing Penny's admiring acolyte, saying, "That's extraordinary, Sister, I don't know how you find the energy," and "Of course you deserve to be a supervisor. Who's better qualified?" and "That sounds just like you; you always made people feel better just by being around them."

The conversation was as unsatisfying as the bland meal. Ivory left the hospital annoyed with herself for falling into old habits, for not establishing a new and more equal relationship between them. Next time, she promised herself. Next time.

As she went down the steps toward the waiting taxi, she met Nathan coming up. His eyes lit with pleasure. "Ivory! What are you doing here?"

"I was visiting that friend of mine I told you about, remember?"

"Oh yes. Sister Immaculata. Look, Ivory, I don't have the time to go into it right now, but I'd like to talk to you about that friend of yours."

"Why?"

"Well, I'd like to know how close you are, and how much you know about her, for starters."

Ivory stiffened. There was something guarded in his voice that immediately raised her own defenses. "I don't see that it's any of your business, really, Nathan," she told him.

"I'm not trying to tell you who your friends should be, don't take me wrong. It's just that I've had . . . some dealings of my own with Sister Immaculata and I'd like to find out more about her."

They were facing one another on the broad stone steps, with the sunlight making them squint. She wanted to read his face and his thoughts, but it was impossible in this setting. He should be sitting across the low white formica table on the set of "Headliners," the strong camera lights leaving no shadows for secrets to hide in.

"We'll have to make it some other time," she told him, turning away. "I'm in a hurry myself this morning. Call me, will you?"

He called her that same afternoon and they agreed to meet for dinner, at her apartment this time, with her newly hired housekeeper to do the cooking.

"Monique's a treasure, you'll love her poulet Marengo," Ivory assured Nathan.

"I love her already on the strength of that name," he laughed. "Monique. Sounds like exotic perfume and silk stockings."

"That's hardly Monique. Or if it is, it's a part of her I've never seen. I interviewed her and hired her within the space of an hour, so she's probably got some facets I don't know about."

"Are you sure it's wise, taking some stranger into your home that way? Did you check her references?"

"I'm a grown woman, Nathan. I can make my own judgments about people. Besides, I've been in a position rather like the one Monique's in, and I developed a good rapport with her from the beginning. She's all right; in fact, she's just fine."

"You're too trusting, Ivory," he told her.

"Don't bet on it," she replied.

That night at dinner, he brought up the subject of Sister Immaculata again.

"The first time I mentioned her name, you made it plain you didn't want to talk about her," Ivory reminded him. "What's changed?"

"Us."

Be careful, she warned herself. Keep it light. "Is there an 'us'?" she asked with a tinkling laugh. "I don't know that I'm ready for that, Nathan."

"It wasn't in my game plan, either," he admitted, "but I found myself writing your name on a prescription the other day instead of my patient's. So obviously you've barged into my thoughts and made yourself at home. You have a way of doing that, in case you didn't know. I've never met anyone like you . . . and that's why I'm concerned about your friendship with Sister Immaculata, Ivory. I've never met anyone like her, either."

She blotted her lips with her napkin and pushed her plate away. Smiling slightly, she leaned her elbows on the table and let her shoulders droop a little; vulnerable. "Tell me," she said.

He seemed slightly nervous about it. "When I first met her, I thought she was an extraordinary woman, one of the most tireless and dedicated nurses I'd ever met. And then, she's so damned beautiful you can't help but notice, in spite of her uniform."

"Habit," Ivory corrected unconsciously.

"Habit. Then we had some run-ins, small things at first, the kind of things doctors and nurses often disagree on. But she took it so seriously! Much more so than the issues warranted. She has, as they say, a whim of iron, and she's absolutely determined to have her own way. When I was forced to pull rank on her, she did as neat an about-face as I've ever seen and came at me from another direction."

Maybe that isn't nervousness, Ivory thought. He seems more embarrassed than anything else. "What direction, Nathan?"

He toyed with his fork, pushing the remnants of the food around on his plate. "She . . . well, she used her considerable charms on me, to put it in a nice way. I was astounded; I'd never had a nun flirt with me! And I have to say I was flattered; who wouldn't be? But still, that changed my view of the woman. Coming on to a doctor didn't square with the image she had around the hospital; some of the other staff seem to think she's practically a saint."

Ivory kept her face carefully blank, hiding the picture she had in her mind of Penny flirting with Nathan Scott. Penny, the most skillful and irresistible of flirts. Penny, who had proudly proclaimed she was through with men. Sister Immaculata in her nun's habit, virtuous and chaste.

"Nuns aren't saints," she said. "They're women like other women, and they don't turn off their emotions when they put on their habits. Maybe she really found you attractive."

"Don't sound as if that's so incredible!" he teased. "Maybe she did, I don't know, but it bothered the hell out of me, especially when she followed it up with another effort to get my support for some of her own policies."

"Were they such bad policies?"

"Let's just say they were totally unacceptable for a privately funded Catholic hospital."

Ivory was getting annoyed. "Look, Nathan, so you and Sister Immaculata have had some differences of opinion and there are things about her that you don't like—so what? My friends don't have to like each other, and I certainly wouldn't want to be drawn into any dispute between the two of you. All I can tell you is I've known her for many years, and she was a friend to me when I didn't have any others. I'll always be grateful for that. Now, can we drop it?"

After that they both tried to smooth over the rough surfaces interjected into the evening. Neither of them mentioned Penny again, and they laughed and talked and drank more wine than Ivory usually allowed herself. She enjoyed being with Nathan Scott; she felt a certain resentment against Penny for having intruded her own personality into their relationship and causing friction. And she was aware that later, when she was alone, she would want to think about Penny and Nathan Scott, to try to analyze what the doctor had told her.

You can get anything you want if you're willing to do whatever it takes. How far would you be willing to go to have your own way at Allenboro Memorial, Penny? Ivory wondered. Surely not . . .

But Nathan Scott didn't give her the opportunity to dwell on Penny. He was warm, and charming, and the wine was filling her veins with a heavy sweetness that somehow made everything else seem far away and unimportant.

When Nathan's mouth closed over hers, she felt a brief flash of panic, but he was simultaneously strong and gentle, his hands asking, not demanding, and the panic subsided. Then her body was answering the questing hands eagerly, and her mouth was returning his kisses as if she had just reached the oasis in an endless desert. He wasn't brutal, like Randy, or tentative, like Boo Colby. He was eager and hungry but respectful, going just to the limits she allowed him, but then persuading her with his tender passion to allow him to go farther.

Step by step he led her toward the moment she had been denied all her life, the moment when she felt totally surrounded and engulfed by love, freed to relax and take part in it. His body moved on hers with a rhythm exactly matched to her own. His hands touched her just the way she wanted to be touched. He kissed her at the moment of entering her, and his kiss lost none of its tenderness in spite of the driving hardness of his body. *Now* was the time. *At last!*

"Ivory," he said just once, with a tone almost like worship.

Then he was thrusting and demanding and she was arching upward to meet him, welded to him, giving and taking at once, and though she did not know it, she was smiling.

Afterward, as she lay in his arms, drowsily content, for some reason the image of Penny's lovely face flitted across her consciousness.

This is mine, she said silently to that watching face. He wants *me*.

And then sometime later, she was dreaming of herself in a hospital corridor, seeing Nathan come toward her and Penny in a beautiful blue dress step out of a doorway to intercept him. She put her hand on his chest, she smiled up at him through her heavy lashes, she said something softly and he wasn't looking toward Ivory anymore. He was looking down at Penny.

Fifteen

THE MOMENTUM GATHERED, the excitement became more intense, until eventually the day dawned that was to mark the official launching of "Headliners," with Ivory Talbot Reynolds. It was a day of promises fulfilled. Though Ivory had spent many hours at LBS, this would be the first time she entered as the star of an officially scheduled program. She would be taking possession of her own office and her own staff.

Ev sent a limousine for her—the first time he had done that—and the doorman of her new apartment respectfully ushered her into it. A limo, she thought to herself as she sank into the upholstery, trying out the abbreviated name, trying to make it sound as if she were used to whisking through New York in a limo.

At first she enjoyed the ride, but then she became aware of people staring at her at red lights. I thought New Yorkers were supposed to be so blasé about celebrities, she thought, aware that her face had been in all the papers for the last few days. But they aren't blasé, or cold and unfriendly, any more than Texans are really like the image outsiders have of them.

At least, not all of them. She shuddered.

The limo carried her to the Avenue of the Americas, still known as Sixth Avenue to the natives, the pulsing heart of the East Coast television industry. Between 54th and 49th streets stood the monoliths of ABC, CBS, LBS, and NBC, known waggishly in the trade as "Hard Rock," "Black Rock," "Bedrock," and "30 Rock" respectively, because of their style, their architecture, or their addresses.

LBS shunned an actual Sixth Avenue address and considered itself the only building on Bedlington Park, a tiny patch of flower beds and weeping birch trees surrounded by concrete walks and redwood benches and named for the founder of the network. The building itself was stylistically somewhere between the fading Art Deco of NBC and the black granite modernity of CBS. An impersonal gray former skyscraper, diminished now by comparison with some of the giants in its neighborhood, LBS still boasted carved stone bas-reliefs beneath the windows of the Production Center on the lower levels, and a lobby that managed to look both prosperous and homey.

Ivory tucked her briefcase under her arm and walked across Bedlington Park with a measured pace that belied her racing heart. The façade of the LBS Building was embellished with a shallow Greek portico and Doric columns, giving it a vague resemblance to a bank. LBS fostered that impression of being an institution, a solid, stable influence in a neighborhood that had coined the term "rat race." Closely packed within the concrete canyons, talent agencies, film corporations, ratings bureaus, syndicators, public broadcasting, and various small packagers were fighting with fang and claw for survival among the titans. Gossip had it that the nickname "Bedrock" had come from the executive suites of LBS itself, to stress the desired image of a survivor.

At the top of the steps, Ivory took a deep breath and looked through the heavy glass doors into the lobby. She had been here before, many times, but never as the official star (star!) of a confirmed and scheduled show. "Here we go," she said under her breath and pushed the door open.

The lobby was carpeted in a plush dark-green, with matching runners to protect the heavy traffic areas. The walls were paneled and hung with oil paintings, conservative representational art, discreetly lighted. Clusters of comfortable armchairs filled the expanse of space between the curving reception desk and the first bank of elevators. The cubicle occupied by the security guard was placed to give him a sweeping view of the room without making him an obvious feature of it.

Behind the reception desk sat a lacquered blonde with a professional smile, almost hidden behind an enormous basket of flowers. "Miss Reynolds!" the girl called cheerily. "Am I glad to see you! I was just going to have to call someone to take these upstairs, but now you can do it."

Ivory stiffened. Carry flowers, like a porter? What happened to the star treatment? But then, I should have expected it, she thought almost at once. Nobody would really be fooled into thinking I was . . .

"These are for you," the receptionist's voice interrupted. "There are more in your office, from your producer, I think, but these just came. Aren't they gorgeous?"

They were indeed. Ivory hunted among the profusion of white roses and blue irises for a card.

"Did the florist say who sent these?" she asked the blonde behind the desk.

"No. Isn't there a . . . oh, here it is, it must have fallen off." She handed the small white oblong to Ivory.

It was difficult to get the card out of the envelope, and

when she did, it took her a minute to recognize the name, because it wasn't what she had expected. She thought the flowers would be from one of the people connected with the network, or the show—or perhaps from Nathan Scott.

The card read, in the difficult, scrawled handwriting of some florist's assistant, "All the luck in the world. You deserve it. From your friend, Penny."

Ivory closed her eyes and blinked back the sudden rush of tears. Her throat ached. Not Sister Immaculata, not God Bless You.

Your friend, Penny.

During the hectic early weeks of establishing an audience for "Headliners," there were times Ivory felt like giving up. The commitment had to be total, it took all her mind and body and demanded more. She worked ceaselessly at projecting the right image on-camera, while behind the scenes she had to work equally hard to smooth over the frictions that threatened the production staff. How could so many skilled, well-established people suffer so many insecurities? When she considered herself, she had the answer, and was able to go on being patient and kind, most of the time.

She got to know the other women on the staff, the ones who were routinely assigned to the boring details the men didn't want to do, and she empathized with them. They were still second-class citizens, in spite of women's lib. Good writers, capable administrators and technicians, they were relegated to secondary positions in reality, though their titles often sounded impressive. More often than not, their true status showed on their paychecks. She began to realize how lucky she was, being one of the fortunate few who had made it to the top.

"I earned it, though," she told Penny in one of their telephone conversations. "I got myself a thorough grounding in this business in Texas. I took courses I couldn't afford, I wrote copy somebody else took credit for, and I learned how to get along with the Establishment and follow orders. Believe me, I made my share of the coffee. I earned my chance at this."

"There's a price to be paid for everything," Penny said evenly, with the complacency of one who long ago paid an enormous price.

"A lot of women are still paying the price for me to get where I am," Ivory told her. "We've come a long way, and the girls just coming into the job market today have no idea how different it is from a generation ago, but you can't say we have true equality, either in our earnings or the way we're treated. The television industry, for one, is very slow to change. They pay a lot of lip service but . . ."

"Are you still so militant?" Penny asked with a note of amusement.

"Me? Oh no. I've grown up and I've had a lot of time to think. And to observe. You'd be surprised how much some of my opinions have changed."

"How so?" It was Penny's questioning voice again, the one Ivory had modeled hers on so well, gently encouraging, promising unlimited interest and sympathy.

It asked her to reveal more of herself than she really wanted to reveal anymore, especially to Penny. But as soon as she thought that, she scolded herself for being a coward. Penny can't hurt you, she told herself sternly. You're strong now. "The war in Vietnam," she said with conviction. "I've come to the conclusion—especially since I've gotten to know the communications industry from the inside—that we let the media control our emotions about the war and dictate their own policy. The result was that a lot of soldiers who believed in their country and fought honorably for her ideals came home to be treated like second-class citizens instead of heroes. We went on a rampage of destroying our heroes, of battering everything down to rubble, and the media encouraged it."

"So you haven't changed so much after all, Ivory. You're still fighting the Establishment, only this time it's the communications industry. Still run by men, according to you."

"Maybe I am. But I know better than to get up on a platform and make a lot of frantic speeches from a position of ignorance. I've learned to work inside the system." Soon she would really be in a position to help other women, to use the medium of television to create her own influence, but she did not say that to Penny. She did not want to discuss ambition with Sister Immaculata.

"What about abortion?" Penny asked in an uninflected voice. "Have you changed on that?"

"Why?" Ivory asked, meaning to tease, "have you?"

The silence on the other end of the wire was almost palpable. At last Penny said, through tight lips, "The Catholic church can never sanction abortion."

Ivory, who had interviewed many people with secrets, and uncovered some, recognized the sound of something hidden in the voice. Something guarded; something feared. "But what about *you*?" she asked sharply, not giving the other any more time to collect her thoughts. "Is it possible that you feel differently about abortion after all these years? Now that . . ."

"They're paging me. I must go now," Penny interrupted, cutting off communication with finality. Ivory recognized that voice, too; that chill, I-will-not-discuss-it voice from their days in the motherhouse together after Penny returned from Europe.

There was a click and then the incessant whine of the dial tone. Ivory stood, holding the receiver in one hand and staring at it. Is it possible? she wondered. Could dogmatic Sister Immaculata have secretly changed her own attitude toward abortion after all this time? But why not? Look how much I've changed. If it has happened, it's something very private with her and she obviously won't talk about it. Look what happened to that nun called Sister Catherine when she espoused abortion!

She hung up the phone and gazed off into space, wearing a bemused expression. Well, well, as they used to say—will wonders never cease?

The next morning, at the booking meeting in Ev's office, Ivory broached a topic suggestion for the show. The booking meetings were one of the most important elements of pre-production, the time when the staff went over suggested subjects for interview and determined their availability. Everhardt, his associate producer Doris Wheelwright, three talent coordinators, and a production assistant, or tech rep, routinely went over a list of headliner names furnished by the talent coordinators, the TCs. Ivory's presence was tolerated but not mandatory; Ev liked to keep absolute control over every element of the show, especially during its fledgling phases, and had not encouraged her to make suggestions. Usually she sat comfortably in a leather armchair off to one side, watching Ev rule his little fiefdom from behind a horseshoe-shaped desk.

Today was different. Today she wanted to be acknowledged. Instead of sitting down, playing Star, letting them do things for her, she walked directly to the desk and stood with feet planted wide, meeting Ev's gaze steadily. Even before the TCs could begin reading the names on their various lists, she said, "Ev, I have an idea for the next 'Headliners' and I'd like to discuss it."

The program was still new; the relationships were not yet solidified. Thinking he sniffed an incipient mutiny, he scowled at the woman in front of him. "Reynolds, we have plenty of topics to work with for now, it's just a matter of deciding when we go with who. There's the son of that banana republic dictator who got himself assassinated; that's hot, and I'm really interested in your interviewing that diva from the Met who . . ."

"What about a program on abortion?"

Everhardt reared back in his big chair. The scowl became a glare, warning her, but this reply was mild enough. Better not make the talent defensive. "Good idea, always topical, but there are a lot of other things I think we should look at first."

"Why? What's more important than a question of life and death? Haven't you been reading the papers, Ev? There are a lot of those pro-life groups forming all across the country, and there's a serious push underway to get the legalization of abortion totally reversed." She wouldn't just drop it; she leaned toward him, trying to convey her own intensity. "I want to do a hard-hitting in-depth study of both sides of the issue, pro-choice *and* pro-life. Really open up the discussion!"

Everhardt cleared his throat and laced his fingers across his belly. He was annoyed to think perhaps he had misjudged this woman. In his relations with her up until now, she had been so docile, so refreshingly compliant and disinclined to argue—a result of her convent training, no doubt —that he had enjoyed her more than anyone he had worked with in years. After all the temperament, all the demands, it was so good to have a budding star still saying yessir and nosir, figuratively if not literally. That was one of the reasons he had gone out on a limb to get the unknown Ivory Reynolds for "Headliners," when he didn't really want to take chances anymore. But she was such a submissive, easily handled unknown. Or appeared to be. Now she seemed to be getting some ideas of her own that had to be turned off, fast.

"We'll talk about this later, Reynolds," he said brusquely. "Let's settle our immediate business first, shall we? Wheelwright, when did you say you wanted to schedule the Margo San Angelo interview?"

Temporarily dismissed, Ivory sat down and waited. With

folded hands. She watched as Everhardt manipulated his staff and fired out his orders. It won't always be like this, she promised herself. If the ratings keep climbing . . . someday I'll have the power. Then they'll be willing to listen to me. Then I can show them. Then I *will* show them.

The meeting concluded, the diva agreed upon, Doris Wheelwright left to start blocking out the framework of the proposed interview with "Headliners'" team of writers. Some established talk show hosts worked up their own interviews to varying degrees, but no one had suggested that Ivory could, in spite of her experience at Channel 5 in Texas.

Everhardt, the talent coordinators, and the production assistant chatted in industry shorthand for a few minutes more, then the office emptied and Ivory was alone with her producer.

"Sorry I had to cut you off like that," Ev began, shaping his heavy features into a fair imitation of an apologetic smile. With no witnesses, he could afford to be friendlier now, less officious. "I just like the team to see me keep a firm hand on the reins. I'm in charge here, Reynolds, and while I'm always open to suggestions, of course, it would set a bad precedent if some member of our team seemed to be arguing with me in front of the others. You understand."

She nodded.

"Besides, the real problem with your abortion show is on the fortieth floor," he added.

"Why?"

"The executive suites. The president of the network, Michael Mitchellson, and his lifelong buddy on the board of directors, Frank Basquette, are both devout Catholics. Very devout, if you get my meaning."

"And they have editorial control over 'Headliners'?" Ivory made herself stifle the sudden flash of resentment.

"Of course not!" The reply was too quick. "Nobody controls Clinton Everhardt! But I know for a fact they wouldn't be happy about our giving a lot of coverage to the pro-abortion side right now, and to do the kind of balanced interview you're talking about, that's what we'd have to do.

"Listen, Reynolds, when I first suggested you for the host spot and told them a little about your background, they were very happy with the whole concept. Let's keep it that way, shall we?"

"That's why you wanted me?" she asked with dawning suspicion. "Not because of my abilities, whatever they were, but because I'd been a nun and you thought that would give you an edge on the fortieth floor?"

"That wasn't it at all. Your background could have hurt, if we'd made an issue about why you left the convent. But we lucked out there; it didn't come up at the time. It would now, if you start doing a program on abortion. Now don't get the wrong idea, Reynolds; I hired you because you're good, damned good, and I want to see you go all the way. I'm on your side. But in order to get where I am, I've learned how to play the game; you've got to." (I've heard this speech before, Ivory thought.) "And one way to play it is to keep Mitchellson happy, get him owing you a little. Now in case you didn't know, his grandmother founded Allenboro Memorial Hospital—you ever heard of that?"

Ivory nodded, feeling a band of coincidence tighten around her.

"It's a private Catholic hospital and Mitchellson's pet charity. There's an opening on the board of directors over there, and he said to me just the other day how impressed he was with you.

"If I suggested that he arrange for you to join the board—it's pretty much a ceremonial position at that particular hospital, the Mitchellson family actually runs the place to suit themselves and the staff—I think he'd go along with it. He has quite a gleam in his eye when he talks about you, the old goat. Anyway, that would give us a little edge, you understand? It never hurts in this business."

The game. The rules; ingratiate yourself with the power structure; appear to do it their way. The rules had never changed; Penny had just recognized and accepted that long before Ivory did. And it wasn't even limited to women, men had to play, too; look at Ev trying to make points with Mitchellson and Basquette.

It's time I made my own points.

"I'm sure you're right, Ev," she said, smiling sweetly. "You know this industry and this network a lot better than I do. If you really think I have a chance at being on the board, and it might help solidify 'Headliners'' position, of course I'll be glad to do it. As long as it doesn't take time away from the program. There's just one thing, though. I happen to know a couple of people on staff at Allenboro Memorial—will that make any difference? I mean, might it be construed as some sort of prejudice?"

"Friends or enemies?" Everhardt asked quickly.

"Friends."

"They wouldn't oppose your nomination, then; that's all that's important. Hell, if I know you, in a few weeks' time, every member of the staff over there will be your friend. You've sure cut a wide swath around here since you came in. Everybody's singing your praises."

Ivory smiled demurely once more and left the office. Yes, Ev, I'm making friends as fast as I can. That's another art I've studied. I'm building my own power base, my own way, she thought as she rode down in the elevator. Imagine what Ev would say if he could listen to the inside of my head; he thinks he knows me. He seemed genuinely surprised and annoyed at my temerity in making a suggestion; that didn't fit with his image of me.

The television industry is the creation of images. How true. You select one from all the many possible and put it up there on the screen and people believe it, as people believe they're seeing the real Ivory Talbot Reynolds. But I don't know her much better than they do; I haven't decided yet who she is. An ambitious lady who wants to show the world how badly it underestimated her? To show my father? An independent career woman? A would-be wife and mother? Gentle and trusting and optimistic, or a cynic schooling herself in the arts of manipulation?

Damn. Who knows?

The elevator doors slid open to reveal the foyer of the floor housing the private offices and dressing rooms of the network stars. The decor was twenty-first-century spaceship, chrome-and-track lighting and hard edges, with green plants trying to appear natural beneath unvarying fluorescent light. Ivory stepped out and the doors closed again on the tinkling background music of Mantovani, a distant heavenly choir. The green light winked on, indicating that the elevator was redirected upward.

Ivory looked around at the foyer. Totally forgettable. Perhaps all life was like that, a series of impersonal way stations through which people moved on their journey to somewhere else.

A person's ultimate destination is God.

Except I got off the train early, she thought. She shook her head angrily, slinging away the idea, and headed for her own new little suite: office, dressing room, and secretary's cubicle.

For Ivory's arrival, the walls of the suite that was to be hers—smaller, less impressive than those of the established stars—had been repainted, a soft powder-blue instead of the ubiquitous Devon cream found everywhere throughout the building. Cream walls, cream halls, cream everything above lobby level; a butterfat shade destined to attract smudges as city snow attracts soot.

Sharon MacCandless was waiting for her. A narrow-shouldered young woman with hips already beginning their secretarial spread, Sharon had tilted hazel eyes magnified by reading glasses, and a drift of freckles across her pleasant, farm-girl face.

In the short time since she had been hired for Ivory, Sharon MacCandless had proved herself to be indefatigable, both at working and talking. Ivory was her first "celebrity" employer, and she was touchingly starstruck, though Ivory was as new to the big time as she was.

"Oh, Miss Reynolds," she began nervously, her words running over each other in their rush to be spoken, "I just got your daybook organized and this man called from upstairs with a message about three o'clock—you know about that?—and I have something else down here for three o'clock and I'm just afraid . . ."

"It's all right, Sharon," Ivory said kindly, though it probably wasn't. A message from "upstairs" about three o'clock doubtless meant a command appearance at an unscheduled, high-tension, last-minute conference, the kind of constant in the television business that strained Ivory's determined surface serenity. "Take it easy. We'll work everything out. By the way, I brought you something. I happened to have coffee with Kensington Mallory this morning before the booking meeting, and I remembered to get his autograph for you. On a napkin from the commissary, with the LBS logo."

Sharon grinned and reached eagerly for the scrap of paper. The scrawled signature of the legendary LBS anchorman was something she was still too shy to have requested on her own. "Thanks a million, Miss Reynolds! It's awfully nice of you to take an interest in my little brother's autograph collection."

"I hope he likes it," Ivory replied, keeping her face straight. She had seen Sharon's file; the little brother was a fiction. Autograph hounds usually claimed to want signatures for relatives, children, friends. For some reason, people were often reluctant to admit they were so vulnerable to celebrity themselves, so eager to have a signed name for show and tell. When people indicated they wanted her autograph for themselves, Ivory tried harder to write beautifully and to add a brief message, as a tribute to honesty.

She stood by Sharon's desk and sifted through the unopened stack of her personal mail. From the beginning, she had requested that all mail and phone calls be directed to her at the network; nothing, even a personal call, was to be allowed to violate the privacy of her apartment. Now she glanced at bills from Bendel's, Bergdorf's, American Express. She refused to have a business manager, preferring to pay her own bills and balance her own checkbook. It gave her a sense of control.

There was a letter from Lou Ellis Colby, fat in its envelope and heavy in the hand. Had another argument with Buford, no doubt, and wanted to talk about it. A note from Boo telling the other side would probably be in tomorrow's mail. Everybody wrote her, everybody kept in touch. Not just because she was becoming famous, but because it had become a habit. Ivory could be counted on to listen to the details of trips to the dentist or fights with lovers or problems with the IRS. She tolerated the repeated retelling of childhood memories or visits to Atlantic City; she sat through verbal playbacks of old movies and television shows only the teller thought interesting; she let people tell her the plots of books they had read twenty years before and she always smiled and nodded and listened.

Many people thought of Ivory Reynolds as a friend. "She always has time for you; she really cares," they said of her.

When Ivory thought of the word "friend," the only face she saw was Penny's.

Sometimes, after spending an interminable time listening to others, she went home and faced herself in the mirror, seeing the boredom and exhaustion plainly written there, and said, "Sucker." But the next time someone wanted to talk to her, she went through it all again. Even to the extent, in this early stage of their relationship, of allowing

Sharon to talk her arm off. The girl was a compulsive, and pity encouraged patience.

She got to the bottom of the stack of mail, the invitations and bread-and-butter letters and endless supplications to buy, invest, contribute. Underneath everything else was a card from Nathan Scott showing a winsome panda bear. Nathan had written across its tummy, "This little panda wants to come and live with you. See you both tonight."

"You know, Miss Reynolds, I could at least open the mail for you before you come in," Sharon volunteered, not for the first time. "I mean, it would save you some time, and that's what a secretary's supposed to do, isn't it? I wouldn't look at it or anything, I'd just slit the envelopes, you know."

During the period of postulancy, you must hand any letter you write, unsealed, to your superior, and all incoming mail will be opened and examined before you receive it.

"No, thank you, Sharon," Ivory said firmly. "Let's just say I'm different from other employers and some exceptions are going to have to be made for me, all right?"

Sixteen

THE ULTIMATE, TOTAL SUCCESS was elusive. It always seemed to be just around the corner; it was never recognized as having arrived. "When you get a thirty share, Ivory," they told her. And after that, "When you make the cover of *TV Guide*," and then, "When foreign heads of state start inviting you to interview them on their own turf . . ." No matter how much she achieved, there seemed to be some new level not yet reached, some criterion not realized.

She pushed. She worked harder than she ever had in her life, reading an incredible number of magazines and newspapers, courting those who could further her career, winning friends to be in her corner against any foreseeable adversity, driving herself as if nothing mattered.

But there were times when she looked in the mirror and knew that wasn't true. A lot of things mattered. Real friendships, that rarest of achievements. Self-knowledge. Peace.

Love.

I can handle it all! she told herself fiercely.

Nobody can handle it all, the face in the mirror seemed to warn her. And you're not doing it. You've got a career and a lover but what else? What about that house in the country? What about those children you really wanted . . . once?

The years were going by. "Headliners" was a big hit, but she had passed her fortieth birthday. If she was ever going to have a family, she would need to get started soon.

If . . .

When their affair was new, Nathan had not mentioned marriage and neither had she. It was delightful to be *un*married and lie in a man's arms, in his bed. She felt gloriously free, as if she had stepped out from behind walls. This was one of the liberations worth fighting for! Then, inevitably, she began to grow uneasy. Why hadn't he even raised the subject in passing? Didn't he want to marry her? Were his tender declarations of love only lies?

Everyone came to Ivory Reynolds for advice, but she had never gone to anyone but Penny. How could she now ask a nun for guidance on handling a love affair? Besides, the friendship was changed, even more changed than Penny knew. The first time Ivory had sat down and read all the way through the research file she had compiled in Texas, the file labeled ENDICOTT, the relationship had changed forever. She did not know what impulse had made her go through with that particular bit of research, after she uncovered the story of Kellam Endicott's trial while preparing an interview on criminal justice in the Lone Star State. She did not know what further impulse had made her bring the file all the way to New York, to lie buried in her desk drawer like an unhealed wound. But it was there, and she had read it, and she would never look at Penny the same way again.

No, she could not ask Penny's advice.

When she and Nathan were together, the lovemaking was perfect. It was hard to remember how unpleasant sex had been before, with Randy, or how much she had hated it. Nathan Scott replaced all the bad memories with good experiences. Almost all the bad memories.

She rarely invited anyone to her apartment, preferring to keep it hers alone, off limits to the rest of the world. They usually went to Nathan's apartment on 83rd Street, just off the Park, and hoped his service wouldn't interrupt them with a phone call. Yet there were rare, special moments when she felt moved to ask him home with her. In her private place, behind her walls, lovemaking seemed somehow intensified, so they went to sleep with bodies locked and wakened in the morning the same way. Their early morning lovemaking, joyous and tender, then wrapped the entire day in a rainbow.

It was on one of those occasions that Nathan finally asked her to marry him.

And give up "Headliners."

It was a one-two punch, she was hit with happiness and horror and her face reflected her confusion. "What do you mean, give up the show?" she demanded to know, even before she had time to think. "Are you crazy?"

"No, I'm in love with you. Or maybe that is crazy, me with a career gal when I've always been attracted to the apron-in-the-kitchen-type. But I just can't see the two of us holding down two jobs as demanding as my being a doctor and you being a television celebrity. We wouldn't have any time left for each other, or for our kids."

"So I should give up something I love and have worked so hard for, is that it? Why me? Why do women always have to do the sacrificing?"

"I'm not asking you to sacrifice, I make a good living and I can take damned good care of you. You'll have everything you want, I promise you; all I ask is that you be there for me when I need you. Is that so unreasonable?"

She felt terribly threatened. Just when you get it, they

want to take it all away from you. "Yes! Yes, it is unreasonable! Why didn't you tell me sooner how you felt about marriage?"

He was uneasy. "I didn't want to bring it up too soon. I know your first marriage wasn't happy, from the little you've told me, and I didn't want you to feel rushed into another one. I wanted to give us time to know each other and be sure it was right for both of us."

"Well, you don't know me at all if you think I want to give up 'Headliners'!"

They had been lying in each other's arms. Now he pushed the covers aside and got up, beginning to gather up his clothes. She watched in disbelief as he started to dress. "Where are you going?"

"Home."

She was exasperated. "Oh, come on, Nathan, aren't you even going to discuss this?"

"What's to discuss? You've made it pretty obvious how you feel. You're not interested in marriage, you just want to go on being the hostess of 'Headliners,' and I'm not interested in being Mr. Ivory Reynolds. So there we are."

It was incredible. She couldn't believe he would accept her flat statement so flatly, without trying to negotiate or convince her. What had happened to all his sensitivity? Didn't he know she had been waiting, hopefully, fearfully, for that proposal? Didn't he realize how much she loved him? Surely they could talk this thing through, make it right . . .

She lay looking at him, saying nothing, anger growing in her. Why wouldn't he make the effort?

When he finished dressing, he went into the bathroom to tie his tie and came back with the knot crooked, as usual. It suited his face, his boyish indifference to himself. There was a quality of casual ease about Nathan Scott that was all the more precious to her because it was native to him, not studied. He looked especially dear now, and she hated him for it. She would hate him more if he actually left her apartment with all the important words unsaid. Men had that terrible superior way of avoiding the complicated layers of emotion that characterized the feminine psyche. Twentieth-century men, who held all the cards and knew all the rules, were so reluctant to let women into the game; they kept sex and love in different neat compartments and could walk away, or so it seemed.

Could walk away.

She gritted her teeth and refused to go an inch to meet him. I won't beg, either. This time I won't roll over and play dead. I'll be just as tough as he is.

"If that's the way you feel," she said, turning over in bed so that her back was to him. She did not see the look in his eyes, the long moment when he paused in pain before he left, closing the door firmly behind him.

After a few days, he called her again and they went to the theater together like two friends who had never been intimate, enjoying the play, laughing at the same lines, talking about everything but themselves. They were both aware of a deep crack in the relationship, but neither wanted to expose it by putting pressure on it. And neither one wanted to give up the relationship completely. When Nathan let a couple of weeks go by without calling her, Ivory found herself calling him, angry with herself for having done so, and this time they went on a long drive upstate together. Eventually, they were reestablished as a pair; lovers, not two people headed for marriage. There were bruised areas they must always tiptoe around.

Ivory did not trust herself. She was afraid, that if he ever did bring up the subject again, she might give in. But he did not mention marriage and she found it hard to forgive him for that.

She had struggled so hard to gain a small measure of independence and then he wanted her to surrender it, but was not willing to fight her to get her to do it. It seemed a sort of rejection.

The quarrels began, always about other things. She criticized his clothes, his choice of words, his habit of always being a few minutes late, any small thing that would serve as a safety valve to let off steam. Instead of fighting back, he took it like a small boy, grinning and waiting for her to lose her momentum.

They were at his apartment, and she had lost her temper (Imagine Ivory Reynolds losing her temper! she thought) because he insisted on paying for the cab she had taken to meet him there. Even after they made love, she went on picking at the wound. "This is the nineteen-eighties, Nathan. You shouldn't be such a, well, this is a cliché, but such a male chauvinist. I was very embarrassed! I'd already given that cabbie his money when you came charging out there and paid him."

"I pay for the cabs and the dinners and the tickets," he told her, not for the first time.

"I have friends who . . ."

"I don't care what arrangements your friends have. The old customs are still alive with me, and that's that."

She knew, deep inside, that was just what she wanted, a man of her own generation who lived by the traditions she had accepted as a child. At the same time, illogically but with the persistence of dogma, she wanted him to be the docile one, accepting her control. The impossibility of both desires being fulfilled made her angrier still and the quarrel moved to a new level of heat, until at last Nathan began to take part in it as well, his manhood stung.

"I shouldn't have let myself get mixed up with a career woman," he almost shouted. "They're all hardheaded bitches."

"Better a bitch than a son of a bitch!"

"I don't want you talking like that, Ivory; it doesn't suit you."

"Now you're going to tell me how to talk? Oh no! I'm not taking any orders from you. Men always think they know just what's right for women but they're wrong, they don't know anything!" It felt good to yell at him, to release the temper she had bottled up for so many years. Nathan was the only person she could vent her rage upon; she let herself surrender to the rare luxury of it. Ev could fire her, her friends could desert her. But Nathan, who loved her, seemed willing to stand there and take it. In her anger, she could not tell if that was a strength or a weakness.

"I know you're suffering from a bad case of wanting to have your cake and eat it, too," he told her. "You want to be a celebrity, and at the same time you want to be a private person. You want to be a lady and to swear like a trooper. You want to possess me and stay free yourself. The truth is, you don't know what you want; but don't take it out on me, I didn't make you that way."

It was the truth and she recognized it; that's why it made her so furious. No one should see into her so clearly, it violated her privacy. She stormed from his apartment wrapped in a thin dress and righteous indignation, only to find herself on the streets of New York on a foggy night with a chill wind blowing and no taxicab in sight, no doorman to get one for her.

The streets seemed unusually dark, long stretches of blackness between pools of misty light. Where was everybody? Her high heels gave off a hollow sound as they struck the sidewalk. She had never been fearful in New York; she laughed at others who were nervous on the streets and spoke of muggers and crime as inevitable. New York was her good luck place, nothing would hurt her here.

The street was very dark.

The next cross street was the best place to get a cab, she

decided. Lights, traffic. She began to walk briskly toward the corner, not allowing herself to glance into dark doorways. This was the East Side, this was her home.

Two men of undeterminate age and build were sauntering down the other side of the street, coming toward her. They stopped, watching her. One seemed to be saying something to the other one and then they started together across the street, straight toward her. She glanced quickly over her shoulder, back to Nathan's building, but there was a third man there, also closing in on her, coming down the sidewalk as quietly as a cat. She would be caught between them.

She went quickly up the steps of the nearest building, a handsome limestone structure with a double glass door barred by an elaborate grille. The door was locked and the lighted interior seemed empty. A foyer, closed doors beyond. She looked frantically for a button to push and stabbed it again and again with her finger. Hail Mary, full of grace, the Lord is with thee, blessed art thou amongst women and blessedisthefruitofthywombJesusHolyMaryMotherof . . . come on, come on, answer, you've got to answer!

"Hey there!" called a voice. A rough voice, full of menace. "Come 'ere, you!"

They were right below her at the bottom of the steps. She flattened herself against the door and pounded on it uselessly with her fist; there was no time left to try to go to another building. "Let me in!" she cried aloud. "For God's sake, let me in!"

"Eddie, you old fart, how long has it been, hey?" The solitary man threw his arm around the shoulder of one of the pair and the men began clapping each other on the back and making the jovial noises of hounds reunited with the pack. Two friends met after an interval apart. Then they became aware of Ivory at the top of the steps, calling hysterically for admittance. They stared up at her. "What's the matter, lady, you get locked out?" one called to her. "Want me to see if the super's in the basement?"

She slumped against the door, feeling as if the calcium had been drained from her spine. Not muggers, then. Only monsters in her own imagination. "I'm all right," she said weakly. "I . . . uh, I seem to have the wrong address."

"You sure? Hey, you shouldn't be out here like this, this late. Can we help you?"

The panic seemed to be rising in her again. "No, really, I can take care of myself! Thank you," she added belatedly, hurrying down the steps and pushing past them. She walked as fast as she could without running toward the cross street and the lights. Her serene, measured convent pace was not important anymore.

When she succeeded in hailing a taxi, she collapsed into it, fighting tears. "Fool, fool, fool," she muttered to herself.

"What say, lady?" the cabbie wanted to know.

"Nothing!" she shouted at him so vehemently that he said no word to her for the length of the drive, merely nodding when she gave him the address and keeping his eyes fixed on the street ahead.

The next morning she was still angry. She marched into Clinton Everhardt's office with snapping eyes and color in her cheeks not put there by blusher. "Ev, we have got to do a program on crime in the streets and how it affects women psychologically," she announced, not making it a suggestion.

Over the months of "Headliners'" steady climb up the ratings charts, Ivory's status had changed. The network of friends she had painstakingly created for herself had given her a weight felt all the way into the executive suites. Without appearing aggressive, she had learned to be assertive, to have her ideas listened to and championed, to get many things done her way. Doris Wheelwright, or Morey Feldman, or any one of a number of others whose allegiance she had won would put in a word here, call in a favor owed there, and Ivory's subtle influence was felt.

But sometimes she could not wait for that silken network to operate. This morning she felt an urgency to take direct action, herself. Attack Ev head on, with no beating around the bush. Flex her muscles.

He did not ask her to sit down. Clinton Everhardt never offered anyone a chair when he wanted to stress the point that his was the ultimate authority. Ivory was amused by the ploy because it was rendered ineffective by her own training. She was perfectly comfortable and at ease standing up. *To sit unnecessarily is an indulgence.*

"What do you mean, 'have to,' Reynolds?" Everhardt demanded to know. "When did you start choosing the topics?"

I've chosen more than you know, she thought silently. "I leave that up to you experts, Ev, but I'm part of that same viewing public we're trying to reach, so I have some strong feelings about what's important today. Crime on the streets is important. It's made us a nation of cringers and I hate that. I think of myself as a pretty self-sufficient person, but last night I thought I was going to get mugged and I simply panicked. It seemed so inevitable, somehow."

Suddenly Ev was leaning forward, listening tensely. "You nearly got mugged!" His precious property could have been damaged!

"No, but I thought that's what was happening, and my re-action to it has made me curious about the overall psychological effect on women, in particular, resulting from the high incidence of violent crime. I wonder how much it's changed people. I'd like to interview women who've been victims, and women who are merely fearful they will be, and see how they're coping."

Fortunately, they were alone in the office. Everhardt allowed himself to consider her request and be interested.

"Well, okay, I think you might have something there, Reynolds. We can take a look at it. Why don't you talk it over with Wheelwright and, if she likes it, have her get back to me, will you? It's probably a good time for a crusade against crime in the streets."

That's what I need, Ivory said to herself. A crusade. A way to blow off steam. And while I've got him in the habit of saying yes, why not go a little further?

"One other thing, Ev . . ." She softened her voice and her expression, deliberately putting herself in the suppliant position he liked from women. "Remember our discussion last year about the abortion program? The issue is hotter than ever, and all our competition's done programs on it. . . ."

Everhardt pushed his chair back from his desk a few inches, widening the space between them. "I thought I explained that to you, Reynolds. It's a sensitive issue for LBS, and it would be just as sensitive for you, on the board of the hospital. Don't you think that would encourage somebody to bring up the subject of your activist days and accuse you of a lack of objectivity now? If the public was reminded that you used to defend abortion . . . well, the board might have to take a long, hard look at 'Headliners.' Now let's drop this whole issue, okay? I don't want to talk about it anymore. Whole thing's insane anyway."

She wondered suddenly how the producer personally felt about abortion. Any other subject seemed possible, but not this one. Everyone in the country seemed to have intense feelings about the abortion issue, one way or the other, and in many cases the feelings ran so deep they could not be articulated.

Unless a program like "Headliners" articulated them.

It should be done. She could appreciate the sensitivity and understand the risk of having the former Sister Catherine hosting the interviews, but surely, in the 1980s, some issues were too large to be set aside for personal considerations.

I won't be a cringer, she thought. I'll start bringing some subtle pressure to bear and get my friends to lay the groundwork for me.

Doris Wheelwright sat behind a desk overflowing with stacks of paper and file folders. A jelly glass filled with blunted pencils teetered atop one pile; another was garnished with a spike holding a rainbow of unanswered pastel memos. The thick smell of cheeseburgers with onions greased the air and a cup of cold coffee waited, forgotten, as Doris concluded a telephone conversation with an unseen irritant.

"Yes, you cretin. How many times do I have to tell you? Now call me back with those stats PDQ and let's get rolling!"

Doris glanced up as Ivory entered her office. She grinned and waved toward the row of plastic chairs opposite her desk, each one piled high with files, scripts, boxes, and miscellany. "Sit anyplace," she mouthed to Ivory, then snarled into the phone, "Shit on you too, Hillenbarger," and slammed the receiver down.

Doris didn't seem to care if anyone liked her or not. She sailed through life protected by the invulnerable armor of the insensitive, saying just what she thought, doing just as she pleased. She never wasted valuable time trying to understand or empathize with anybody else, and if her ambition was held against her she didn't mind at all. Ivory marveled at her. Doris often said, "Life's too short for me to worry about what other people think of me," and Ivory, who would always care what other people thought, envied her that.

Doris lived in an unfashionable section of Brooklyn with two Siamese cats and a brother in a wheelchair, and her figure reflected her supreme unconcern about the opinions of others, resembling a sack of sugar tied in the middle with a string. Doris ate whatever she pleased and wore whatever was comfortable. Today that meant a pair of khaki fatigues and a thrift shop blouse, unevenly buttoned. She was also the best associate producer at LBS, and she cared very much about that.

She hunted among the litter on her desk and found the remnants of her cheeseburger. "Want a bite?" she offered before she tossed it away. "What can I do for you, Ivory? If it's about that money I borrowed to get my car fixed, I'll give you a check on Thursday, we just had to take Tom to a new therapist and . . ."

"Forget it," Ivory said. "I mean that, Doris. That wasn't a loan, it was a gift. You have so many responsibilities and I hardly have any; it's the least I can do. I'm not trying to take care of a brother in a wheelchair and a houseful of freeloading cats."

Doris laughed. "It's the cats that do me in; my brother's no problem. He at least tells me jokes and if he has a sex life, he's not noisy about it. But one of these days I'll be a full producer with no fucking 'associate' tacked on the front, and get my hands on the cookie jar. Then I'll support 'em all in style. Now, what's on your mind?"

They discussed the crime topic and Doris scribbled notes. "Terrific," she commented. "Your own idea? And Ev accepted it?"

"You know as well as I do he's accepted quite a few ideas of mine, thinking he'd had them himself. I just put this one to him up front instead of slipping it in his coffee. But the program I really want to do, and I'll need your help on this, is about abortion."

She outlined her ideas for the show and Ev's objections while Doris listened with interest.

"I'm surprised we haven't done that one already," the assistant producer commented. "I don't really think the executives would be that upset about it—hell, they'd keep quiet if we programmed the Crucifixion as long as it got a forty

256

share. If the show is strictly nonpartisan, no one's likely to make an issue about your background. Y'know, I've worked with Ev for a lot of years, and he didn't use to be such a nervous Nellie. Must be male menopause," she added with a malicious chuckle.

Ivory recognized the undertone of jealousy, the twist of the knife. An adroit word now would put Doris more soundly in her camp.

"There's a lot of talk about female instability during menopause," she commented, "but I think some men are a lot worse."

"Ain't it the truth," agreed Doris, who had already known her share of hot flashes and depressions and never missed a day's work. "Since Ev hit the shady side of fifty, I can tell the difference in him. He's beginning to run scared. The network's bringing in new blood, you know—they all are— kids so fresh from school they can't fill out a business suit. We see them here all the time, hot-eyed young Turks with big ideas who think TV is the real world and are just dying to take over. Ev's always been in solid with the Estab- lishment and he's desperate not to lose that edge, I can tell you.

"Those youngsters are breathing down his neck and he knows it. I personally think we could have done several things that were a lot more controversial if he weren't scared of rattling the wrong cage. I've presented some damned good ideas myself. There was a time when he would have leaped at them, but now . . ." She paused.

The unfinished sentences hung in the air and Ivory stud- ied them. There was latent hostility there, and a sharp com- petitive edge. Shapes she recognized. "Men wear out more quickly than women, don't they?" she asked Doris. "I think we stand up under stress better. There certainly hasn't been any slackening in your pace, you're always the first one here and the last one to leave. But if you think Ev is missing some opportunities, for whatever reason, maybe you and I working together can do something about it. We both want 'Headliners' to be the best it can possibly be, don't we?"

"Right on, sister. Hey, you sure you don't want the last bite of this second cheeseburger? Made a damned good breakfast."

Satisfied that Doris Wheelwright would begin to bring her own pressures to bear to urge an interview about the abortion issue, Ivory went back to her office. She started going through the stack of material she had already begun collecting on her own on the abortion fight, rereading the impassioned arguments, both logical and visceral. Everyone who spoke to the issue seemed threatened by it in some deep and frightening way. This wasn't just another topic. This one struck at the very basis of human life. It was hard to be a human being and not feel some emotional involvement; formulate some point of view.

And behind the individual human beings were the institutions, already polarized along the lines of what they perceived to be their various self-interests. The medical profession, the government, religion . . . and the media.

Institutions. Giant organisms composed of so many cells, each individual deemed expendable so long as the whole survived. Institutions struggling for growth and life, under attack from within and without, in a constant state of flux, never quite what they appeared to be.

Institutions like television networks. Like the Church.

Political, emotional, cynical, idealistic, ambitious, generous, riddled with jealousy and ambition and intrigue, capable of creating beauty or offering hope or inflicting pain.

Institutions built on piles of human bodies.

Abortion is not an issue for institutions to decide, she thought with a fierce anger. We can't be moved about like pawns; we can't substitute mass media influence for individual responsibility. No matter how this issue is ultimately decided, someone is going to be permanently angry over the result.

And I'm not even sure how I feel about it anymore, she realized with astonishment. I took for granted . . . but now I question. I wonder.

Damn it, I have to *know!*

Seventeen

NATHAN DIDN'T CALL to apologize. Of course not. He was the man. It was up to the woman to patch things up—wasn't that part of the code he honored? His role, her role. Each time the phone on her desk rang, she jumped and reached for it too eagerly, only to hear the wrong voice on the other end of the wire.

Nathan Scott was one of the few people on earth to whom she had given her private number at the apartment, but he did not call her there, either. Even Penny—especially Penny—did not have that number. If Penny wanted to speak to Ivory, she had to call the studio and have her message relayed, as Ivory must call the hospital and have her message relayed, either through the nurses' station or to the residence.

With the abortion interview very much on her mind, Ivory called Penny and arranged for the two of them to meet. "I'm off duty tomorrow until noon," Penny told her. "Can you come out here around nine or nine-thirty?"

She must always go to Penny. Penny had never seen the network, her suite, the success that surrounded her. "I'll be there," she agreed.

The two women sat together in the solarium of Allenboro Memorial, surrounded by lush plants and wicker furniture, trappings meant to give the feeling of a resort rather than a battlefield where pain and illness must be fought.

"I'd like to ask your help, Sister," Ivory began rather formally.

Penny smiled, pleased. "Certainly, you know that. What can I do for you?"

"I want to do an interview on 'Headliners' about the whole abortion question: the Supreme Court decision, the Church's position, the pro-abortion groups and the Right to Lifers, the whole thing. From every side, if possible. Perhaps not just one show, but a series exploring every aspect, so there will be plenty of time for viewers to see and hear all of it, enough to get the whole picture. Like so many other issues, the public is being presented with bits and pieces, not the entire package. One side always seems to get the majority of attention on any given program or in any written articles. I want to divide it right down the middle, an exact fifty-fifty, and let everybody have their say."

For once, Penny's composure slipped slightly. "Wow! You certainly have a tall order there!"

"I know. And I'm going to have to fight like . . . like mad to get my producer to go along with it. I just happen to think it's extremely important."

"Oh yes, no doubt about it," Penny said fervently. "Extremely important. But where do I come in?"

"Would you be willing to go on the show and represent the Church's point of view? You have the added involvement of being a nurse, and I thought . . ."

Penny's face was a closed door. Locked and barred. "No. Not under any circumstances. I'm sorry, Ivory."

"Don't you think you could get permission?"

"It isn't that. I'm good at getting permission from the hierarchy, as you know. And I'm sure the Church would want to have its position explained on your program. It's just that I personally would not be willing to publicly condemn abortion."

The sun-filled room seemed to echo with silence. Ivory stared at the woman in the white habit. "You *what?*"

"I'm only speaking for myself, you understand, and I trust this will remain just between us. But I do not agree with the anti-abortion position and I would not be willing to support it."

"My God! I got the idea several months back, from a conversation you and I had, that you might not feel as strongly as you used to about abortion, but I never expected to hear you say what you just did. What changed your mind?"

"Being a nurse in a Catholic hospital. Seeing young women—children, really—come in here with their lives all messed up, children who have every right to expect their Church to care about them and help them, and are told instead that they have to carry and give birth to an unwanted child that will change their futures forever. You argued with me about this many years ago, Ivory; you tried to tell me then that I could save myself a great deal of heartbreak if I didn't go through with the pregnancy."

"And now you wish you'd listened to me?" Ivory could hardly believe what she was hearing.

Penny dropped her voice and glanced around the room. "My life would have been very different. *I* would have been very different."

"I suppose you would have. You might not have wound up in a convent, for one thing."

The nun's face filled with an almost fanatic light and she replied fervently, "God would have put me here anyway! I can see that now, more than ever. It was His plan for me to go into the order and become a nurse, because it's given me an opportunity I wouldn't have had otherwise. I'm in a unique position to counteract much of the evil done to women in the name of love. *Love!*"

"What are you talking about, Sister? What are you doing that's so unique?"

Penny glanced around the solarium again; a guarded, furtive gesture that made Ivory tense with apprehension. When she was satisfied no one was within earshot, the nun said, almost in a whisper, "I'm helping women who find themselves in . . . in a very special kind of situation. Catholic women, most of them just naive young girls, the way I used to be."

Ivory heard Nathan Scott's voice suddenly, an echo at the back of her mind. ". . . policies . . . totally unacceptable for a privately funded Catholic hospital."

She looked intently at Penny, who had always loved secretly breaking the rules while pretending to obey them more devoutly than anyone else. "What do you mean, Sister?"

Penny seemed on the verge of telling her, then something extinguished the light in her eyes as surely as if a switch had been thrown. The nun sat up very straight and said in a formal voice, "I can't discuss this with you, Ivory. I'm afraid I forgot for a moment that you're on the board of directors here."

"That doesn't make any difference between us," Ivory protested, but Penny's walls of defense were already up.

"I appreciate your invitation to appear on 'Headliners,'" she said politely, "but I simply can't do it. Let's leave it at that, shall we? Now, do you have time for a cup of tea with me?"

Now Ivory had an excuse to call Nathan, an excuse other than the apology she would not, could not offer. When he answered the phone and recognized her voice, he sounded as if the quarrel had never happened. That annoyed her, too.

Didn't it hurt him as much as it hurt me? Has he forgotten it already?

She matched his voice with a casual tone of her own. "I wouldn't have bothered you, Nathan, but I just remembered something you hinted to me about Sister Immaculata quite some time ago. I wasn't ready to listen then, but now I'd really like to know, if you wouldn't mind meeting me and discussing it."

"Sure. Are you free for dinner? I'll get us reservations at Wee Willie's."

He took for granted her willingness to go to Wee Willie's; his right to choose the time and place. But she accepted it; it seemed more important to find out about Penny than to continue that painful, no-win argument. Perhaps if she just let herself drop it, they could mend the cracks in their relationship and go on as if nothing had ever happened.

Maybe.

If she was willing to do all the giving in.

All through dinner they made small talk, two people skirting the edges of a swamp, careful not to overstep the boundaries and sink into quicksand. They were both relieved when the meal was finished, their coffee served, and Ivory could begin discussing the third-person matter of Sister Immaculata.

Nathan looked grim. "I've got a pretty good idea what she's doing," he told her, "though I don't have any real proof. And if I did, I don't know what I'd do about it. That friend of yours is running a highly selective kind of abortion service."

"Are you kidding me?"

"Nope. She came to me about it last year, wanted to know if I'd be willing to get involved either as a surgeon or by referring prospective patients. I didn't want any part of it then and I told her so, though she tried pretty hard to convince me."

Ivory found his statement difficult to believe. "But abortion is legal as of right now, Nathan! Women can get abortions on demand. Why on earth would a Catholic nun be involved in such a thing? It doesn't make any sense."

"Catholic women get inconveniently pregnant just like anybody else. Maybe they're not married, or they are and can't afford any more kids, it doesn't matter what the reasons are. The fact is, they're Catholic and the Church forbids abortion. I know you've drifted away from organized religion the same way I have, Ivory, but you must admit it still has a very strong hold on some people."

"No question about it," she agreed.

"So here we have some woman, or more likely a young kid, scared to death, doesn't know what to do, goes to her doctor and describes her symptoms, and hopes like hell he'll tell her it's all a big mistake, she isn't pregnant. Because if she is, her conscience won't let her seek an abortion.

"It happens many, many times in this town. If the doctor is one of those in the network Sister Immaculata has set up, he contacts her and refers his patient to the surgeon she's gotten involved with her in this.

"Instead of coming right out and telling the woman she's pregnant, this surgeon examines her, tells her she has a minor gynecological problem and a D&C will fix her up. No mention of a baby, a fetus. With Sister Immaculata in attendance, they do the job in the surgeon's office or clinic, wherever they've got the thing set up, and when the patient wakes up everything's fine. She's not pregnant and she has no sin on her conscience. She just had a little routine female surgery. And I imagine the patients are desperately eager to believe that.

"Sister Immaculata is deliberately breaking the law of the Church to do what she perceives as helping these women, and I assume if she gets caught there'll be dire consequences for her."

Ivory nodded. "She'd have to leave the order, for starters, and that would be the most cruel thing anyone could do to her. The order is her whole life."

"Yeah, I suspected as much. That's one reason why I haven't said anything to anybody about this. Hell, I don't even know who the surgeon involved is, though I suspect it's a doctor on staff at Allenboro. Someone more amenable to persuasion than I was. But I do think there were a couple of witnesses to at least one of the procedures, student nurses who might be persuaded to talk; if they're not already too far under her influence."

"No wonder Penny was unwilling to discuss this with me," Ivory said. "I'm on the board of directors. I could bring it all crashing down."

"Maybe somebody should," Nathan Scott said. His eyes, usually so warm, were bleak.

The waiter appeared to pour more coffee but neither of them paid any attention to him. "Why do you say that, Nathan?" Ivory asked.

"Have you ever seen an abortion procedure? Well, I have. I could show you photographs from medical journals that would chill your blood. I'd like the business of abortion on demand to be stopped once and for all. If women don't want to have babies, let them prevent conception; we can tell them how to do that. This is just me being purely emotional and not coldly professional at all, Ivory, and it has nothing to do with my religion or lack of it. I just happen to know how beautiful and complex and miraculous—yes, miraculous!—human life is, at any stage of its development, and I don't think somebody has the right to destroy one life at the whim or for the convenience of another. I guess I'm an old-fashioned man, probably the chauvinist pig you've been calling me in your own mind for the past several weeks—ah, I'm right, I can see it in your eyes—but that's how I feel.

"Sister Immaculata and her partner are performing a little

medical sleight-of-hand to salve come Catholic consciences, and if they get found out there'll be a big stink at Allenboro, but I have no doubt they'll make all kinds of noble arguments on behalf of the poor women they've helped. I'm just afraid there aren't enough voices raised on behalf of the unborn children who have an equal right to life, as far as I'm concerned."

He spoke the last words with a note of defiance, as if he expected her—liberated woman Ivory Reynolds—to argue with him. But she had no argument to make.

There was a painful silence, then at last Nathan said, "Well, that's the story. What are you going to do? As I told you, I don't have any concrete proof and I haven't tried to get any. Maybe I've been wrong, closing my eyes to the situation. But when I see the law on one side and morality on the other, and I'm aware my own morality doesn't agree with everyone else's, then what the hell am I supposed to do?"

That's everybody's problem, isn't it, Ivory thought. None of us know what to do. Except Penny. She's doing for others what she needed someone to do for her, taking the responsibility and the sin—if it is sin—onto herself. Sister Immaculata. The saint. Making a virtue of a sin.

She realized she was neatly pleating her linen napkin into tiny, perfect pleats, a nervous outlet for hands that refused to stay quietly folded in her lap. "I don't know what I'm going to do, Nathan," she said in a tired voice. "I'm like you; I don't want to blow the whistle on her, either. I've known Sister Immaculata just about all my life."

"You think she's right, then?"

Ivory stared off across the restaurant, seeing nothing but life and death and hard decisions. "Fifteen years ago, I could have answered that," she told him. "I didn't know anything then, and so I was very certain. Now I'm not so sure."

He reached across the table and covered her hand with

his. His skin was very warm. His eyes, meeting hers, were gentle and kind. "I know this has upset you," he told her. "It puts you on the spot, I realize that. But you wanted to know."

"Yes, I wanted to know."

"Look, don't think about it any more tonight. Come home with me. I've got a new album of smoky old sexy New York-at-night saxophone music. I'll put it on the stereo and we'll pile some cushions on the floor and forget all the prickly moral issues. Be a little immoral. Kick off our shoes. What do you say?"

Oh yes! an inner voice urged. Just close your eyes and say yes. Let him make the decisions, let him tell you what to do. Be soft and feminine and trusting. It would be so easy.

"No," she said. "I'm sorry, Nathan, but I can't. I've got a briefcase full of work waiting for me at home that I just have to get to, all the background reading for the next interview I'm doing on 'Headliners.'"

"Is that really the reason?" he asked directly.

She felt very tired. She wouldn't go over the files in her briefcase and she knew it; she would stretch out on the couch in the living room and stare at the ceiling, smoking cigarettes, drinking coffee, trying to sort out a tangle of thoughts. But she didn't want to lie to him, so she just sat there, looking down at her cup.

He stood and came around the table until he was standing next to her chair. His proximity made her skin tingle. She wouldn't look up. He reached out and laid his hand very gently on her hair. "You're a proud, stubborn lady," he said fondly. "I wish . . . I wish I was unselfish enough to meet you halfway, but maybe I'm just not the man you're looking for. Hell, I wish I had the courage of my convictions enough to expose Sister Immaculata's little abortion business myself! But I've got a career to protect, you understand? There's another doctor involved in this, somebody who no doubt feels there's nothing wrong with abortion and thinks he's doing a real service. My profession doesn't look kindly on one physician who gets another one in trouble. If abortion were illegal . . . but even when it was, not many doctors reported others who did abortions on the side. We all protect each other to save our own skins; it's the way of the world. Nothing's simple any more; nothing's black and white."

She tilted her head back and looked up at him. She saw a kindly, humorous face, strong and weak and human, and her love for him clutched her heart like a hand. "Nothing's black and white . . ." she echoed. Like a nun's habit.

"Can you show me those medical journals you were talking about, Nathan?" she asked briskly, summoning energy from some dead-tired space within herself. "Can you give me a crash course in the medical aspects of abortion, so I know what I'm dealing with, biologically?"

"For 'Headliners,' you mean? You've got plenty of staff researchers who can do that, don't you?"

"Yes, but I like to do my own research as much as I can. I want to do this for myself, so I know."

"No soft cushions on the floor? No smoky saxophone?"

She shook her head. "Not just now. Maybe later."

"Career woman," he said. She could not tell from his tone of voice if he meant it as a criticism or not.

The next day she sat in his office and studied the material he brought her. The complicated text, the all-too-simple pictures. The beautiful, minuscule creature, floating in assumed security in its protective sac, tiny and perfect but not yet recognizably human. Yet alive, by every medical standard. Possessed of flesh and blood, being formed by marvelous workmanship from components already in place. Pictures from later in the developmental stage, with the blue bulge of the eye clearly shown in the outsized fetal head. "It's sucking its thumb," she breathed in wonder, touched by the classic position with its inherent helplessness and trust.

"Yes," said Nathan, looking over her shoulder. "By that stage, most of them are doing that."

"And yet they're aborted?"

"Look at the next pictures."

She turned in sickened disbelief to picture after picture of the products of abortion, the tiny hacked limbs, the soft flesh burned by acid, the mutilated mess ripped from its mother's womb with nothing remaining to show its humanity but a fringe of little toes.

The last picture showed one single disembodied hand, opened like a star.

She turned her head away, fighting tears. "I never visualized it like this," she said in a low voice.

"People don't want to."

He brought her a cup of coffee, so black and bitter it might have been medicine, and it had a bracing effect. He sat on the edge of his desk, swinging his foot, and waited for her to recover her composure.

"What's the right answer, Nathan?" she asked at last.

"I honestly don't know. I only know it's my personal belief, based on my medical training and experience, that life begins with conception. The unborn child, the fetus if you will, has property rights under the law that have been upheld in court for years. It's only the right to life that's been legally taken away from it.

"There is more than adequate information available about the prevention of conception, free for the asking. It's criminal of people to be careless or lazy and then substitute abortion for contraception."

"The best contraception techniques fail sometimes," she reminded him.

"I know that. It's too bad, but there are no one hundred percent guarantees of anything in this life. We all get a bad throw of the dice from time to time and have to make the best of it."

"What about the victims of rape and incest?"

"Do you know what a small percentage that really is? In situations like that, I'd be willing to consider therapeutic abortion. But the hard truth is, most of the women who want abortions don't fall into either category. They just want a surgeon to correct their own mistakes, and to hell with everybody else. Save me; slaughter my child. You've seen the pictures. Those are little people, no matter what dehumanizing label you stick on them. As for population control, hell yes, I'm in favor of that—and that brings us right back to contraception. Not to murder."

Marching into the ovens . . . She shook her head, slinging away the picture it offered.

"How about some lunch?" he suggested. "Get your mind off it."

She had no appetite, but she let him take her to the hospital cafeteria, hold doors open for her, and light her cigarette once they sat down at a table; she waited while he went through the line for both of them and brought her a salad and another cup of coffee. She sat with folded hands, watching him come toward her across the room, balancing two trays and still managing to smile at her when their eyes met.

The congregation awaits the Celebrant.

When the meal was over, Nathan asked, "Well, what are you going to do?"

"About the show? I don't know yet. I still want to do it, more than ever. It's going to take a lot of fighting to get it done the way I envision it."

"I meant what are you going to do as a member of the board of directors here at the hospital, now that you know about Sister Immaculata's sideline? How seriously do you take your responsibilities to the hospital?"

"Rat on a friend? That's never been my style," she told him. "Penny and I always kept each other's secrets. But you're right. I do have responsibilities here. I took the position just as a political move, really; my producer thought it would put me in good with the men at the top of the pyramid at LBS. But I have tried to do my best since I've been involved with the hospital, and I think certainly any other board member who knew what I know would be duty bound to say something about it, friendship or no. False diagnoses are being given, plus the laws of the Church are being broken. But a lot of people would say it's in a good cause. Oh, Nathan, I dunno." She sighed deeply and shook her head. Nathan, sitting next to her, put his arm around her shoulder and pulled her against him, letting the warmth and strength of his body comfort her. But he didn't tell her what to do.

You're a big girl now, Ivory, she reminded herself. Tough. Independent. You wanted it that way. You have to decide what to do all by yourself.

"Well, well, isn't this cozy?" said a familiar voice.

Ivory glanced up to see Penny standing beside their table, looking down at them. She tried automatically to pull away from Nathan but he kept his grip on her shoulders. "Hello, Sister," he said coolly.

"I had no idea you two were so well acquainted," Penny said, with acid in her voice. She gave Nathan a look of intense dislike.

"Ivory and I have been close for quite a while," he told her.

"I see." The nun widened her eyes slightly, obviously surprised. Then she said, to Ivory, "You should really be more selective, my dear. I would have thought you could do better." She turned abruptly on her heel and walked away from them, carrying her tray to the far side of the cafeteria.

"She doesn't like me very much," Nathan commented. "And she didn't like the idea of us being together. Maybe she's afraid I'll tell you about her."

"You've known what she's been doing for a long time," Ivory pointed out, "and you haven't exposed her yet. She should be feeling pretty safe as far as you're concerned."

"How can she feel totally safe?" Nathan asked. "A woman like that must always have the feeling God is looking over her shoulder. You've known her; would you say she's intensely religious?"

"Yes. At least she has been ever since she went into the convent. I see what you mean, Nathan. Now she's breaking the very law she's lived by and it has to be hurting her deeply, yet she feels strongly enough about it to go on. Of course she's afraid of being exposed! She must be really suffering."

"Or crazy," Nathan commented. "There's something not quite right about that woman; she's just too intense about everything. It makes me uncomfortable to be around her, and she knows I feel that way. Bad blood, bad chemistry, something. She made a serious miscalculation when she tried to enlist me for her team."

Ivory looked across the room at the white-robed woman, methodically eating her food, already surrounded by a cluster of other nurses, drawn to her like moths to a flame. Penny, the perennial star.

Sister Immaculata raised her head just then and her eyes locked with Ivory's across the room. The two women stared at each other, each face expressionless. Penny was, perhaps, trying to guess just how much Nathan Scott might have told her. And Ivory was looking at that once-known, once-loved face and wondering if there was any truth in Nathan's guess. After all that had happened to her, was it possible Penny was no longer completely sane? The white, set face, the glittering blue eyes could belong to someone who was determined to hold her power at all costs. Penny had her little empire here, life and death in her hands—literally. If what Nathan had said was true, and some instinct warned her it was, then Penny was playing God, arbitrarily arranging death for unborn infants who would have lived otherwise. Evil done in the name of good.

If abortion were evil.

If.

The question everyone had to answer for themselves.

"If you want my advice," came Nathan's voice, scattering her thoughts like toys on a summer lawn, "I'd keep my mouth shut in the board meetings, at least for a while. Don't make waves. This is a nasty little mess and bringing it out into the open could hurt a lot of people, yourself included, I suspect. Your friends at LBS wouldn't thank you for uncovering a scandal here, would they?"

Don't make waves. She looked at her hands in her lap, not folded now, but clenched, white knuckled. Don't make waves. Play the game; follow the rules. Don't defy the hierarchy; don't argue with the lawyers; accept things as they are; accept, accept.

Penny wasn't accepting. Penny was defying the Church, for her own reasons.

"I have to make my own decisions, Nathan," Ivory told him. "Thanks, anyway." Her voice was crisp and cool.

"Sure. But look, if things ever go against you at LBS and you decide you've had enough of the TV industry . . ." He hesitated. A slow, gentle smile curved his mouth.

"Yes?"

"You know there's a position open as a doctor's wife, if you want it. Full-time. House full of kids, no abortions. How does it sound?"

She made herself stand up so she could look down on him as she asked, "And no outside career?"

"You know how I feel about that; I can't help my feelings."

"And you know mine." She dug in her handbag for enough money to pay for her own lunch and dropped it noisily on the table as he got hastily to his feet. "I'll say one thing for you, Nathaniel Fraser Scott—you've got the worst sense of timing I've ever seen!"

She left him there and walked briskly across the room, her head high and her eyes burning.

Sister Immaculata's eyes followed her.

Eighteen

HAIR WASHED AND BLOWN DRY, pores cleansed and tightened, nails enameled, Ivory Reynolds lay stretched on the daybed in her dressing room with astringent soaked cotton pads over her eyes ("We'll just tighten up that skin a little before you go on-camera, Miss Reynolds") and a light mohair blanket folded across her legs. Below the level of conscious thought she was aware of the faint hum of electronic life upon which the existence of the Lincoln Broadcasting System depended, sustaining the human and nonhuman servitors of the megalith. Air conditioning and fluorescent lights and computers, elevators and cameras and cables running to and from the numberless outlets that poured their energy into the whole complex system.

The electronic hum was a familiar theme to every Manhattanite who occupied an office building or a high-rise. The background music of the city dweller, the familiar sound of heart and arteries and veins. Occasionally that power flickered and failed, a life-support system not to be completely trusted. The lights could go out. The air conditioning could go off, leaving you to breathe your own effluvia in suddenly still air. You could get caught in an elevator, frozen between planes of existence.

You could get trapped in a subway with a thousand other panicked souls.

She lay quietly, ankles crossed, listening to that subliminal hum.

Beyond the door of the dressing room was the faint chatter of Sharon's Selectric, churning out warm, friendly form letters, seemingly personal replies to notes from star-struck fans. Sharon herself was sick today with one of the new viruses proliferating to stay ahead of baffled medical science, and a girl from some typing pool had been pressed into service to handle the routine mail. It would never do for the hostess of "Headliners" to be without a servitor of her own.

Elsewhere in the building were other extensions of Ivory's power. Doris and Morey Feldman and the many friends and allies she had cultivated would be mentioning, whispering into this or that important ear, the value of considering a "Headliners" segment on abortion. Or better yet, why not a whole series? Something to consider. Just a suggestion. A lot of interest out there, growing all the time. Better get on the bandwagon, don't want to get caught behind. No trouble with Mitchellson and Basquette; they'll be tickled pink if the ratings are high enough. Sounded Basquette out about it myself over lunch the other day. Did you know we play handball in the afternoons sometimes? Good guy, open to suggestion. Do you think Ivory'd do it?

Power, carefully used, carefully targeted.

Ivory lay with crossed ankles and folded hands, aware of the expanding limits of her power.

Power, of itself, was amoral, neither good nor evil. Like the power of Popes and princes, the power of the television industry was nothing more than a tool to be used. After a lifetime of being at the end of the chain of command, I have power, Ivory thought. And I'm learning how to use it.

How can Nathan ask me to give that up?

And why can't I have it both ways—a husband and family as well as a career? Other women do. All that fighting we did back in the sixties, all that struggling for women's rights and women's lib, there's a whole generation benefiting from that now. Sharing household chores and child-raising and all the rest of it with their husbands, while going ahead with their own careers. Maybe they get a little tired sometimes, but they have it all, don't they? They have it both ways?

Except not very many of them are of my generation. Ours was the war—theirs is the victory.

She lay at the heart of a power grid and thought about the long, hard way she had traveled, and the way Nathan Scott's slow smile lit candles in his eyes.

The intercom buzzed, startling her. She pushed the mohair blanket aside and sat up, reaching for the phone.

"Miss Reynolds? There's a lady for you on line two, she gave her name as Sister Immaculata."

"Thank you." Ivory pressed the lighted button and heard the familiar voice with a touch of surprise. It was unlike Penny to telephone her.

"Ivory, I need to see you," Penny began. "We have something very important to discuss; can you come over here this afternoon?"

Ivory looked around at her beautiful, perfectly appointed dressing room, the satin chairs, the shelves filled with the latest books, the collection of framed and inscribed photographs of herself with celebrities and statesmen. She listened to the soft rush of conditioned air.

"I can't get away this afternoon, Sister," she said. "I'm doing an interview this evening and I have to be here and ready to go on-camera. Can you come to LBS?"

There was silence at the other end of the line. Ivory urged, "I know you'll need to have another nun come with you, of course, but perhaps someone . . ."

"That won't be necessary," Penny said. "I can make arrangements to come alone as soon as I'm off duty."

Of course you can, Ivory thought. For the Pennys of the world, special arrangements and exceptions can always be made. But for once you're going to have to come to me if you want to see me, Sister Immaculata. You're going to have to come to my turf. Sometimes those of us who are your everyday, standard-issue human beings—not saints at all—have to show off, just a little. Sometimes we have to say: Look at me; I made it, too!

You're not a very nice girl, Imagene, she told the face in her bathroom mirror. But it wasn't Imagene's face, it was Ivory's, and it looked back at her with a self-satisfied smugness she could not condemn. I may not be a nice girl, but I've made myself a damned handsome woman, Ivory's lifted eyebrow reminded her. Nice girls don't necessarily finish first anyway. Would you say that Penny is nice?

She thought of the file locked away in her rosewood desk. The file labeled ENDICOTT: subtitled ELAINE; KELLAM.

She checked her hair and face one more time to make certain everything was perfect, then went into the dressing room to wait for Penny.

Within the hour, the security guard called to announce her. "Send her right on up, please, Mike," she told him. "And give her specific directions; she's never been here before. I'll have my girl meet her in the foyer and bring her the rest of the way."

The visitor must always be accompanied by a member of the community.

There was a discreet tap on the door—Sharon would have knocked with a doubled fist—and Sister Immaculata was ushered into the private suite of Ivory Talbot Reynolds. Her manner did not betray the urgency that had brought her outside the walls of the hospital; she was composed and lovely as always, her smile gracious, the warmth carefully measured out by the milligram to be appropriate to the occasion.

She did not seem to take any notice of her surroundings. She did not even glance at the photographs of Ivory with potentates and movie stars.

"It's nice of you to see me on short notice like this," she began graciously, seating herself on a straight-backed chair. Ivory curled up on the daybed, feet tucked beneath her, determined to appear relaxed and very much at home.

Penny got right to the point. "When I saw you in the hospital with Doctor Scott, the two of you were having a very serious conversation before I interrupted. Were you talking about me, by any chance?"

"What makes you think that? As Nathan told you, we've been friends for a long time; we've talked about a lot of things."

"Close, he said," Penny replied, being precise. "Doctor Scott said you were close, and I assume he meant more than just a friendship." There was a hard edge to her voice, almost like anger.

"I really don't see that it's any business of yours," Ivory said pleasantly, being careful to smile.

"We're friends and I feel protective toward you."

"Really? Isn't that interesting? Nathan once had much the same reaction when your name came up."

"You have discussed me, then!" Penny leaned forward in her chair, the nun's serenity replaced by a tension like a live wire. Ivory, whose business it was to read and interpret body language, noted the change. "What did he tell you about me?" Penny demanded to know with the authoritarian voice of a head nurse. "Did he discuss our . . . personal relationship, or . . ." she paused again, ". . . business?"

Ivory was disconcerted. "What do you mean, 'personal relationship'?"

Penny narrowed those beautiful blue eyes slightly. "There was a time when Doctor Scott made it obvious his feelings for me were those of a man for a woman he, ah, desired. As a professed nun, of course, I had to make it clear to him that the intimacies he sought would be impossible. He did not take my rejection very well, I'm afraid."

"Are you trying to tell me Nathan Scott made a pass at you?" Ivory asked incredulously.

Penny looked at her from the vast, haughty distance of the always beautiful, the always desired. "Yes. It's happened before. I always seem to be cursed with that problem; even the habit isn't perfect protection. How lucky you are to have avoided all that."

Ivory gritted her teeth. "I find it hard to believe of Nathan Scott," she said. "He's a very decent man."

"He's a very attractive man in his own way," Penny commented. "A sensual man, one might say." She went on talking about him, describing him as if compelled to keep his name and face before her. Ivory, watching, was reminded of the human need to discuss one's beloved. Once Penny had spoken of no one but God and her relationship to Him. Now she seemed obsessed with discussing Nathan Scott. Given her background, was it possible the nun had at last fallen in love after all, in spite of her vows?

When had the rules applied to Penny if she chose to disregard them?

Nathan had said she . . . how had he put it? . . . "used her considerable charms" on him at one time, to gain something she wanted. To gain, according to him, his cooperation with her involvement in abortion. But suppose it were more than that? Suppose she had actually propositioned him—Penny, who had always loved flirting with the forbidden—and he had rejected her physically?

Or maybe it was as Penny said, and he had made the advances. But the more she studied Penny's face, the more convinced she became that it was the nun who had been rejected. The anger still simmered just beneath the surface; it glowed in her skin; it flashed in her eyes. Penny had once more reached out to the forbidden and her pain at Nathan's refusal to respond had turned into rage when she saw him with Ivory. Plain little Imagene Tutt, who was not, never could be, any competition.

"Men like Nathan Scott don't care about anyone but themselves," Penny was saying. "His only interest is in furthering his career, and he doesn't care how he does it, if you ask me. As soon as I realized the two of you were involved, I knew I had to talk to you about him and warn you. He has no morals at all; he'll use you and then dump you. Listen to me and stay as far away from him as you can, Ivory—Nathan Scott's no good for you."

"Really." Ivory's voice was noncommittal.

"I mean it, and I care about you or I wouldn't be telling you this. I don't know what kind of line he's given you, trying to get close to you, but I can assure you he's the sort who'd do whatever he could to butter up somebody on the board whom he thought could help his career. It's no secret he has his eye on the post of chief of staff when old Doctor Fitzgerald retires in the fall."

"And you think Doctor Scott has been playing up to me to get my support when the time comes to appoint a new chief?" Ivory felt cold and hard inside. Penny was blithely assuming no man could be interested in her, no man could care for her—not after he's seen the exquisite blond woman facing her across the quiet, humming room.

Penny was too involved with her own feelings to be aware of Ivory's resentment. Once she would have seen it and rushed to salve it with that eager sensitivity that had been hers, but those days were gone. Now all her awareness was focused in the struggle in which she was involved. "Doctor Scott will go to any length to get control of the hospital," she told Ivory, "and I will go to any length to keep that from happening. I know he's telling lies about me—the man's morally depraved; you've got to understand that—and I just want to know what he's saying so I can be prepared. I won't let him discredit me. I'm needed; I can do too much good."

The fanatic light was in her eyes, heightening her beauty. Ivory had to ask the question; she had to be sure.

"Nathan tells me you're arranging certain surgeries on your own that are against hospital policy," she said, choosing her words very carefully.

The blue eyes flashed. Penny stood up abruptly, a movement alien to the grace she had always shown. When she spoke, her voice was high-pitched with nervousness and defiance. "I told you the man would do anything he could to destroy me! Is he spreading that story all over town?"

"I don't think he's spreading it at all; he only told me because I insisted on knowing what was wrong between the two of you. Is it true—about the operations?"

"Nathan Scott doesn't understand!" Penny said vehemently.

"But you are arranging abortions for Catholic women by getting some doctor to give them a false diagnosis to ease their consciences, then taking the fetus without ever telling them they were pregnant? Unauthorized abortions? That's playing God, Penny! You have no right to make that kind of arbitrary decision, nor to encourage a doctor to break the law by performing an unauthorized procedure!"

"I have every right. I understand these women. I can tell when a pregnancy would be a disaster. Unmarried girls, scared to tell their parents they've been sleeping with a boy. Harried mothers with too many children already. They can't even turn to their Church. But I can help them, and I do. I have a very special mission in life and I've been put in just the right place to enable me to do it."

Her face was radiant. I can never be what she is, Ivory

thought. Nothing touches her; nothing destroys her. She can go through the utmost depravity and come out looking like that—so beautiful, so assured—it isn't fair.

"Abortion is a mortal sin in the eyes of the Church, Penny," Ivory reminded her unnecessarily, "and even if it is legal today, I'm certain the way you're doing it isn't. Those women should be told and not aborted without their actual permission. That's an appalling responsibility to take on yourself!"

"That *man* has turned you against me, hasn't he?" Penny accused. "Has he convinced you to tell the board about this?"

"Don't you think it's my responsibility to tell them?"

"Responsibility! You were a nun; you know that our responsibility is to the helpless of the world who have nothing to depend on but God's love. Except for you, the board of directors at the hospital is a clique of self-righteous old men who want to keep women in the bondage of the Middle Ages, powerless and in childbed. Don't look so surprised! You used to say the same things about the hierarchy of the Church.

"But my responsibility isn't to the board of directors, it's to the people who really need me. Don't you see? All that dogma that holds Catholic women paralyzed was created by men for just that purpose! God doesn't want it that way! God wants them free, and I am privileged to be in a position to help."

"You think you are a direct instrument of God's will?" Ivory asked incredulously.

The proud lift of Penny's head was so familiar. She had always known she was special. "I have been given a unique opportunity," she replied with assurance. "I can sacrifice myself for others. I can actually take their sins onto myself, in a way, as . . ." She faltered, her eyes roaming restlessly around the room before they came back to Ivory's. ". . . as a propitiation for my own sins."

Ivory could see it clearly in her mind. The manila folder. ENDICOTT.

Penny's eyes were moving again, going back for a second look at something only briefly noticed. She took a step toward Ivory's desk so she could examine the framed color photograph prominently displayed there, as loved ones are often displayed on desks. It was not a black-and-white glossy of Ivory Reynolds with a movie star or statesman; it was a candid snapshot of Ivory and Nathan Scott on a swing in Central Park. Ivory was on his lap, head thrown back, hair loose and blowing, and they were laughing.

It was the sort of picture lovers cherish.

Penny studied it closely, then turned to Ivory. "If any charges are brought against me before the board," she said slowly, measuring the effect of her words, "I'll bring charges myself. I'm a nun; people are very inclined to believe my word over the word of a layman. Those pompous Catholic men on the board have a reverence for the habit, you know. And I have friends, *good* friends, who will back up anything I say." She accented the word "good" as if drawing a line under it and using that line to separate Ivory from those she now considered her trusted allies. "If I should accuse one of the doctors on the staff of making sexual advances to me . . . explicit sexual advances . . . that man's career would be ruined like that!" She snapped her fingers. "This may be a liberated age, but there are still certain moralities a man can't disregard. How badly would it hurt your precious Nathan Scott to be known as . . ." she lowered her voice, deliberately injecting something salacious into it, whispering dirty talk with malicious pleasure, ". . . as the kind of man who would try to ram his cock up a nun's ass when he cornered her in a hospital linen room?"

"He didn't!" Ivory exclaimed.

"I can produce witnesses who say he did. They'll say I screamed and they opened the door just in time to stop him."

"They'd lie for you?" Ivory asked, already knowing the answer from the look of triumph on Penny's face.

"Let's just say I suggest you forget Scott's vicious allegations about me, and I won't make any charges either."

"But you'll go on with the . . . abortions? You and your friend? Or friends? Have you gotten several people involved in this?"

"I know what's right and wrong, better than you do," Penny said with finality.

How could she be so certain? What must it be like to be so sure? For Sister Immaculata, everything obviously *was* black and white, as if God Himself were dictating directly to her.

"Tell me something honestly," Ivory requested. "I promise it won't go beyond this room. Just how much power are you trying to get at the hospital, and for what?"

Penny seemed mildly amused. "I'm not trying to get power, Ivory," she said. "I have it. Don't you realize that? God put it in my hands by giving me the ability to influence others, and I'm starting to use it for the purposes He intended."

Ivory felt chilled. More than just the complicated question of abortion was involved here. The nun had obviously developed a strong sphere of influence within the hospital. She was the kind of charismatic leader who could persuade followers to break rules, defy laws, ignore morality itself if she chose. "What purposes?" Ivory asked hoarsely.

"There is so much that's wrong with the world as a result of the lusts and greed of men," Penny told her, her mouth twisting briefly into an ugly shape of hate before resuming its customary placid smile. "So many unwanted children. More people than the planet can support. We know how to take care of that quite humanely, of course, but *they* won't let us do it. It has to be done in secret to circumvent the hierarchy. You understand.

"There are so many times when abortion—or sterilization,

or euthanasia—would fix everything; don't you see that? I have the gift of persuading others to help me, and eventually we'll be able to accomplish quite a lot. Yes, quite a lot. It's so easy. Just a few private moments and there's another mess straightened out, with no one the wiser. It's so easy in a hospital.

"But I can't let you interfere, now that I've found what God wants me to do. If you try to stop me, I'll smear your Nathan Scott with the sort of nastiness that can cripple a man in his profession. Stories like that are never forgotten, not when doctors are involved. People like their doctors to be gods, you know," she said. She did not seem aware of the irony of her statement.

"Abortions," Ivory said as if to herself. "Sterilization. Euthanasia." Lies and secrets. Randolph Reynolds. Old people being neatly tidied up and thrust out of life. June Bug Colby.

"In time," Penny said complacently, "we will be able to do more and more. Don't you see why I can't let you interfere? We were both helpless once, you and I, but I'm not helpless anymore. I have power now; God has given it to me so I can do His real will, and I won't let anything or anyone stop me. Religion has become a way of keeping people in bondage, but I can set them free. And I know in my heart you're with me on this, now that you understand." She paused, locking Ivory's eyes with her own. "Now that you understand *all* the ramifications." She deliberately looked at Nathan's picture again, then turned with all her old grace and went to the door.

With her hand on the knob, she said over her shoulder, "I really do have to go now. I'm sure I've taken too much of your time. But I'm glad we had this little talk. I always knew I could count on you, 'Gene." She smiled radiantly. "Always."

There was a swirl of white through the doorway and she was gone.

Ivory sat bolt upright on the edge of the daybed, staring at the closed door. At last she made herself get up and go to her desk. She unlocked the bottom-left-hand drawer, the one always kept locked, and took out the thick file labeled ENDICOTT. It had been a long time since she read that file; she had brought it from Texas with her, carried it around like some sort of talisman, locked it away and tried not to think about it, but it had been there all the time, waiting. The past, waiting for both of them, still exerting its influence.

The manila folder was limp, its stiffness exhausted by time. There were smudged fingermarks on the light-colored edges. We all have fingermarks on us, Penny, she thought sadly. We are touched and molded and changed by so many people.

Barney Tutt and Penny Endicott and Randy Reynolds and Nathan Scott. And all the others. How many others, for Penny?

She opened the file. The material about the girl who had been Elaine Endicott was on top: a brief biography, a record of awards for scholarship and music and sodality leadership, a confirmation portrait, a listing of the graduating class of St. Mary's Academy. Not much to reveal a life.

It was the information and the newspaper clippings about ENDICOTT: KELLAM that gave the file its size and weight. Black headlines with their lip-smacking recounting of perversion and tragedy, still as startling to Ivory as they had been on the day she first discovered them while researching the lurid history of Texas criminal justice.

It was all there. In his pursuit of power, his eagerness to join the most wealthy, most prestigious inner circle of Texas, Kellam Endicott had always sought publicity. There were numberless stories of his relationships with prominent politicians; his business successes; a public photohistory of himself with his family. Kellam Endicott, the devoted husband and father.

She flipped through the collection, seeking the chronicle of the final year before the scandal broke. There was a mention in the society section of the Anson *Bugle* about the Endicotts' sudden trip to Europe just before Elaine was to have attended her high school commencement, and then a thick packet of clippings from the European tabloids that loved to recount the excesses of rich visiting tourists. Those she took from the file and set aside on her desk.

Underneath them were the stories of the return of Kellam Endicott and his wife, alone—no mention of Penny now. And then a brief announcement that Mrs. Endicott had checked into a private sanitarium near San Antonio to convalesce from "an undisclosed chronic illness."

It was while she was in that latest institution that news of her husband's arrest reached her and broke her, what little remained of the woman to be broken. She hanged herself from the hinge of a closet door, and a newspaper was found beneath her dangling feet, the headline screaming PROMI-NENT EXECUTIVE INDICTED FOR CHILD MOLESTING!

There were other headlines; Ivory only glanced at them. "Kellam Endicott, shown at right with governor's aide, is accused of nineteen counts of statutory rape. Prosecutor alleges victims were eleven to fifteen years of age, and were mostly daughters of Endicott's friends and associates."

How much had Penny known about this? Both she and Penny had still been in their novitiate when the story broke. A dry voice in Ivory's head reminded her: *A novice nun need not concern herself with worldly affairs. You will see no newspapers during your novitiate; if there is anything Mother Superior feels you need to know, she will inform you herself. We must be dead to the world and it to us.*

Need to know. No one had told her about Kellam Endicott's trial and conviction; there was certainly no need for her to know. And very possibly Penny had been protected from the news as well—Penny, whom everyone loved. The gates had already closed behind her, the break was final and she wanted it that way. Mother Superior would have shielded her, kept her safe and apart in her new identity.

Ivory scooped the material back into the file and thrust it into its drawer, turning the key with a savage twist of her wrist. Then she gazed thoughtfully at the little pile of clippings she had set aside.

She telephoned Nathan Scott. "I just had a long talk with Sister Immaculata," she told him, "and I'm convinced she must be stopped. She, of all people, shouldn't be playing God with the lives of others. Will you go before the board with me?"

"Ivory . . . I've got a career to think of. And so do you."

"Yes, I know." She looked around at the elegant suite; she looked down at her manicured hands, glittering with jewels she had lovingly selected and bought for herself. For the first time, she realized just how tenuous was her hold on the things she had fought for and earned; an angry network executive such as Mitchellson could take them all away as quickly as a habit could be removed from a nun.

And what would remain, underneath?

"I know," she repeated. "But I know Sister Immaculata, too. And I've got to speak out. I just want to know if you'll stand with me. There's one other thing I have to tell you though, Nathan—she's threatened to make some pretty ugly accusations against you if I say anything. She thinks she can blackmail me, both of us, into silence. Can she?"

"What kind of accusations?"

She told him and then listened to a hollow silence. After a long pause, Nathan Scott chuckled, but without humor. "Hell hath no fury like, I guess," he said bitterly. "Of course I didn't do that, Ivory, but I suspect she's got friends who will swear I did. She's built up quite a network in that hospital; there are people there who think she's practically perfect."

"Then that's all the more reason she should be stopped, Nathan; can't you see that? If you and I speak out together . . ."

"I think that would be a mistake for both of us. Damn it, I'd like to sit down with you and talk this thing through, but I'm on duty tonight. How about tomorrow evening? You don't have a show and I'll be off duty."

"The next day is a board meeting, Nathan," she reminded him. "That's when I want to bring up the matter of the secret abortions. You said there might be a couple of witnesses?"

"Wait, listen! Don't make any moves until I have a chance to talk to you, okay? Let's not rush into anything, Ivory."

She could feel the frost in her voice as it passed her lips. "Are you afraid to put everything on the line for something you believe in? I thought you were against abortion."

"I am, but . . . hell yes, I'm afraid."

"Well, I'm not!" she told him, and slammed down the phone.

She went into the bathroom and looked at the face in the mirror. Liar, liar, she said to it. You're scared to death. You've just made it to the top and you're about to take the risk of throwing it all away.

You can always get what you want if you're willing to do whatever it takes. Even fight dirty. Even hurt someone you used to love.

Oh, Nathan, why couldn't you just come right out and say you'd back me up! Be brave and gallant and . . . and all the things I want you to be.

Only nobody's perfect, are they? And if somone pretends to be, look out. Maybe I'd be very lucky to settle for a human man with some human flaws.

She gathered up the little pile of clippings she had taken out of the Endicott file and put them in her handbag before she left.

Nineteen

MONIQUE WAS DELIGHTED to hear Nathan Scott was coming for dinner. "Will he be staying overnight?" she asked with a Gallic glint in her eyes.

"I don't know." Ivory still found it hard to answer such questions; she appreciated the casual freedom but was simultaneously embarrassed by it.

Amused at her employer's discomfiture, Monique smiled to herself with the wisdom of a woman who presides over mysteries. "I'll fix sweetbreads with white wine and brandy sauce," she said. "He'll stay. What are you going to wear?"

"I don't know. That peacock-blue brocade caftan, I suppose. With a silk teddy."

Monique put her hands on her ample hips. "Those teddies are all in the bag to be washed and I haven't gotten to them yet. My meringues weren't working out today; I spent my time on them. Besides, I didn't know what was clean and what wasn't, the way you wad up your clothes and cram them into your drawers and then just fold the top layer so it all looks neat. You're not fooling me." She gave a superior sniff.

I'm not even fooling myself, Ivory thought. Lists and labels and a neat surface.

"I don't mind if you're a bit of a slob," Monique told her. "It is not so good for you anyway, all this driving yourself. Makes you thin and tense. Bad for your liver."

Nathan arrived on time, for once, with a bouquet of flowers and a shy smile. Monique fussed over him, bringing him a drink immediately, settling him in the most comfortable chair, admiring the cut of his slightly rumpled suit. After she left the room to get a tray of hot canapés, Ivory said, "Monique's been annoyed with me because you haven't been here for a while."

"I haven't been invited," Nathan reminded her. "You like to keep this place for special occasions, don't you? And there haven't been many special occasions for us lately."

She thought she heard a subtle censure in his voice, as if whatever tensions were between them were entirely of her making. How like a man, she thought, to avoid accepting any blame himself. But then, because she was Ivory, she admitted to herself that she didn't want to accept blame, either. She didn't want to give in. Let him do it.

If he loved me, he'd do it, and let me be selfish. And he wouldn't make me feel guilty about being selfish, either. And it would only rain at night and no one would ever get cavities and all the gentle things of the earth, the rabbits and the babies and the little girls, would be cherished and protected.

Stupid. It just ain't gonna be that way, and you know it!

The dinner was delicious but they ate it in near-silence, with a glass wall between them. When she finished serving the coffee, Monique set out a crystal decanter of brandy and two snifters, then made a conspicuous departure to her own room, shutting the door loudly. Ivory and Nathan sat together, but not touching, on the long couch, facing the view, and the night city spread below them offering all the sparkling temptations of the world.

Each waited for the other to begin conversation. They sipped their brandy and stared out at the lights. Ivory, who was better at waiting, won.

"So what are you going to say to the board tomorrow?" Nathan asked, not looking at her.

"What I have to."

"What's that supposed to mean?"

"A long time ago, Nathan, I spoke out for some things I believed in—then—and got in a lot of trouble. So I said to myself: Okay, lesson learned, from now on you play the game the way the winners do. Follow the rules. Give people what they want—particularly those people who have power over your life. And it seemed to work pretty well. But lately I've felt the real me surfacing and wanting to have more of a say."

He looked at her now, lifting his eyebrows slightly. "And who is the 'real you'? I guess it's too much to hope she's a wife and mother."

"Maybe; maybe those are parts. But there are a lot of parts that aren't me, that I put together from someone else's personality, and I have to excise those and come to terms with what's left. Does any of this make any sense to you?"

She had curled up in the angle of the couch, and for once her hands were not neatly folded in her lap but were balled into fists and tucked in the bend of her knees.

"I suppose so," he told her. "Does any of this have anything to do with what you're telling the board tomorrow?"

Chief of staff, she thought, the words flashing electrically across her consciousness. He doesn't want to be involved in a mess that would cost him his chances of being chief of staff. Ambition.

Like mine.

Cowardice.

Like mine.

She bit her lips and made herself sit up a little straighter. "I've discovered that I have a very active conscience. Not because I'm a devout Catholic anymore, but because I'm a human being sharing this spaceship we call a planet with a lot of other human beings, and I have to accept some responsibility for my fellow passengers. I have to use what power I have to help where I can."

That's what Penny thinks she's doing, too, a voice inside reminded her, but she ignored it and went on. "As part of my maturing process, without my even being aware of it, I seem to have changed some of my views. I used to think abortion was an answer for a woman in trouble; now I feel it's a very bad answer. No matter what the law says, life is sacred, and no human life, once lost, can ever be replaced exactly as it was or might have been. I've done 'Headliner' shows on random violence in the streets, on wife beating and on child abuse, and I see abortion as just one more example of the low value we've come to place on human life. Maybe when we made abortion legal that was the message we were giving out. When you condone one kind of murder, you open the door to many kinds.

"Even when that murder is done in the name of kindness, it has widespread and destructive effects. When Sister Immaculata convinced others to cooperate with her in this, she was damaging them. Tomorrow I intend to stop her, one way or the other, and I want you to make a commitment to stand with me if I need you."

"If she makes the charges she threatened, you know what it will do to my career, Ivory." He shifted uncomfortably on the couch. "My parents sacrificed a hell of a lot to put me through school and see me become a doctor; how could I explain it to them if I threw it all away now? They're old and they're proud of me; I'm all they've got. Until the grandkids," he added, putting in the screws.

All our lives are so tied up to other lives, she thought with resentment. We're never really free. We grow old still carrying on incomplete dialogues with our parents, trying to court them, to justify ourselves, patch up the wounds or balance the scales. And it can't be done.

It can't be done, Penny. In the end, all that is left is simple and primitive. Good or evil, right or wrong. We each have to choose.

"You're the one who told me you wanted abortion stopped," Ivory reminded him. "Opening up a scandal at Allenboro Memorial could hurt me a lot, too, you know. But I have to go through with it. Aren't you man enough to take your lumps with me?"

He groaned in exasperation and reached for her almost blindly, pulling her against his chest. His body was so warm; she slumped against him with eyes closed, wanting desperately to give in and stay there, to let the battles of the world go on without her. At a comfortable distance, in that city of light beyond the windows.

"Oh baby," Nathan murmured, his lips against her hair. "You really are a scrapper, aren't you? Who'd have guessed it? You even fight dirty."

Yes, she thought, I can fight dirty. She pushed out of his arms reluctantly so she could see his face. "What about it, Nathan? Will you testify if I ask you?"

His face was unreadable. Nathan had a private inner place to which he could retreat without taking her, just as Penny did, and she felt left out. "Why be in such a hurry, Ivory?" he asked carefully, feeling his way among the words. "How about giving it a little time and a lot more thought. Maybe there's a way to handle it without a direct confrontation that could get everybody hurt."

Now was the time to tell him about the file. She almost did, then bit off the words. Capitulation. Doing it his way.

Oh please God, for once let him agree to do it *my* way!

"I can't put it off any longer, Nathan. I've talked to Sister Immaculata and I think she has other plans; she has more good works she means to do without authorization, and she has to be stopped now. She's got a warped vision of herself dispensing some kind of heavenly justice to right the wrongs of the world!" Her voice was shaking with passion, but she couldn't help it.

It was his turn to study her face, searching for meaning.

"Are you after Sister Immaculata for some reason I don't know about? You two go back a long way. Is there some sort of rivalry between you, and is this your way of winning?"

"No!" she answered quickly; too quickly. For once, she had given herself away. "Well, yes," she amended. "There is a . . . kind of competition between us, but she never knew it. I was always the one competing. But that's not what this is about."

There was an angry set to his jaw. "Then what is it about?"

You have been a Bride of Christ. Live in such a way as to make your Bridegroom proud of you.

"It's about abortion," she told him. "That's all."

"I don't think it's that simple. It looks like a catfight to me, and I'm the one who's going to get caught in the middle. Or is that okay with you, too, because I wasn't willing to be Mr. Ivory Talbot Reynolds?"

"I'm not hitting back at you for that, Nathan!" she protested. "I love you!"

"Well, you've got a damned funny way of showing it. I'll tell you this right now, Ivory. I wear the pants in my family and I don't want any woman telling me what I should do."

"And I don't like being bossed by any man!" she flung back at him.

They glared at each other. "When did I ever boss you?"

"All the time," she heard herself saying. "All the goddamn time!"

"I don't think there's any point in my staying here if that's the way you feel," he said. But there was something else in his eyes.

"You can go home whenever you want to. The door isn't locked." She got to her feet and he automatically stood up as well.

That seemed to make him angrier. "Well, it should be, damn it. This city isn't safe for women who leave their doors unlocked."

She was suddenly back on the street, the dark, cold street, with the men closing in on her and the pounding of her heart shaking her body. "I can take care of myself!" she flung at him.

"Can you?" He stepped forward and grabbed her so suddenly she knew a moment of genuine panic. He held her with a measured strength that stopped just short of hurting her, but kept her captive as he carried her into the bedroom. Crushed against him, head thrown back, she could see a muscle clenching and relaxing rhythmically in his lean jaw.

He dropped her on the bed. "You're a woman, Ivory," he said, looking down at her as he unbuttoned his shirt. "I'm a man. There's a big biological difference, and I don't care if it isn't fashionable to recognize that difference anymore. It's still there and all your tough talk won't change it. You don't have to play little girl for me—except when you want to, and sometimes you *do* want to, whether you acknowledge it or not. But you don't have to go to the other extreme, either.

"There's nothing wrong with being a little bit dependent on somebody. I love you, and that makes me dependent on you to some extent, emotionally. I'm not afraid of that. If you have to hide behind walls and shut me out because you're so damned scared of being equally dependent on me, then we don't have any chance at all. Maybe we ought to just call this one for the road."

Then his hands were on her, pulling away the brocade caftan, jerking the pins out of her hair. There was something cold and implacable about him, as if the act of love were part of a set ritual and had to be performed in this certain style, with no deviation into the tenderness they had always shared before. He was not brutal, he could never be brutal, but he insisted on being in total control.

He left the lights on so she could see him above her, his broad shoulders pinning her to the bed. His eyes locked with hers and he watched her with a curious, tense, waiting look until passion made its own claim and his eyes closed involuntarily, his mouth twisted by helpless pleasure. Against her will, Ivory was carried with him into a place where she had no will at all and the surrender itself was part of the ritual, and part of the shuddering, incredibly sweet joy that lasted forever and ended too soon.

Afterward, he wouldn't look at her. He got up, took a cigarette from his shirt pocket, and lit it without asking if he could, knowing she hated smoking in the bedroom, ignoring her rule. He smoked the cigarette to the end, standing beside the bed looking down at her again, and neither of them said anything. She tried to keep her face set and unyielding, knowing the battle was not over. When the cigarette was a glowing stub, he carried it into the bathroom and flushed it down the toilet. Then he came back to her, still without speaking, and got back in the bed.

She lay waiting until he reached for her and then she tried to pull away, but he clamped his hands like iron on her shoulders. "No!" he said, in a hoarse voice.

In the morning, when she awoke, there was nothing left of him in her bed but the smell of sex on satin and the scent of his aftershave on her pillow.

The next morning Nathan Scott's car was just pulling into the doctors' parking lot as Ivory got out of the taxi in front of Allenboro Memorial. He started to call out to her but then he stopped himself; she probably hated him this morning. He watched as she stood at the foot of the steps, looking up at the building. He saw her square her shoulders and take a deep breath, and he thought how vulnerable she looked, there in the sunlight. Stubborn lady. He could tell from the way she carried herself that she was going to go in there and blow the whistle on Sister Immaculata, all right. And without a doubt, Sister Immaculata would take swift revenge. By tonight the whole hospital would be buzzing with a scandalous story about Doctor Scott and the head nurse; a story that might haunt him for the rest of his career. As for Ivory, how would the president of LBS take this? Allenboro Memorial could choose a different chief of staff, and "Headliners" could get a new host. Only the individuals were expendable.

Then he watched the slender woman reach the top of the steps and open the door, disappearing from his sight, and suddenly he knew that the individuals weren't expendable at all. At least, that one wasn't. Not to him.

Ivory followed the long corridor marked with strips of colored tape, meant as pathways to various parts of the hospital. Yellow for radiology, red for surgery, blue for administration . . . she chose the blue, walking with her head down and her eyes on the tape. She didn't want to see the faces around her.

She paused at the door to the conference chamber where the board meeting would be held. It was still early; no one would arrive for another twenty minutes. The polished mahogany table gleamed in readiness, pads of paper and sharpened pencils waiting. She looked at it in silence for a long time, then passed by.

The little office of the head nurse was at the very end of the hall. She knocked once and opened the door without waiting to be summoned.

Penny sat on the other side of a small desk, its papers and supplies neatly arranged at right angles. She glanced up when Ivory entered and noticed the attaché case under Ivory's arm immediately. "Have you something to present to the board this morning?" she asked in an icy voice.

"Perhaps. But you and I need to talk first. Privately."

Penny swiftly crossed the room and locked the door. Her gestures were not so graceful now; they were abrupt, almost jerky. She was watching Ivory closely. "I trust you're not going to do anything this morning that you . . . and your Doctor Scott . . . are going to regret?"

"I'm hoping I won't have to speak to the board about the procedures you've been arranging. Or those you plan to arrange."

Penny gave her a bland look. "What on earth are you talking about?" Her voice was uninflected.

"You know what I mean. The world hasn't treated you very kindly, has it, and you've decided to start arranging things your own way. You began with aborting babies you didn't think should be born, but you won't stop there.

"You're right; you do have a great gift for influencing people, and I have no doubt you've got at least one doctor who's willing to go along with . . ."

"A woman doctor," Penny said smugly. "Fitting, isn't it? But there will be more. We're only just beginning. The men who've been running the Establishment have made such a mess of things, letting people suffer unnecessarily, it's time those of us with true compassion took over. And even some of the men themselves will join us. You'll see. I've been working on them. Why, there are doctors right here in this hospital who . . ."

It was Ivory's turn to interrupt. "No, Sister. Penny. I can't let this go on. You may have the best intentions in the world, but your judgment is warped and you'd be the last person to realize that. If abortion is necessary, or euthanasia is a kindness, you're not the one to decide. I want you to stop this right now and release whatever hold you've got on those people who've been helping you. Give it up, Penny. You can't play God."

"I'm not playing God! I'm doing His will, I tell you! If you try to interfere, I'll smear Nathan Scott and you, too. I'll get you thrown off the board here. Just watch me!"

Ivory's stomach felt cold. Penny could do just that. Who would be believed, if it all came out in the open?

"That threat works two ways, Penny," she made herself say.

"What do you mean? What can you do to me? Tell about my unfortunate pregnancy all those years ago, or the fact that I was raped by my own father? That would only get me more sympathy. Don't you know that?"

Ivory set her attaché case on the desk and opened it. Before she took out the file she said, "You've always had a terrible need for others to see you as perfect, haven't you? You've tried so hard to foster that image. And I was convinced of it for years. You were wild and mischievous, but those were just youthful pranks and I admired and envied you. And then . . . the pregnancy, and your father . . . I saw you as a victim, and as you say, I was sympathetic. You suffered through the fire and seemed to come out purified. I tried to be like you, but I never could live up to that.

"I thought I was a failure because I couldn't be what you were, Penny. It's kind of funny, but in the convent I rebelled against the habit, yet when I got out I created a sort of emotional habit of my own as a disguise. I finally forced myself to become my own version of you. But I lost myself in the process. You can't wear a habit that doesn't fit without having it start to chafe. But I kept right on, stubborn me—that's one part of me that's all mine, anyway—trying to live up to this idealized version of womanhood. Then I read this."

She took out the file and laid it on the desk between them. Penny glanced down at it and her face went hard. "That's my father's name on the file," she said.

"And yours. Imitating you, I'd learned to do everything a hundred and ten percent, remember? That included my research. When I read the information in this file, I got one hell of a shock. You weren't what I thought you were at all; you weren't what any of us thought. Saintly Sister Immaculata. For all I know, the entire person I'd tried to model myself on was just a clever construction of yours to get what you wanted from other people.

"And you were so good you even fooled them in the convent. That's remarkable. The religious life has a way of weeding out pretenders, but obviously one occasionally slips through the cracks. If she's very plausible and persuasive. Like my dear friend Penny, who'd been a willing sexual partner for her father in half the resorts of Europe!"

Penny's face was as white as her habit, with two hectic red splotches beginning to burn high on her cheekbones. Her voice was hollow as she cried out, "What are you saying?" She seemed to lose her balance slightly; she clung to the edge of the desk for support and stared, not at Ivory, but at the file.

Now was the time. Now when Penny, who had thought herself safe, was exposed and defenseless. Now you raise the gun and sight along the barrel; now you blow the poor damn thing into a bloody rag. God forgive me, she thought. I'm doing this for love, Penny, but you would never understand that. Poor little girl who got twisted out of shape. You can't make the world all neat and tidy again, no matter how hard you try.

"I have the dates right here," she said, struggling to keep her voice dispassionate. Journalistic objectivity, not the fanatic's intensity. "After your mother was hospitalized, you didn't go directly to Switzerland, and from there to the convent. Switzerland was just the last stop on a grand tour you and your father took across Western Europe, to all the glittering playgrounds. The European tabloids, the paparazzi, they love Americans who spend money like water; they write about them and photograph them with the most malicious glee. Weren't you aware of that then? Your whole odyssey was chronicled. With pictures, for the periodicals who cater to that sort of taste."

She opened the file and took out the magazine clipping

on top, holding it up so Penny could see. It was a close-up
taken with a telephoto lens on a Riviera beach. In the fore-
ground, a muscular middle-aged man was caressing the
body of a blond girl in a topless bikini. Glistening with oil,
the two lay close together on a beach towel. Their faces
were startlingly clear to the camera's expensive eye, as was
the nature of their caress. The man's hand was cupping the
girl's breast, playing with her nipple. She was propped on
one elbow with her other hand inside his swim trunks. Her
eyes were half-closed, her lips slack with lust.

The caption read, "North Americans enjoy topless sport at
the Riviera."

No names, but no names were needed. Both faces were
clearly recognizable: the blunt, distinctive profile of Kellam
Endicott and the lovely features of his daughter Elaine.

"There are other pictures," Ivory said, without allowing
herself to show mercy. "People seem to lose all their inhibi-
tions when they're a world away from home. I don't suppose
your father had registered you as father and daughter, had
he? At least he must have taken that precaution."

Penny sagged as if the air had been sucked out of her
lungs. When at last she spoke, her voice seemed to come
from very far away. "He really wanted me, you know," she
said. But she wasn't talking to Ivory. "For a while, he
wanted me. We were closer than two people had ever been,
after that first time he came to my bed. It was our secret
and nobody knew. The places we stayed, they thought we
were lovers. He said he loved me."

She looked up with a ravaged face Ivory hardly recognized. "He said he loved me!" she repeated. "But then . . ."
The plaintive voice sighed away.

"Go on, Penny," Ivory said with all the gentleness she
possessed. Trust me, tell me. I won't judge.

"But then he changed. He pulled away from me. By the
time we got to Switzerland, he was . . . finding fault with
me again, and he didn't want me . . . didn't want to make

love to me . . . anymore. He said his conscience was bothering him, that what we were doing wasn't right. But that was just his excuse, it wasn't the real reason. He'd started watching the younger girls in that special way of his. He'd decided I was too old, you see. He liked little girls and I wasn't a little girl anymore. And there wasn't anything I could do about it. But I was the only one who loved him!"

Her shoulders were shaking, but it was a grief beyond tears; her eyes burned blue in her pale face, tearless and tortured.

"What happened then, Penny? Did you actually run away from him?"

"Oh yes, I ran away. I thought he'd follow me, but he didn't. There was a little child in the hotel where we were staying, a beautiful girl with shiny black curls and a mama who encouraged her interest in the rich American . . . I went to the convent, as I told you. And eventually took my vows. But I didn't forget.

"I didn't forgive." Her eyes burned now with malice.

"What did you do?"

"How do you think the police in Texas got onto him? An anonymous tip, that's how; that's the only way a story like that would have ever surfaced. The girls wouldn't have talked; they were too intimidated to tell. I sent him away to prison for a long, long time. I hope he dies there. I hope he gets old, old, old, with no one to put him out of his misery!"

The room was very quiet except for a faint, pervasive electric hum. The mechanical servitors of the hospital went on functioning, doing their duty. Illuminate or electrocute, it was all the same to that harnessed power.

Ivory put the clippings back in the file and closed it. Penny was sitting with her hands folded on the desk and her head bowed over them. Her voice was muffled as she asked, "Are you going to . . . make public what's in that file? All of it? Would you actually expose me like that?"

Ivory tried not to let herself feel anything. "If I have to. To as many people as necessary."

Penny flung out her hands. "These people love me! They admire me! When I walk down the halls of this hospital, I see the student nurses watching me and wanting to be just like me. If I have something to say, they all listen. If they knew . . . if they started picturing me with my own father . . ." She could not say anything else. Her face was naked with pleading.

Recognize temptation in all its guises.

Ivory bit her lip. "This group you've put together—your surgeon, and anyone else who might be involved—would they continue without you as the guiding force?"

Penny hesitated before answering. She sounded embarrassed to admit, "No, not yet. It's because of their belief in me . . ."

"Their belief in you," Ivory echoed. She lifted the file and held it so that Penny couldn't help focusing on it again, then slid it into her attaché case. And waited.

The two women looked at each other in the quiet room.

It can't come down to this, Ivory thought. I can't fight blackmail with blackmail, destroy my best friend, and then walk away. "Penny," she said, very softly.

The nun's face was bleak. It was as if she did not recognize the name. Something inside her was irrevocably broken.

"Penny," Ivory said again. "Do you remember how it was when we were girls in school together?"

Watching her face as if for some hidden clue to salvation, Penny nodded slowly.

Ivory went on, "You were always the one who had the ideas, and I was the one who got in trouble carrying them out. Remember? And you would go to Mother Superior or one of the teachers and argue my case to get me out of trouble. Sometimes you even shared my punishment; if I got grounded, you kept me company. I could count on you.

"Now you can count on me. I don't want to humiliate you publicly, and I certainly don't want to do anything that might result in your having to leave the religious life. But I think this has to end, here and now. And I think you should give up nursing; maybe even consider becoming a contemplative, the way you once told me you wanted to. I'll stand by you. I'll help you any way I can."

"I'm the one who helps people," Penny said tonelessly.

Ivory ached with gentleness and pity. "Yes. You always tried to. But what you're doing now is hurting them; if this surgeon who's working with you is discovered, it could ruin her career; it would be a lot worse than just being grounded in a girls' school. I don't think you want that.

"Penny, the God you've always loved so much is a forgiving God. A loving father." It was painful to say that; she saw her own pain echoed on Penny's face. "You were forgiven for what you did long ago. Now you have to forgive yourself. Don't sacrifice yourself anymore, don't try to take on sins for others. That was done almost two thousand years ago.

"I don't want to have to use this file, Penny. Let me ask you to do this, not because I've threatened you, but because we were friends. Give it up. Spare yourself and everyone else."

Penny made one last try. "I am needed . . ."

Ivory shoved the file aside and stretched her hands across the desk, seizing Penny's ice-cold fingers and squeezing them, hard. "*I* need you, Pen!" she pleaded. "Don't make me expose you! I'll do it if I have to, but how do you think I'm going to be able to go through the rest of my life with your destruction on my conscience?"

The moments ticked on and on, the two women caught, frozen in them, hands and eyes locked. Finally Penny disentangled her fingers from Ivory's and stood up slowly, like an old woman, rounding her shoulders and raising herself from her lower back. "I'm tired," she said. "You know, I think I've been working too hard."

She crossed the room to the window and looked across the parking lot to the oily glint of the river. "I've always tried so hard," she said plaintively. "I have friends, dear, dear friends, who've tried to tell me I was pushing myself too much, but I would never listen. I thought I had to . . ." She sighed. The light from the window lent a pale glow to her skin that was almost ethereal. She began unconsciously pleating the curtain. "Perhaps I should do something selfish, for once," she murmured. "Something just for me."

Ivory sat without moving, held by an iron discipline until Penny at last turned to face her. The nun's face was calm; she had already moved past another milestone. "If I should transfer to a contemplative order, would you come to see me when it's allowed?" she asked Ivory. "I have no family, you know, and even the strictest orders occasionally allow visitation now. Perhaps every year or so. If you came to see me, you could see . . . how well I was doing."

And put a gold star on your chart, Ivory thought, agonized. "Of course I'd come to see you, Penny."

The nun nodded. "I might be very happy in a strictly enclosed order," she said with a trace of a smile, as if already anticipating a treat. "Do you really think that would be best for me?" she asked with the slightly breathless quality of her long-ago childhood, a little girl asking a grownup's permission. The discipline, the proof of love. "Would everything be all right then?"

I won't cry, Ivory promised herself, trying to hold back the tears stinging her eyes. "Yes, Penny. I think that would be the right thing to do."

Penny nodded obediently. "All right, then. You know, in an enclosed order the world can't touch you anymore at all." She smiled her heartbreakingly lovely smile. "I'll apply for a transfer as soon as possible. I don't think I'll have any trouble getting one, do you? People always seem to be willing to do things I ask of them." She wandered back to the window again and her fingers resumed pleating the curtain. She did not seem to notice when Ivory picked up her attaché case and left the room. Penny continued to gaze out the window, her face as serene and pure as a marble statue.

By the time Ivory reached the conference room, the other board members had already taken their seats. She made her way down the table to her customary place without noticing anyone; all she could see was that last glimpse of Penny. She was not aware that Nathan Scott was sitting next to her until he spoke her name.

She glanced up, startled. "What are you doing here?"

"I've come to testify if you need me."

A tide of happiness rose, flooding through her. It filled the aching void in her chest and thickened her throat so that she could not answer him for a heartbeat or two. In the silence that bound them, they carried on a dialogue with their eyes. It was about his strength and her strength, about matching them and finding them compatible. It was about compromise instead of conquest. It was about the tenderness in him and the need for tenderness in her, the need to be soft without surrendering the hard-won integrity of her inner being.

"I won't need your testimony after all, Nathan," she told him finally, with relief. "But I'm awfully glad you're here. I think I am going to need you, in a lot of ways. For a very long time."